THE CHAPERONE

THE
CHAPERONE

M HENDRIX

sourcebooks
fire

Published by Sourcebooks Fire, an imprint of Sourcebooks
P.O. Box 4410, Naperville, Illinois 60567–4410
(630) 961-3900
sourcebooks.com

Cataloging-in-Publication Data is on file with the Library of Congress.

Printed and bound in the United States of America.
MA 10 9 8 7 6 5 4 3 2 1

For all the young people out there who dream of a better world.

And in memory of my father,
the first person to teach me the importance of equality.

EMBRACE PURITY.
NAVIGATE THE WORLD WITH CARE.
RESPECT YOUR CHAPERONE.

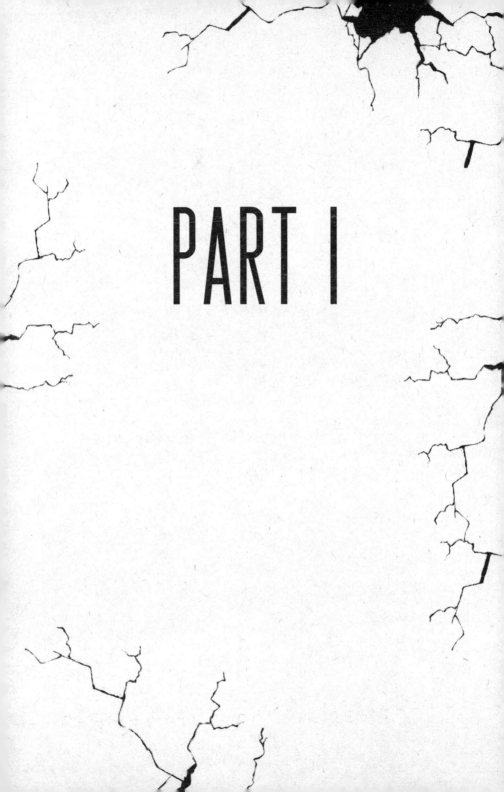

PART I

CHAPTER 1

I hear it while I'm in my room getting ready for Sunday Visitation.

A thump so loud it sounds like a piece of furniture falling to the floor. Did it come from the other side of my bedroom wall? Sister Helen's room is on the other side of that wall.

In the annex.

But if the thump came from...that would mean...

I put my ear to the wall at the same time that my hand goes to the base of my neck. I'm still clutching my throat when a door slams so hard it shakes the windows.

I drop my hand and dart for the hallway.

CHAPTER 2

My mother comes out of her bedroom the same time I do. We meet on the landing above the marble staircase. I'm greeted by the smell of her vetiver perfume. She holds out her hands like she's stopping traffic. I have no choice but to wait.

Everything about Mom is impeccable. Take away the fluffy white slippers, and she could be in an ad on the Freedom Channel. Her makeup is perfectly applied, highlighting her full lips and high cheekbones. And her golden-brown hair falls across her gray-blue eyes in the exact same way mine does when I follow her instructions. People always say we look like sisters, but I don't see it.

"Did you hear that?" I ask Mom.

"Stella, why aren't you dressed? Levi will be here any minute." In Mom's eyes, my V-neck and leggings seem messy. Unkempt. "And you really should take off that necklace. It draws too much attention to your…"

She doesn't finish. But I know what she means.

Embrace purity.

Of course, Visitation is all Mom cares about. All she cares about are appearances.

"Mom." I don't hide the impatience in my voice. "Did. You. Hear. It?"

She nods an almost imperceptible nod at the same time Shea steps out her bedroom door, looking at us with fear in her eyes. Even at the age of seven, she's thinking the same thing I am. *Is someone in the house? Have they come for us?* We live in a constant state of paranoia.

"What was that?" Shea says in her *I'm-scared* voice. I should be braver than Shea, but I'm scared too. I'm scared all the time, because every week another girl goes missing.

"Go back in your room," Mom instructs Shea in a voice colder than necessary.

I put my hand on Shea's shoulder, as tiny as a doll's. "It'll be okay." The truth is, I'm not certain it will be.

Mom wags a finger at Shea. "And lock the door."

Shea must be more frightened than normal because she doesn't argue. She steps back and turns the lock when her door clicks shut.

Mom turns to me. "Where's your father?"

"In the garage?"

That's where Dad hides when he's not at work. Mom shakes her head in frustration, a common response when Dad comes up.

"We should see if—"

"Stella, I'm sure everything's fine. Your father will check when he gets back."

Even though everything in me is telling me not to wait, she's right. Dad is the only one with a gun. A Glock 9mm. It's on his hip at all times. Women aren't allowed to carry firearms. It's the job of men to protect us.

Navigate the world with care.

I look her right in the eye. "Mom, please."

That's when we hear the scream.

It's the kind of scream you hear in movies from Old America. The ones about a serial killer taking out teenagers. Before it's all over, every single girl ends up dead.

And that scream definitely sounded female.

I start down the giant staircase, Mom right behind me. She must've kicked off her slippers.

"Stella, wait!" Mom whisper-yells as I reach the first floor, but I ignore her.

I'm at the other end of the house—through the sprawling dining room and the massive kitchen—in seconds. The first floor is dead quiet. Everything untouched. There's no sign of anything out of place.

Mom catches me when I get to the threshold that crosses into the annex, throws an arm in front of me so I can't start up the back stairs. She leaps past me and takes the steps two at a time. I'm right behind her, remembering what we heard.

The thump.

The door.

The scream.

"Hello?" Mom pushes open the half-closed door of Sister Helen's room. That's when I see her.

Sister Helen.

On the floor.

Clutching her neck like she's choking.

CHAPTER 3

I rush past Mom into the room, dropping to Sister Helen's side. Strands of white hair stick to her sweaty forehead.

"Sister Helen, are you okay?" Tears come to my eyes, but I fight them. She doesn't look at me. "Sister Helen, it's me. It's Stella."

It's like she doesn't even know I'm here.

I glance over my shoulder at Mom. "Mom, do something!"

Mom shakes her head, a hand over her mouth. "I can't, Stella."

"Mom, please!"

"Your dad will be here soon."

I turn back to Sister Helen. "Will you look at me? *Please*?"

Sister Helen finally angles her head in my direction, her lavender scent washing over me. Only today it's mixed with the unmistakable odor of urine. Has she wet her pants? In her green eyes, there's a sadness I've never seen there before. Sadness and pain. For the first time I notice the many lines around her face, lines I've always missed because of her warm smile. But now they stand out, reminding me that, at sixty, she's no longer young.

Sister Helen puts one hand on my face, cradling my cheek. Her other hand is balled into a fist. I choke off tears. I must stay strong. I must be brave. Sister Helen opens her mouth, but nothing comes out.

"Sister Helen? What happened?"

Her eyes stare into mine as she lifts her fist to my hand. When she finds my palm, she opens her fist and drops something inside. It's the white quartz pendant she's worn since the day I met her.

Why is she giving it to me?

I look to Sister Helen for an answer. Her lips are moving, but I can't hear anything. She wants to say something. She grips my arm, forcing me closer. I turn my ear to her mouth.

"Ain." She croaks out one word at a time. "Jell."

I glance at Mom, searching for the explanation she never has, before turning back to Sister Helen. "What did you say?"

She tries again. Almost no sound emerges. I read her lips. "Ain." She mouths the words. "Jell." She says it another time. This time faster. "Ain. Jell."

"Ain Jell?" I ask her out loud. And then I understand. *Ain Jell…* *Angel.* "Angel?"

Her pupils go up and down.

I nod though I have no idea what she means.

Her eyes still, and something in them shifts. It isn't sadness I see anymore. It's terror.

"Sister Helen, what's happening?"

Her gaze bores into mine. She's trying to tell me something.

"Sister Helen, don't leave me!"

I haven't even gotten the words out when her eyes lose focus, moving from side to side like a metronome. A moment later, they stop and roll to the back of her head. A trickle of blood leaks out of the side of her mouth.

Now I'm the one who screams.

CHAPTER 4

Dad rushes into the room.

He doubles over, puts his hands on his knees. He's breathing so hard his salt-and-pepper hair lifts with every breath. His shirt is soaked with sweat. "I got here as soon as I could. I was all the way out in the—" He pauses and looks around, as if seeing the space for the first time. The solitary wood dresser. The neat stack of books on the bedside table. The simple white quilt on the small twin bed. His gaze lands on me.

"Stella, my God."

I flinch. He could get arrested for saying that word.

"Are you okay?"

"Dad, you have to...just please...help her!"

He takes in the scene. Me on the floor. Sister Helen in my arms. Blood all over her white caftan. Her head rolled back so far her body arches into a back bend. "My God. What happened?" He glances at Mom before moving to my side.

Mom shakes her head, completely mute.

"Did she have a heart attack?" Dad asks. "A stroke?"

I jerk my head up. "What do you mean?"

"She was getting older, Stella."

"She was in perfect health."

"We don't know that."

He's right. Sister Helen seemed healthy—she did crow pose with me every afternoon at yoga, and we often hiked fifteen miles on weekends like it was nothing—but what if it wasn't nothing? What if she was struggling, and I didn't know it?

"But, Dad," I plead, "someone was here. A door slammed. We all heard it." I glance at Mom for support, but she doesn't even return my gaze. "Whoever it was got away."

Dad waves a hand at me. "It was probably just the wind, Stella. Do you have any idea how strong the wind is today?"

"I have *no* idea." I'm not allowed outside alone, but I don't dare voice that frustration.

"Stella, we need to get you out of here."

I'm supposed to obey him. That's how a proper daughter acts, that's how *I* act, but for some reason, I don't move. I can't leave her. I just can't.

Give obedience.

Dad drops to one knee. I smell his strange mixture of after-shave and hospital. "You have to leave, Stella." He puts two fingers on Sister Helen's neck.

What is he doing?

I take a deep breath and try my best to hold in the tears. "Dad, what's happening?"

"I'm sorry, Stella."

This can't happen. Sister Helen cannot be dead. Because there is *no way* I can live without her. My chest tightens so much I feel like I'm choking on my own lungs. I wipe tears away, but they keep coming.

I don't even realize how hard I'm crying until Dad says, "Please don't cry, Stella." Dad lifts his hand to my back, his touch as shocking as a slap. What is he doing? He's not supposed to touch me. Not ever. I can't remember the last time we were this close. It's been years.

"Stella," he says, making me look into his gray eyes. "You have to let her go. She's in God's hands now."

His voice is too calm. Doesn't he understand what's happening?

"We have to call the constables. The police too."

"The police?"

Everyone knows the police don't know what they're doing. They haven't solved a crime in months. The Minutemen are the ones with real power. Their party controls everything in New America. From the top branches of government liberty, purity, and security—all the way down to the military constables. Even the prime minister is a member of the Minuteman Party.

"You can't be here," he says.

"I don't care." I look directly at Dad. "I'm not leaving her." I've never talked back to him before. Hearing my defiance out loud is terrifying.

"Stella, honey." He pats my back the same way he did when I was little. I look into his face but see no sign of recognition. Does he realize what he's doing? Ever since I became a woman, Dad hasn't been allowed to touch me. It's against the rules. "You feel that way now, but later...you'll understand. You *have* to say goodbye."

Mom hovers in the doorway. Mouth flat, arms crossed. She doesn't say a word. This is how it always is. Dad doing, Mom watching.

"Go ahead, Stella," Dad says. "Take your time. We'll wait."

I wipe my nose on my sleeve.

Dad flips a crisp, white handkerchief out of his pocket. He passes it to me before returning his hand to my back.

The warmth of his touch is reassuring. It's been so long since I've felt anything from him besides judgment. Too long. It's Sister Helen who holds me when I cry. Sister Helen who offers me encouragement when I need it. How can I say goodbye to the person who knows me better than anyone in the world? When we read Emily Dickinson together, Sister Helen made me memorize one line. *That it will never come again is what makes life so sweet.* She taught me not to fear death, but she never showed me how to let go of the dying. I got incredibly lucky when Sister Helen was assigned to me. She never wanted to control me the way some chaperones do. She wanted me to be my own person. But the truth is, I have no idea how to do that. I have no idea who I am without her by my side. How can I possibly go on alone?

That's when it hits me.

I *won't* be alone.

After Sister Helen is gone, after I sit through my Days of Grief, they'll send another.

CHAPTER 5

Dad tells Mom to take me back to my room, and she does exactly what he says.

Shea peeks out when we pass her bedroom. "Mommy?"

Mom shushes her. I want to offer Shea a smile, but I can't summon a brave face.

My room feels cavernous. Barren. Every corner reminds me of Sister Helen. Sister Helen sitting in the armchair next to my desk. Sister Helen selecting a book from the shelves on either side of my windows. Sister Helen perched on the bench at the end of my bed. She's everywhere.

I watch for the constables out the windows.

"Stella, don't," Mom says.

I jump, forgetting she's behind me.

"Don't what?"

"Don't watch for them." She's biting the edge of her thumb, something I haven't seen her do in years. "It will look suspicious."

"What do you mean?"

"We don't want them thinking…well, that we had anything to do with this."

"Anything to do with what?"

"With Sister Helen."

"They would never think that," I insist, but when I see the fear in her eyes, I understand she doesn't believe it. "Right, Mom?"

She doesn't respond, instead turning away just as Shea sneaks in the door. Mom scoops her up like a kitten. Shea has tiny tears in her eyes, and Mom pushes her head down on her shoulder. "Shhh, don't cry." My throat clenches. I'm the one who needs comfort.

"Stella," Mom says, "why you don't lie down? I'll check on you in a little bit."

She's out the door before I can protest.

I grab the white scarf Sister Helen knitted for me last winter and climb into bed. Cold air blasts out the vents, a losing battle against the oppressive heat of August. I wrap the scarf around me, pull the quilt up to my face. I close my eyes, trying to forget. But the image of Sister Helen on the floor plays over and over inside my head. A horror movie on repeat.

I was only eleven when Sister Helen came to us. It was almost six years ago. A few months before my twelfth birthday.

Mom submitted the report to the constables when I got my first period. Adolescent girls are required to have a government-assigned chaperone. Some families can't afford a private one. Those girls are sent to the government school, but I never worried about that. Dad is president of the largest auto manufacturer in New America. I always knew I'd get my own chaperone. I hadn't even stopped bleeding when Sister Helen arrived on our doorstep.

Dad requested certain things. He wanted her to be educated

and physically active. He wanted her to be older than thirty and a nonsmoker. But ultimately it's the constables who decide which chaperone is right for each of us. The prime minister has bestowed that power upon them.

My first thought was that Sister Helen was beautiful. Yes, she was older than most chaperones, but the white hair that fell to her shoulders in silky wisps made her seem timeless. And her jade-colored eyes were the brightest I'd ever seen. They were alive with intelligence. She wore the white caftan required of all chaperones, but she paired it with gold drop earrings, gold and white bracelets, and the white pendant she had pressed into my hand just minutes ago.

My life was never the same. Chaperones have freedom and respect other women don't, but they also give up their own lives to follow a higher calling. Teaching girls like me how to be respectable women is their sole purpose. I was Sister Helen's top priority, and we bonded immediately.

The night she arrived, she told me about the day she became a woman. Back when Old America was just America, and everything was different. She started her period while her family was on vacation in Florida. Her dad made her go to the beach even though she wanted to stay in the hotel room and cry. It sounded exactly like the kind of thing my father would do. Not long after she moved in, I shared every thought with her. I'm closer to her than I am to my own mother.

Was closer. I *was* closer.

That's what they want. For us to become so close to our chaperones that we trust them over everyone else, even our own family. People talk about mothers who try to drive a wedge between their daughters and their chaperones, even mothers who try to get their daughters out of the country, but those stories always end in tragedy. The family gets fined or—worse yet—shunned.

Once you're shunned, your whole life is ruined. You can't go to college. No boy will come to Visitation, much less marry you. If you do marry, you won't be able to attend social events or keep your friends. Mom knew a woman who was shunned after trying to get her daughter out of a marriage arranged by the constables. She was never allowed to see Mom again, and her daughter never did marry, instead becoming a chaperone, which some people say is a way for girls of a certain class to become respectable.

I never had to worry about Mom interfering. She claimed the chaperone program was a godsend because it saved her from being responsible for my education. Like all mothers her age, Mom was raised in Old America, and that makes her nervous about following the rules here. She never talks about it, but I learned in New American History class that life was really different in Old America. People had strange ideas about freedom. They wanted everyone to be able to do whatever they wanted. But it didn't work. People would fight about it, even getting violent.

That's why women in Old America could do things women can't do here—choose their husbands, have careers, drive cars, own guns, play sports, open bank accounts, even dress however they wanted. But some women didn't want to give those things up, so they left when New America was founded. I was just three years old then, so I don't really remember, but I guess a lot of younger women left. That's why they want us to have babies right away.

Honestly it's kind of confusing.

I want to have choices, but at the same time I know they can be dangerous. That's why we were all glad when Sister Helen arrived. She learned all about how to stay safe at the conservatory.

But what about the person they send next? What if she doesn't know how to take care of me? What if she doesn't fit?

CHAPTER 6

I wake to the sound of sirens.

I jump out of bed, dashing to the windows at the end of my room. Two squad cars and three red SUVs sit in the circular drive, their flashing red-and-blue lights bouncing off the twelve-foot brick wall surrounding our property. One SUV is much longer than the others.

That's where they'll put her.

When the door of the first SUV opens, I step behind the curtain. Mom is right. Who knows what they'll think if they see me? Constables blame girls for all kinds of things. I peek from behind the curtain, but it isn't a constable I see. It's Levi Edwards walking around the SUVs on his way to the front door. Levi Edwards is in my Family Development class at Bull Run Prep. He's wearing a navy bow tie and carrying a small bunch of pink zinnias in his right hand.

Dad forgot to cancel Visitation.

This is the third time the constables have granted Levi a Sunday visit. He's nice enough, but he tends to say the same thing. *You look so pretty, Stella. You're so nice, Stella. You're sweet, Stella.* Talking to

Levi is like talking to a toddler. I like boys who surprise me. There's one in my Musical Expression class who says the craziest things.

Mateo de Velasco.

Even his name makes me catch my breath. It's like a poem.

But Mateo's never been to Visitation. And I'm afraid if Levi keeps coming to visit, he'll be expected to bring up the subject of marriage. I don't want to get married. Not yet. I want to go to college. At least a few years. Then I'll be ready to marry, have kids. All that. But it doesn't matter what I want. Visitation is mandatory for girls my age.

The whole thing is totally artificial. Sitting with some boy I barely know. Making small talk. Acting like we don't know why we're there. I do it because I have no choice. Sister Helen says I have to choose my battles, and Visitation is not something worth fighting.

The doorbell rings, and I sneak to the top of the stairs. But I'm too far away to make out what they're saying. As soon as the front door closes, I dart back to my room. I get to the window just in time to see Levi throw the flowers in the bushes and skulk away. A few stray petals color the pavement pink. Levi stops when he gets to the gate and turns back, studying the full driveway, his face filled with longing. His gaze floats up to me, and our eyes meet. He puts his hand to his mouth and blows me a kiss. I don't acknowledge him in any way.

Deflect attention.

People gawk on the sidewalk out front, but the brick wall is too high to see over. Two constables emerge from the front door rolling a stretcher between them. A long black bag rests on top.

It's her. It's Sister Helen.

When I pull my eyes from her body, I see a constable staring up at me. He has pale splotchy skin and hair so blond it's almost colorless. He doesn't look old enough to be a constable, but he wears their uniform—gray pants, gray button-down shirt, gray tie, red armband, and an automatic rifle slung across his back the same way I carry my yoga mat. I throw the curtain across the windows and step back. But it's too late.

He's seen me.

CHAPTER 7

t's the morning of my first Day of Grief.

Girls who lose a chaperone are required to spend five days mourning before returning to the real world.

When Mom knocks on the door a half hour after I wake, I know it's her because Shea never bothers to knock. "Stella? Are you going to get out of bed?"

"Why?" I say through the closed door.

Mom pushes the door open just enough to see me. "Don't you want breakfast? You need to come to the table."

I have no desire to eat, but I do as she says. When I pull my shirt over my head, goose bumps alight on both of my arms. Something isn't right. I go to the windows and throw open the curtains.

A red SUV is parked in the driveway.

Again.

~~~~~~

Shea sits at the giant kitchen island, a stack of fluffy pancakes in front of her. The smell of frying oil is nauseating. Mom hovers over the stove with a spatula in her hand. It's only seven o'clock in the morning, but she's already camera-ready. Tiffany, our housekeeper, stands behind her at the sink, washing last night's dishes.

"Pancakes?" Mom's voice is annoyingly cheerful.

"I'm not hungry." I pull my scarf around me. Even though it will be nearly 100 degrees outside today, the kitchen is freezing.

Tiffany turns off the faucet and looks over her shoulder at me. "I'm so sorry, Stella. I know you meant the world to Sister Helen."

A wave of emotion rushes through me, but I hold it in. "Thank you."

Tiffany stares at me like she wants to say more.

"What is it?"

"It's just…well…maybe she spent time with the wrong people."

"What do you mean?"

Mom wheels on Tiffany, her spatula a weapon. "Tiffany!"

"I'm sorry, Mrs. Graham, but—"

"Get back to work."

Tiffany's eyes meet mine for only a second before she returns to the dishes. *Maybe she spent time with the wrong people.* What does that mean?

I study Mom while she flips pancakes. "Is that why they're here?"

"What are you talking about, Stella?"

"The constables? Are they here because Sister Helen knew people she shouldn't?"

Mom lets out a long sigh before scowling at Tiffany over her shoulder. "I have no idea what Sister Helen did in her free time, Stella. She certainly never confided in me. As for the constables, they're here to make sure we're safe."

"Safe?" I ask as Shea lifts her head from her pancakes.

Mom shakes her head. "I don't mean it like that, Stella. I just mean…well, you know."

I know exactly what she's trying to say. What I've known since I was young enough to read. Girls get attacked and kidnapped every day, and if we aren't vigilant—about how we act, how we dress, where we go, who we're with—we put ourselves in danger.

I walk toward the annex. Dad's office is on the first floor, under Sister Helen's room.

"Stella Ann." Mom uses her most serious tone. "Don't even think about going back there."

"I know, Mom."

As soon as the words are out of my mouth, the door of Dad's office creaks open. I back away.

Dad appears in the kitchen minutes later. Sister Helen is dead, but for some reason he's whistling. And dressed as if he's going to work. Dark gray suit, striped shirt, matching tie, onyx cufflinks. Even the silver streaks in his chestnut hair are combed perfectly in place. His eyes go to Mom, staring at her from across the room as if she's as bright as the moon. He takes off his jacket, revealing the pistol on his hip. The sight of it makes my chest hurt.

Mom slides a plate of pancakes across the island, and Dad takes the stool next to Shea.

"Are you going to join us, Stella?" Dad asks over his shoulder as he lops a giant pat of butter on his pancakes.

I can't remember the last time I had butter or syrup. Pancakes, Mom insists, are a treat all by themselves.

Mom isn't eating either. She's still at the stove, pouring batter onto the griddle. It's not unusual for her to cook while the rest of us eat.

"No, thank you." My stomach tumbles as he swirls syrup like it's art. "I'm not hungry."

Dad spins around. "What's wrong, Stella?"

What's wrong? What does he mean, *What's wrong?* But I can't be disrespectful, so I choose my words carefully. "Is everything okay?" Dad raises his eyebrows, giving me permission to go on. "Are we in danger?"

Dad turns back to his plate. "You know the world is a dangerous place, Stella." He picks up a forkful of pancake but doesn't put it in his mouth. "You know you need to remain vigilant at all times."

"But, I mean, will the people—the people who did this to Sister Helen—will they come after us?"

Dad puts his fork down and glances toward Tiffany, who's finished the dishes and started wiping out the fridge. She must sense his impatience because she closes the refrigerator and says, "I might have a smoke. If that's okay."

Tiffany's smart enough to know when to get out of Dad's way. He doesn't normally let her take breaks in the middle of a shift, but today he nods right away. After she pulls the back door shut, he turns to me. "I don't want you talking about this in front of Tiffany, Stella." When I don't respond, he adds, "Do you understand me?"

"Yes, sir."

"The constables were here to talk about Sister Helen." He picks up his fork again. "They wanted to go over what's next."

"What do you mean, 'what's next'?"

"We're all going to have talk to the police, be fingerprinted. Provide a DNA sample."

"We will?"

"It's routine, Stella. Nothing to worry about."

"Do they know what happened?"

He takes a bite. "Happened?"

"To Sister Helen." I have to force the words out. "Do they know how she was killed?"

Dad swallows. I don't know if it's irritation or pancake going down. "She was an old lady, Stella. Old people die. It's part of life." His jaw is set in anger. He's not happy about my questions. Gossip is a sin. Apparently there was a lot of it in Old America.

"May I please be excused?"

Dad looks at Mom who closes her eyes and shrugs.

"Of course," he says. "You're still grieving."

I spin away and run up the stairs. I just want everyone to leave me alone. And for some reason, my wish comes true.

No one knocks on my door.

No one checks on me.

For the first time in my life, I experience true loneliness.

CHAPTER 8

Mom doesn't drag me out of bed the next day, sending Tiffany to my room with a tray of food every few hours. All I can think about is getting on the internet. I need to find out if they're talking about Sister Helen on the news.

It's after eleven before I can sneak downstairs.

Shea's been in bed for hours, and Mom and Dad went into their room a while ago. The master bedroom is two doors down from mine. Sometimes they go right to sleep. Other times I can hear their smart screen in the hall. That's the best time to get online—when they're distracted.

I wrap my scarf around my silk nightgown and creep down the stairs as slowly as possible.

A few years ago, I was at Brooklyn Liu's house for a sleepover when she bragged about figuring out her mother's internet password. The names of Brooklyn and her siblings strung together like a poem. *SavannahBeauBrooklyn*. We stayed up until sunrise that night, watching movies from Old America. Some things are blocked, but the stuff that isn't too racy is still there.

I was with my best friends, Bonita and Liv, when we figured

out our mothers all use the same kind of passwords—some variation of our names with an asterisk or numbers at the end. My mother didn't even bother with that. Her password is *StellaShea*. It took me several tries to get it right because I assumed Shea's name would be first. Now I get online whenever I can. I like to search for information about the latest disappearances and message my friends. It's the only way we can talk without anyone listening. If I have time, I'll watch an episode of old TV too. But mostly we save that for sleepovers. That's how we learn about the things no one talks about—dating, sex, drinking, drugs, even gay people.

As soon as I sit at Mom's kitchen cubby, I automatically turn to check the windows on the detached garage behind the house. When I see the blue reflection of the smart screen in Mom and Dad's bedroom, I know it's safe to log in.

The second I finish typing Shea's name, the neighbor's dog breaks into a frenzied bark. I freeze, but the barking stops as quickly as it started. Probably just a cat in the alley. I go back to the screen, and a bubble pops up.

A new message for Mom from someone named RoseInReality.

I shouldn't open it, but I can't help myself. When I click, words fill the screen.

I guess this means there's one less chaperone in the world.

My jaw drops right when the barking starts again. I ignore it and reread.

> I guess this means there's one less chaperone in the
> world.

What does that mean? Is this Rose person saying it's good Sister Helen died?

The barking outside gets louder, and I rotate my body toward the garage at the same the blue light from Mom and Dad's room goes out. I immediately power down the smart screen. If they find out I know the password, I'll never be able to get on the internet again.

The neighbor's dog is howling relentlessly. I move to the tall windows overlooking the courtyard. Moonlight hits the giant fountain Mom had installed a few years ago. She claimed it made the courtyard less prisonlike. I can't see the neighbor's house from inside, but when I peer in that direction, the barking stops.

Suddenly everything is quiet.

My breath fogs the glass. Behind it, a full moon as big as the sun hovers above the horizon. *What would happen if...*

A breeze rushes in when I unlock the door, sending a shiver down my back. I pull the scarf tighter. As I walk down the steps, the courtyard grows dark, the moon hiding behind a cloud. The brick pavers tickle my bare feet.

A second later, the courtyard brightens. I look up in time to see the moon reemerging. It's the most beautiful moon I've ever seen. Is this what it looks like every night?

The gate creaks, bringing me back to reality, and I drop my eyes in time to see a man racing out the back gate. He's wearing the uniform of a constable—gray shirt and pants, red armband. I open my mouth to scream, but no sound comes out. I can't speak, and I can't move. I'm paralyzed by fear.

Why was a constable here? How did he get in?

The sound of the dog barking madly from the neighbor's yard jars me of out of my paralysis. I race back to the house, slamming the door behind me so loudly I'm sure Dad will come running. I throw the lock and back away.

When my heart stops racing, I work up the courage to step up to the door. With my hands around my eyes, I peer into the darkness.

The courtyard is empty, the constable gone. But something on the ground catches my eye. Did he drop something? It's long and white. Is it a flag? I lean closer, and that's when I see it clearly...

My white scarf.

Laying on the bricks next to the fountain.

I reach for the lock but stop before turning it. I can't. It's not safe. And it's against the rules.

Navigate the world with care.

I glance over my shoulder. Why hasn't anyone come downstairs? Where is Dad? He must be sound asleep. How can he sleep when danger is all around? Even in our own backyard. Even in Sister Helen's room.

The message from RoseInReality comes back to me.

I guess this means there's one less chaperone in the world.

Is that what Mom wants? One less chaperone?

CHAPTER 9

I wake early the next morning and go to the windows overlooking the front drive.

I want to study Mom.

A few minutes later she steps out the front door to walk Shea to school. She must feel my eyes on her because she looks back, offering me a sad smile. Shea turns too, her eyes landing on mine, but doesn't smile, holding my gaze for a second before turning away. The two of them disappear beyond the gate a moment later.

Hours later, Mom brings me lunch but doesn't say a word, silently sliding the tray onto the bench at the end of my bed. I want to ask her about RoseInReality, but if I do, she'll change her password. I'm surprised when she comes back a little while later, right after walking Shae home from school.

"Stella?" she says after knocking. "There's someone here to see you."

I jump to my feet. "Who is it?"

Mom pushes the door open. "*It* is actually *two* of your favorite people." Mom steps aside to reveal my best friends behind her,

Bonita and Liv. The skin around their mouths is pulled tight. They look terrified.

I haven't talked to them since Sister Helen died. Only adults can have phones, and I didn't want to risk sneaking on the internet again to message them.

"Go on in, girls." Mom turns to them. "Tiffany will make tea for your chaperones while they wait downstairs."

They do what they're told, shuffling in like it's a jail cell.

Bonita's shiny black hair is so perfect she looks like she just came from the salon. In contrast, Liv's hair is pulled back in a messy ponytail with stray blond strands hanging out. I lean against the bed while Bonita slides onto the bench. Liv crosses the room and perches on Sister Helen's chair. No one has sat there since Sunday.

Neither of them speaks, and I wonder if we'll just sit there, mute. But eventually Bonita says, "Are you okay, Stella?"

Her words push me over the edge. I try to fight the tears, but it's impossible.

"Oh, Stella." Bonita moves from the bench to the bed, pulling me into her arms. I cry so hard her shirt grows damp under my cheek. When the sobs finally slow, she leans back and looks into my face, her rich brown eyes full of empathy.

"Are you going to be all right?"

I take a deep breath.

"I mean, we get it." Bonita looks at Liv, who nods at her. "Sister Helen was the best. She was more like your friend than your chaperone."

Liv finally speaks. "She really was." Her eyes are so wide I can see their amber color from across the room.

I wipe my nose on my sleeve. "I know."

"A million times better than Sister Sophie," Liv adds.

"How did it go Sunday at Visitation?"

Bonita rolls her eyes, and Liv shakes her head.

"What happened?"

"She made me wear heels."

Bonita and I love to get dressed up, but Liv loathes it. Even at school dances, she pairs modest dresses with flat sandals. "I'm sorry."

Liv goes on. "It's just not *me*. I felt like someone else. Like an imposter." Bonita and I exchange a look. When we noticed Liv gazing at Brooklyn Liu like she was a painting in a museum the year before, we decided she was probably more interested in girls than boys. Ever since then we've been collecting evidence to support our theory. But we can never breathe a word to anyone. It's the kind of thing that gets people shunned.

Bonita changes the subject. "At least Tucker Jones isn't a creep."

"That's true," Liv admits. "He *is* a nice person."

"Don't forget swoon-worthy," I add. "Remember when he dedicated that song to you in the talent show?"

Bonita jumps in. "When he leaned into the microphone and said, 'This is for Liv.' Now *that* was romantic."

Liv's face scrunches in distaste. "I couldn't believe he did that. He's *so* not my type." Bonita and I lock eyes.

"I guess," Bonita says, "but Olu Parker isn't anyone's type."

Bonita has been fighting off Olu for years.

"He's a total Climber," Liv admits.

The Climbers are the most annoying boys in school. They wear clothes more appropriate to middle-aged men and talk constantly about their careers. They act like they're too good for Bull

Run and have no intention of sticking around after high school, though a few of them, like Olu, want to find a girl to marry first. The others are known for getting grabby when no one is looking. Most kids in our school hate them, and the three of us are no exception.

"He refuses to give up." Bonita looks me right in the eye. "He brought up homecoming."

Homecoming is one of only two nights this year when we can get dressed up and dance with boys. Homecoming and prom. No way Bonita is wasting one of them on Olu.

"He didn't." Liv says.

"Oh, yes." She nods at Liv. "He did."

"He's not ruining that for you," I say. "For us."

"Not a chance."

"Did you tell him you weren't interested?" I ask.

"Like a hundred times." Bonita shakes her head at the floor. "Why won't he take the hint? It's not even a hint. I told him *exactly* how I feel. Why doesn't he get it?"

Her question sounds rhetorical, but Bonita holds her hands out, waiting for an answer. Liv pulls on the sleeves of her button-down, a nervous tic.

"What is it?" Bonita turns to me. "Stella?"

"You know, B." I don't want to admit out loud the reason Olu has been infatuated with Bonita since middle school.

"No, I don't, Stella."

"Do I have to say it?"

"Yes," she says with a dramatic nod, "you *have* to say it."

I use a finger to pull on my bottom lip. Sister Helen always said that's how she knew I was rolling an idea around in my head.

"Maybe he doesn't want to give up because you're the only Black girl in our grade."

"I don't see why that matters."

"He's a Climber, Bonita. You know what they always say? They want *traditional* marriages."

"That's just another reason I'm not interested. He shouldn't care if I'm Black or white. None of them should. That's so Old America."

"No, it shouldn't, but it clearly matters to them."

"I told Sister Anne I don't want him to call on me again." Bonita pauses before adding, "And I told her about Mason."

"You did *what*?" I ask her.

"I told her about Mason."

"What did she say?"

Liv squeezes her eyes shut as if she's heard the whole story.

"She said he isn't a good match for someone like me and that I can't marry a boy like Mason because his family isn't in the same class as mine."

Liv's eyes flash open. "She has you marrying him already?"

"That's all they care about, Olivia," Bonita says. "That's all *anyone* cares about. Getting married and having babies."

Unlike most of the girls in our school, the three of us desperately want to go to college before we get married. But it's really hard for girls to get in. Like impossible hard. And if we don't, we'll have no choice but to marry. Those are the only acceptable options for girls like us.

Bonita goes on. "She even pointed out his sister is at govie. Like I care."

"But—" Liv starts and then stops.

"But what?" Bonita looks at me, knowing Liv will never admit what she's thinking.

"What she means is—" I'm not sure how to put it.

"Just say it, Stella."

"You don't want to be forced to send *your* daughters to govie."

And there it is. If Bonita marries a boy like Mason, a boy unlikely to go to college and make enough to afford a chaperone, her daughters would be forced to move into the government school. No one wants their daughter to go to govie because that makes it almost impossible to marry well. Forget about college. Govie girls become servants, chaperones if they're lucky.

Bonita puts her hands over her face. When she drops them, she looks right at me. "You are so lucky, Stella. Sister Helen was amazing. She really took care of you. She taught you all the stuff no one ever talks about."

"You mean, I *was* lucky."

The truth sits between us like a bomb. I *was* lucky when I got Sister Helen. But I have no idea who they'll send next.

CHAPTER 10

The doorbell rings at four on Sunday afternoon. I know who it is without opening the door.

I don't open it. I just stand there.

Staring.

There are actually two front doors, both made of thick teak panels crisscrossed with heavy iron nailheads. No intruder could get past those doors.

Mom comes running into the foyer. "Stella, what are you doing?" She must read my mind because she says, "Oh, Stella. It's going to be okay." She puts the dish towel in her hands on the pedestal table and walks to the door, looking over her shoulder before opening it. "Ready?" she asks, and I nod.

On the other side is a woman much younger than Sister Helen. She looks thirty, maybe a young thirty-five. She has dark curly hair that falls to the middle of her back and wears her white caftan over black leggings with cowboy boots and large tortoiseshell glasses. Behind them, her watery blue eyes study me. She looks like a hippie in a movie from Old America. I've seen chaperones like her before, but it's still jarring after Sister Helen's elegance. "You must be Stella." She zeroes in on me, though Mom is the one inviting her inside.

"Hi." I lean forward and shake her outstretched hand. Was it this formal with Sister Helen? Of course not. I wasn't even twelve.

"I'm Sister Laura."

"Welcome, Sister Laura," Mom says with enthusiasm. "We're so lucky to have you."

I glare at Mom.

"That's kind, Mrs. Graham, but it isn't luck that brings me here. Sister Helen was a special person." She turns toward me. "I can only imagine how difficult this must be for Stella."

How does she know exactly what I'm thinking?

I say nothing, following the two of them through the house like a puppy. Mom makes small talk about the almanac predicting the weather will be hot through October this year as she shows Sister Laura every single room in the house. Like she's a prospective buyer, not an employee. But I get it. The house is Mom's domain. She wants to show it off.

Thirty minutes go by before we cross through the dining room and the kitchen to the annex. We climb the stairs to the second floor without speaking, but when we stop outside Sister Helen's room, it all comes back to me. I haven't been here since...I take a deep breath, and Sister Laura swivels her head in my direction, eyes wide.

She turns back to Mom. "Is this Sister Helen's room?"

"Yes, of course."

"And where is Stella's room?"

"On the second floor of the main house. With the other bedrooms."

"The main house? That seems awfully far."

"It wasn't a problem for Sister Helen."

"Yes, but that was before."

"Before what?" Mom asks.

"Before Stella lost her guardian."

It takes everything in me not to roll my eyes. Bonita, Liv, and I make fun of chaperones who call themselves guardians. It's *so* pretentious.

"I'll need to be closer." Sister Laura scratches her nose. "Now that Stella has suffered such a loss."

"But—"

Sister Laura interrupts. "Who else has a bedroom near Stella?"

"We do, of course. And Stella's little sister, Shea, is right across the hall—"

"I'll take Shea's room. That will be perfect."

"And where will Shea go?"

"She can have this room." Sister Laura tilts her head at the still closed door behind her.

"It's too far. She's only seven—"

"Stella has experienced a great loss, Mrs. Graham. She needs more support than ever. I simply must be close to her."

I want to object, but I'm speechless. How could someone who doesn't know me help me get over Sister Helen? Mom will *never* put Shea in Sister Helen's old room. But to my astonishment, she gives Sister Laura what she wants.

"I suppose we could move Shea into the upstairs library."

"Perfect."

It's typical of Mom. Whenever anyone challenges her, she just gives in.

CHAPTER 11

Sister Laura surprises us again by showing up for dinner an hour later.

"Oh." Mom's mouth holds its O shape while she continues assembling the salad. "You'd like to join us tonight?"

"Not just tonight. Every night, Mrs. Graham."

It's true Sister Sophie eats with Liv's family, but she's the most uptight chaperone I've ever met. She never lets Liv out of sight, watching her do homework, eat her meals, get ready for school, everything. Recording all of it in her weekly reports. Will Sister Laura be that way? Documenting every move I make?

Mom's lips stretch across her face like she's as uncomfortable with the idea as I am. "Sister Helen never ate with us."

"It would be best if I observed the family as a whole."

Mom continues working her way around the formal dining table, dropping exactly six cherry tomatoes onto each salad. "Let's ask Mr. Graham, shall we?"

As if summoned, Dad's Roanoke appears in the driveway behind the house. I have no doubt he won't want Sister Laura at dinner every night.

When he walks in the door, Mom introduces them. Sister Laura offers her hand, but Dad gets out of shaking by holding his palms in the air. "Better not. Had to check the oil on the way home." I've never seen Dad check the oil in my life, but I've never seen him shake hands with a woman either.

Mom clears her throat.

"Yes, Mary Beth?" His tone makes it sound like Mom works for him.

"Mitchell... Sister Laura would like to eat with us."

"Tonight?"

Sister Laura responds in a firm voice. "Every night."

Dad turns back to Sister Laura. "*Every* night?"

"If you don't mind, Mr. Graham, that would be best. I need to stay close to Stella, especially given what happened to Sister Helen."

What happened to Sister Helen?

Dad ignores this comment, shaking his head. "Sister Helen never ate with us."

"That's true, Mr. Graham, but I'm sure you'll agree we have to do things differently to help your daughter recover from the trauma she's experienced."

She makes a good point, but I'm still stunned. Sister Helen never asked anything of Dad.

He holds Sister Laura's gaze so long I expect him to fight. But a second later he pulls away. "I suppose that will be fine."

Does he understand she doesn't have to ask his permission?

~~~~~~

The dinner conversation is even more awkward than usual. Dad asks Sister Laura about her education and experience. Like it's a job interview. Even though she already has the job and it isn't Dad's place to decide if she gets it.

When he runs out of questions, the five of us grow quiet. Will the clatter of sterling silver against bone china be the soundtrack of our dinners from now on?

"I did want to ask *you* something, Mr. Graham."

Dad doesn't look up from his plate. "Yes?"

"I was studying the calendar...and, well, I noticed there isn't anything scheduled during the week for you and Stella."

"For me and Stella?"

"Yes, the two of you."

I jump in. "Is that allowed?"

Dad snaps at me. "Stella!"

Don't speak unless spoken to.

"Why would we schedule something for the two of us?"

"Why, so you can spend time with your daughter, of course."

"That would be highly unusual." Dad's eyes dart in my direction before looking away again. "Stella is a seventeen-year-old girl in the throes of puberty. I hardly think it would be appropriate for us to spend time together."

"It might help Stella during this difficult time. And what better way for Stella to learn to interact with adult men?"

Dad lets out a barely audible sound. I can't tell if he's clearing his throat or laughing, but I know exactly what it means. *Why would my teenage daughter need to interact with adult men?* He's ranted many times about women who try to talk to men. *Women shouldn't be around men at all. Unless they're married to them. They need to tend their own gardens.* But he doesn't articulate any of this to Sister Laura. "I don't think—"

Sister Laura interrupts him. "Mrs. Graham says you're a dedicated runner."

"Well, yes—"

"Perhaps Stella could join you."

"Join me?"

She pushes her glasses up her nose. "Run with you."

I almost choke on my brussels sprouts.

Dad puts his fork down hard enough that the wood table shakes. "This seems like a highly unusual request." But even as he says it, he deflates, his shoulders drooping. He can't have her fired. The constables decide who should be placed in our home.

Dad starts to speak again but stops, as if searching for another threat but coming up empty. "I'm not sure—" He starts to say something but never finishes.

We've all heard stories about parents who try to get a chaperone fired. It's never worth it. The chaperone training is long and intense. Once a chaperone is confirmed, she's seen as almost sacred. Families who complain about chaperones can be shunned.

I keep my eyes on Dad, hoping he'll let it go.

It's never good to question the Minutemen.

CHAPTER 12

A few hours later, the kitchen is dark. I check for the blue reflection of Mom and Dad's smart screen before walking my hands across the countertop in search of the donuts. Dad picks up a dozen at the Great New American Donut Shop on Sundays after church, our only real indulgence. I'm allowed one, but Dad and Shea eat as many as they want before Tiffany gets the leftovers. Mom says Dad shouldn't buy so many if they're just going to tempt us.

"He really shouldn't," I say out loud before lifting a giant éclair out of the box and putting it on a gold-rimmed salad plate. I'm licking icing off my fingers when I hear a floorboard creak overhead.

I need to hurry.

With the éclair in one hand, I use the other to log into Mom's smart screen and type, "How to adjust to a new chaperone." A few sites pop up before I see something strange.

Warning. Do Not Enter. Sensitive Information.

I push the key and brace for what's next, half expecting an

alarm to sound, but only a small red box appears, vibrating in the middle of the screen. "*Access denied*? What does that mean?"

"You must have done something you weren't supposed to."

I spin around, expecting to see Mom, but instead come face-to-face with Sister Laura.

"What are you doing?" I hiss at her. "Sneaking up on me like that? You scared me to death."

"I heard something." Sister Laura scratches the top of her nose while glancing toward the wall of windows at the back of the house. "I wanted to make sure everything was okay."

Every night they have warnings on the Freedom Channel. About all the kidnappings around the country. Seems like there's one every week, but there still hasn't been one in Bull Run.

"Don't worry. Nothing ever happens in Dull Run."

Sometimes I wish a girl from my high school *would* go missing. At least that would be exciting. Or maybe it would be terrifying. I follow Sister Laura's gaze, wondering if anyone is out there. If the constable is back. Or someone more dangerous. A few summers ago, Liv, Bonita, and I snuck out to Bonita's screened-in porch with our sleeping bags. We'd barely closed our eyes when we heard someone rustling in the trees. We all screamed, Bonita yelling, "Who's there?" But whomever it was ran into the woods behind the house. Bonita's parents called the police, but no one was ever caught. Ever since then, I worry someone is watching.

"Let's hope you're right," Sister Laura says as she turns away. Before she leaves, she peers over her shoulder. "Enjoy your éclair."

A shiver runs down my spine. Now I *know* someone is watching.

CHAPTER 13

I avoid Sister Laura the next morning until it's time to leave, dodging her in the kitchen but making sure she's watching when I grab a bran muffin, so she can put it in her report. It's her job to walk me to school, but I have no desire to talk to her. Or anyone for that matter. It's my first day back, and I know everyone will have a million questions.

What happened to Sister Helen? How did she die?

How do I respond when I don't know the answers myself?

It's late August, the hottest part of the year in Bull Run. Many things that are normally green are now brown and dry. The manicured lawns. The colorful lantana planted with hope at the beginning of summer. Even the trees appear lifeless.

Bull Run Preparatory Academy is just a mile from Gaslight, the neighborhood where we live. Sister Helen walked me to school every day, and it's hard not to think about her. Breathing the fresh air. Smelling every flower. Noticing the tiniest crack in the sidewalk. Tears well up in my eyes, but I'm determined not to cry. Sister Helen would tell me to think of the strong young women I've read about—Anne, Jo, Elizabeth, Bird, Celie, Jane. I try to summon their bravery, but it's useless. Sister Helen gave me every book I love. My whole life is saturated with her.

"Can I ask you something, Stella?"

I jump, having forgotten Sister Laura next to me. "What is it?"

"I was serious about you running with your father." I say nothing, and she goes on. "Will you do that for me?"

"But why?"

"Because it's important for you to learn how to navigate relationships with men."

"I don't know a single dad who *wants* to talk to his daughter." I say this even though I know full well Bonita and her dad still spend time together. But, to me, he's the exception that proves the rule.

"Some men don't know how to act with women. Your dad is afraid of us, so he avoids us." It is true Dad keeps his distance. He never stays in a room any of us are in, always fleeing to his office or the garage. "But he *does* want to have a relationship with you. I can see it."

I pause on the sidewalk to face her. "How?"

"The way he looks at you. He beams when you talk about school. He's proud of you. Even if he isn't allowed to show it."

I flash back to the day Sister Helen died. Dad's hand on my back. Like I'm more important than any rule.

"Fine."

"Fine?"

"I'll do it."

"Excellent. Well, here we are."

I expected to be nervous when I arrived at school after a week away, but it's a relief to escape Sister Laura's interrogation.

"See you at three?"

Respect your chaperone.

"I guess."

What I really want to say is: Would you please just go away?

My pulse quickens as I pass two constables stationed outside the school. Is one of them the constable I saw running out the gate last week? Normally I don't even notice the machine guns strapped across their backs, but today the sight of them makes my chest tighten. Bonita and Liv stand just inside the intimidating iron fence that surrounds the high school. The girls gather on the right side of the courtyard, the boys on the left, but I don't dare look in their direction. Yet, strangely I find myself wondering if Mateo de Velasco is there yet.

Deflect attention.

Bonita's chaperone is gone, but Sister Sophie lingers, insisting Liv button her blouse all the way up.

Bonita watches Sister Laura walk away. "Is that her?"

"That's her."

"She seems..." Bonita leans close. "I don't know. Creepy, I guess."

"Totally. She snuck up on me last night in the kitchen."

"Shadows are the worst."

We both glance at Liv's chaperone to make sure she didn't hear. Sister Sophie lets out a resigned sigh before turning to leave. The three of us start for the entrance. All the other girls watch us.

No, not us.

Me.

They're watching *me*.

"I don't know why they're so obsessed with you." Bonita waves her hand in a dismissive fashion. "They should be worried about the kidnappings."

"Was there another one?"

"The put out a new Red Alert Friday."

"Why didn't you tell me?"

Bonita shrugs. "You were too...you know." She doesn't finish. She doesn't have to.

"Where did it happen?"

"Close," Bonita says. "Antietam, less than an hour away."

Liv whispers the girl's name like a prayer: "Cynthia Reed."

"Snuck out alone last week." Bonita shakes her head. "Without her chaperone."

"But why?"

"No one knows. She was the one who refused to get married."

Liv shudders with such force she sounds like a helicopter.

"Olivia." Bonita leans across me and puts her hand on Liv's arm. "You *have* to stop worrying. Sister Sophie never leaves you alone. All the girls who have gone missing were alone. As long as you obey the rules, you'll be fine."

We walk by Brooklyn Liu and a group of girls we've known since grade school. I expect them to say something—*sorry* or at least *hello*—but instead they gawk. I make eye contact with Brooklyn, and she averts her gaze. The others follow her lead, looking away in one quick motion. As if my eyes will turn them to stone.

"Ignore them, Stella." Bonita takes my hand and pulls me toward the building.

"What's going on?" I ask.

"People are saying—" Liv starts before Bonita swings her empty hand in front of Liv, cutting her off midsentence.

"Just tell me," I insist, pausing to let them know I mean it.

Liv's eyes drop to the ground.

"It's stupid," Bonita says. "People are scared. No one's ever lost a chaperone before. They're worried you might be shunned."

"Shunned?"

"Just forget it. It's not even worth talking about."

There's no way I'll forget, but I don't want to talk about it either. Not yet anyway.

CHAPTER 14

B ull Run Preparatory Academy is divided into two distinct halves.

I've never stepped foot in the boys' half of the school, but I've heard rumors. Supposedly they have an exceptional science lab, a state-of-the-art technology center, and a fancy gymnasium with a fifty-foot climbing wall and ten-lane lap pool. Even though girls can't attend sporting events, we all know the boys' swim team has won the New America championship three of the last five years.

The girls' half of the school isn't run down—it's always sparkling clean—but it couldn't be described as anything but functional. Besides our regular classrooms, we have several kitchen facilities and a large multipurpose room where they hold everything from fitness classes to all-girl assemblies.

Even though they're both housed inside the same giant building, these two halves might as well be different schools—divided right down the middle by a thirty-foot-wide hallway with girls' lockers on one side and boys' on the other. That's the only place we run into each other besides the cafeteria. It's a layout designed to shield us from temptation.

Abstain from sin.

Our classes are segregated too. Except for a few electives and the one class we're all required to take: Family Development, where we're supposed to learn to talk to each other about getting married and having kids. They figure that's the best way to make us hurry up and start a family since they're desperate to grow the population. It's not lost on us how stupid it is to *take a class* to learn to talk to each other rather than just *letting us* talk to each other.

But I got lucky this year. I have a coed elective: Musical Expression. The class with Mateo. Most girls are put in single-sex electives. Like Culinary Arts or Floral Design. Consumer Math or Dietary Health. Reproductive Science or Midwifery, which they offer at the beginning, intermediate, and advanced level. The rest of my classes this year are only for girls. Gynecological Fitness, New American History, Basic Literacy, and Public Safety, which is where they teach us how to keep from getting kidnapped or attacked. It's where we first learned the DANGER method: *Deflect attention. Abstain from sin. Navigate the world with care. Give obedience. Embrace purity. Respect your chaperone.*

When I walk into Family Development, Levi Edwards catches my attention from across the room. He sneaks a look at Mr. Russell before moving toward me. It's against the rules, but boys still try to talk to us. I'm not in the mood to make small talk with Levi, so I fake a cough.

Mr. Russell looks up. "Levi Edwards, what on earth do you think you're doing?"

Levi's eyes plead with me. What does he want *me* to do? I don't make the rules. Still, I can't help but notice how beautiful his eyes are when they're sad. It's actually sweet. Maybe I've been too hard on him.

"You both need to sit." Neither one of us moves. We're still locked on each other. For the first time, I almost feel something for Levi. Mr. Russell clears his throat. "Now!"

I turn away before Levi does but feel his gaze on my back. We definitely shared a moment, but Levi isn't my type. He's too *something*. Too easy. Sister Helen once called him simple.

Mr. Russell watches me too. Making sure I do as I'm told. He's always watching. All of them are *always* watching. It's more penitentiary than school.

Mason Stiles offers me a sympathetic smile as I move to my seat. Bonita is right. Mason is different. I don't blame her for not wanting Olu Parker with Mason around.

Liv is already in the desk next to mine.

After Mr. Russell returns to his grade book, Liv whispers, "What just happened?"

"What do you mean?"

"With Levi."

"I don't know, but I have to sharpen my pencil." I jump up before she argues.

From the back, I study my classmates, people who seemed perfectly normal a week ago but now seem remarkably naive. Don't they know everything can go wrong in an instant? A girl sitting at the end of our row—Willow Howard—flashes me an irritated look. Was I staring? I drop my eyes and put my pencil in the sharpener, moving the crank as slowly as possible, so I can eavesdrop.

"Can't go this week," Willow whispers to Lana Lucas, the girl sitting next to her.

Where does someone like Willow Howard go? We're not allowed to go *anywhere* besides the library and church. Sure, we have sleepovers on rare occasions, but we never go *out*. If I'm being honest, Willow is not like other girls at Bull Run Prep. She's more like a girl who goes to govie. Tired. Worn out. She pulls her long tea-colored hair back in a bun and wears the same shirt days in a row. She clearly doesn't care what anyone thinks. I've heard rumors about Willow and her friends going to secret parties. I know boys go to parties. But girls? How would they get away with it?

"Why not?" Lana asks Willow.

"Pop found my stash."

I pause the crank.

"Is he angry?"

"Are you kidding? He was more than happy to keep it for himself."

"What a jerk," Lana says with conviction in her voice. "You sure you can't swing it? It's going to be a rager."

A rager?

I pull out my pencil and step up to Willow. "Are you talking about a party?"

Willow spins in my direction. "What the—?" She gives me the meanest scowl I've ever seen. "Were you eavesdropping?"

"No, I just—"

"If I ever catch you listening to one of my conversations again"—she pauses, glancing over her shoulder at Mr. Russell—"I'll kick your ass from here to Old America."

In between classes, everyone stares. Not just the girls. Boys too. I can't go anywhere without eyes on me.

A few girls put aside their fears to say something supportive—

I'm so sorry, Stella. How awful. Are you okay?—but mostly people just whisper and squirm out of my way. Their words float behind me like accusations. *Is that her? What happened to her chaperone? How did she die?*

By fifth period, I just want to go home, but instead I endure the pageantry of lunch. Girls in the right line, boys in the left, sizing us up like we're the real meal.

After a week away, it strikes me how much we look alike. Every single girl wears an A-line skirt—some solid, some plaid—that falls below her knees with socks that kiss the bottom of the fabric. We pair them with modest shirts: neat button-downs, plain blouses, striped tops. Not one of us wears anything as casual as cotton or as eye-catching as satin. The colors are muted—washed-out blue or green, blah gray, lackluster brown, deep plum, or barely noticeable pink. No red, orange, yellow, fuchsia, purple, or violet. And no jewelry besides a watch. The rest is banned.

It's not a uniform, but it might as well be.

Deflect attention.

In my tan corduroy skirt and blue striped button-down, I'm no different.

A group of Climbers passes the girls' line on their way to the other side of the cafeteria, and one of them lets out a long whistle.

Our collective response is to flip our heads in their direction and then immediately turn away. They leer at us like a pile of juicy steaks. We don't acknowledge them. If we're caught responding, we'll be the ones disciplined—detention, suspension, or worse—not them. It's our job to keep them at bay. We're the ones with the power of seduction. We're the ones who have to stop that from happening.

Embrace purity.

I focus on the tray in front of me, so I won't be tempted to peek at the boys again.

Abstain from sin.

The cafeteria workers dish our food without meeting our eyes, but I overhear their flirtatious chatter with boys on the other side. *Having a good day, Liam? How are your classes, Blake? Would you like more fries, Drew?* Boys get steak frites, pork loin topped with fried onions, pizza loaded with meat, but girls are expected to eat low-cal, low-carb foods that taste like nothing. If we want anything else, we have to find it on our own. Liv is an expert, stealing money from her father's wallet and paying for contraband. Today we're eating overcooked salmon and green beans with an apple for dessert. It could be worse. It could be chicken again. Or tofu.

"Salmon?" Bonita says when we sit down. "Again?"

Before the words are out of her mouth, a teacher with a pinched expression stops at the end of our table. They take turns monitoring us. We pick up our forks before he tells us to eat what's in front of us.

Give obedience.

"That was creepy," Bonita says when he's out of earshot.

"I know, right?"

"I hate shadows." Liv turns to me. "Is your new chaperone like that?"

"Yup. And she's already annoying me. She's changed everything."

Respect your chaperone.

"What did she change?" Bonita asks.

"She took over Shea's room. She's insisting on eating dinner with us."

"Just like Sister Sophie." Liv nods. "You better pray she's not as bad. Did I tell you how excited she is about Mandy Martin?"

"What about her?" I ask.

Liv gasps. "Oh my gosh, did you not hear?"

"No, what?"

"She got engaged. It was, like, over a week ago."

"But she hasn't even finished high school."

Bonita gives me her best don't-be-ridiculous voice. "You know this happens every fall, Stella. One girl in the senior class gets engaged, and all the others follow."

"Doesn't she know what happens to girls who get married too young? Hasn't she heard of *Jane Eyre*?"

"I guarantee you," Bonita says, "no one in all of Dull Run has read that book besides you. Sister Helen let you read books the rest of us aren't even allowed to look at."

"Brooklyn read it."

"But she—" Liv's head turns, tracking something across the cafeteria.

"What is it?" I follow her gaze.

Two uniformed police officers are walking into the cafeteria. Principal Terry appears at their side, pointing them in our direction.

"Are they here for me?"

When they get to our table, the principal says my name. "Miss Graham?" I stand, and the whole cafeteria goes quiet. "These officers are here to...uh, ask for your assistance." When he glances at them, they nod for him to continue. "This is Officer Alvarez and Officer Poole." He points to each of them. "They're with the Bull Run PD."

I'm too afraid to speak.

The shorter one, Alvarez, folds his hands in front of him. "There's no reason to be afraid, Stella. You're not in any trouble."

"Then why are you here?"

"Just protocol, Miss Graham," the taller one, Poole, says.

Alvarez holds a hand out in the direction of the hall like a game show host. "We'll start at your locker."

"My locker?"

Poole jumps in. "Just a formality."

Officer Alvarez starts for the hall, and Poole gestures for me to follow. I have no choice but to do what he wants.

They take everything out. Books, backpack, sweater. Even the linen pouch where I keep my feminine products. It's humiliating. Blood races through my veins as I try to remember if there's anything incriminating. Any contraband or banned books.

After they return the last item, Officer Alvarez turns to me. "Very good, Stella."

I let out a long sigh. "What were you looking for?"

Poole gives Alvarez a look that says, *Don't tell her.* So they *were* looking for something. What did they hope to find? A knife? A gun?

Officer Poole glances at his watch, impatience oozing off him. "We need to keep moving."

Alvarez holds his hand out. "One more stop in the nurse's office, Stella, and then we'll let you get back to class."

Everyone who sees us drops their mouth in astonishment. Who wouldn't? I'm walking down the hall with the principal and two police officers just days after my chaperone has dropped dead. I'd stare, too.

In the nurse's office, Officer Alvarez presses each of my fingers on a moist black pad and a clean sheet of paper. My prints are more art than fingertips. At the sink, I can't get the ink to wash off.

Alvarez rolls a long Q-tip along the inside of my cheek. Now I know why we came to the nurse's office. It takes everything I have not to vomit. Nurse Weeks writes me a hall pass and shoves me out the door. Is she hurrying so she can tell people?

When I arrive at Public Safety halfway through sixth period, every girl in the room stops what she's doing and watches me move to my seat. I share a table with Lana Lucas. The horrified look on her face tells me she's less than thrilled when I sit next to her.

I want to yell, *Things aren't going well for me either!* but I say nothing and wait for this awful day to end.

CHAPTER 15

Musical Expression is my last class of the day. And my favorite. Not only is it the class I have with Mateo, it's interesting and the teacher isn't awful. As long as no one acts up, Mr. Jeffrey is actually kind of great. He plays us all kinds of music, even songs by women. All we have to do is listen. After each song, Mr. Jeffrey talks about the history and what he likes about it.

Today we're listening to something called "If You See Her, Say Hello." Mr. Jeffrey tells us this was one of his father's favorites: "One of the great love anthems of the twentieth century."

I look around the room until I find Mateo in the back. His eyes are closed, and he's nodding. Does he listen to music with *his* dad? I've never once heard my father listen to music. I don't even know if he likes it.

The song begins. We've heard this man before. He's one of Mr. Jeffrey's favorites. The beginning sounds more like he's talking than singing. But then he gets louder.

She might think that I've forgotten her. Don't tell her it isn't so.

His voice is the saddest I've ever heard. It's like he's standing next to me, crying his heart out.

The bitter taste still lingers on,

Now he's wailing.

from the night I tried to make her stay.

His pain is so real I feel it in my gut.

When it's over, the room is cloaked in silence. No one can speak after hearing such a pure outpouring of heartbreak.

"Wow," Mr. Jeffrey says before telling us how the musician recorded two versions and claimed it wasn't autobiographical. *Wasn't autobiographical?* How could he sing like that and not feel every word in his soul?

Mr. Jeffrey calls on Mateo. Every head in the room swivels toward him. We never know what he'll say. "But none of that is as important as how the song made *us* feel, right?"

"I suppose you're right, Mr. de Velasco. How *did* you feel?"

"I felt like Dylan ran a knife down my chest, yanked my skin open, and gripped my heart in his hands. I felt like a fish he'd gutted."

Several people in the room gasp. Others laugh. Most of the girls turn away from Mateo's honesty. *Deflect attention.* But I can't pull my eyes from him. That's *exactly* how I felt. A second later, he notices me staring at him. Even though I know it's not right, I let myself be caught in his gaze.

His focus is so intense, it almost hurts as much as the song.

CHAPTER 16

An hour later, my first day back at school is over.

I cannot wait to go to yoga and reset.

But when I meet Sister Laura at the gate, she says, "I have an idea."

No, no, no. No ideas. No change. Just stop changing things.

She goes on. "I'm taking you to a safety class."

"I already take Public Safety at school."

"That's different. This is about women protecting themselves, not society. It's called Feminine Safety, but that's a silly name."

"That's a requirement for most classes, isn't it?"

Sister Laura lets out a laugh. It's the first time she's laughed around me, and I'm surprised she does it so easily. "It does seem that way. These days anyway."

"What do you mean?"

"Oh, nothing." She gives me a dismissive wave as she walks away from the school. I have no choice but to follow. Not doing so is against the law, not to mention dangerous. *Respect your chaperone.* When I catch up to her, she says, "It's actually a self-defense class."

The teenage girls on old TV shows are always going to self-defense classes. "Really?"

"Yes, really." She stops and looks at me. "You up for it?"

I gaze across the street to the gravel path that meanders through Freedom Park and ends at the library.

"I just want to go to yoga."

Sister Helen took me every day after school. It was part of our routine. Yoga at the library on weekdays and hiking or kayaking on Saturdays. I was lucky Sister Helen liked to exercise with me. Bonita and Liv's chaperones make them work out in their home gyms and weigh them every morning. Sister Helen was never like that. She made sure I was healthy, but not by constantly monitoring my progress. When she filled out her weekly reports, she would often just write what the constables wanted to hear. She said being too strict about that kind of thing would make me less healthy, not more. Yoga, she insisted, was a way to stay fit without overdoing it.

"I want to zone out."

"You've had enough of that."

The class meets in the basement of an abandoned gym in Shake Rag. I've never been to this part of town before. Dad says it's not the kind of place where people like us spend time, but it looks normal to me. The houses are smaller than they are in Gaslight, repair shops dotted between them, but the lawns are neatly mowed, showing off late-summer asters and concrete birdbaths in nearly every yard.

A metal door in the back of the gym leads into a room lined with lockers and gym equipment. Sister Laura goes up to the last locker and pulls on the handle, revealing a secret door hidden behind three lockers. We make our way down a crumbling cement staircase to the basement where we find a handful of women changing clothes in a long hallway.

Sister Laura pauses before going any further. "There's one more thing, Stella."

My eyes go to her involuntarily.

"These classes are forbidden."

I feel several faces turn in our direction.

"And we can't go in until you agree to keep them a secret."

A secret? What is she talking about?

"You'll see some things here that might surprise you. But you can't tell anyone about them. Do you promise not to tell?"

Every woman in the hallway is watching me now, waiting for my response.

"Yes, of course." I have no idea if I mean it, but I feel like I have no choice.

We go through another set of heavy doors and come to a large paneled room with a giant square mat. A man with light red hair kneels in the middle. He's bent so far over that his forehead rests on the mat. His wide-leg white pants are identical to the ones in the karate movie I watched with Bonita and Liv last summer, but he's paired them with a long-sleeve white shirt, the words *State Street Gym* emblazoned down one arm.

About twenty women kneel around the outside of the mat, almost all of them wearing sweatpants and the same large boxing gloves Sister Laura handed me in the hallway. Most are adults, but there are two other teenage girls. Each sits next to a woman I presume is a chaperone though, like Sister Laura, they've changed out of their caftans.

"It's crowded," I say to Sister Laura.

She rubs the top of her nose, "With all the kidnappings, people are scared." *Is that why we're here?* She leads me around the mat and points to the floor when we get to the back corner. "Kneel here."

The redheaded man lifts his head gently off the mat, rising so slowly he's barely moving. When he sits back on his heels, he speeds up, jumping to his feet in one quick motion. He spins in a circle, arms out like a ringmaster before clapping his hands together. "Good afternoon, ladies."

Every person in the room responds the same way: "Good afternoon, Master."

"I have a question for all of you." I'm shocked no one laughs at how seriously he takes himself. "Are you ready to learn how to protect yourselves from men like me?"

"Yes, Master!" they shout in response.

"I see we have newcomers." The Master points his chin in our direction. My face gets hot. "You must submit to our terms."

A few women murmur agreement.

"I started these classes just over ten years ago. When my daughter became a woman." He moves in the direction of a young woman with long hair the same soft shade of red as his. "Tommi, please come to the mat."

The young woman leaps to her feet just like the Master did minutes before, her ponytail flipping from side to side. She strides across the mat, bowing when she reaches her father.

He bows back and resumes his slow spin. "I fully believe in what we're doing in this, our brave new country. I believe it is the ethical duty of men to protect women. But I also believe avoiding danger is not the only way for women to protect themselves."

The Master stops turning and lunges at his daughter, who grabs his arm and twists it behind him, pinning it against his back. He tries to wriggle free but eventually goes slack. I look around the mat, waiting for someone to say something about what they've done, how many rules they're breaking, but no one seems to notice.

"Women also need to be able to *physically* defend themselves."

The Master peers over his shoulder at his daughter, who wears a smile wide enough to crack her face. "Thank you, my dear Tommi."

She lets his arm go and bows before returning to her place.

"I believe I have given Tommi a great gift. The gift of inviolability. It is my goal to give the same to all of you. This is no longer a popular idea in our society, but it is what I believe. If you agree, you will always be welcome here. If not, you are free to leave. But please respect our work enough not to report us."

The Master's eyes rest on the two of us. He wants a response, but I don't know how to answer. Is this even allowed? Can we get in trouble? Everyone stares, waiting for us to speak. I turn to Sister Laura. She, too, is watching me.

"Well, Stella? Do you want to stay?"

I don't know what I want. I don't know what's right.

Sister Laura faces forward. "We agree, Master."

The Master goes over basic moves—jab, cross, uppercut, hook— for thirty minutes before instructing everyone to return to the edge of the mat. He spins in another circle. "Does anyone in this room feel ready to stand against me?"

I have to stop myself from yelling, *No!* Are there women brave enough to fight a man, especially a man who teaches people how to fight?

I expect no one to volunteer, but then a voice yells out: "I am, Master."

I'm shocked when I turn and see Sister Laura's hand in the air.

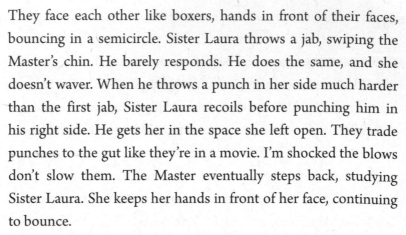

They face each other like boxers, hands in front of their faces, bouncing in a semicircle. Sister Laura throws a jab, swiping the Master's chin. He barely responds. He does the same, and she doesn't waver. When he throws a punch in her side much harder than the first jab, Sister Laura recoils before punching him in his right side. He gets her in the space she left open. They trade punches to the gut like they're in a movie. I'm shocked the blows don't slow them. The Master eventually steps back, studying Sister Laura. She keeps her hands in front of her face, continuing to bounce.

The Master laughs and says, "You fight like a girl, Sister!"

Sister Laura's hands drop, her mouth falls open. The Master lunges forward and throws a cross-hook at her face, following that with a straight-on kick to her gut. Sister Laura flies backward, landing on the mat with a thump. Everyone gasps.

Her fingers go to her mouth. Even across the room, I see blood on her hand. She shakes her head before jumping to her feet and bowing at the Master.

When she returns to my side, I whisper, "Are you okay?"

"I'm fine," she says, but her teeth are clenched tight.

The Master raises his hands in victory, spinning around for the whole room to see. "Anyone else?"

No one takes his challenge.

~~~~~~~~~

Outside, I feel obligated to ask again if she's all right.

She shrugs and starts walking. "I'm fine."

"Did he have to kick you so hard?"

"It wasn't that hard."

"What a jerk."

"It can be hard to tell, but his heart's in the right place."

"He punched you *in the face*."

"I barely felt it."

I point to her lip. Even from a foot away, the metallic smell of blood reaches me. "You're *bleeding*."

"It's a tiny bit of blood. It's nothing."

"Still, I could never—"

Sister Laura stops and puts her hands on her hips. "Don't underestimate yourself, Stella. I'm confident you could handle it."

"I don't think so."

"Well, I do." She shakes her head, the disappointment in her eyes as clear as the cloudless sky above. "That's *why* I fought him. I want you to understand what you're capable of. We're stronger than they want us to believe, Stella."

Sister Laura might think that, but she's wrong. I could never fight a man.

"The truth is, I'm more pissed than hurt."

"At him?"

"No, at myself."

"Why?"

"For letting my guard down. I just couldn't believe he said that."

"I mean, you *are* a girl. Of course, you fight like one—"

"He didn't mean it that way. He didn't mean it as a statement of fact. He was insulting women. Saying we're not as good as men." She pushes her glasses up her nose. "You think I'd be used to it by now."

I have no idea what she means, but I'm not about to ask. I didn't want to act unconcerned, but I also don't want to let her in.

CHAPTER 17

The library is exactly the same as before. The giant oak table. The worn-out carpet. The serious armchairs. The books scattered like left-out toys. The only thing missing is Sister Helen. At least Sister Laura sticks to this part of our routine, letting me hang out in the library until it's time to go home for dinner. I'm rereading *A Wrinkle in Time*, the first book Sister Helen and I read together.

When I get to the part that says, *Believing takes practice*, I remember Sister Helen saying, "I think that's true, Stella, don't you?" I wipe my eyes before Sister Laura notices, but when I glance at her chair, she isn't there anymore. *Thank God.*

I drop my gaze back to the book but can no longer concentrate. I crane my neck, searching for her. She was here a minute ago, and now she's gone.

My pulse quickens. *Why isn't she here?* She's *supposed* to be here. That's her only job.

That's when it hits me.

I'm alone.

In public.

For the first time in my whole life, I'm out in the world alone.

CHAPTER 18

I 've *never* been alone in public before. Not that I remember. Before Sister Helen, I never went anywhere without Mom or Dad.

But now I am really and truly alone.

Alone.

My heart thumps in my chest like one of those rap songs from Old America. It's terrifying. And exhilarating. But what if something goes wrong?

Moving my head in a slow circle, I search for Sister Laura, scanning every crevice and corner. Between the rows of books. Behind my chair. Under the table. Even up on the ceiling. But I can't find her.

What if someone sees me? Being alone in public is against the law for a girl my age. I could be arrested. Or shunned. What if someone attacks me? On the way in, we passed a few Climbers sitting around a smart screen near the circulation desk. Will they come after me? I know all too well what happens when girls my age are left alone with a group of men. The inappropriate comments. The unwanted grabbing. Or worse. They've been teaching us about that as long as we've been in school. That's *why* we have chaperones. To protect us from all the evil in the world. But *my* chaperone has abandoned me.

Cortisol courses through my blood. The body's natural response to danger. They teach us that too. The fight-or-flight instinct.

Should I run? Or look for a place to hide? But where? If I leave the library, it's even more likely I'll get assaulted. Or kidnapped. Or run into a constable. Girls who sneak out alone get expelled and sent to govie. If that happened, I couldn't get into college or make a good match for marriage. My whole life would be ruined. No, I can't run. It's too dangerous. I have no choice but to sit here. Sit here and wait. Pray no one sees me.

Praise God for protecting women from harm.

Please, please, God. Please protect me from harm.

A minute later Sister Laura strolls out of the stacks and plops down in the chair next to me like it's the most normal thing in the world for her to do.

"Where were you?" I hiss at her.

She nods toward the far wall. "I was in the stacks."

I glance in that direction and back at Sister Laura, but she's flipping through the book in her hand like nothing unusual happened.

Like she didn't just break the biggest rule in the world.

I'm still livid on the walk home.

A convoy of red SUVs fly past us like they're headed to a fire. When they pass, a shiver runs through my entire body. What if they had caught me?

As soon as they're gone, I wheel on Sister Laura. "How could you leave me?"

"Oh, don't be silly. I didn't *leave* you. I was a few feet away."

"What if something happened?"

"I would have heard you. Besides nothing was going to happen. I promise."

"You can't know that. Being in public is dangerous."

"Oh, please. This town couldn't be any safer. There are constables on every corner. You have nothing to worry about."

"Then why did we go to self-defense?"

She slows her pace and tilts her head in my direction. "You have to try new things if you want to grow, Stella. And learning how to be on your own—and stay safe—is a big part of that."

"But being alone is against the rules. What if I had been attacked?"

"You were *fine.*"

"How do you know?"

Sister Laura increases her pace without answering my question. Neither of us says another word until we're nearing the old planetarium. "I want to ask you something."

I make the mistake of glancing at her.

"Why were you afraid?"

"*Obviously* because I was alone."

"Are you sure that's what frightened you?"

"Yes, of course."

"Maybe it was something new, something you never experienced before, giving you that rush of adrenaline."

"That wasn't it. I was really afraid."

Sister Laura stops abruptly, and I stop too. She catches my eye before I can look away. "Did you *really* think you might be attacked, Stella?"

I'm so infuriated, I start walking again. How dare she ask me— yet again—if my emotions were real. Of course, I was afraid.

Wasn't I?

CHAPTER 19

At home, I go straight to the kitchen where I know Mom will be cooking dinner. I will Sister Laura to her room, but she follows me like a hungry dog.

I call out as soon as I see her. "Mom?"

She's stirring something on the stove. "Yes, Stella?" Shea sits at the table drawing a bright red monster. I expect to see Tiffany, but there's no sign of her.

"Where's Tiffany?"

Mom returns my stare and lets out a sigh. "She's at the police station."

"The police station. Why?"

"Everyone who was in the house that day has to be questioned and fingerprinted, Stella. Tiffany is no exception. I don't like it any more than you do. But we don't have a choice." Mom puts her wooden spoon down. "Did you need something?"

"This isn't going to work." I flick my eyes at Sister Laura and then back at Mom. "*Sister Laura* isn't going to work."

Mom's slams a lid on the pot in front of her. "Stella, honestly, do we have to do this today? I had to spend hours with the police—"

"You too? Why?"

"I just told you why."

I have more questions, but I'm desperate to tell her what happened. "Sister Laura left me alone at the library today."

"Alone?" Mom's tone changes from irritation to surprise as she turns to Sister Laura. "Really?"

"I was wrong to let Stella believe that, Mrs. Graham. What she doesn't understand is that I could see her, but she couldn't see me."

"You're lying! You said you could hear me, but you never said you could see me."

"I was testing you, Stella. I wanted to see how you would respond."

Mom raises her eyebrows. I'm ready for her to chastise Sister Laura, but instead she turns back to me. "We don't want to bring the constables into this, Stella."

"Do you even care?" I spin toward Sister Laura. "Do either of you care that something could have happened to me? That I could have been kidnapped?"

Mom glances at Sister Laura, and something passes between them. A knowing look. As if they have information I don't. Like Mom is siding with Sister Laura. I shake my head in disgust.

"Stella—" Mom uses the pleading voice she uses to defend something she can't possibly defend, but I don't hear the rest. I'm gone before she feeds me a totally unbelievable explanation.

I yell over my shoulder loud enough for them to hear. "I'm telling Dad the minute he gets home!"

As soon as my face hits the pillow, I scream as loud as I can. I don't care if they hear me. I *want* them to hear me. It's not lost on me that I'm acting like the teenage girls in the movies from Old

America. For the first time, I get why they slam doors and roll their eyes so much. *No one understands.* I flip over and stare at the ceiling, wishing I had stars stuck there like the movie teenagers do.

Sister Laura's words come back to me. *Are you sure that's what frightened you? Maybe it was something new, something you never experienced before.*

She's wrong. I *am* afraid of being alone in public.

Aren't I?

My bedroom is the only place I'm allowed to be alone. A beautiful cell decorated like it belongs in a photo shoot. Directly across from my bed is a marble fireplace. On the other side of the room, in front of one of three large windows, my desk sits under a beaded chandelier. The desk is giant—big enough to spread out at least a dozen books. It belonged to my maternal grandfather. My mother says he was highly intelligent, sometimes claiming I remind her of him. Built-in bookshelves line the walls on either side of the windows, packed with books from top to bottom. Some were given to me by Sister Helen, the others belonged to my mother and her mother before her. The women inside those books didn't do what was expected of them. They pushed themselves. They set out on their own.

They weren't afraid.

Am I really afraid?

Or is that just what I've been taught?

Is Sister Laura right?

She's only been here two days, and I already hate her. But I also can't stand that she thinks I'm afraid.

It hits me as clearly as the Master hit Sister Laura.

I don't have to *like* her to get what I want out of her.

And what I want is freedom.

CHAPTER 20

I figure things will start slowly, and at first they do.

After dinner, Sister Laura brings me a stapled booklet with the words THE ALLEGORY OF THE CAVE stamped on a plain brown cover.

"Keep it inside another book." She runs her finger across my bookshelves until she comes to I *Capture the Castle*. "This one." She taps it. "A castle is like a cave."

"You want me to hide it?" Sister Helen gave me books to read all the time, but she never told me to hide any of them.

"I want you to be the only one who knows it's here."

The first paragraph doesn't grab me, but once I find out the people living in the cave have been kept in chains since birth, I can't stop reading. When I get to the part where one of them is freed, I feel my heart racing. What would that be like? To be free after being chained your whole life?

But it's when I read about what happens to the person who leaves the cave that I start to cry. The idea that you could spend your entire life in the dark and then suddenly be exposed to light is both heartbreaking and beautiful at the same time.

By the time I close the booklet, I have goose bumps up and down both arms.

In the morning Sister Laura doesn't mention the booklet or anything else. We walk in silence along the tree-lined streets. What would it be like to make the trip by myself? Would I be afraid? Would I be worried someone was watching? Or would I feel liberated? Like the person who gets out of the cave?

I tilt my head back and close my eyes for the briefest moment as I imagine that kind of freedom. The sun warms my face, and I breathe in the sweet smell of late summer clematis. Yes, it would be scary in some ways, but it would also be intoxicating. When I open my eyes, Sister Laura is staring at me.

"What?"

"*You* tell me."

I take in a deep breath and let go of the fear. It will be different this time because it will be my choice. "We can try again."

"Try what?" The flicker in Sister Laura's eyes tells me she knows exactly what I mean.

"Don't make me ask."

"Okay, I won't."

"Maybe you're right. Maybe I was afraid because it was new. All my life I've been told that if I went out in public alone, I'd be attacked. Or kidnapped. Or worse. I never thought it was safe."

"That's what they want you to believe."

"I want to find out for myself."

A tiny smile emerges on her face. She's pleased. And I have no idea how that makes me feel.

At the library I try my best to act normal, taking out the book Sister Laura found for me, but I'm too excited to process the words. I read the first line over and over, but nothing gets through. I can't wait for her to go.

She must sense my impatience, getting to her feet right away. I see her moving out of the corner of my eye but don't react. I close my eyes and count. When I get to one hundred, I open them and look over both shoulders to make sure she's really gone. I turn back around and that's when I see them.

Two eyes.

They're behind the row of books directly in front of me, peeking through an empty space on the shelf.

I know those eyes.

Those are the eyes of Mateo de Velasco.

Normally he stares out the window in the back of the classroom with longing. As if he's gazing at the ocean instead of a parking lot. But now it's me he's contemplating.

Our eyes lock on each other, and my whole body flushes with emotion. Even from fifteen feet away, I notice his irises are the same color as the moss that grows on the banks of Shanty Hollow.

Am I supposed to say something?

But that's against the rules. Especially in public. Especially alone. And who knows who's watching?

He holds a single hand up. It's the simplest wave I've ever seen, but it says so much. *I don't care about the rules. I want to reach you.*

I glance behind me. No one is there. I let out the breath I didn't realize I was holding.

When I turn back around, Mateo has vanished.

I gasp out loud, covering my mouth when I hear the sound.

He's gone.

CHAPTER 21

S ister Laura and I stroll toward home. The sun hasn't set, but
its intensity wanes. Dusk takes over with its ethereal magic.
Sister Laura hasn't said a word since we left the library. She
seems to intuitively understand when I need space. I *could* tell her
about Mateo—she'd never breathe a word to anyone—but doing
so means letting down a wall I haven't let down yet. It means letting her in.

"What is it?" she asks as if she can read my mind. I must have
peeked at her. I keep walking and weigh my options. I can tell
Bonita or Liv and risk them letting it slip. Or I can tell Sister Laura.

I don't have much choice. She's my shadow. I can befriend the
shadow or make it my enemy.

I choose the former.

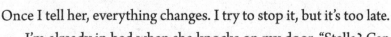

Once I tell her, everything changes. I try to stop it, but it's too late.

I'm already in bed when she knocks on my door. "Stella? Can
I come in?"

This is exactly what I was afraid of. Now that I've let down the wall, I'll never be able to put it back up. Regret sits in my chest like a hard tumor.

"Okay." I use a voice I hope is too soft to reach her. But she must have supersonic hearing because the knob turns a second later.

She's wearing sweatpants and a gray T-shirt with a white squirrel on the front. It's only the second time I've seen her without a caftan. She looks so normal. Her right hand is lifted high in the air, as if she's carrying a gift. She comes to the bed and holds it out to me: a glazed donut on a linen napkin. Underneath it is a blue book.

"*Where* did you get that?"

"I have my ways," she says cryptically as she pushes the donut toward me. "Go ahead."

It's clearly a bribe, but I take it. I'm not about to turn down a donut in the middle of the week. "Thanks," I say in the least thankful voice I have.

She holds up the book. "For you." A simple drawing of a white room appears under the words *A Room of One's Own*. She pulls *A Room with a View* off the bookshelf and removes the dust jacket. "Both have the word *room* in the title."

Is this becoming a habit?

"So only I know it's there?"

"That's right."

"Am I *allowed* to read books like these? Aren't they banned?"

"Technically, yes, but books shouldn't be banned. Ignorance should not be a goal."

"You mean, like the people in the cave?"

"Exactly." She glances at the chair on the other side of the bed. Sister Helen's chair. "Can I sit?"

"I guess so."

I bite into the donut as she gets settled: pulling her legs underneath her, cleaning her glasses, and finally leaning against the chair like she intends to stay a while.

How can I get her to leave? Can I say the donut is making me sick? Would she believe me if I claimed to have a test in the morning?

Sister Laura must not sense my apprehension because she smiles and starts talking like we're going to have a real conversation. "I'm so glad you told me what happened today. It's good to have someone to confide in."

"Uh-huh." I take another bite of donut.

"Sooooooo." Sister Laura lets the word drag out. "Do you know him very well?"

"Who?"

"Mateo, of course."

She clearly isn't taking the hint. I respond as shortly as I can. "Kind of."

"Is he in one of your classes?"

"Musical Expression," I say before I realize she's tricked me into giving up information.

"What's *that* like?"

"You didn't take it?" I ask, again figuring out too late what she's doing.

"No." She shakes her head. "I finished high school early. Right before New America was founded. Before the Minutemen renamed every city they took over."

"Bull Run used to be called something else, didn't it?"

"It was called Bowling Green until the Minutemen named it

after the second Battle of Bull Run, one of the bloodiest losses for
the Union."

"The Union?"

"That's what they called the first army that fought to save
America."

"Why would they name a town after something so awful?"

Sister Laura narrows her eyes. "All of our cities are named after
Civil War battles now. I guess they don't teach you that in New
American History?"

I'm not sure which war she means, but I decide not to admit
that's something else they don't teach us. "No, but I bet they didn't
teach *you* how to express yourself through music."

Sister Laura lets out a laugh. "That's true. We had old-fashioned
music classes—choir, band, piano, guitar, that kind of stuff. All the
other classes were different too. Algebra, geometry, calculus, world
history, biology, chemistry, physics."

"You took classes for boys?"

"Well, they weren't *just* for boys back then."

"Huh." I'm interested but don't want to show it. I put the last
piece of donut in my mouth.

"Don't get me wrong—they still told girls they weren't good
at science and math. But they never actually kept us from taking
those classes. Still—" She wants to say something else.

"What?"

"It's nothing." She rubs her nose and looks away.

"Just say it." She wanted me to talk to her, and that's exactly
what I'm doing.

She lets out a sigh as loud as a cleansing breath. "I was going to say
that, yes, it was similar to what happens here but wasn't *nearly* as bad."

My mouth drops open. "You think what happens here is *bad*?"

"Are you shocked to hear me say that, Stella?"

"Uh, yeah. You're a chaperone."

"Then you know why I hesitated."

"I guess."

"Are you upset with me?" She tilts her head to the side like a dog. "For telling you what I think?"

"No, it's just—no one ever talks like that."

"It's good to be honest about these things." When I don't respond, she asks, "Do you agree?"

"No one ever is."

"Well, maybe it's time things changed."

I don't say it, but an answer forms in my head.

Maybe it is.

Sister Laura studies me. Does she know I agree with her?

"Is that what you want, Stella?"

"Sometimes."

"How do you think things should change?"

I take in my own cleansing breath.

"I won't tell anyone, Stella. I don't work for them. I work for you."

"I know." The truth is, I didn't know that. Yes, Sister Helen supported me unconditionally. That's why it was so hard to lose her. But I'm not sure I can trust Sister Laura, though I have to admit there's something about her. She's not like anyone else. She and Sister Helen have that in common.

I take in another deep breath before I exhale to the count of ten.

And then I tell Sister Laura what I wish could change. "There are too many things I don't know. Like what you said about the Union. And the Civil War. I don't know what those things are."

"I'll teach you."

"And, of course, I want to do things on my own, but—"

"Yeah, not possible. Not here anyway."

Not here? I want to ask, but I'm not ready. "I hope this doesn't sound boy crazy, but it would be great if I could, you know, actually spend time with boys. Or *a* boy."

"A boy meaning Mateo?"

I feel myself blush. "Sure."

"You want to be alone with him?"

My face gets even hotter. "Uh, yeah."

It seems like an obvious answer, but Sister Laura appears to be processing. Now she's the one glancing down at her hands. "I'll have to teach you some things." She squints. "All the things they don't want you to know."

"Like what?"

"Like how to stay safe."

"You think Mateo is dangerous?"

She lets out a laugh. "Of course, that's what you'd think. That's what they've taught you. I don't mean that kind of safe. I mean, safe…you know, when you're romantic with someone."

Sister Laura is talking about sex. And I don't think she means sex after marriage.

Embrace purity.

"If and when things get heated."

"But—"

She pushes her glasses up her nose. "I know it sounds wild to you, Stella, but the truth is, it's perfectly normal for teenagers to have sex."

I think about this all the time. But I'm not going to admit that to Sister Laura.

"As long as they do it safely and with consent."

Everything in my body alights. It's the same rush of emotion I experienced when Mateo and I locked eyes in the library.

I can feel it.

Everything is changing.

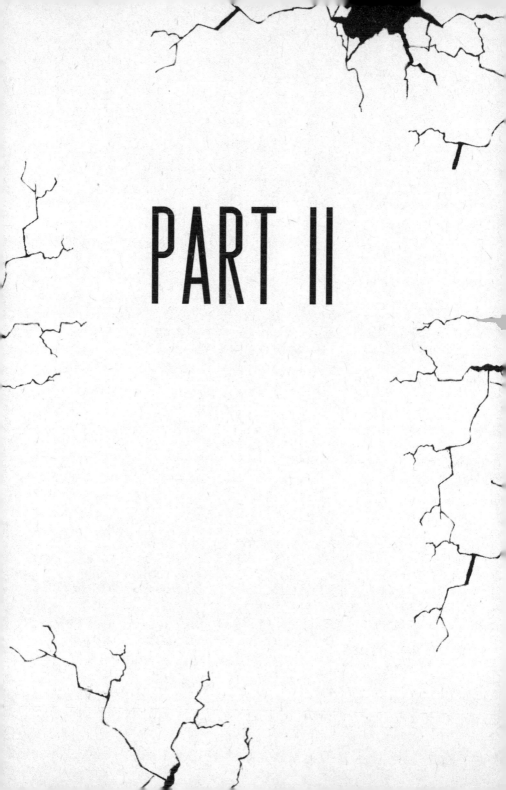

PART II

CHAPTER 22

Sister Laura brings a small pile of running gear to my room early Friday morning. The clothes are hers, the shoes from Dad. He bought them the day before. I didn't think he'd give in so easily.

"Meet him downstairs in fifteen minutes. And don't be late."

It's still dark out, the house even colder than usual. I sleepwalk through putting on the roomy shirt and sweatpants.

Dad is at the door when I go down the front staircase. I can't help but notice the pistol is not on his hip. Does he usually wear it when he goes running? He doesn't look happy *or* unhappy. He looks focused.

"You ready?"

"I guess so." I have no idea how this will go. I've never run outside of gym and haven't taken a real gym class in almost four years. Boys take it in high school, but girls take Gynecological Fitness, which is more about keeping our bodies primed for pregnancy than exercising. There's no way I can run more than a mile without passing out. And I'm betting Dad runs farther than that.

The humidity smacks me in the face.

Dad rotates his arms in circles as he strides to the front gate. I follow, not sure if I should imitate him. On the sidewalk, he tilts his head to the left, and before I know what's happening, we're running.

He moves slowly at first. For my benefit, I'm sure.

We run away from town. I'm surprised how invigorating it is to cover new ground. I can't remember the last time I've gone this way on foot. Pretty soon we've climbed the hill out of the Gaslight district and gone down the other side into the government campus. This used to be a university. Limestone classroom buildings now house offices I've never been inside. The old dorms at the bottom of the hill have been transformed into the conservatory where chaperones train. Dad peers into each lobby, nodding at security guards like he knows them. He must run this way every day.

I'm already winded, but Dad blasts ahead. We leave campus and cross into the residential area behind it. Cedar Ridge. It's old, but not as old as our neighborhood. Bonita lives here, and we run toward her house like it's our destination. My breathing gets louder, uneven, but Dad doesn't seem to notice. Bonita's house is in the distance: white brick with black shutters. From the street, it looks like it's only one story, but the backyard slopes down to a giant field surrounded by woods, revealing a ground floor not visible from the front. When we were little, Bonita's parents let us camp in a tent out back. We might as well have been on another planet.

"Would Bonita be surprised to see you running?"

I'm taken aback by how upbeat he sounds but only have the energy for one word: "Definitely."

He smiles. "It's good to surprise people, Stella. Keeps them guessing."

I know the rules. *Speak when spoken to.* I choke a few words out. "I hope I can make it."

"You should never get your hopes up, Stella. That's a sure way to be let down."

What's the point of living if you don't get your hopes up? "Yes, sir."

We're climbing the giant hill in front of Bonita's house, and I'm wheezing too much to say more. I come to an abrupt stop, bending over at the waist. Dad is twenty-five feet ahead of me before he turns around.

"You can do it, Stella."

I shake my head. "I can't."

"Keep going!" He rotates his arm in a circle, waving me forward with out-of-character optimism.

I straighten up "You go ahead. I'll catch up."

He wipes his hand across his mouth, glancing up and down the street before walking back to me. "It's okay. We can head back."

"Don't you want to keep going?"

"No, it's fine."

It hits me. He *can't* go on without me. He *can't* leave me. For the briefest moment I forgot I'm not allowed to be alone.

Dad lifts his hand like he's going to pat my back but, at the last second, pulls away. "You did well, Stella. Now let's go home."

CHAPTER 23

A week later, the temp climbs above 100 again. The weather man on the Freedom Channel brags about breaking more records. Even though I showered after running with Dad this morning, I'm sweaty all over again just two blocks from home.

Sister Laura wipes a hand across her forehead before she says, "You need to come up with other things you want to try, Stella."

"Like what?"

"Little things. Things that aren't against the rules but, for whatever reason, you don't do."

Sister Laura has been right so far.

Sitting alone in the library. Going to self-defense class. Running with Dad. It's been exhilarating. Why not do more? And what do I *want* to do? My absolute number one is going out alone, but that isn't happening. Going on a date, like a real movie date, is up there too, but I don't see that happening either. If nothing else, it would be nice if the boys who come to Visitation could be boys I actually like. Or even if I was allowed to talk to boys outside of Visitation. Like at school or the library or wherever. But, as it stands now, I don't even talk *in front* of boys in class. Girls *never* talk in coed classes. It's just a thing. Like an unwritten rule or something.

That's when it comes to me.

I want to talk in class.

⁓⁓

The hardest part is just trying.

I've never seen a girl raise her hand in a coed class. Not since elementary school when every class except gym was coed. But starting in middle school, we were separated by gender. In class, at lunch, at church, even at social events. *Deflect attention.* As soon as that happened, girls stopped talking to boys. It was like we'd all received the same announcement. *Girls who are menstruating can no longer talk to members of the opposite sex.* We got the message. Once we were old enough to have a chaperone, it wasn't safe for boys and girls to converse.

But I'm not doing it anymore.

⁓⁓

I give myself a pep talk in the restroom before Family Development. In the mirror, my skin appears flushed, almost splotchy. "You can do this," I say to my reflection. "It's just talking."

I march into Mr. Russell's classroom with my head up, shoulders back. I'm ready.

It's Liv who questions me. "Are you okay, Stella?"

"Why?"

"Your face."

I move a hand to my cheek.

"It's bright red. And your hands." She points at them. "They're clenched."

I unclench my fists. "I'm fine."

Mr. Russell clears his throat from the front of the room. "If you need to see the nurse, Miss Graham, do so before class begins. I don't want your…your cycle…disrupting my discussion."

My cycle? Is he assuming that just because I'm worked up I have my period? And is he saying my *period* would be disruptive?

"I'm fine."

"Then take a seat."

It takes Mr. Russell fifteen whole minutes to ask a question. "What *is* the appropriate age to start contemplating marriage?"

An easy one. Everyone knows we're supposed to start thinking about marriage when we begin puberty. I shoot my hand in the air.

Mr. Russell's eyes flatten. My hand wavers, but I force it back up. He rolls his gaze back and forth over the tops of our heads like a sprinkler.

He points at a boy on the other side of the room. "Cal, how about you?"

He clearly went out of his way not to call on me.

I throw my hand back in the air.

Mr. Russell goes back to his desk and pulls a notepad out of his drawer. "I'm writing you a pass, young lady." He looks up from the paper and glares at me.

"What? Why?"

"You're obviously not well."

"I'm fine, really."

Mr. Russell strides back to me and pushes the pass in my hand. "Skedaddle."

Mr. Russell does everything but physically push me out the door. It's all I can do not to give him a cross-hook to the face.

"Do you feel better, Stella?" Liv asks when the three of us sit down at lunch with identical meals: plain chicken breast, steamed broccoli, and an overripe peach.

"You're sick?" Bonita turns to face me, dropping her fork back to her tray. "Homecoming is next Friday, Stella. You *cannot* get sick."

"No." I shake my head with disgust. "I am *not* sick."

"Your face was bright red in Russell's class. You looked feverish."

I blow out a puff of indignation. "I was worked up, Liv, *not* sick."

"Worked up about what?" Bonita asks.

Before I can respond, Mason Stiles approaches our table, his eyes trained on Bonita. He doesn't stop—that would draw too much attention—instead walking as slowly as possible past our table. He does this every day. It's one of the ways he and Bonita are able to be together without actually *being* together. Their connection is so intense I have to look away. I glance at the boys' side of the cafeteria. Mateo isn't in our lunch shift, but if he was, would he do the same thing? Would he walk by our table every day just to look in my eyes?

"Stella," Liv says, pushing her chicken around on her plate. "Is this about Sister Laura?"

Of course Liv would think that. Her chaperone is a dictator. "No, it's not her. She's actually okay."

Bonita swings her attention back to us, Mason finally out of sight. "She's *okay*? I thought she was ruining your life."

They both stare at me with wide eyes.

"She's really not that bad."

Neither of them says a word.

"You just have to trust me."

Bonita finally speaks. "If you're sure, Stella."

"I'm sure."

"So you got lucky with your chaperone *again*?" Liv says.

I swivel toward Liv. "You're not implying Sister Helen's death was lucky, are you?"

"Of course not. But still."

I roll my eyes at her. "I'm not sure about Sister Laura yet, but I have decided something."

"What?" Liv asks.

"We always act like we have to obey them. Our chaperones."

"And?" Bonita says.

"And we don't. They work for us. We can stand up to them."

Liv jumps in. "It's too risky. If we get caught, we'll be shunned."

"But what if we don't get caught?" I turn to Bonita. "You and Mason are constantly finding ways to connect."

Bonita smiles. "We're pretty sly though."

"What about the time he stormed into New American History just to tell you he had to see your face?"

"Okay, that was the opposite of sly."

I turn to Liv next, pointing to the Moon Pie in her lap. "And you buy contraband all the time."

"That's different. No one gets in trouble for sneaking junk food. Disobeying our chaperones is on another level."

"That's why we won't get caught."

Bonita and Liv exchange a look. I'm not sure what emotion I see on their faces. Is it fear? Concern?

"Stella." Bonita puts her hand on the table like it's a buzzer. "What's going on with Sister Helen?"

"What do you mean?"

"The case. Brooklyn Liu keeps saying she's heard things. From her dad." Brooklyn Liu's dad is head of the Bull Run PD.

"*What* case?"

Bonita glances at Liv and then back at me. "You don't know?"

"Know what?"

Liv answers. "They're investigating…you know…"

"No, I don't know."

"People are talking, Stella." Bonita takes a deep breath. "People are saying it was murder."

When I walk in the door of Musical Expression an hour later, everyone glares at me. Now I finally know why.

They think Sister Helen was murdered.

I hurry to my seat and bend over my textbook like I'm reading.

If I don't let them in, they can't hurt me.

"Studying hard?"

I look up and see the same moss green eyes from the library staring back at me.

Mateo.

My heart races. "Pardon me?" I say, managing to get out two words before looking over my shoulder to see if anyone is watching. No surprise—everyone has eyes on us.

Mateo's black hair falls across his flawless skin in long wisps. "I said, *Are you studying hard?*"

I have no idea what to say. I repeat the response I've heard Dad give: "Hardly." It's a weird thing for Dad to say because he works all the time. But whenever he says it, the other guy laughs. Like it's some kind of man code for being normal.

But Mateo doesn't get the joke. "You don't like this class?"

"No, that's not what I meant." I glance at Mr. Jeffrey, who sits hunched over his desk at the front of the room, oblivious. "I actually do like it." I'm not lying. It's the *only* class I like.

"Cool. It's my favorite."

"It is?"

"Highlight of my day. If you know what I mean."

And then, just before he turns and heads for his seat in the back of the room, he does something I don't expect.

He winks at me.

He totally winks at me.

CHAPTER 24

Adrenaline buzzes through my body.

I actually *enjoy* going to self-defense today, punching Sister Laura's gloves with joy instead of resignation. At the library a tiny part of me hopes to see Mateo, but another part knows I won't get lucky twice in one day. I breeze through the book Sister Laura found, *The House on Mango Street*, finishing the whole thing in one sitting. Sure, it's short, but never before have I read an entire book without looking up from the page. The effect is exhilarating.

By the time I get home, I'm bursting with all kinds of different emotions—about Mateo, the book, what Bonita and Liv told me. It's no surprise I interrogate Mom as soon as I walk in the door.

Tiffany is vacuuming the dining room. She lifts her gaze from the rug and watches me beeline across the house. Before I get to the kitchen, she flips off the vacuum. "Sheesh, you're in a hurry. Almost like you're running from something."

Is that an accusation? Does she know about the investigation?

Mom is in the kitchen making sourdough.

"I need to ask you something."

"Yes." Her impatience is obvious. Do I really want to bring this up? *You have to try new things if you want to grow, Stella.*

"Remember when the constables were here?" I pause until she looks up from the mixing bowl. "After?"

"After?"

"You know. *After.*"

"Oh, that."

"Do you remember what you said?"

Mom uses her I-told-you-so voice. "I said a lot of things that day, Stella. We all did."

"You said we didn't want to look suspicious."

Mom turns to the cabinet behind her.

I talk to her back. "You said we didn't want them to think we were involved."

Mom returns to the counter and pushes the heels of her hands into the lump of dough. The scent of flour and yeast reaches me on the other side of the island. My stomach quakes.

"I don't know why you're doing this, Stella."

"Doing what?"

"Dredging up the past." She picks up the dough and shapes it into a ball.

"It's hardly the past, Mom. It happened less than two weeks ago."

"You know what I mean."

"No, I don't."

"It's over, Stella." She drops the ball of dough on the pastry mat. "Sister Helen is dead. You have to get over it."

My jaw drops, but that doesn't deter Mom.

"She wasn't your mother, Stella. She was just your chaperone. She wasn't family."

"She lived with us for five years, Mom."

"Almost six. Sister Helen lived under our roof for five years and ten months." Mom's eyes bore into mine, and as much as I want to, I can't pull away. "I know Sister Helen liked to act as if she was the most important person in your life, Stella—Lord knows she'd love all the carrying on that has gone on in her absence—but the truth is, she was just the hired help, and sometimes I wish she'd acted like it."

"How can you say that?"

"It's the truth, Stella. She was nothing more to us than a servant."

I'm too stunned to respond. But now I know for sure. Mom hated Sister Helen. The only question is, how much?

CHAPTER 25

As soon as dinner is over, I go to my room and flop onto the bed. How could Mom say those things about Sister Helen? Did she *want* Sister Helen gone? Could she have hated her enough to kill her? I try to put it all together—the message from Rose, what Mom said about Sister Helen, the investigation, but I must fall asleep at some point because the next thing I know I'm jolted awake by the sound of a car door slamming.

I'm still wearing my school clothes, but it's pitch dark outside. The last thing I remember is a pink-and-orange sunset slanting through my bedroom windows.

I tiptoe to the window. Parked in front of the annex door is a single car. A red SUV.

A constable is here.

Again.

A tall man dressed all in gray with a red armband and a gun as big as an oar crosses the driveway. I don't recognize him. His thick dark hair and pronounced jawline make him look like a movie star. Even though it's after eleven, Dad steps out the annex door and gives him a long handshake.

It's almost like he expected him.

I linger at the window, waiting to see if the constable will come right back out, but nothing happens.

What's going on?

I slide my arms into my cashmere robe before putting an ear to the door. But all I hear is the sound of the air-conditioning roaring through the house. This is my chance. I crack the door and peek out. The hallway is deserted. I pull the door shut behind me as quietly as possible.

I'm down the stairs in less than a minute.

The first floor is so quiet it's eerie. Like the house has been muted. I tiptoe through the dining room and kitchen and peer into the annex hall. The door to Dad's office is closed, but I can see light under the doorframe. That's when I hear them.

Dad and the constable.

Their voices are louder than they should be at this hour, but not so loud we could hear them upstairs. This close I have no problem making out what they're saying.

"You've got to put a stop to it." The irritation in Dad's voice is unmistakable.

"How am I supposed to do that?"

"I don't care *how*. Just do it."

It almost sounds like Dad is giving the constable orders.

"But people think—"

"People think what?"

Before the constable responds, I hear shuffling. Are they moving toward the door? I slide back almost to the kitchen. Now I can only make out snippets of what they're saying.

"Your wife."

"Nonsense."

"Investigate."

"Goddamn it!" Dad yells, and then something slams. I run to the other side of the kitchen, crouching behind the island.

A door squeaks open, and their voices are clear again.

"I don't want to have this conversation again," Dad says.

"Understood, sir."

Sir? Why is the constable calling Dad sir?

"And I don't want another single person to call my wife a murderer."

CHAPTER 26

I don't get a chance to inspect Dad's face until Sunday morning when the five of us go to church.

Dad pulls his brand-new Corvette Wilderness SUV up to the front door. He gets the latest model as soon as it rolls off the assembly line. Everyone who lives in Bull Run knows the Corvette was a flashy sports car created a long time ago by a company called General Motors. But after New America was founded, the people who worked at the Corvette plant in Bull Run broke off from GM and started a new company, which they named after the car that made their town great. Now the Corvette Motor Company is the biggest auto manufacturer in the country.

When he opens the door for me, I search Dad's eyes for some hint about what he knows. I see nothing but impatience.

"Go ahead, Stella." He tilts his sweaty head toward the back seat. It's hotter than it should be this early in the morning.

Sister Laura is in the third row. Our eyes meet, but she doesn't say a word.

When Dad gets in, he immediately tunes into Freedom Radio.

As usual, we don't speak, instead listening to the Sunday morning experts screaming about all the babies being killed in Old America.

Infanticide is a daily—no, hourly, no, minute-by-minute— occurrence in the hell-on-earth that is Old America, folks. Women actually put coat hangers up their vag—

Dad lunges at the dashboard, flipping off the radio before the commentator can finish. I don't know why he bothers. We all know how women kill their babies in Old America. It's one of the reasons everyone hates it so much. I glance at Shea, who holds her new Girl of Faith doll in her lap, stroking its long hair. No, Shea doesn't know *exactly* how women in Old America kill their babies. She doesn't know about the hangers. But she knows they do it. As soon as she was old enough to recite The Divine Praises, she was praying for those babies.

It used to bother me. When I was Shea's age, I would cry about it. But I cried so many tears and said so many prayers it stopped seeming real. It felt like something happening in a story or book. I don't know a single woman who's committed infanticide, a crime punishable by death.

We're pulling into the church parking lot before I can figure out if not praying for those babies anymore means there's something wrong with me.

"I have an announcement," Dad says before he comes to a stop. No one speaks.

"Chief Liu called this morning." Chief Liu? He must mean Brooklyn's dad. "He called to tell me they've closed the investigation."

"What?" I can't help myself. It just comes out. "Why?"

"It's as we suspected, Stella. Sister Helen was old, and she died. That's what happens when you get old."

My eyes go to Shea. Should she be hearing this?

"Anyway, this means we can all move on." He tilts his head like it's a form of punctuation. "Sister Laura is with us now. She's taking good care of you. And to be honest, I've heard enough speculation and gossip about this situation. It's time for us to move on." Dad catches my eye in the rearview. "All of us."

"Yes, sir," I say because I know his words are directed at me.

Dad pulls up to the front of the church, putting the Wilderness in park. Two constables appear on either side to open our doors. First Mom and Dad's doors, the constable shaking Dad's hand like they're friends. When the back doors open, a constable with wavy blond hair and unnaturally blue eyes holds his arm out to me. It's one of the only ways I can touch a man—when he's helping me out of a vehicle. I grab hold of him as I teeter out in my kitten heels.

Sister Laura brushes off the constable holding the door for her, refusing help but still offering a polite greeting. "Good morning, Constable." She smiles warmly. "Thank you for your service."

Inside, Dad doesn't even glance back at us before striding to the front of the church. I could swear Sister Laura slits her eyes at him, but her face morphs into a smile before she says goodbye and heads toward the stairwell. The chaperones sit in the choir loft though they never sing.

Women aren't supposed to talk in church, but Mom leans close enough to whisper. "Get us a seat." She nods at the pews behind the three-foot barrier separating men from women. "I'll take Shea to Sunday School."

I search for Bonita or Liv. Bonita's family doesn't usually come to services, and Liv is often late. The Grahams are *never* late. We're always right on time. There's plenty of room in the first pew, so I throw my sweater over the empty seats, hoping Liv and her mother join us.

There's nothing to do but people watch. My eyes rove over the congregation until I come to Dad standing next to a group of men in the Minutemen Party. The party officials sit in front, the constables right behind them, their tall guns leaning against the pew as if holding it up. After what happened the other night, I can't help but notice how friendly Dad is with them. Shaking hands, smiling, even letting out a little chuckle. The other dads keep their distance.

Why is he so comfortable with the men in the Minutemen party?

"*Who* are you gawking at?"

I flinch before turning to see Liv sitting next to me, both of our mothers on her other side.

I ignore her question. "You're late."

"Almost."

"Shhh," Liv's mom says as she presses a finger up to her lips. "You girls need to quiet down. You're going to get us all killed."

Church is just like class. The men talk, the women listen. It wouldn't be so bad if they didn't say the same thing every single time.

Praise God for showing us the true way to follow Him.
Praise God for teaching us our proper place in society.
Praise God for letting us see how to best revere mothers.

Praise God for allowing us to follow good men.
Praise God for protecting women from harm.
Praise God for rescuing us from the sins of Old America.

It goes on and on and on.

I'm so bored I push back my cuticles with the nail of my index finger.

A minute later Mom leans across Liv and her mom and whispers in my direction. "I'm going to the restroom."

She jumps up and starts toward the vestibule before I can say I have to go too. Everyone sitting anywhere near us turns to watch her go. It's no surprise. As usual, Mom looks stunning. Today she's wearing a vintage Dior dress that highlights her tiny waist, and her hair is swept into an Audrey Hepburn–like updo. Not to mention her expertly applied makeup. Several men sitting in front of the barrier let their eyes follow her and a woman behind me hisses the words, "My gracious."

Deflect attention.

This is why they separate us.

Because of women like Mom. Because of men who can't stop leering. Because of how people talk. If only Mom would…I don't know…stop being so beautiful. Stop dressing like that. If only she would act like she's supposed to act.

After we turn back to the minister, all I can think about is Dad yelling at the constable last night and the fact that I still have to go to the bathroom. But I can't go without Mom. I peer over my shoulder. What's taking her so long?

A few minutes later, I realize I can't wait any longer. I jump up before I reconsider, climbing over Liv and her mother to get out. Several people swing their heads in my direction. An O shape forms on Liv's mouth. I rush down the aisle and bolt through the glass doors, praying no one stops me.

But the vestibule is empty.

In the ladies' room, I expect to see Mom at the mirror, touching up her makeup. The stall doors stand open. I examine each of them, but she's not here.

She's gone.

I push the swinging door open just a crack, hoping Mom is outside the door, looking for me. But there's still no sign of her.

Instead a dozen men are standing around the vestibule talking and laughing.

I let the bathroom door fall closed and wait.

Organ music reaches me from the other side. The glass doors into the nave must be open. I peek again. The men are gone, and Mom is still nowhere in sight. I tiptoe toward the rear doors of the church, sneaking outside, something I would have never dared a few weeks ago. The heat immediately attaches itself to me. I fan my face and scan the parking lot for Mom.

When my eyes get to the playground, I see her.

She's leaning against an oak tree as if she doesn't have a care in the world.

And she's smoking.

"What are you doing?"

"What do you mean?" Mom holds the cigarette away from her mouth. "Isn't it obvious?"

"That's illegal, Mom."

"Smoking is not *illegal*, Stella. It's just frowned upon. There's a difference."

"Still," I say with outrage in my voice. "You could be shunned. We could all be shunned."

Mom waves her empty hand at me as if I'm being ridiculous. "That would *never* happen."

"How can you be so sure?"

"Because your dad is one of the most powerful men in the country, Stella." She drops her cigarette on the ground and smashes it with her toe. "He's president of one of the largest corporations in New America. What are they going to do? Shun him because his wife snuck one measly cigarette in the church parking lot?" She lets out an uncomfortable laugh. "Don't be ridiculous. Besides, they don't care about women like me. Middle-aged women too old to have babies. They only care about young women like you. Women who can procreate."

It's the most I've heard Mom say in years.

"Come on, Stella." She nods toward the church. "We should get back. We don't want anyone to know we have minds of our own, do we?"

CHAPTER 27

We're ten minutes into class the next morning when Mr. Russell starts his questions. I let a few go, but when he asks about the role of the wife, I lift my hand as gracefully as I do for triangle pose. Levi glares at me, raises his hand at the same time. One girl scrunches her face, but two others smile. Do they know what I'm doing? Mr. Russell calls on Levi, doesn't even acknowledge me. This process repeats itself two more times. Until Mr. Russell asks a more embarrassing question.

"For instance, are there certain things a woman should do for her husband?"

I'm the only person to raise my hand, but Mr. Russell doesn't even glance my way. His eyes do the sprinkler thing again. Back and forth. Back and forth. Is he really going to pretend he doesn't see me?

"Should I repeat the question?"

It's Mason who raises his hand next.

Mr. Russell calls on him. "Yes, Mr. Stiles."

"Stella has her hand up, sir."

"I'm sorry. *What* did you say?"

"Stella, sir." Mason points at me. "She has her hand up."

Mr. Russell pivots toward me and drops his mouth in faux surprise. He can't pretend he didn't see me. I *know* he saw me. And I know *he* knows I know. "Stella," he says in a ridiculously fake voice. "I didn't even see you."

"That's okay." What *can* I say?

Mr. Russell claps his hands together. "But it appears we're out of time." He swings his face to the clock on the wall behind him. "It's quarter till. And we still have homework to review."

No one says a word. The room is so quiet I can hear myself breathing.

We never review our homework in Family Development. *Never.* Mr. Russell gave us a syllabus at the beginning of the year and sticks to it. He obviously doesn't have any problem lying. As long as it means I don't speak.

"I'm so sorry, Stella."

Behind his eyes I see a spark of some kind. He's angry but there's something else there too. It takes me a minute to identify it.

Joy.

He's *enjoying* this.

And he's never going to let me speak.

～～～～

I'm fifty feet from my locker when I see him.

Mateo de Velasco.

How does he know where my locker is?

I slow my pace, allowing myself to enjoy the moment. His eyes on me. My eyes on him. *Is this really happening?*

When I'm just a few feet away, he peers over his shoulder. He turns back and holds up a folded piece of paper in one hand before pointing at me with the other hand.

The piece of paper is for me.

I hold my breath as I make up the short distance between us. Before I reach him, I look behind me to make sure no one has noticed us. But there isn't a single teacher in sight. I stop right in front of Mateo and allow myself to breathe again.

He rotates his head in a half circle, taking in the entire hallway, before landing on me again. He holds the folded paper out to me. "For you," he says in a voice so low it's almost a whisper.

I take his offering.

"Dylan's great," he explains, "but this is one of my favorites."

I know I should thank him. The problem is I'm too stunned to speak.

"And it reminds me of you."

Before I can utter a word, his eyes dart around my head, as if he sees something behind me. I follow his gaze. Mr. Washington is coming right toward us. In a few seconds, he'll see us.

Mateo's eyes come back to mine, and he holds a single hand up. It's the same wave he gave me that day in the library. Then, without saying a word, he walks away, as if nothing happened between us.

I unfold the paper. The words *Bye Bye Pride* are scrawled above a page full of lyrics. When I read the first line of the third stanza, my breath catches in my chest.

But I didn't know someone
could be so lonesome.
Didn't know a heart

could be tied up
and held for ransom.

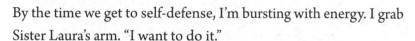

By the time we get to self-defense, I'm bursting with energy. I grab Sister Laura's arm. "I want to do it."

"You want to do what?"

"Fight the Master. I'm ready."

Her head shakes like it's come loose. "You're not ready."

"I am. I'm ready."

She must see something in my face that convinces her because her eyes soften. "If you say so."

When the Master makes his usual request—"Does anyone feel ready to stand against me?"—I force my hand in the air and yell, "I am, Master!" without waiting for him to call on me. I can do that here. It's allowed.

He smiles when his eyes settle on me. "Young Stella. Are you sure you're ready?"

I nod quickly. "I am."

He motions me toward the middle of the mat.

My stomach tightens, but I manage to walk with purpose. The Master taught us not to show fear.

He bows slowly, his eyes on me. I do the same. After I rise, he moves in a semicircle, jabbing the air with his fists. I mirror his movements. We do this for what seems like forever but is probably only a minute or two.

He leans forward and whispers softly enough that only I can

hear. "Hit me, Stella." When I don't respond, he repeats himself in a normal voice. "Hit me."

I've made a mistake. I'm not ready.

"Jab to the mouth, Stella." Now he's even louder. "Pull back and land a jab to my mouth."

I do exactly as he says. I pull back and throw my fist into his mouth, as if it's on a spring. It's different than hitting Sister Laura's boxing gloves—his skin has more give but reverberates the same way. He shakes off the jab. My instinct is to say I'm sorry, but he's warned us about that. *Don't ever apologize for protecting yourselves, ladies. There is nothing wrong with self-defense.* We return to circling each other like adversaries.

"Again, Stella!" he commands.

I pull back and send another jab to his face. But this time he blocks me, his left hand knocking my right away. I gasp and examine my hand as if it's bleeding even though I'm not hurt.

"Again!" he yells.

I fake him out with my right before launching a hook with my left. I throw so hard, my glove hits his jaw and keeps going.

His eyes light up. He's surprised.

I steel myself for retaliation, but instead he drops his hands and smiles. "Very good, Stella." He nods like a proud parent. "Very good. You're learning."

CHAPTER 28

'm not waiting this time.

The longer I wait, the more likely it is Mr. Russell will say we're out of time. My hand flies up with the first question the next morning, an easy one about things women shouldn't do while pregnant. Mr. Russell calls on a boy in the next row, but when he says women shouldn't exercise, I jump in.

"There are people who believe exercise is—"

Mr. Russell wheels on me before I can finish. "Miss Graham, I did *not* call on you."

"I know, but—"

"If you know I didn't call on you, then you know you shouldn't speak."

"But Mr. Russell—"

"Don't *but* me, young lady."

Is there any point arguing with him? Then I remember something Sister Laura said. She told me to make my own attack rather than be put on the defensive.

Mr. Russell turns away like he's done with me, but I keep going. "It seems like you don't want to call on me because I'm a girl, Mr.

Russell." Someone gasps out loud. Nearly everyone else, includ-
ing Levi, gawks at me like my head's on fire. Only Mason nods his
encouragement. I always knew Levi wasn't my type.

Mr. Russell swivels back to me, making up the space between
us in no time. "What did you say, young lady?" He shakes a finger
in my face.

"I said, 'Are you not calling on me because I'm a girl?'"

Mr. Russell retreats two steps and folds his arms across his
chest. "That's it, Miss Graham. Pack up your things and go."

"Go where?"

"To the principal's office."

"But why?"

He holds up an index finger. "Not another word, Miss Graham.
Pack up and get out."

I don't say anything, but I don't move either.

"Now!" he yells.

I close my book and grab my backpack. Mr. Russell stares at
his shoes, as if he can't stand the sight of me. But I keep my eyes on
him the whole way to the door. I want him to know.

I'm not giving up.

CHAPTER 29

In the hallway, I nearly collide with Principal Terry, who's rushing toward me like a Derby winner.

He comes to an abrupt stop when he sees me, his hands out in front of him. "Miss Graham." He scratches his temple. "I was just looking for you."

"You were?"

"Sadly, yes." The gold clip on Principal Terry's tie catches the light as his chest rises and falls with an elaborate sigh. "The police...well, they're in my office. Again. And to be honest, Miss Graham, this isn't exactly good for me."

"You?"

"Yes, me." He jerks his head to the left as if someone has called his name. "The constables...they don't...well, they don't want this to continue."

"They don't?"

"No, they don't. And I don't want to make them unhappy. So I'm hoping you can wrap this up today. Put it behind you." He leans forward. "You need to send the message you've told them everything you know."

"Yes, sir," I say though I have no idea how *I* can get the cops to wrap things up.

"Wonderful. They're waiting in my office."

Principal Terry closes his door behind us. "The officers just have a few more questions for you, Miss Graham." He gestures to the chairs opposite his desk. Alvarez stands next to one chair, and Poole leans against the window with a tiny black notebook in his hand. I sit in the chair closest to the door.

"Is this about Mr. Russell?"

"Mr. Russell?" the principal asks.

"He sent me here."

"Oh." Principal Terry offers me a reassuring smile. "Don't worry about that."

Alvarez jumps in. "Stella, we have a few questions about the day…well, the day your first chaperone died."

"Did something else happen? I thought the investigation was closed."

"Closed?"

"That's what I heard." I don't mention Dad is the one who said it.

"I heard the same thing," Principal Terry says.

"Wishful thinking," Alvarez says.

Wishful thinking? On Dad's part?

Poole jumps in. "Please tell us exactly what happened that day."

I squeeze my bottom lip between my thumb and index finger, telling myself not to cry. Do I really have to go through all this again?

"Just walk us through it, Stella," Alvarez adds. "Step by step."

Principal Terry closes his eyes and nods, and I tell them every-thing I remember.

When I finish, Alvarez asks, "Had anyone else been to your house that day? Sunday... It was a Sunday, right?"

Poole flips open his notepad. "Yes, Sunday the 15th of August."

Levi was supposed to come to Visitation, but that was *after*... Before that, it was just us. Mom, Dad, Shea, Sister Helen, and me. Oh...and Tiffany. *Tiffany.* Do they know about Tiffany? "Tiffany was there too."

"Tiffany Keene?" Poole puts a finger on his notepad as if her name is already there. "The cleaning person?"

I nod. "She comes every day."

"Even on Sunday?"

"Yes, of course."

Poole raises his eyebrows.

"Just a few hours. She's gone before we get home from church. You don't think Tiffany hurt Sister Helen, do you?"

Alvarez glances at Poole before saying, "No, nothing like that, Stella. But in my experience, the housekeeper knows every-thing going on in a home. Kind of like the chaperone. Speaking of your chaperone, Sister Laura told us your dad never locked the annex where Sister Helen stayed, making it easy for some-one to get in."

Why would Sister Laura tell them that? Is she the reason they're questioning me again?

Alvarez goes on. "Is it possible Tiffany knows something too? Something that could've put Sister Helen in danger?"

Maybe she spent time with the wrong people. That's what Tiffany said the next day. I glance at Principal Terry, remembering his request to put this behind us. It's the same thing Dad has wants me to do. "I'm not sure."

Poole looks up and inspects my face. Does he know I'm lying? "So no one else was at the house that day?"

"I don't think so. But I was at church all morning."

Poole scribbles in his notebook.

Alvarez says, "But your mother left church early that day, right?"

"My mother?"

"Yes, your mother," Poole says. "Someone said she left church early on the 15th."

My mind flashes to Mom smoking in the church parking lot a few days ago. But that was *this* Sunday. I can't remember if she left church early the week Sister Helen…

"I don't remember."

The principal offers me a square smile. He's forcing it. Poole scratches in his notepad again before looking up, but it's Alvarez who speaks.

"Let's move on to something else, Stella. This is going to sound strange." He lets out a laugh that sounds completely fake. "Have you ever seen any funny-looking beans around the house? Maybe in the kitchen. Maybe somewhere you wouldn't expect."

"Beans?"

"Castor beans. They're brown and gray."

"Why are you asking about beans?"

It's Poole who answers. "They're used to make ricin."

"Ricin?"

"It's a kind of poison."

Poison? "Did someone poison Sister Helen?"

"I didn't say that."

"But you're implying it." I would've never had the nerve to make such an accusation three weeks ago, but I'm a different person now.

Poole flips his eyes to Alvarez, who takes over. "We just want to know if you've seen anything like that around the house, Stella."

I shake my head. "I don't remember seeing any beans."

"Did you see anything else strange or out of the ordinary?" Alvarez asks. "Did anyone say anything unusual?"

"Anything suspicious?" Poole adds.

Suspicious. That's the word Mom used when Sister Helen died.

I look Poole right in the eye and lie. "No, *nothing* like that."

It's easier than I expect.

CHAPTER 30

As soon as I see Sister Laura at the gate, my instinct is to scream at her. But I hold it in until we get to the gym. Neither of us says a word until we're kneeling at the mat. I lean toward her and hiss into her ear. "You should have told me."

She swivels toward me. "Told you what?"

"About the police."

"What about them?"

"They questioned me again."

The Master starts class, and we get to our feet, moving to our places on the mat.

"You didn't know?"

"How would I?"

The Master runs through each move. I stop talking to listen to his instructions. When he finishes, I put my gloves up so Sister Laura can practice her jabs.

"You have your ways, right?"

She doesn't respond but keeps jabbing.

"Besides, they *said* they talked to you."

She drops her hands to her side. "They talked to *everyone*." Her face wrinkles in thought. Is she hiding something? "I had a suspicion, of course."

"I knew it."

We trade positions. She holds her gloves up, so I can practice my jabs.

"I wasn't *sure*." Her calm demeanor tells me she was *completely* sure. "Besides, what good would it have done to tell you?"

"I would've been ready."

"It's almost better not to know. You don't want to seem like you got tipped off. Then they'll ask how."

Now I'm the one to drop my hands. "So you didn't tell me *on purpose*?"

"Maybe." She shrugs as if uncertain.

I'm not buying it.

"It worked out, didn't it? You had nothing to hide. It's not like you know anything about Sister Helen's death."

I don't say anything.

"Do you?"

I throw a cross hook so close to her face she backs up, her eyes widening. I don't plan it. It just happens.

"You were safer not knowing, Stella."

"I doubt it."

"You're not a very good liar. They would've seen right through you."

This time I let the cross hook fly for real, slamming my fist against her mouth so hard I feel teeth through the glove. Her hand goes to her face as she stumbles back. She doesn't fall, but doubles over.

I hold out my boxing gloves, now useless. "I'm sorry." The
Master won't approve, but I don't care.

Sister Laura wipes blood from her lip. "I'm not."

CHAPTER 31

S ister Laura doesn't come to dinner that night, her empty chair louder than a real person.

Mom and Dad don't ask where she is, but Mom has Tiffany take Sister Laura a tray before we eat. Like she knows she's not coming.

It's been weeks since it was just the four of us at the table. Dad doesn't say anything for a few minutes, so we eat in silence—catfish tacos with black beans and oranges. I relish every bite. Ever since Sister Laura arrived, I've been eating more. Between running with Dad and self-defense, I'm famished.

"Sheesh, Stella," Dad says, "you'd think we didn't feed you."

"I'm hungry."

"Well, slow down. It's not ladylike to shovel food in your mouth."

I put down my taco even though I'm nowhere near full.

"I want to ask you all something," Dad says. "Have you heard about the latest girl to go missing?"

Mom looks at her plate, so I answer his question. "Cynthia Reed?" I pick at my taco shell, breaking off little bites.

"So you *did* hear about her?"

I nod, not wanting to admit who told me.

Dad looks each of us in the eye before going on—Mom, Shea, then me. "First of all, you shouldn't be talking to people about this. You never want to give gossip a listening ear."

Abstain from sin.

But what if it's not gossip? What if it's true?

"Second, I want to make sure you all know this could've been avoided. If this girl, this Cynthia, if she had followed the rules, if she'd stayed with her chaperone, she would've been fine."

Does Shea know what happens to girls who go missing? I learned in Feminine Safety they found another girl in a ditch by the side of the road, her skirt above her waist, her arms tied behind her back, her mouth gagged. Shea is only seven. I hope she doesn't know these awful details.

"I don't understand why girls aren't more careful," Dad says.

Navigate the world with care.

Mom's lips flatten into a straight line.

"Don't they know how important it is to do what we say?"

Mom won't answer, but I itch to speak. What was it Sister Helen used to say? *What about the man who did this? Isn't he the one responsible?*

But I don't breathe a word.

My job is to be seen, not heard.

CHAPTER 32

The weather shifts overnight.

The temps have dropped to the high 80s. For the first time in months, I don't sweat as soon as I walk out the door. It won't last, but I welcome the reprieve. More people clutter the sidewalks. A young mom pushes a double stroller past us. She doesn't look old enough to be out of high school. A middle-aged man in a blue suit rushes toward the government campus. If I didn't feel obligated to say something, I'd happily soak up the scene and walk in silence. But I have to make things right with Sister Laura.

I get right to it. "I'm so sorry. I really am."

She stops to face me. The leaves on the trees behind her droop so pitifully she looks like a sad painting. "You don't have to apologize, Stella." But her voice still sounds hurt. "It's normal for teenagers to rebel against their parents…or, in your case, your chaperone." She offers me a smile that tells me we're okay. "Do you want to know the truth?"

"Of course."

"I'm proud of you, Stella. I really am."

Liv slings her tray down on the lunch table like it's a bag of trash. Bonita rolls her eyes at me.

"What is it, Liv?"

"Didn't you hear?"

"Hear what?"

Liv squeezes her eyes shut and clutches the cuffs of her sweater. I turn to Bonita.

"They found her, Stella." Bonita lets out a long sigh. "I mean, they found her body."

"Who?"

"Cynthia Reed."

Cynthia Reed? Is this why Dad brought her up last night? Did he know something? Did the constables tell him she had been found?

Liv's eyes flash open. She leans across the table, and both Bonita and I move closer to her. Liv's words come out in a whisper. "Did they kill her?"

"Who?" I ask.

"The Minutemen." She peers over her shoulder before going on, her voice still low. "Did the prime minister have her killed because she wouldn't get married?"

"No." I shake my head, but Bonita's eyes widen. She's considering it. "No, Liv. She was kidnapped. She went out without her chaperone and got kidnapped." I turn from Liv to Bonita. "That's what happens when you go out alone, right?"

Neither of them answers me. The truth hits me in the gut.

They aren't sure.

As soon as I find my seat in Musical Expression, I feel him standing next to me. "Stella?"

I look up without thinking.

Mateo.

"I heard what you did."

"You did?"

I have no idea what he's talking about. Did he hear about my fight with Sister Laura? Is he talking about Cynthia Reed?

He glances over his shoulder before sitting in the desk next to me. The boy who normally sits there will show up any minute.

Mateo leans forward, elbows on his knees, and looks right into my face. "I heard you stood up to Russell yesterday. Mason told me last night. That's pretty spectacular."

I try to play it cool but feel myself blushing. "Thanks."

When he speaks again, it's in a whisper. "I love that you're not afraid of them. I love that you don't care about their stupid rules."

Emotion whips up inside me like a tornado, but I manage to meet his gaze. "You do?"

"Yeah. It's all so dumb. Why can't we talk to each other? It's normal for us to want to get to know each other." He puts his hand on top of my desk and slides it toward mine until the outside of our fingers touch. All the oxygen goes out of the room. I look at the place where our hands meet and then back at him.

"Mr. de Velasco!" a voice booms across the room.

Mateo yanks his hand away, and my breath rushes back to me.

Mr. Jeffrey starts toward us. "I don't know what you think you're up to with this Barry White routine, young man, but you better knock it off right now and get to your seat."

"Actually I feel more of a kinship with Joni Mitchell, sir."

"*Now!*"

"Okay, okay."

Mateo jumps to his feet, but before he goes, he catches my eye one more time. Something passes between us. An invisible current of energy that leaves my whole body charged. As he walks away, his arm brushes mine, the warm feeling of his skin causing a shiver to pass through me.

It isn't an accident.

CHAPTER 33

It takes almost three weeks, but I'm finally faster than Dad.

The lights of Bonita's house flicker on as we approach it. Later today, I'll be there, getting ready for homecoming. But, right now, my focus is Dad. I've been wanting to ask him all week what's going on—with the constables, with Mom, with the investigation—but I can't just interrogate him, especially since he told us on the way to church we had to let it go.

Give obedience. Speak when spoken to.

Dad and I used to talk all the time. When I was young, our favorite topic was dogs. We spent hours searching for different breeds on the internet. But that was before I became a woman.

I can't interrogate him, but I can mention what I saw.

"Was there a constable at the house last Friday?"

We're chugging up the biggest hill now. It's hot again, the cool reprieve at the beginning of the week already over, and Dad's breathing is labored. He takes his time responding. "What are you talking about?"

"A constable. I saw a red SUV in the driveway. Before I went to sleep."

"It was nothing. Nothing for you to worry about anyway."

I'm not letting him off that easy, but I wait until we crest the hill to go on. "Is everything okay, Dad?"

He slows and looks at me out of the corner of his eye. "Yes, of course."

We run in quiet another block before he finally says, "Didn't you hear what I said on the way to church, Stella?" He doesn't give me a chance to answer. "It's time for all of us to move on. It's time for *you* to move on." When I don't respond, he says, "Have I made myself clear?"

Give obedience.

I have no choice but to say yes.

But I wait until I'm a foot ahead of him to say it.

CHAPTER 34

Why did I think Bonita could be low key about homecoming?

I told her I didn't want to make a big deal this year, not after what happened to Sister Helen, but Bonita's never done anything low key in her life. And we always go all out for homecoming.

It started freshman year. We were nervous, so we decided to dress alike—all three of us wearing black dresses made of silk organza. Everyone loved it so much, we made it a tradition. And we saved the best for last: teal sequins in honor of our school colors. I'm wearing a floor-length A-line with spaghetti straps, Liv has a mini dress with long sleeves, and Bonita's mother somehow found her a teal-sequined jumpsuit. No way we're going low key.

It isn't lost on us how bizarre it is that we're allowed to dress this way for dances. The rest of the time our dress code is super strict—no leggings, no shorts, no jeans, no skirts above the knee, and definitely nothing sleeveless, backless, or strapless. But for five nights of our high school career, we're allowed to dress however we want. Sister Helen used to say people who grew up in Old America are nostalgic for their own high school dances. They see it as a rite of passage. Just like those ridiculous father-daughter dances they used to make us attend.

We meet at Bonita's house, Liv and I dragging our chaperones along like pets. Sister Sophie usually helps Liv get ready, but we banish her to the basement with the other two and take over the bathroom Bonita shares with her little brother.

Bonita attempts to style Liv's hair while I do my makeup in the mirror. Liv has managed to get her hands on some chocolate truffle cookies, and we scarf those while we get ready. The bathroom reeks of cocoa and baby powder.

"Can you believe this is our *last* homecoming?" Bonita says to our reflections. "Where do you think we'll be this time next year?"

Liv takes a breath so big her T-shirt lifts above her flat stomach.

"Have you eaten anything besides cookies today, Olivia?" Bonita asks.

"No, why?"

Bonita and I trade frowns. I shoot Bonita a look that says, *Let it go.*

She picks up a section of Liv's hair before dropping it in frustration. "Your hair is too thin, Liv. It won't hold anything. Stella, on the other hand, inherited her mother's perfect hair." Bonita turns to me. "You look more like her every day."

"Oh, gosh, that's not true."

I study our faces in the mirror. We look different with makeup and hairspray. Like grown-up versions of ourselves. Despite Bonita's complaints, Liv's hair looks perfect, cascading down her back in a way she doesn't normally let it. Bonita's hair is pulled into a glamorous updo held together by three twists that wrap across her head, and her makeup is as flawless as Mom's. The two of them have never looked more beautiful. They could be models. But when I look at myself, all I see are caterpillar eyebrows and a square chin.

"Who knows where we'll be in a year?" Bonita says, bringing me back to reality. "I mean, hopefully we'll be in college, but—"

But what?

I put down my cookie and turn to look at Bonita for real. "What are you saying, B?"

It's Liv who answers. "Maybe they won't let us go to college."

"Seriously," Bonita says, "do you know any girls who've gone to college, Stella?"

She's right. We don't know any.

Bonita slides a jeweled headband across her hair. "Maybe they'll make us get married. You know they're obsessed with us having babies. Look at my sister. She's twenty-five and already has three of them."

"They can't *make* us do that," Liv interjects.

"Uh," Bonita says, "yes, they very much can."

"They can't *make* us," Liv insists. "We're not slaves."

"True," I say, "but they *can* make it so we don't have much choice."

"How?" Liv asks.

"One," Bonita holds up her index finger. "They can tell us we didn't get into college even though we're smarter than boys who get in. You know they do that, Olivia." Bonita raises her middle finger next. "Two. They can threaten to take stuff away from us, from our families." Then Bonita lifts her ring finger. "Three. They can make sure we don't get invited to stuff. It's not shunning, but it might as well be." Bonita shakes her three fingers in the air. "The bottom line is if they want us to have babies bad enough, they might do anything."

I jump in. "They can make our lives so miserable we have no choice but to give in."

"Not me." Liv stares at us in the mirror. "I'm not doing it. Not ever." She shakes her head so hard I'm afraid she'll hurt herself. "I swear, I'm not."

Bonita pats Liv's shoulder. "Okay, Liv."

But Liv doesn't stop. "I can't do it. I just can't."

I put my hand on her arm. "It's okay, Liv. We get it."

"Do you?" Her big eyes well up with tears.

"We do."

Liv's tears start flowing for real, but she manages to choke out a question. "What do you mean?"

"About what?" Bonita asks.

"You just said you get it." Liv turns from Bonita to me. "What do you get?"

I glance at Bonita, and she shrugs, giving me permission to say what we're both thinking. "I mean, we know you're not into..." But I don't want to say it. Liv should say it. I don't want to steal that from her. "You know..."

"Boys?" She sniffs, wiping her nose with her sleeve. "You know I'm not into boys?"

"Yeah." The tears build inside me too. "We know."

Bonita squeezes Liv's shoulders. "It's okay, Olivia."

"You're not upset?" Liv says through her sobs.

"Not a chance," Bonita leans down and wraps her arms around Liv from behind. "Why would we be upset?"

"Of course not, Liv," I add, thinking of the book about the boy who went to Iran. Darius, that was his name. The one who was afraid to admit he was gay, even to himself.

"We love you." Bonita reaches an arm out in my direction, and I scoot closer, letting her wrap both of us in her arms. "And this is who you are."

We cling to each other, Liv sobbing softly while Bonita and I wipe our eyes.

But then Liv pulls back. "But what if they make me get married?"

"We won't let that happen." I don't let myself think about how impossible this is. "I promise."

CHAPTER 35

Dozens of heads turn in our direction when we pause under the glowing paper lanterns framing the doorway into the gym.

By the time we start walking, all eyes are on us. Most faces light up when they see us, but one girl squeezes her mouth into a pucker. "Sequins?" she snorts with disapproval. I tell myself I don't care. This is our last homecoming. I'm going to make the most of it.

In the middle of the dance floor, Bonita throws her arms around Liv and me, the three of us forming a tight circle.

"This is it, girls," Bonita yells over the music. "Senior year!"

Liv pulls us closer. "I love you both."

"Me too," I say, and I mean it.

"Let's do this," Bonita says, squeezing our hands before we slowly back away, easing into the music.

Tonight I'm going to forget about everything that's happened.

Tonight I'll let it all go.

～～～～～

We make eye contact across the dance floor during the second song. He comes right to me. Like we're attached by an invisible string.

"Wow," Mateo shouts over the music. "You all look amazing!" He puts his mouth to my ear. "*You* look amazing."

I feel myself blush but refuse to give in to embarrassment. "Thank you," I say, channeling my inner Elizabeth Bennet. "You too."

He's wearing a white button-down shirt, a narrow black tie, black suede sneakers, and tight black jeans that draw my eyes to places they shouldn't go. *Embrace purity.*

The only thing is—he isn't dancing.

I point at his feet. "Why aren't you dancing?"

He lets out a nervous laugh. "I'm out here, aren't I?"

I laugh too. "Yes, you are."

He slides one foot away from the other, lifts his arms in front of him, and starts swaying back and forth with the beat.

Bonita raises her eyebrows. Before I can respond, Mason Stiles appears behind her and boldly rests his hand on her hip. She spins around to face him. For a second, I think she's going to kiss him, but she holds back, looking over her shoulder. All of our chaperones line the perimeter of the gym. Like white sharks waiting to attack. Even at homecoming, they're watching us.

The music slows. I move closer to Mateo as if it's the most natural thing in the world for me to do. When we lock eyes on each other, it happens again. A jolt of something passes between us. We blush at the same time.

"Oh, wow," he says. "I'm sorry."

"What? Why?"

"I don't know." He seems shy, nervous. Totally different than his normal, confident in-class self. He's looking at his shoes so hard I wonder if he dropped something. When he finally looks up again, I just say it.

"Do you want to dance?"

He lets out another laugh, but this one is laced with relief. "I really, really do."

He holds out a hand, and I put my hand in his, his heartbeat pulsing so hard I can feel it between our palms. He puts his other hand on my hip and slowly pulls me closer, our bodies brushing each other every time we move. This is the only time we're allowed to be this close. The only time it's socially acceptable to touch.

I will myself to lift my chin and look into his face. The song will be over in minutes. I have to make the most of it.

I'm surprised his eyes are already on me. I could let myself get lost in those eyes. He holds my gaze so long another shiver passes through me. This isn't just kinetic energy. It's something else. This is desire.

"I've waited so long for this," he says.

"You have?"

"I really have."

I blush before saying, "I didn't know."

"You didn't?"

"You haven't even been to Visitation."

"I know. I hate those things. They're so fake."

"I guess that's why I didn't know. Not until that day anyway." Over his shoulder I find Sister Laura sandwiched between two older chaperones who could be her grandmothers. "That day in the library."

"Oh, yeah." His voice is full of wonder, pulling my attention back to him. "That was *intense*."

"I know."

"How did that even happen? I mean, why were you alone?"

"I don't know." I don't want to lie to his face, but I also can't look away from him. "One minute my chaperone was there. The next she was gone." Technically it's the truth.

"You looked so beautiful that day."

My heart is in my throat, but somehow I manage to speak. "In the library?"

"Yes, in the library." He nods and goes on. "And in class. In the hallway. Everywhere. You always look beautiful, Stella. And you look more beautiful now than ever."

I want to kiss him more than anything in the world.

But it isn't allowed. Not until we're married.

His hand tightens on my hip, pulling me closer. So close our bodies press against each other. This is against the rules. *Be sure to leave room for the Holy Spirit,* Sister Sophie says to Liv before every dance. My eyes flip to the wall, but we're in the middle of the dance floor. They can't see what's happening below our necks. And I don't care if they do. I want to kiss him. No matter the consequences.

But as soon as I start to move my lips toward his, someone starts shouting.

CHAPTER 36

Olu Parker is yelling at Mason.

Bonita and Liv stand on either side of them, Mason's hand still holding Bonita's.

"Oh, hell." Mateo looks at me with so much longing I could cry. "I'm sorry, Stella." He drops my hand and moves toward Olu and Mason. I don't know if he's apologizing for the curse or for letting me go.

Olu shouts at Mason over the music. "You can't do this!"

Everyone nearby has stopped dancing and formed a circle around them. A bunch of Climbers push their way to the front of the crowd like they're more important than everyone else.

"Do *what*?" Mason yells back.

He nods at Bonita. "You cannot possibly be with her."

Mason steals a look at Bonita before letting go of her hand and turning back to Olu. "Why not?"

"I think you know, Stiles."

"No. I don't." Mason shakes his head like he doesn't get what Olu is implying. The hair on his forehead glistens with sweat.

"Do I have to spell it out for you, Stiles?" Olu forces a laugh. "Or is spelling not a thing for guys like you?"

That's all it takes.

Mason launches himself at Olu, grabbing Olu's stiff shirt in his fists and then pushing him in the chest. But Olu doesn't fall. He recovers and shoves Mason back. Soon the two of them have their arms around each other, simultaneously wrestling and struggling to get free. This goes on a full minute. Mateo looks at me with a question on his face. No one knows what to do.

Finally Mason pulls free of Olu. He catches his breath, shakes himself off, takes a survey of everyone crowded around him, and glances back at Olu. It seems like it might all be over. But then Mason hauls his fist back and punches Olu in the face so hard he stumbles backward.

I flash back to Sister Laura's fight with the Master, the way she stumbled right before he finished her off. But when Mason charges toward Olu, the other boys jump in—Mateo too—pulling Mason back before he can knock Olu to the ground and dragging Olu in the other direction. That's when Principal Terry pushes through the crowd, screaming at all of them to go to his office before he calls the constables.

Mateo looks over his shoulder at me, closes his eyes, and shakes his head.

And then he's gone.

CHAPTER 37

The weekend is interminable, the longing weighing on me like a heavy blanket I can't get out from under.

When Sister Helen died, everything sped up. Life on fast forward. But after Mateo shakes his head at me, it slows down. All I want is to go back to school and see him again. And on Sunday, insult is added to injury when I'm forced to go through the ritual of sitting with yet another boy I barely know, much less like.

His name is James, a freshman at Lee University. I've never met him before. He's a terrible conversationalist and smells like a wet dog. I excuse myself to go to the bathroom, my attempt to end things quickly.

Sister Laura brings the entire box of leftover donuts to my room not long after Mom and Dad go to sleep that night. There were six left, and we've already eaten four.

"Can Mateo come to Visitation?" I ask her.

"Is that what you want?"

"Yes, of course."

"I can put in a request. They don't usually honor them, but it doesn't hurt to try."

I flash to Dad saying I should never get my hopes up. I don't want to be disappointed.

"Is there any reason Mateo wouldn't be a good match?" Sister Laura asks. "It helps to know these things in advance."

"He's not poor if that's what you're asking."

"How awful is it that such a thing is considered when matching people?"

Sister Laura says these kinds of things all the time. I still haven't gotten used to it. No one else talks like she does. Even Sister Helen didn't criticize so much.

"It is kind of awful now that I think about it."

"Disgusting." Sister Laura spits out the word. Why become a chaperone if you hate the system so much? Why not go to college or get married? The truth is, I can't see Sister Laura married. She doesn't like people telling her what to do, and all Dad ever does is order Mom around. She's more servant than wife. "I'm going to give you my copy of *The Outsiders* tomorrow. Put it inside *Of Mice and Men*. A book about boys that starts with O."

By now I'm used to this. My collection of banned books has grown quite large. When I ask where she gets them, Sister Laura says the chaperones pass them back and forth.

"Do you know what Mateo's father does for a living?" Sister Laura asks. "And can I just say it pains me to ask these questions?"

"I think he's some kind of doctor."

"And is he a good student? Mateo?"

"I *guess* he's a good student. I only have one class with him."

Sister Laura frowns.

"He's not like Mason. He's going to college."

"Who's Mason?" Sister Laura unfolds her right leg. We've been sitting on the floor for fifteen minutes.

"Mason is the boy Bonita likes. The one who got in the fight at homecoming."

"Oh, him." Sister Laura collects the remaining glaze from the donut box on her finger and puts it in her mouth. "My papaw would've said he's from the wrong side of the tracks."

"What does that mean?"

"It means he's working class. It means his parents didn't go to college."

"So why is that being from the wrong side of the tracks?"

"It used to be people who didn't have money bought houses outside of town—literally across the tracks from town—because it was cheaper."

"Was that in Old America?"

Sister Laura lets out something that sounds like a cross between a laugh and a growl. "Yeah, Old America. Sure."

"What do you mean?"

She suddenly gets serious. "It's nothing. I just thought of something that made me laugh." She scratches her nose. "You need to get some rest before going back to school tomorrow."

CHAPTER 38

When I finally get to school, I can feel him in the building. I don't know where he is, but I know he's there.

It doesn't take him long to find me.

The first bell hasn't even rung. I close my locker, turn around, and he's standing right behind me.

My breath catches in my throat.

We aren't supposed to talk to each other at school beyond saying things like *please* and *excuse me*. Social niceties, Mom calls them. But he doesn't say anything. He just stands there, staring at me as if he can't look away. I stare back, our eyes locked on each other like magnets.

"de Velasco!" a teacher shouts.

Mr. Washington, the physics teacher, stops right next to us. "What are you doing?"

It's agonizing when Mateo pulls his eyes away from me. "Nothing, sir," Mateo says.

Mateo doesn't move. Mr. Washington looks from Mateo to me and back again. "Well, then, get moving, de Velasco."

"Yes, sir." But before Mateo turns to go, he glances back one more time and holds up a flat hand. The same wave he always gives me.

My body melts into the linoleum.

This is what *it* feels like.

This is what they talk about in books.

~~~~~~~

I'm impatient now. I want more.

So when Willow Howard walks into first period, I zoom over to her desk.

"I need to talk to you," I say as she pulls a book out of her backpack.

She takes her time looking up, offering me a blank face. "I don't really care what you need, Sequins."

"What?"

"How much did that dress cost anyway? Probably as much as my parents pay for rent."

Did she really notice my dress? And then it hits me. That's the point. We *want* people to notice.

I shake my head. "I don't know."

"You don't *know*?" There's more than a little judgment in her voice. "You mean, you didn't even look at the price tag? Well, that is rich. And I mean it literally."

I ignore her insult. "Listen, I need your help. I need to know about those parties."

"You don't *need* anything. On the other hand, what I need I can't begin to count. But here's a start. I *need* you to get out of my face before I tell Russell you still have your period." She nods in the direction of his desk.

r my shoulder, Mr. Russell's eyes are trained

"I'm desperate."

I don't do charity work for privileged brats."

~~~~~~~~~

dy eating when I set down my tray.

ything yet?" I ask Bonita.

day night at Bonita's. We stayed up until

e who might know what happened to

twin brother, Beau, is best friends with

d her online, asking if she knew anything.

was home by one in the morning, but she

auled away by the cops.

s wistfully. "Have you?"

Word around the school is he's still in jail,

her if the rumors aren't true.

xcept—"

er. "Except what, Olivia?"

ace for Liv's hemming and hawing, so I

"People are saying he got arrested. But

for?"

is as serious as it's ever been. "I looked

rently it's against the law to just go and

nita's father is a lawyer, so she's always

—Liv looks for a teacher before she

s over our heads, searching too. "And

I follow Bonita's gaze to the boys' side of the cafeteria.

That's when I see Mateo.

This isn't his lunch shift. What's he doing here?

He says something to the person behind him. Another A bunch of seniors are standing in a group by the doors. boys. And then I remember. They're starting college vis week, taking the bus to Wilderness University, where they' a campus tour, sit in on classes, eat in the dining hall. The l this, but the girls apply blindly, guessing at which college right for them.

Mateo turns back around. That's when he sees me. H light up. I want more than anything to go to him, but allowed.

I'm not allowed to talk to him.

I'm not allowed to go on a college visit.

I'm not allowed to do anything.

CHAPTER 39

I have to find a way to be alone with him.

Willow. She's in our lunch shift.

I leave the table a few minutes before the period ends and move in her direction, hanging back so she won't see me. When the bell rings, I'm ready.

I follow her.

Because I suspect a girl like Willow can get time alone with any boy she wants.

Willow's locker is on the opposite end of the school from mine, behind the gym. My locker is near the classrooms. I've been here before—Bonita drags me along to stalk Mason   but I don't know anyone else who has a locker this far down. Why do some kids get lockers close to everything while others are banished? Tailing Willow, I finally get it.

Everyone who has a locker near me has money, dads with good jobs. We live in big houses and wear expensive clothes. Everyone near Willow's locker is middle class. Willow's dad works at the post office. I'm surprised they can afford their own chaperone. And she's not alone. No one in her hallway is going to college. They're assigning us lockers based on class. They're separating us into groups.

When Willow closes her locker, we come face-to-face with each other.

"I need to talk to you."

"Jesus," she says, and I wince. This is one of the rules everyone takes very seriously. Willow breaks it without thinking. "I already told you, Sequins. I don't give a shit what you want."

"Yeah, I know. I'm a spoiled brat."

"Pretty much." This close, the yellow lightning bolts around Willow's pupils shimmer like gold. She's even more striking than I realized.

The warning bell rings, but I refuse to let her pass, blocking her like a constable when she tries to step around me. She goes the other way, but I block her on that side too, holding my arm up so she can't pass.

"What the hell?"

"Just tell me what you want."

She laughs. "Are you kidding, Sequins?"

"No, I'm not."

"You want to know what *I* want?"

"I do."

She gazes at the lockers on the opposite side of the hall. "What does anybody want?"

Love? Happiness? But I know that's not what she means. "Money?"

"You guessed it."

"Fine." I nod. "How much?"

"How much you got on you?"

"Nothing." Girls aren't supposed to carry money. It makes us more vulnerable. "You know that's against the rules. What if I got mugged?"

She doesn't laugh out loud, but her eyes mock me. "Yeah, right. What if?"

"So how much?"

She looks me directly in the eye. "A thousand."

I gasp, but the truth is, I have double that in the jewelry box hidden in the bottom drawer of my dresser, cash aunts give me for birthdays but I have nowhere to spend. I've definitely got enough.

"No problem."

Willow scoffs. "Of course, it's no problem for you. So let's make it twelve hundred."

I want to say no, but she'll walk away if I do.

"Tomorrow. Meet me here. I'll tell you what you want to know."

"No." My voice is louder than I intend. The one boy left in the hall glances in our direction. "Tell me now. You know I'm good for it."

"What do you want to know?" It's a challenge more than a question.

"The parties."

"The HH parties? You wouldn't like them."

I have no idea what HH means but try not to show it.

"You can't even hear someone curse without flinching, Sequins. You couldn't handle the shit that goes down at HH."

"I don't care what you think. I want to know about them. I want to go."

"That's not up to me."

"Who is it up to?"

"Your chaperone."

Does Sister Laura know about the parties? Why didn't she tell me?

Willow sighs in resignation. "Maybe you could bribe her. Some people bribe chaperones."

Bribe her? "Girls bribe their chaperones to take them to parties?"

Her face goes darker. "No, stupid, the boys bribe them."

"What do you mean?"

She lets out another irritated sigh. "Sometimes boys pay chaperones to bring girls, but usually it's the government teachers." I must still look confused because she adds, "To bring girls from govie."

"But why?"

"Are you really that clueless, Sequins? So they can get them drunk and take advantage of them."

"But they're supposed to protect them."

"You know they don't all take that seriously, right? And some of them really need the money."

"For what?" Chaperones don't have to pay for food or rent, a fact that irritates Dad to no end.

"Jesus," she says loudly, and I wince again. "I don't know if you're clueless or just stupid." She shakes her head. "For their families. You know, some of them are only in this godforsaken country because they can't afford to leave."

I didn't know that, but Willow has called me clueless twice, so I keep my mouth shut.

"Anything else? I'm already late to class."

"What does HH stand for?"

Willow smiles. If I didn't know better, I'd think she was starting to like me. "*Hush Hush*. In other words, keep your mouth shut, okay?"

I nod.

"And bring the money tomorrow. Before school starts. If you're not here, I'll find you."

CHAPTER 40

S ister Laura is walking fast. Faster than normal.

"What's going on?" I ask as a red SUV streaks by us.

The SUV screeches around the corner. Sister Laura scratches her nose before turning back to me. "It's nothing. Just not myself."

"Why is that?"

"Haven't you noticed?"

"Noticed what?"

"There are constables *everywhere*." At that exact second, another red SUV heads in the same direction as the one before. This one whizzing by even faster.

"Is that different than normal?"

"You're right." She looks over her shoulder. "Like I said, I'm just not myself."

I don't bother pointing out she still hasn't answered my question. She's not going to reveal anything anyway. As much as we talk about my life, we never talk about hers. So instead of questioning her further, I jump into what I really want to discuss.

"I want to go."

She stops so abruptly it looks like she might fall forward. "You want to go?" Her voice is full of confusion. "What do you mean?"

"I want to go to one of the parties," I explain. "The HH parties."

Sister Laura doesn't respond. Instead she turns and starts walking again. I stay put, not willing to follow her. But when another siren wails behind us, I run after her. We walk in silence for half a block.

"They're dangerous, Stella." She doesn't look at me. "Those parties."

Navigate the world with care.

"I don't care. I can't live like this anymore."

Sister Laura peeks over her shoulder. "You sound certain."

"I am."

"There are other ways, you know?" She rubs the side of her nose. "Other ways to have a different life."

"Of course. But college is too far away. I can't wait any longer. I want...I *need* to live now."

Sister Laura stops in the middle of the sidewalk, lets out a long sigh, and looks to the sky. I follow her gaze. The electric blue surprises me. Everything else is dying and devoid of color. It's been hot too long. "You think you'll be free if you go to those parties, but the truth is, you're never really free. Other people can always stop you from doing what you want. All you can control is how you respond to what's in front of you."

"And how hard I try to change things."

"Yes, that too."

"I want to try. I'm ready."

CHAPTER 41

The next morning I hand Willow a yellow envelope thick with cash. "When is the next party?"

She flips through the bills with her fingertips. "What the hell?" There's real anger in her eyes. "This is only half."

"Half now and half when we get there."

"Jesus."

I do my best not to wince.

Willow studies the lockers on the other side of the hallway, as if considering her options. Someone behind me says, "Hey, Willow." She smirks a half smile, taking in a deep breath before returning my stare. "Fine."

"When is it?"

She closes her locker. "A week from Wednesday. Weeknights are safer. They're less likely to get busted."

"That's only eight days away."

"No refunds if you chicken out—" She starts to walk away.

"No." I put my hand on her arm. "I want to go. Where is it?"

"Your chaperone will know who to ask." She jerks her arm away from me. "Meet me there at midnight. And don't be late."

"I won't."

She shakes her head at me. "You're so stupid, Sequins. And you don't even know it." She lifts her backpack and shoves the envelope inside. "Once you do this, there's no coming back. But I guess your loss is my gain." She zips her backpack and walks away without saying goodbye.

CHAPTER 42

Sister Laura comes to my room every night that week to help me get ready. We sit across from each other on the floor and talk about what will happen. And to my surprise, she makes me drink.

At first she brings beer. I like the way the cold, wet can feels in my hand, but when I pop the top, the whole room smells like dirty socks. I'm finally used to the heavy sensation of it on my tongue when she shows up Saturday night with two of Mom's crystal Baccarat glasses and, to my surprise, a small bottle of amber liquor. She holds it up like a prize. "Bigger than an airplane bottle. That's all I've been able to get for months."

"An airplane bottle?"

"That's what they serve on planes."

"You've been on an airplane?"

"All the time. Before"—she frowns—"before everything changed. Before New America."

"What was it like?"

"Before?"

"No, flying." I realize too late I want to know what everything else was like then too.

"It's kind of scary." Her eyes grow big, but she smiles. "It doesn't feel natural. But it's exhilarating too. The takeoff? Your heart's in your shoes. But when you're in the air, there's nothing in the world like the view from miles above the earth. I'm sure even Dull Run looks stunning from that high up."

I let out a little laugh.

"I always had a drink before takeoff." She lifts the bottle. Red wax covers the cap and the top of the bottle. It looks like melted red crayon. "To calm my nerves."

It takes a minute for her to pull the wax back and open the bottle. She splashes some of the alcohol into the glasses and hands one to me. What would Mom and Dad say if they knew? The glass is heavier than I remember, and the smell of industrial cleaner hits me in the face.

"Drink the whole thing at once."

"What? Why?"

"You'll never finish it if you don't." She must see the disbelief on my face. "You have to be able to hold your liquor at these parties, Stella. Unless you don't want to go anymore."

"No," I insist. "I want to go."

"Then throw it back."

I look into the glass and then at Sister Laura.

"Like this." She picks up her own glass and demonstrates, drinking it all in one swallow. After she gulps it down, she shakes her head from side to side like a wet dog. "Wow." She sticks out her tongue. "It's been a while since I've done that."

"I don't know if I can."

"You don't have to, but if you don't, I'm not letting you go."

"Why not?"

"Because you'll *have* to do it there. They'll expect it. And I'm not going to put you in the position of doing shots for the first time in your life with a bunch of horny, privileged, entitled, shit-faced teenage boys."

"Geez!" I laugh.

"It's actually not funny, Stella." Her face is as serious as her tone. "Despite what they want you to believe, there's nothing more dangerous than those kinds of boys. They want everything, and they have no qualms about taking what you don't give them."

I've never seen Sister Laura this worked up.

"Now get going." She gestures toward my hand. "We haven't got all night."

Respect your chaperone.

I imitate Sister Laura, lifting the glass to my lips in one quick motion and throwing my head all the way back. The liquid is a shock going down, like swallowing a lit match that explodes when it reaches my chest. "Oh my gosh." I shake my head and stick my tongue out. "You should've warned me."

Now it's Sister Laura who laughs. "It wouldn't have changed anything!"

"I know, but—" I let out a little shudder. "Wow."

Sister Laura taps a finger on the rug between us, accentuating each word. "Now. You. Understand. This is why you have to practice."

"I guess."

She sits up. "You did well. Lots of people don't handle their first shot with such grace."

"They don't?"

"I've seen boys your age throw up."

"Really?"

"Well, maybe not a shot of Maker's Mark, but still. You didn't embarrass yourself."

"I hope I don't embarrass myself at the party."

"So what if you do?" She throws her hands up in the air. "Are you really that worried about what people think of you, Stella?"

"I just don't like being embarrassed."

"It's part of life, Stella." Sister Laura crosses her arms over her chest and examines me. "What's the most embarrassing thing that ever happened to you?"

I don't even have to think about it. "Seventh grade."

"Middle school is hard." She frowns. "What happened?"

"Brooklyn Liu's birthday parties were always big. For her thirteenth, it was a pool party." Is the alcohol giving me the courage to talk? "She lives in a giant house in the country. There's no one for miles, so it's safe to swim there."

Sister Laura squeezes her eyes shut like something poked her.

"I'd been swimming there before. Bonita and I were kind of close to Brooklyn when we were kids. The three of us hung out a lot. Until this party."

"It must have been bad."

"It was...I don't know...humiliating." I force myself to go on. "Everyone changes into their bathing suits in the pool house. When we come out, we're all standing around, waiting for Brooklyn to jump in. But she looks at me and says, 'My gosh, Stella, you have thunder thighs.'" As soon as I say the words out loud, I'm back there.

Seventh grade.

Brooklyn's pool.

Me half-naked on the concrete.

"Everyone just stood there gawking at my stupid thighs. Some of them even laughed."

"I hate when girls do that to each other. And your thighs aren't even big. Forget about being thunderous."

"You haven't seen me in a bathing suit."

She waves her hands dismissively. "Besides, some people find that attractive. During the Renaissance, big thighs—not to mention breasts and stomachs—were considered beautiful."

"The what?"

Sister Laura lets out a breath so long it sounds like a deflating bike tire. "Never mind. The point is you can't take it too hard. It's part of growing up. Everyone gets called names."

"Did you?"

Sister Laura tilts her head at me. "They called *me* Laura the Leper."

"What? Why?"

She pushes her glasses up her nose. "It started when I got mono junior year. I don't know why it stuck—back then *everyone* got mono in high school—but for some reason, I was the poster child. I must've gotten it first." She rolls her eyes and lets out a small laugh. "And *maybe* everyone accused me of spreading it all over school."

"Why is that funny?"

"Oh, Lord, that was such a *long* time ago." Sister Laura shakes her head and laughs at the same time. "It's funny because mono was the kissing disease. And, okay, I'll admit it. I kissed *a lot* of boys."

"You did? Really?"

"That was what we did for fun back then. That and this—" She picks up the bottle. "They kind of went hand in hand. To be honest, I had a lot of fun. And I regret nothing. I mean, except being called Laura the Leper all of junior year. *That* put a bit of a wrench in my kissing game."

"Weren't you embarrassed?"

"Of course. But you're probably not normal if you haven't had a mortifying nickname."

"Kind of like you're not normal if you haven't bled through your skirt in public?"

Sister Laura eyes light up. "Exactly."

"I had something even more humiliating happen once." I never imagined sharing this with Sister Laura, but right now I feel like I could tell her anything. "You have to promise you won't mention it to my parents. They *never* talk about it."

"Your parents know?"

"They were there. It was sophomore year. When I was baptized."

"Oh, no. What happened?"

"It was spring, but so hot it felt like summer. I mean, it was *really* hot." I smooth the fibers of the rug we're sitting on as I work up the courage to tell her. "I was at the baptismal font in front of the church. Everyone was staring at me. It was too hot up there. I started to get dizzy, and before I knew what was happening, I was on the floor. I passed out in front of the entire congregation."

Sister Laura's hand is over her mouth, but I make out the trace of a smile. "I really wish I could've seen your parents' faces."

"They weren't happy. I didn't get baptized that day. I had to go back when no one was there. With just Mom and Dad. The minister didn't even bother with the baptismal font. He just dribbled some water on my head in the church office."

Sister Laura shudders so hard it shakes her whole body. "What is it?"

"Oh, it's just...that made me remember something."

"What?"

"It's hard to talk about." Her right hand goes to the pocket of her sweats like she's going to pull something out, but she just lets it rest there. "It's a sad story."

"What is it?"

"Maybe I shouldn't tell you."

I lean forward. "I *want* to know."

She turns her head to the right. She's eye-to-eye with the top of the bed as if the past is sitting on it. "It's a storm I can't get out from under." She looks at me again, now with real pain in her eyes. "It happened in a church office. That's what made me think of it."

This is big. I can feel it. I sit up straight.

"I was with my older sister. Samantha."

Sister Laura's never mentioned anyone in her family before. I didn't even know she had a sister.

"This was years ago. I was only fourteen." Sister Laura's eyes dart back to me before losing focus. "Samantha was your age— seventeen. Back then, there were many different kinds of churches. Not just churches like the ones here. Churches for people who believed...well, how do I say it? People who believed different things than you were raised to believe." Sister Laura peers at me. "People who believed in things like equality and women's rights. People who believed it was okay to be gay."

"Churches? Really?"

"Yes. We went to a church like that. My family. We didn't go every single week. Just when we felt like it. More important than going to the service was being part of a community that shared our values."

Sister Laura reaches past me for the glass of water on my bedside table, drinking half of it before continuing.

"Samantha was picking up some flyers. At church. I tagged along because I worshipped her. The pastor told her the flyers were supposed to…" She pauses, considering me over the top of her glasses. "Well, it doesn't matter what they were supposed to do."

I have more questions, but I sense I should just listen.

Sister Laura lifts her head to the chandelier. "It was just the three of us. And I was small for my age. I wasn't strong. I hadn't learned how to defend myself." She pauses and breathes in deeply. "The pastor was tiny too. She was barely a hundred pounds. My sister wasn't much better. And she was pretty. *Too* pretty."

It's the first time I've ever heard Sister Laura say anything remotely like what we're taught in school. *Don't make yourself look too pretty. Don't wear clothes that are too revealing.*

"Did you say 'she'? Your pastor was a she?"

"That wasn't uncommon back then. Even in some conservative churches. The irony is Samantha and I were just about to leave when they got there. These men. These…" She sneaks a look at me. "Well, anyway, they were very angry men."

What men? What was she going to say? She's leaving things out, but I don't want to interrupt.

"They didn't like our church. They wanted women like us put in our place. And that's what they did that day."

I'm overwhelmed with feeling this is a story Sister Laura has been needing to tell me all along. I'm afraid of what she'll say next, but I also know I need to hear it. "What do you mean?"

Sister Laura's head sways back and forth like she's following a curvy road. "Two of them dragged the pastor away. Took her into the equipment closet. They dragged me in there next. Tied us with computer cords. They left us there and went back to where my sister was alone with the others."

I have to work hard to keep myself from gasping.

"I tried to fight. I did. But it was no use. There were too many of them. Four or five. Maybe six."

She hesitates, but I *need* to know the whole story. "What happened?"

Sister Laura's eyes meet mine for a long moment before looking away. "We couldn't see them, but we could hear them." She sucks in a quick breath and holds it in her mouth. When she can't hold it anymore, she lets it go so slowly I see her chest falling. "It was horrific." She looks right at me. "Totally horrific."

Everything in my body goes cold. She squeezes her eyes shut before tilting her face back to the ceiling. I can see the tears pooling in her eyes. She wipes them away and replaces them with the most crooked smile I've ever seen. "And this wasn't the only time. Terrible things happened to women in order to keep them, to keep us, quiet."

I reach for her hand, and she lets me take it. "I'm so sorry."

"Me too, Stella. Me too."

We sit for a minute, me holding her hand like it's the only thing keeping her from slipping into the past. Finally, she lets go, her fingers going to her pocket again. This time, she reaches inside and pulls out a piece of yellowed paper folded into a tiny square.

She holds it up with a sniffle. "I kept it."

"What is it?"

"It's one of the flyers we were supposed to pass out that day. A piece of it anyway. I didn't realize until it was all over: I'd been gripping it in my hand the whole time." She studies the square of paper. "I keep it with me all the time." She looks directly into my eyes. "So I don't forget."

"Is that why you became a chaperone?"

Sister Laura's face flattens into surprise. "How did you know?"

"Because that's your job now. To protect girls."

"Oh." She pushes her glasses up and wipes her nose again. "You're right. I suppose that's true too."

CHAPTER 43

When I come downstairs and head for the kitchen the next morning, I hear a voice behind me.

"Good morning, Stella."

I whip around and see Dad sitting in one of the club chairs in the living room.

His eyes lock on mine. "We need to talk."

The flatness of his voice tells me something's wrong. Is it me?

"Yes, sir."

"When was the last time you were in this room, Stella?"

My eyes roam over the space as if I don't know every inch of it by heart. The marble fireplace. The gray sofas. The Degas painting. All of it. "This room?"

"Yes, Stella." His voice is so devoid of warmth it's almost unrecognizable. He's not just troubled. He's irate. "This room."

"I don't know, Dad. I—"

He interrupts me. "You do know."

I involuntarily repeat myself. "I don't know... Yesterday, maybe."

"Why would you need to come in here on a Saturday, Stella?

This is the *formal* living room. You have no business in here unless you're entertaining guests."

"I needed to—"

"Don't lie to me, young lady."

I don't speak. What I can I say that won't anger him further?

Dad uncrosses his legs, gets to his feet, and makes his way over to the bar cart between the tall windows in the middle of the room. He pauses there, examining what's in front of him. That's when it hits me. He knows. He knows what we've been doing.

Dad has his back to me, but I can still see him move his index finger from one bottle to another. Like he's counting. "Almost eighteen years ago, I was given a small bottle from the first limited edition Maker's Mark Wood Finishing series."

Maker's Mark. That's what we drank last night. Did Sister Laura steal it from Dad?

Dad is still talking. "This was a few months before it was even released. It wasn't a bottle of Pappy, but it was nothing to scoff at either." Dad turns around to face me. "Even though it wasn't the most expensive, it was very, very special to me. Do you know why it was so special, Stella?"

I shake my head.

"It was special because it was given to me on the occasion of your birth."

I try to swallow, but my mouth is dry.

"I'd always planned to open that bottle, Stella Ann, with your future husband when he proposed marriage. An appropriate moment because, at that point, I would have successfully completed the job of raising you."

Everything in me tells me to admit it, apologize, but I'm too afraid to speak.

"I've looked at that bottle nearly every day since you were born. So you can imagine how I felt when I came in here this morning and noticed it was gone."

"Dad, I—"

He shakes his pointer finger at me. "Don't you dare speak, young lady."

"What's going on?"

We both turn our heads at the same time. Sister Laura stands in the foyer. She's dressed for church, her caftan paired with flowing white pants and understated silver jewelry.

Dad drops his outstretched hand to his side and clears his throat. "Since you asked, Sister Laura—" He turns back to the liquor cart and reaches for a clear bottle with amber liquid inside, opening it before he continues. "It seems you haven't done an adequate job of keeping an eye on your charge."

Sister Laura looks at me with a question in her eyes, but I don't have time to warn her before Dad turns around with a small glass of bourbon in his hand. I have to stop my jaw from dropping. It's nine in the morning. I've never seen Dad have a drink before dinner is over, let alone on a Sunday before church.

Sister Laura ignores his drink. "What do you mean, Mr. Graham?"

"Stella stole a bottle of bourbon that was very special to me. Did you know she had started drinking, Sister?"

Sister Laura's face is so painted with red I can't imagine she'll be able to lie. Dad takes a sip from his glass while he waits for her answer. She takes in a deep breath. "This is my fault, Mr. Graham."

Is she really giving in so easily?

Dad slams his drink down on the cart behind him and takes five swift steps toward her, stopping in front of her like an invisible wall stands between them. Sister Laura doesn't even flinch. "Of course, it's your fault. You're in charge of her upbringing."

"No, I mean, I am the one responsible."

"What are you saying?"

I hold my breath, waiting for her answer. If she tells him what we've been doing, everything will fall apart. Sister Laura will be dismissed. I won't be able to go to the HH party. A new chaperone will be assigned. I'll have to start all over. Again.

"I mean, I'm the one who took the bottle."

No one says anything for so long it's like we've been muted. I don't dare let out the breath I'm holding.

Just when I feel like I'm going to burst, Sister Laura says, "A friend of mine lost her mother yesterday. She was only fifty-nine years old. Fifty-nine. Can you imagine? I just wanted to console her, Mr. Graham. It was such a small bottle. I didn't think you would notice."

"You took it?" Dad's voice conveys disbelief.

"I know this is grounds for dismissal, Mr. Graham."

"That's right, it is."

What is he saying? Does this mean he believes her? Does he believe it was for her friend and not me?

"I just wonder if there's any way you can give me another chance."

"Another chance?" Dad lets out a laugh so loud it echoes across the room. "You must be joking."

"I wouldn't joke about something this serious."

"I can't possibly tolerate this breach in protocol. How would it reflect on me if people found out?"

I can't believe it. She's managed to take his focus off me and put it on her.

"It's just that, well, if I'm being completely honest, sir, it's Stella. I'm doing so well with her. And she's turning into exactly the kind of woman New America needs. Respectful. Modest. Polite. Not to mention beautiful. You must be so proud."

Dad can't help himself. He glances at me, and his eyes gleam with pride. She's saying exactly what he wants to hear. And he has no idea she's manipulating him.

"I know you're a man who's advocated for mercy in the past. I know you've helped other people get second chances."

What is she talking about?

Dad leans toward her as if he can't hear. "Excuse me?"

"The Appomattox Six. The men who…"

"I know who they are, damn it." He glances at me and then back at Sister Laura. He doesn't want her to say who they are. He doesn't want me to know.

"I know you helped pay for their defense."

"How could you possibly know that?"

"I just—"

Dad cuts her off, pointing a threatening finger at her. "Don't say another word." His eyes narrow. He looks almost…frightened. Something has shifted between them. "I did what needed to be done." He shakes his head. "I solved a problem. A problem ripping our country apart. But if people found out, if they…well, they'd think I approved."

What are they talking about? Approved of what?

"You're correct, sir. They might say that. But, of course, as Stella's chaperone, I'd never breathe a word to anyone."

Dad closes his eyes and puts his hand across his mouth like he's trying to hold it shut.

Sister Laura speaks next. "I'll go pack my things."

Why is she giving up now? Just when she was starting to get him to listen?

She turns toward the stairs and starts up them, but before she gets to the landing, Dad says one word: "Wait." Sister Laura looks over her shoulder, and he holds her gaze for a long moment before going on. "Since none of this is Stella's fault…" He glances at me. "Perhaps we could…I don't know…come up with a solution. A punishment of some kind if you will."

Sister Laura walks back down the stairs. I don't know how she does it, but she manages to look penitent.

"I suppose I could let you stay if it was on a probationary basis." She holds his eye. "Whatever you think is right, Mr. Graham."

He points an index finger at her. "But if one more thing goes wrong, if either of you steps out of line one time, that's it. You will have to leave immediately."

I can't believe it. He's going to let her stay.

"Of course."

"And you won't take your meals with us anymore either."

Sister Laura winces the tiniest bit but doesn't respond out loud.

"You can eat after we've finished. On your own."

This isn't about the missing bottle. This is about Dad taking control. For the first time since Sister Laura moved in, he thinks he's the one making the rules. Little does he know Sister Laura is manipulating him.

"And you can be sure I'll be keeping a much closer eye on you and everything that goes on in this house."

I'm so relieved, my eyes are closed when Sister Laura says, "Understood."

"And if anything else like this ever happens again…"

He doesn't finish. He doesn't have to.

CHAPTER 44

For three long days, we don't break any rules, doing only what's expected. Sister Laura still comes to my room every night to go over exactly how it will happen. I'm desperate to ask her about the Appomattox Six, but I'm afraid if I do, it will distract her from getting ready for the HH party. And when the day finally arrives, I'm ready.

We can't leave until Mom and Dad are completely asleep. Over an hour after they go to their bedroom, Sister Laura pushes my door open, a finger on her lips. I'm sitting on the bed, fully dressed. It took me hours to settle on a blouse with tiny blue flowers, the corduroy skirt I wear to school, and Sister Laura's cowboy boots. I even put on a little makeup.

We move slowly, knowing the floors will creak if we're not extremely careful. And if Dad catches us, it will all be over.

At the top of the stairwell, I glance down the hall, making sure no one is watching. But when I try to move my foot to the first step, I can't find it, tumbling forward and crashing into Sister Laura's back.

She twists around, putting her hands on either side of me to stop my fall. Her voice is a frustrated whisper. "Stella!"

I mouth the words *I'm sorry* before we both look back down the hallway, waiting to see if anyone will appear at Mom and Dad's door. It's dead quiet, but a second later, a loud whoosh sounds across the floorboards.

Sister Laura puts her hand over my mouth. "It's just the air-conditioning," she whispers. "We need to go. *Now.*"

We quicken our pace, rushing quietly down the steps and out the back door. We're in the alley behind the house before I dare glance at Mom and Dad's windows. The blue light of their smart screen is still off. They didn't hear us.

Sister Laura's ancient Mercedes rumbles to life.

"What if they hear?"

"They'll think I'm going to a prayer meeting."

I look at their window one more time and hope she's right.

It's a long drive. Almost twenty minutes and farther out in the country than I've been. Sister Laura turns down a gravel road that runs between fields of corn. Dry stalks loom over us like sentries. It's a mile before we come to an old white farmhouse.

Sister Laura cranks a handle on her door. Her window goes down in jerky motions. I've never seen anything like it.

Two bearded men, one middle-aged and one not much older than I am, sit on the front porch. Sister Laura slows to a stop, and the older one leans over the railing. Sister Laura puts an index finger to her forehead. The man does the same before waving her forward and pointing to a barn behind the house.

"What was that?" I ask after she cranks the window back up.

"What?"

"That signal you gave him. When you touched your forehead."

"That's how we know we're on the same side." She lifts a finger to her head again. "It means 'We're thinking.'"

The same side?

The barn is ancient. Yellow light seeps between the decaying boards. At least two dozen cars and trucks sit next to it. Are that many people willing to break the rules?

Sister Laura's jacket brushes against the seat when she turns to me. "Are you sure you want to do this, Stella? It's not too late to change your mind."

"I'm sure."

Sister Laura walks me to the door, pulling a phone out of her pocket before I go in. "I'll be back there." She nods to the farmhouse. "With the others. Come find me when you want to go. And if there's an emergency"—she points to the phone screen—"call this number."

"Thank you so much for helping me."

Her eyes stay flat. "Just be careful, Stella."

She walks toward the farmhouse like it's the most normal thing in the world to leave me alone outside a strange barn in the middle of nowhere.

My heart races.

I open the door.

CHAPTER 45

As soon as the thin door slaps shut behind me, heads turn in my direction. It's hard to see even though bare light bulbs hang from the ceiling. Clusters of people sit or stand in front of a plywood bar while others hover around a ping pong table. A string of lights hangs from a loft. It's festive, but my gut tells me this is not a welcoming place. Something feels off.

I go to the bar, searching for Willow's bun. A girl with perfect makeup and long wavy hair turns toward me.

"You're late, Sequins."

It takes me a second to recognize her. The long hair. The makeup. She's a glamorous version of herself.

"I'm right on time."

She squints at an expensive-looking smart watch, the kind girls are not allowed to have. "It's three minutes after twelve."

"Isn't that on time?"

"Whatever." She stands from the oak barrel she's sitting on, puts a hand on my shoulder, and pulls my ear to her mouth. "Do you have it?"

I look into her face and nod.

She leans close and whispers in my ear again. "Okay, here's the deal. You can give it to me in the bathroom. But we need to act girly and stupid first, so they don't think we're up to something." She's talking fast. "When I count to three, start giggling like an idiot. You should be able to handle that, right?"

She doesn't wait for an answer, immediately counting down. When she gets to one, she leans back and laughs hysterically.

It takes me a few seconds to catch up. Once I do, I laugh so hard I have to cover my mouth.

Willow bumps her hip against mine. "You're hilarious, Sequins." She links her arm in mine and pulls me away from the bar.

The guy sitting next to her looks over his shoulder. "Where ya goin', babe?"

I didn't realize they were together.

"Pee break, baby." She winks at him. "Be right back."

Willow drags me to a corner of the barn where a burlap curtain hangs on an oval shower curtain rod. She yanks it open, revealing a plastic bucket of urine next to a roll of toilet paper. The smell is so toxic I have to work hard not to gag.

She throws the curtain shut behind us. "Okay," she says in a serious voice, performance over. "Where is it?"

I pat my jacket pocket.

"Let's see it."

I pull out a wad of bills.

Willow sneers while she counts. "I can't believe you have this kind of money laying around." She stuffs the money into a pocket and zips her green Army jacket. "Okay, we're done."

"You're not staying?"

"Not a chance. I know you think I'm some kind of whore, but—"

"I do *not*." I say this even though we both know she's right.

"Whatever, Sequins. Anyway, this isn't really my scene."

"It doesn't look so bad."

"You're so stupid, Sequins, I don't even know what to say." She reaches for the curtain but hesitates, looking back over her shoulder. "If things get weird. And, I mean, weird in even the slightest way, just leave, okay? Find your chaperone and leave."

Why is she pretending to care about me?

She throws open the curtain, and everyone looks in our direction. The guy sitting next to Willow at the bar, the guy she called baby, waves. Willow waves back, and he returns to his drink. I turn to say goodbye, but she's already headed for the door. Before I know it, she's disappeared, leaving me alone in a room full of strangers.

CHAPTER 46

I wander back to the bar and slide onto Willow's empty stool.

"Where is she?" He peers around me like I'm in his way.

"I don't know." It's obvious she ditched him. I feel obligated to help her get away. "What did you say your name is?"

He stares at the door for another minute before looking me in the eye for the first time. "Aren't you that bitch who killed her chaperone?"

Everyone nearby turns to look at us. All the saliva in my mouth evaporates. I'm still trying to figure out what to say when he asks another question.

"Is she coming back?"

I shrug. "She didn't say."

"What the fuck?" he says.

I cringe. I've never heard anyone say that word in real life.

He gets to his feet, and the bartender loudly clears his throat. Baby reaches into both pockets and throws a bunch of crumpled bills on the bar before starting for the door.

He's gone before I can protest.

I tell myself Willow can fend for herself. She's probably already found her chaperone. Some part of me knows she's in danger. But what can I do? That's when I remember the phone in my back pocket. The emergency number.

But if I use it, my night will be over. Sister Laura will get me out of here so fast I won't have been here long enough to describe the bartender's face.

So I tell myself again Willow's the kind of girl who can handle herself.

I tell myself she'll be fine.

The guy behind the bar brings me a plastic cup of flat beer. I thank him, and he sniffs in reply.

I'm not surprised when the bitter taste hits my tongue. Sister Laura has trained me well. After a few sips, I take in my surroundings. Baby's empty barrel is on one side of me and a group of boys from school on the other. All Climbers. No surprise.

Farther down, a girl I recognize—Leslie something—sits between two guys I don't. Both of them hang on her like she's furniture. A row of copper-colored shots sits in front of them. They count to three before throwing them back. Sister Laura warned me about doing too many shots, but Leslie calls for another round. At school she's a quiet sit-in-the-front-row type. Maybe that's all an act.

At the other end of the bar, two guys play a game with straws, pushing something around the bar top. They lean forward and put their noses on the straws. White powder explodes in one of their faces. Cocaine. Just like the rich guy in the movie about the redhead who makes her own prom dress.

A Climber approaches the bar, stops in front of the others.

"Brittney Hurley's good for the go." He hooks a thumb over his shoulder. "Some good ole boys got her naked in a rusty bathtub out back."

Brittany Hurley is only a freshman. What is she doing here?

"You're shitting me," another Climber says. "Well, I, for one, would like to see those massive tits."

"Now's your chance, Jace."

They break into laughter that sounds more menacing than playful.

"Let's finish up and go see for ourselves," the Climber named Jace says. "I'm sure a girl like Brittney Hurley won't mind if we each take a turn."

I choke on my beer. A few Climbers glance at me, but no one says a word.

"Go right ahead, man," another one of them says. "But I prefer not to put my johnson in a trash can."

I don't realize I've finished my beer until the bartender shows up with another, swiping my empty cup before I can speak. I take a long sip. When I put it down, one of the Climbers—the one who mentioned his johnson—slides onto the stool next to me.

Another, a boy I know from grade school named Remy, is at his side. "Well, if it isn't Stella Graham."

"That's me." I stretch a fake smile across my face. I'm more nervous than I expected. My heart thumps like a rabbit in my chest.

"I don't believe we've exchanged a single word since we went to Summit Day together."

"Well, we're not *supposed* to speak to each other anymore, are we?" The words are out of my mouth before I realize how they sound. Bitter. Defiant.

But both of them laugh freely. The boy I don't know says, "She's got a point," before taking another sip of beer.

"Stella, this is my buddy Adam." Remy points to his friend. "He's good people."

"Nice to meet you," I say as if this happens every day. The truth is, it's the most unusual experience of my life.

The thumping in my chest hasn't let up. I feel something akin to happiness. Is it relief? But what I really want is to see Mateo. Now that I'm here, I get this isn't his scene. Too something for him. Too distasteful. That must be why he acted confused when I let it slip I might be here. He probably doesn't even know what an HH party is. Or if he does, he has no desire to go.

"How have I never seen you around before?" Adam asks.

I'm confident it's because Climbers prefer college girls over the ones in their own high school, but I say, "I'm not sure."

"This calls for a toast," says Adam. "It's not every day you end up at a party with the prettiest girl in Bull Run."

I feel myself blushing behind the plastic cup.

Remy nods. "Excellent point. Count me in."

Adam holds a hand up like we're in a real bar. "Bartender? Three Buttery Nipples, please."

It's all I can do not to spit my drink out.

CHAPTER 47

They taste like butterscotch candy, sliding down my throat with none of the fire in Sister Laura's shot. We're on our third round already. My body is warm all over. A good warm. Kind of like descending into a hot bath. I need to slow down, but I want to keep this feeling going. Adam has his arm slung around my shoulder like it belongs there, and every one of my extremities is buzzing. This is exactly what I wanted to feel. Uninhibited. Free. Even if I wanted it with a different boy.

We down our third shot.

"That's my limit." I use the self-assured voice Sister Laura taught me.

Adam smiles like I've made a proposal. "Mine too." He puts his empty shot glass on the bar. "Do you want to go somewhere more comfortable?"

Embrace purity.

"That sounds nice."

He takes my hand and leads me to the area underneath the loft. Overstuffed chairs and couches fill the dark space, most of them occupied by couples on top of each other. Even though he's not Mateo, I want this to happen. I want his lips on mine. I want his body against me. I want to live.

At the first empty couch, Adam pulls me down next to him.

He puts his hand on my face, whispering, "I'm so glad you're here."

It's not the most romantic thing I've ever heard, but I don't care. I just want to kiss someone.

Anyone.

I'm almost eighteen, and I've never kissed anyone.

He leans closer, and I let my eyes shut. His mouth meets mine. It's wet and soft. I want this moment to last as long as it can. He starts slow at first, kissing me gently and pulling away to look in my eyes every few seconds. He's taking his time.

But then things speed up.

He unbuttons my blouse, and the sensation of his fingers on my bare skin is an incredible rush. My body responds in ways I didn't know it could. He slides his hand under my bra before I can object. I don't *want* to object. It feels too good. When he cups my breast in his hand, I moan.

He leans back and smiles. "Like that?"

"Yes." I pull him back to me even though I'm breaking rules I never imagined I would.

We go on like that so long I lose track of time, every minute getting more and more intense. My body is on fire. I've never felt this way before. Sure, I've touched myself. I've been doing that ever since Sister Helen gave me a copy of *Deenie* in eighth grade, but this isn't the same. This is on another level. I want this to happen with Mateo, but Mateo isn't here.

And when I close my eyes, it doesn't matter who it is.

His hands roam all over me. My breasts, my hips, my butt. For some reason I don't understand, I put my hand on his crotch, rubbing him through his jeans. Before I know what's happening, he's putting his hand up my skirt.

And I'm letting him.

A second later he moves to my underwear. It feels forbidden and wrong and oh so right. Knowing it's against the rules makes me want it so much more.

I want this.

Even though I know I shouldn't.

His fingers touch me in a way that feels completely natural.

But then he rotates his hand to a different position before lunging a finger into me like a torpedo. It hurts so much I have to stop myself from yelling out. His finger falls out but stays inside my underwear. This is what I wanted. This is where we've been heading all along. I made this happen. I *let* it happen. So why does it feel like I'm not ready? Sister Laura's words come to me. *If anything doesn't feel right, you can always walk away.*

I pull back, and a question appears in Adam's eye. An accusation.

"I need to go." I lean away until his hand slides out of my underwear. "It's getting late."

I start to get up, but he grabs my arm before I'm on my feet, dragging me back into his lap. "Not so fast. I'm just getting started."

The couple across from us stops what they're doing. We're putting on too good a show to miss. What did Sister Laura say? *Be firm and rely on other people if necessary.*

I run my hand down his torso. He grins. Does he think I'm being flirtatious? That's not how I mean it. I put my hand in the middle of his chest and push against him as hard as I can, jumping up from the sofa. I yank down my skirt and fumble with the buttons of my blouse.

I turn to the couple watching us. "What time is it?"

The girl frowns the slightest bit. "After two."

"I need to go." I speak with conviction. Adam still has his hand on my leg, but I shake it off and turn away. For some reason, this works.

He doesn't grab me.

Doesn't pull me back.

Lets me go when I move away.

Saying the words out loud makes them happen.

CHAPTER 48

S ister Laura doesn't ask questions. We're in the Mercedes heading home without a word.

The sky overhead is blacker than I've ever seen it. There are no streetlights this far out. I didn't notice the stars on the drive out of town, but now I wonder how I missed them. They're so bright they look artificial.

I wait until we've cleared the cornfields to say anything.

"Things got a *little* out-of-control." I hold my thumb and index finger a hair apart to indicate how little it was.

Eyebrows raised, Sister Laura takes a quick glance at me. "Are you okay?"

"M'kay." If I can hear my words slurring, I'm sure Sister Laura can too. "But I think I'm just a tiny bit drunk."

I'm a different person than I was an hour ago.

Everything is different.

Finally.

I work up the courage to tell Sister Laura what happened. "I had some drinks. *And* some shots. *Really* glad we practiced."

"No doubt."

"And…some making out."

"Meaning?"

"Meaning I made out with someone."

"Mateo?"

"Don't think that was Mateo's scene."

"Okay."

"Made out and a little more." I hesitate, remembering what it felt like when Adam kissed me, put his hands on my skin. "It felt good. *Really* good."

"I can imagine. Have you ever done anything like that before?" I shake my head. "*Never.*"

"This is a big deal, Stella." She offers me a genuine smile. "I'm happy for you."

I feel my face turning red as I remember putting my hand on Adam's crotch. "But then things went too far, you know?"

Her head jerks in my direction.

"It's my fault."

"It's not your fault," Sister Laura says. "It's not anyone's fault. I mean, unless he forced himself on you."

"No, no, no. I *wanted* it. But then I wanted it to stop."

"Did you?" There's so much fear in her voice I almost regret telling her. "I mean, did you stop it?"

"You know what?" I turn my body to face her, straining at the seatbelt. "I did what you told me. And it worked perfectly."

"Oh, good." She lets out a relieved breath. "I'm glad."

"But now I feel stupid."

Sister Laura smiles at me again. "Stella, this is a good thing."

"How is it a good thing?"

"It's good you stayed in control. It's good you knew your limits and got out when you'd had enough. That's what matters."

"If you say so." My singsongy words echo off the walls of the Mercedes.

"This is all perfectly normal, especially at your age. Especially when you're new at this. It's normal to experience desire, act on it, and then, sometimes, feel like you've gone too far."

"It's normal to be all secretive and sneak out in the middle of the night? To a secret party? At a secret house?" I say the word *secret* over and over because it's the only word I can remember after doing all those shots. "And kiss a boy you don't even like?"

Sister Laura lets out a frustrated grunt. "You're right about that."

"But *you* said it's normal."

"I mean, it's normal in the real world." She doesn't take her eyes off the road.

"Isn't this the real world?"

She steals a look at me. The fields have disappeared, and small brick houses line either side of the road. "No, Stella, it's not."

My bedroom tilts and spins like a funhouse.

When I climb into bed, my head slips off one side. I'm afraid of falling, so I center myself on the mattress and try to hold my head perfectly still. It helps the tiniest bit though the spinning continues. I close my eyes in an unsuccessful attempt to shut it out.

Sister Laura may think we're not living in the real world, but it's real to me. It's the only world I've ever known.

It's also seriously messed up. I shouldn't have to sneak around when I'm a senior in high school to have my first kiss. I wanted that kiss to be with Mateo, not some Climber. But in my world, there's no way for that to happen. Why do we play by these stupid rules? Why can't we go to the movies? Or out to dinner? Or parking like they do in all the old movies?

That's Sister Laura's normal.

Why can't it be mine?

CHAPTER 49

I wake to the sound of raised voices. People are arguing right outside my bedroom door. Every word pounds against my head.

I cover my face with my hands and will the pounding to stop.

It takes everything I have to push myself out of bed. When I put my ear to the door, their voices are as clear as the pounding. Dad and Sister Laura. She's trying to get me out of running this morning.

"This was *your* idea," Dad insists. "Now she needs to prove she has the follow-through."

"This isn't about follow-through. She's sick."

"But she's not really sick, is she? She just has her—" He doesn't finish. "This is exactly why women can't be trusted to hold positions of power."

"Mr. Graham, I take serious offense—"

"Do I have to remind you, Sister, that you're still on very thin ice around here? One more word, and you're dismissed."

Sister Laura is smart enough not to respond.

I have no choice. I have to run.

Twenty minutes later Dad and I are running toward the government complex. My head is pounding like the giant drum they drag out on Freedom Day. I've been outpacing him for weeks, so if I slow, he might get suspicious. I tell myself to ignore the pain. I tell myself it will be over in half an hour. I can tolerate thirty minutes of pain.

"Stella?" Dad says.

No. No. No. I do NOT want to talk.

But Dad goes on. "I need to discuss something with you." More than half the mornings we run, Dad doesn't say a word. Why can't this be one of those mornings?

The pounding is constant, and each time my foot hits the pavement, a wave of nausea shoots through my body.

"Stella, your eighteenth birthday is coming up."

It's hard to focus, but I catch the word *birthday*.

"It's time I made some decisions about your future." His eyes stay on the road ahead. "I know you're growing up, Stella. I can feel you changing. I know you want to experience new things."

What is he saying? Does he know about last night? I don't dare look at him now. If I do, he'll surely see the truth in my eyes.

"I don't want to stop you from becoming a woman, Stella." He lets go of an uncomfortable laugh. "What am I saying? I *can't* stop that. I can't stop nature from taking its course."

If he doesn't know about last night, he at least suspects something.

"The best thing for you, the best thing for *all* of us, is for you to get married this summer."

I stop running and put my hands on my pounding forehead. Dad stops too.

"What did you say?"

"I know you want to go to college, but, Stella, you've lived a sheltered life." He puts his hands on his hips. "You're not prepared for that. You could get married next summer and then, maybe, if it works out, think about going to college later."

I try to shake my head, but it's too painful. "You don't know me at all."

"Excuse me?"

I realize my mistake too late. I've admitted there are things he doesn't know about me. I've opened the door to questions. I do my best to pivot. "I'm not stupid, Dad."

"I don't think you're stupid, Stella. Just ignorant."

It would hurt less if he'd slapped me.

"I don't mean that as a criticism. Just an observation. I know you're a smart girl, but you know nothing about the world we live in. You have no idea how dangerous it is."

"How could I not, Dad? They teach us about it every day at school. In fact, that's all they teach us. That and how to make babies."

Dad winces but doesn't argue. "Learning about the world in school is very different than experiencing it firsthand. Unless there's something you haven't told me, you have no actual experience in the real world." He looks directly into my eyes. "Do you?"

It's a challenge. I want nothing more than to tell him how wrong he is, to tell him *exactly* where I was last night, to tell him about Adam's finger inside me. But if I do, I'll never have a moment of freedom again.

"I've set up your next Visitation with someone who might be a match for you."

"What are you talking about?"

"Your Sunday Visitation. I've invited a candidate for you to marry. His name is Joseph Clarke. He's a constable, and he's on the right path. That's what you need right now."

The pounding in my head has been replaced by a type of flashing. A cerebral lightning storm. I can barely comprehend what he's saying.

"A constable?"

"That's right."

"Are you kidding, Dad?"

"Not at all. And you better watch your tone, young lady."

I shake my head even though doing so is more painful than anything I've ever felt. I need the lightning to stop. "I'm not getting married, Dad." I start to turn away, but he grabs my wrist, yanking me back. I flash to Adam doing the same thing last night. Is this how they do it? Is this how they control women? By overpowering us?

He barks at me when I look into his face. "You don't understand." His eyes have gone flat, and his hand is so tight on my wrist he could break the bone. His voice drops to a low hiss. "This isn't up to you, Stella. This is my decision."

Give obedience.

I hold his gaze. I could argue. Try to change his mind. Better yet, I could knee him in the groin and take off running when he drops to the pavement. Thanks to the Master, I know exactly how to do that. I might even make it home without anyone seeing me. But what good would that do? It would only delay the inevitable. I have to let him win now and, later, when I'm alone, figure out how to fight back.

It breaks my heart, but I say it. "Yes, sir."

CHAPTER 50

T he two acetaminophen I take do little to stop the pounding. It's so bad I hold my head as Sister Laura and I walk to school.

Sister Laura doesn't speak, understanding every word hurts, but there's something I can't wait until later to bring up.

"I want to ask you about some things you've said lately, and you have to promise to tell me the truth."

Sister Laura nods but keeps walking without looking at me. "It depends on what you ask. Sometimes protecting you is more important than being honest."

I stop and turn my whole body in Sister Laura's direction even though doing so makes my head spin wildly. "Who are the Appomattox Six and what were you trying to say about New America last night? Were you saying Old America is real and New America is not?"

Sister Laura's face contorts through too many different emotions to read. "I can't tell you about the A6, Stella."

"Why not?" I lift my hands in protest, immediately regretting that I've let go of my head.

"You're not ready. And it wouldn't help you. Knowing what

happened would only hurt you." Sister Laura's eyes plead with me, and I decide to let it go. "And as far as New America, I guess it's not true that it isn't real. It's real to you. It's real to your friends. It's all you've ever known. I guess what I mean is it's not right."

"Not right?" Even I hear the skepticism in my voice. "Then why do you live here?"

"It's complicated, Stella."

"I don't see why." I return a hand to my forehead. "You were sixteen when this country was founded. You could've left."

"Maybe there was a reason to stay."

"Like what?"

Sister Laura looks down the sidewalk. "You're the one who recognized the reason I'm a chaperone is to help girls."

"But you *can't* help me. You can't get me time alone with Mateo. You can't get me into real classes. You can't get my teachers to let me talk. You can't get people to take me seriously. You can't get me a driver's license. You can't get me out of Sunday Visitation, much less marriage."

Now Sister Laura is the one lifting her hands to her head. She rubs her eyes, which looks truly painful. "You're right, Stella. You know you're right. But I can help you with other things. Things within your control."

"What if I don't want the things within my control? What if I want the things I'm not allowed to have?"

"I'm sorry, Stella. That can't happen here."

"You mean, in Bull Run?"

She looks over her shoulder. "No," she whispers. "I mean, in New America. You can never have what you want here."

We're less than three blocks from school. I look up and down the street, but there isn't another soul around. The grass of every single lawn is so dry it's the color of hay. The leaves on the trees have turned a gray-brown color. The plants have dried up. Everything around me is dead.

"I wish I didn't have to live here anymore. I wish someone would kidnap me."

"Don't say that, Stella. Don't say that unless—"

"Unless what?"

Sister Laura shakes her head. "Just…just don't say that."

CHAPTER 51

The whispers start as soon as I enter the school. I do my best to ignore them, but the words still reach me.

Missing.

Kidnapped.

Willow.

Willow?

I pass my locker and head straight to Bonita's. Liv is already there. When they see me, Bonita's eyes lock on mine.

"What is it?"

Bonita's eyes widen. "You haven't heard?"

"No."

"Another Red Alert."

"Where?"

"Bull Run, Stella. Someone from our school is missing."

No one from Bull Run has ever gone missing. I take a deep breath. "Was it Willow? Was it Willow Howard?"

Liv tugs on her sleeves for the first time since homecoming.

"What happened?"

Bonita explains. "She went missing last night."

I look at my watch. It isn't even eight in the morning. I saw Willow less than eight hours ago.

Liv's eyes squeeze shut. "They got her, Stella. She's gone."

Mateo appears right after the words leave Liv's mouth.

He stops directly in front of me. As if it's the most normal thing in the world for him to do. "You heard?"

He knows too? Does this mean it's real? Willow is really gone? But I *just* saw her. How could she be gone? That guy. The one she called baby. He followed her out. He must've done something. The pounding in my head comes rushing back. It's too much. I put my hand on the locker next to Bonita's.

"Stella?" Mateo grabs me by the arm.

I drop my gaze to his hand. He's touching me. In public.

"Stella, are you okay?"

That's when everything goes black.

I fall back against the lockers, and Mateo catches me before I slide to the floor.

They take me to the nurse's office, Bonita leading the way. Mateo slings my arm over his neck, and Liv keeps a hand on my back. I'm with it enough to see everyone looking at us, pointing.

The nurse makes me lie down even though I'm starting to feel better. She sends the others to first period. She takes my vitals, tells me to rest. I count the ceiling tiles and wait for sleep to come.

I don't make it to thirty.

I wake to the sound of the bell ringing. It takes me a minute. Willow. Mateo. The nurse's office.

When Nurse Weeks returns, I sit up. "How long did I sleep?"

She looks at the dainty silver watch on her wrist. "Almost three hours."

"Three hours?" I say with disbelief. "But I just heard the bell ring."

"The end of third period."

"What?"

She comes over to my cot, sets a cold hand on my forehead. "You're not warm." She lifts my chin to face her. "How are you feeling?"

"Fine."

"Do you want to go to class? Or should I call your mother to come get you?"

I shake my head. "I can go to class."

She raises her eyebrows.

"Really, I'm fine."

"If you say so." She turns away from me and moves back toward her desk. "But you may just want to go home and sleep it off. I know a hangover when I see one."

I don't deny it but don't admit anything either. If the constables find out, I'll be expelled. Or worse. And what if Mateo finds out? I play dumb and flee before Nurse Weeks asks questions.

I'm at my locker, reaching for my literacy book when I hear it.

Someone shouting the word *slut* across the hallway like an accusation.

It's happened before. It happens to girls like Willow and Lana all the time. I spin around to find the target. Honestly I hope it's Willow. I want her to be standing there, scowling at me, her neat bun back in place. Because then I'd know she's okay.

But instead of Willow, I come face-to-face with a boy I don't know glaring at me from the other side of the hall. He's tall and frighteningly thin. I recognize his blue blazer and plaid tie as the uniform of the Climbers, but his pink skin and strawberry blond hair are unfamiliar. He looks like a blue pencil with a pink eraser.

When our eyes meet, he puts a fist to his mouth, coughs, and spits the vile word into his hand. "Slut!"

Everyone within earshot turns to look at me.

One girl slits her eyes in judgment. Another's mouth stretches in shock.

Boys up and down the hall don't bother to conceal their smug grins. They look like they've won some kind of contest. Like they've beaten me at a game I didn't even know we were playing.

CHAPTER 52

I don't go to class.

I head the opposite way down the hall, toward the doors that lead to the front courtyard.

The bell announcing the start of fourth period rings before I get there, and the hallway empties, all the other students sucked into classrooms by some gravitational pull I no longer feel.

I hesitate. The constables stand right outside, guarding the school like the prison it is.

There's no escape, but I also can't face the girls in Basic Literacy snickering behind my back if Mr. Conlon makes me diagram a sentence on the board. I just don't have it in me. I can handle the whispers and stares. But being called a slut? Why would someone think that? All those times people called Willow a word like that? Was it ever true? What does a girl have to do to deserve such a slur? Does anything make it okay?

I can't just stand there. Sooner or later the constables will look my way or step inside to use the restroom. That's when it comes to me—I can hide in the bathroom next to the cafeteria and figure out what to do with Bonita and Liv at lunch.

But when I turn away from the doors, I'm surprised to see the boy with strawberry blond hair standing directly behind me. How long has he been there?

Our eyes meet for a fraction of a second before I break away from his gaze. I stride right past him, and I sense him following me. I walk faster, but when I glance over my shoulder, he's still behind me, only twenty lockers back. His eyes study the floor so intensely it's like a message is written there. I don't look again until I make it to the restroom. When I get there, I peek over my shoulder and see him gaining ground.

I throw the door open, hurry inside, and push it closed behind me. There's no lock. Why is there no lock? Has there ever been a lock? He won't dare follow me in here. *Will he?*

This bathroom is tiny. There are only two stalls and one sink. Nowhere to hide.

I put my ear to the door but can't hear anything except the sound of my own thudding heartbeat.

He's out there. I can feel him on the other side of the door. A cheetah waiting to pounce. I have no choice but to wait him out. *Navigate the world with care, Stella.* I look at my watch. Fifty minutes until lunch. I'm trapped until then. I go to the sink. There are bags under my eyes. My hair sticks up in back. I have to calm down, pull it together. I take a deep cleansing breath, tell myself everything will be okay.

That's when the door flies open.

～～～～

It's him.

The Climber.

"What are you doing?" I yell. "Get out!"

"I came to see you." He takes a single step, crossing the threshold into the bathroom.

"What for?" Why am I even talking to him?

"I think you know, Graham." He takes another step toward me. I don't say a word this time. "I heard you're easy."

"I don't know what you're talking about."

"You're good for the go. A slut in training wheels. That's what I hear."

My heart is already racing, but the cortisol takes it to a higher level. Fight-or-flight kicks in for real. I have to get out of there. Or else I have to fight.

"I'll scream. I swear."

His response is to take another step in my direction. He's three feet in front of me. Just over an arm's length away. If he lunges, I'll be within reach.

"No, you won't." He smiles. "Because if you scream, I'll tell them where you were last night."

"You can't do that."

Can he? Unlike me, he has nothing to lose. This must be what Willow meant. Once I step into that world, once the rumors start, there's no going back. He's absolutely right. I can't scream.

I have to fight.

The Master's words come back to me. *Draw a line in the sand. If they back away, walk past them. If they cross it, strike first.*

"If you come one step closer, I'll have to defend myself."

He lets out an amused chortle, his eyes lighting up. "Go right ahead, Graham. That'll make this even more fun."

Neither one of us say anything for another long second.

And then he does it. He steps toward me.

He crosses the line.

I know exactly what to do.

I pull back my right hand to fake him out. He falls for it and tries to block me on the right, giving me the chance to attack him on the left. I swing as hard as I can and land a solid hook to the left side of his gut. He doubles over. While he's incapacitated, I grab both of his arms above the elbows, hold him steady, and launch my knee into his groin.

All that's left is to step out of his way before he falls to the ground like a giant bag of books.

There isn't a single person in the hallway when I walk out of the bathroom. No one has heard us. I'm in the clear.

I stroll away like it's perfectly normal for me to be in the hall without a pass, the Climber grunting and cursing in the bathroom behind me. He calls me the word Sister Laura told me to never tolerate. The word that starts with a C.

Now I know for sure.

I want out.

CHAPTER 53

I don't tell Sister Laura right away.

But I bet she knows it's coming. That's what she meant when I said I wanted to be kidnapped.

Don't say that unless—

Now I know what comes after "unless." *Don't say that unless you want to escape. Don't say that unless you want to get out.*

I didn't even know that was an option. Now I'm confident that's what she meant.

It has to be. It just has to.

CHAPTER 54

have to consider what—and whom—I'm leaving behind. When I'm running with Dad the next morning, I try to add it up. We've just crested the hill past Bonita's house when it comes to me.

I need a list.

First is Sister Helen. She's already gone, but I still count her because she's everywhere here, calling to me like a ghost.

Then there's Mom and Dad. And Shea, of course. The three of them plus Sister Helen make four.

I sneak a look at Dad. When I was little, everything was different. He'd crawl on the ground and play Legos with me. We'd build red- and white-striped houses and talk about every idea that came in my head. But we haven't bonded like that since Sister Helen arrived. It's true we have our morning runs now, and sometimes when we're both out of breath at the top of the hill, I feel more connected to him than I have in years. But we almost never talk. And I have no doubt he'd get out of doing this with me if he could.

He turns in my direction. "Are you okay, Stella?"

He must have felt me studying him.

Our eyes meet, but I pull mine away. It's uncomfortable to look directly at each other anymore. *When did that happen?*

"I'm good actually."

Satisfied, he turns back to the road in front of us.

Mom is complicated. Most days she treats me like the help. And then there's the way she talks about Sister Helen. That hurts more than anything. It's like we can't be close with a chaperone in the house.

Shea is the other reason Mom and I never have time together. She's an extension of Mom. There's no room for me in that union.

Bonita and Liv are next. Numbers five and six. Imagining my life without them makes me breathless. I count on them for so much that it's impossible to comprehend letting them go. They always have my back. And they're the only people who make me laugh.

Except for Mateo. Lucky number seven.

But how often do I get to see him? An hour a day and twenty feet apart in Musical Expression. A minute in the hallway each morning. Forget about talking to him. I could count the words we exchange each day on one hand.

Leaving Mateo will be torture, but I don't see the point in staying if we can't spend one minute alone.

And then there's Sister Laura. Number eight. I never would have expected it, but it will be hard leaving her too. No, she's not Sister Helen, but she's still become a part of my life. A person I have difficulty believing I can live without.

"Stella?" Dad stops at the community garden. Is he out of breath? I pause and turn to him, confused. "Are you sure you're okay?"

I don't know why he's asking.

He points at my face. "You're crying."

I didn't even realize. I wipe my eyes. "I'm good now, Dad. I promise."

His attention feels hot on my face. Except for the day Sister Helen died, he hasn't shown this much concern in years. I don't know how to handle it. The worry in his eyes is genuine. He can't fake that. I feel his desire to reach out, comfort me. But that's not allowed.

It's against the rules. It always has been.

It always will be.

CHAPTER 55

Eight people.

Less than a dozen. Fewer than I can count on two hands. Is that enough to stay in a place where I'm not free?

Those eight people remain in my head for three days. But now it's Sunday, and I have to think about someone else. Joseph Clarke.

Mom chooses my outfit. What Tiffany calls my goody-two-shoes-gone-bad dress. Long-sleeved blue lace with a V that's not deep enough to be scandalous but deep enough to attract attention. The only problem is I don't want this person's attention.

The doorbell rings.

I don't move from my spot on the sofa. Answering the door is not my job. I pray Dad doesn't hear it.

But a second later he comes rushing down the front stairs, securing his onyx cufflinks at the same time. His hand is on the door a moment later. He turns to me before opening it.

"You ready, Stella?" He doesn't wait for my answer. Instead he turns the knob and smiles at the person I presume is Joseph Clarke, offering his hand to shake. Even from the other room, I can see their knuckles clench in a manly ritual that goes on so long it seems absurd.

Dad beckons him inside with an outstretched arm. Has Dad ever been so welcoming to a boy at Visitation? But Joseph Clarke is not a boy. He's a man. A constable. Dad backs up, and the constable steps inside.

First I see a black shoe and gray leg. Then the rest of him comes into view. Gray pants, gray shirt, red armband, giant gun slung across his back. He's turned away, so I can't see his face. He lifts the gun over his head and holds it out to Dad like a gift. I've never seen a constable remove his gun before he sits. It strikes me as odd that he offers it to Dad, who gestures to the corner. The constable stands his gun there like a wet umbrella. After it's secure, he turns in my direction.

Pale splotchy skin. Hair so blond it's almost white.

The shock rolls through me like thunder. I put my hand on the sofa to steady myself.

It's him.

The constable who saw me the night Sister Helen died.

And he's here to call on me.

I offer the shortest possible answers to his questions, contributing almost nothing to the conversation. I make it clear I don't want to be here.

Dad is gone. He introduced us, listing Joseph's credentials to me like a job applicant, before shaking Joseph's hand a second time and excusing himself. He'll be back when it's time for Joseph to leave, but for now, we're virtually alone. It's the only time I'm allowed to be alone with a boy. We have exactly one hour, and we have to stay in the living room. Of course, no one is far. Dad and Mom and Sister Laura are in the next room, listening to every word we utter.

He makes small talk about the weather. Joseph hopes it will cool now that September is almost over. Then it's the news. Joseph hopes the prime minister will approve funds to strengthen border security.

He pauses. It's time to get to the real reason why he's here.

"I know I may seem a bit old to be calling on you, Stella."

"Not at all." That's what Mom told me to say if the subject comes up. It's not unheard of for older men to call on high school girls.

"The truth is, you seem more mature than most girls your age."

I could say thank you, but I don't. I'm not giving anything I don't absolutely have to give.

"You seem so sure of yourself."

It's hard not to say thank you a second time, but I successfully fight off the urge.

"And honestly, my gosh, Stella, you're just so beautiful."

I've been polite about looking at him while he speaks, but this is such a violation that I look away, studying the sculpture on the piece of furniture behind him. Why does it pain me to hear him say that? When Mateo says the same thing, my whole body floods with warmth. But now my body tenses, ready to fight. Maybe it's because I've never even spoken to Joseph before today. He's treating me like an object, not a person.

"I'm sorry," he says. "I didn't mean to make you uncomfortable."

This time I don't overcome the obligation to respond, sneaking a quick look at him. "It's fine."

Neither of us speaks. The silence is charged, but I'm not going to help him. He has to do the work himself.

"I just think you're the kind of girl I'd like to spend my life with."

I have to work to keep the horror in my throat. It sits in my mouth like a bubble about to burst, but I hold it there. I don't know what's worse. That he introduces the idea of spending our lives together the first time we meet or that he uses the word *girl* when he does it. Sister Helen never let Mom or Dad call me a girl. "She's a young woman now," she explained not long after she arrived. "If we're going to expect her to act like one, we'll have to call her one too."

But Joseph seems to know nothing about how to talk to women.

"I'm ready for that," he adds. "A wife, kids, a family. I want all of it. The whole picture." Again it's a challenge to keep the bile in my throat. "I want someone who will support me, take care of my home, have my children."

It's not lost on me that he says *my* rather than *our* children.

"Don't you want that too, Stella?"

I've been gazing in his general direction without looking directly at him ever since he said the word *girl*, but now I stare right into his face. I notice there are tiny folds of pink skin under his eyes that make him seem rodent-like. I glance at the pictures on the mantel to distract myself. I refuse to tell him what he wants to hear, but if I reveal the truth—that I'd rather die than be his wife—Dad will be furious. I have to find a way out of this. I have to destroy his chances.

"Where did you say you went to college?"

"Oh." His cheeks flush a darker pink. "I didn't. I went to the Academy right after high school." The Academy for constables, he means. Men who go to college skip right over that and become officers in the military.

"Hmmm." I hope he gets the message. "Did your father go to college?"

The skin on his face has now gone from pink to red. "My father is the Bull Run postmaster." It's his turn to not answer a question. But we both know the answer. People who work at the post office—even the postmaster—don't go to college.

"And do you have sisters?" This is where I've been heading all along.

"Yes." He smiles, wrongly believing he's survived my line of questioning. "Two of them. An older sister and a younger sister. The older one is married to a senior constable."

"The younger?"

"Still in high school." As soon as the words are out of his mouth, his smile vanishes.

"Oh," I say with fake enthusiasm. "What's her name? I'm sure I know her."

Joseph Clarke looks straight into my eyes. He's not quick, but he's finally figured it out. This is a deal breaker. He stares so long it feels like we're having a contest. He doesn't realize there's no way I'll let him beat me. Still, I'm impressed I have to count to fifty before his eyes break away from mine and drop to the floor. "Kayla doesn't go to Bull Run Prep."

"Really?" I act like I don't know the answer. "Where does she go?"

Joseph's eyes flick back to mine. I've pushed him too far. He's gone from frustrated to furious. "She's at the government school."

"Oh." I drag the word out, so it conveys more than it means.

"But—"

I don't let him finish. Instead I do my best to finish him.

"I'm so glad you came to visit today, Joseph." I stand from the sofa and give him a fake smile. He has no choice but to stand too. "My father will meet you at the door."

CHAPTER 56

As soon as the front door clicks shut, I hear Dad charging toward me. His shoes smack the wood floors in the foyer, softening to a dull sweep when he reaches the living room rug. He must stop at the far side of the rug because the smacking doesn't start again. Still, I sense him behind me.

Out the window I see Joseph in his SUV. He hasn't left the driveway yet. For all I know he's still watching.

"Stella." Dad interrupts the quiet that descended after Joseph left.

I glance over my shoulder without turning around.

"Stella, you're going to have to try harder."

I swivel and look right into Dad's face. When we're running, I only glimpse him in profile. I'm surprised to notice three lines creasing his forehead. When did they get there?

"Did you know he didn't go to college, Dad?" I'm not supposed to question him, but at this point I don't even care. There's no punishment Dad could assign that would be worse than a lifetime with someone like Joseph Clarke.

"Of course, I know that. He—" Dad pauses and folds his hands

together. "Things are different now, Stella. If you become a constable, you don't have to go to college."

"His father didn't go either."

"That isn't unusual."

"Maybe not, but you can't possibly want me to be with someone who has sisters at the government school, someone who will
have to send his own daughters there. *Your* granddaughters."

"Oh, Stella." He takes two steps toward me but stops before he
gets close enough to touch. "You don't have to worry about that.
You and your sister? You'll always have enough money for whatever you want."

"What do you mean?"

"You'll have a dowry, Stella. Joseph will have more than enough
money for chaperones once you marry."

The horror that's been in my throat ever since Joseph brought
up marriage finally comes out. "You already have us married, don't
you?"

"He's a good man, Stella."

Sister Laura says when one man calls another a "good man," it's
code. Meaning, *He's in the club. He's one of us.*

"Do I even get a say in this? Do I get to provide any input at all
about who I'm going to spend the rest of my life with?"

"No, Stella." His voice is so severe it gives me a chill. "You
absolutely do not."

CHAPTER 57

If I had any doubts about leaving, they are now completely erased. No way I'm marrying Joseph Clarke. No way I'm living that life. No way I'm going to be a baby machine instead of the person I want to be.

I tell Sister Laura Monday morning. I imagine it will be hard, but the truth is, it's easy.

"I need to talk to you."

She keeps walking but looks at me out of the corner of her eye, a question on her face.

"Remember when you said I can't have what I want here?"

She glances at me before dropping her attention to the ground. "Yes." The hesitation in her voice is so thick I can almost touch it.

"You started to say something else. You said, 'unless,' but you never finished."

She pauses and turns to face me, scratching her nose. She's hiding something. She always scratches her nose when she's not being forthright. "When did I say that?"

"When I told you I wished someone would kidnap me."

Sister Laura winces like someone slapped her.

"You said, 'Don't say that unless—'" I try to read her face, but she won't look at me. "What were you going to say? Unless what?"

Sister Laura finally returns my stare. "Why are you asking me this now, Stella?"

"Because I want to change my life. Because I want to know about unless."

Sister Laura turns and walks faster. I hurry behind her, unable to catch up. She keeps motoring ahead, but I desperately want her to stop and answer my question.

"Are you going to tell me?"

She tilts her head back at me. "We can't talk about this now, Stella. Just keep up."

Respect your chaperone.

I slow my pace, frustrated, and she comes to an abrupt stop.

She spins around, walks back to me, and whispers at me in a harsh voice. "There's a constable up ahead. On the corner." She takes my arm, leading me to the intersection we just passed. We cross the street and walk down the sidewalk on the other side. "Just act like everything's normal, Stella," she says under her breath.

When we're directly across from him, Sister Laura offers the constable a friendly wave. "Good morning to you, Constable," she says as if we haven't clearly gone out of our way to avoid him.

When we're past him, she talks to me out of the side of her mouth. "Later, Stella," she says. "Tonight."

I start counting the hours.

It's after ten o'clock that night when Sister Laura finally comes to my room.

"There is a way." Her voice drops to a whisper "But...it's dangerous."

"Aren't you the one who told me anything worthwhile is dangerous?" This was her response when I read about the Mirabal sisters.

"That's true. Especially here." She glances out the window. "But I still want you to know up front."

"I understand it won't be easy."

Sister Laura lets out a sound that's a cross between a laugh and a gasp.

"What?"

"It's just...you. You've come so far."

"What do you mean?"

"When I got here, you were so afraid. So broken."

"I'd just lost my best friend."

"Sister Helen was your best friend?"

"Of course."

Sister Laura puts a hand over her mouth. "That's really beautiful, Stella. Sister Helen would be so touched."

"You knew her?"

She nods at me. "I met her as soon as I enrolled at the conservatory. We became friends right away. And I saw her at meetings, of course."

"Prayer meetings?"

Sister Laura raises her eyebrows.

"They're not really prayer meetings, are they?"

"It's better you don't know, Stella. But maybe now is the time to tell you I was chosen by Sister Helen. To replace her."

"What do you mean?"

"We talked about you. She saw something in you. She thought you were...how do I say it? She thought you were a special person. And she said she wanted me to take her place if anything happened to her."

"She was worried?"

"We all are, Stella. It's dangerous to teach girls. If you teach them too little, they might make a mistake. If you teach them too much, you might get in trouble with the Minutemen. Remember when you asked why I stayed?"

"Yes."

"That's one of the reasons. So I could be that person for..." She inhales deeply and looks at the ceiling.

"For me?"

"Yes, for you. And for my last charge. And for my next one. For all of you." She drops her gaze from the ceiling and looks right at me. "For anyone who wants to reject what's expected. For anyone who wants to get out."

"Is that why you're here? To help us get out?"

I'm sure it's true now. I'm sure that's what she meant when she said "unless."

"Yes, that's a big part of it. That's not true of all chaperones. But there are more of us every day."

"So you'll help me?"

Her face is a cross of pride and apprehension. "I'll introduce you to someone. She'll help you. I can't actually do it myself."

"Why not?"

Sister Laura lets her eyes drop shut for a second before opening them again. "Because I want to stay alive, Stella."

CHAPTER 58

It happens fast. Faster than I thought possible.

Sister Laura pulls me into the restroom inside the back door of the State Street Gym two days later. I don't see her at first. The woman in the corner. But once Sister Laura locks the door and turns me around, I come face-to-face with her. She has wavy gray-brown hair, tiny brown eyes, and lightly crosshatched skin. She's older than I expected—almost as old as Sister Helen—and doesn't look anything like the kind of person who breaks the law. She looks like someone's grandmother. Maybe that's the point.

"Stella, this is Angel. She's the one who'll arrange your passage."

Angel shakes my hand the same way Sister Laura did when I met her. "It's so nice to meet you, Stella. I'm excited about your journey."

"Nice to meet you too, Angel."

As soon as I say her name out loud, it hits me.

Angel.

That was the last thing Sister Helen said to me. She got it out one syllable at a time. *Ain Jell. Angel.* Is this what she was trying to tell me?

Find Angel?

Get out?

CHAPTER 59

We talk money first.

"I hate to be coarse, Stella, but I have to ask. Can you afford this? Do you have money saved?"

Sister Laura nods. "She does."

I wheel on her. "How do you know that?"

"I know."

"You've gone through my things?"

"It's my job," she says, but her face flushes. She's embarrassed. What she doesn't know is that most of what I had is now gone.

I turn back to Angel. "How much?"

Angel tilts her head, studying me. "I'm guessing you're a girl of means. We use a sliding scale, and you'll have to pay the full rate." I don't say anything, waiting, and she adds, "It's two thousand, Stella."

"Two thousand?" How will I ever get that much money if I gave so much to Willow?

"Can you get it?"

I nod slowly, remembering all the places Mom hides money. I'm not certain I can find two thousand dollars, but I'm going to try. Maybe it will be okay if I just get close.

"I know it sounds like a lot," Angel says, "but the costs are extraordinary. Vehicles, fuel, and food for the three days it will take you to make the journey. And we have to pay people to keep their mouths shut more often than not. It takes a lot of money to have you kidnapped."

"Kidnapped?"

Sister Laura jumps in. "It's not really a kidnapping, Stella. That's just what they'll say on the Freedom Channel after you're gone. So no one knows what really happened. They'll *say* you've been kidnapped. And people believe whatever they're told."

Is that what happened to Willow? Everyone says she's been kidnapped. Does that mean she escaped? Is that why she needed the money?

Angel explains. "They don't want people to know girls are getting out every week."

"Is that what happened to Willow Howard?"

They exchange looks. A conversation of raised eyebrows and head shakes.

Angel turns back to me. "It's better if you don't know, Stella. It's better if neither of you knows."

So that's it. Willow Howard escaped from New America. That's why she needed the money. She was sick of the HH parties, the stares, the rumors, the slurs. She got out.

And I will too.

CHAPTER 60

I wait until everyone has been asleep for hours.

It's after one when I tiptoe to Mom and Dad's room and put my ear to the door. Dad's snores sound more like a breathing machine than a fully grown man.

Mom hides most of her valuables in the bottom drawer of her dresser, but she has other hiding places too. She isn't allowed to have her own bank account, so she stashes cash all over the house. I don't even know why she needs it. Dad pays for everything. One time I saw her putting a roll of bills into the flour sifter. Another time several hundreds fell out of a transparent envelope when she was looking for stamps. It's shocking how careless she is.

The kitchen seems even darker than normal. I open the pantry doors as quietly as I can and carry the step stool to the fridge. The metal creaks beneath my weight. I look over my shoulder, certain someone will be there, but there's nothing behind me except a floor full of marble tile. I open the cabinet doors above the fridge and grab the rolling pin, moving it to the top of the fridge. When I put my hand inside the flour sifter, I feel a Ziploc bag. Inside, there's a roll of twenties thicker than the rolling pin. I was right.

How much can I take without getting caught? I pull half the bills off the roll and return the rest. I slide my hand over the top of the fridge, searching for the rolling pin, but it gets away from me, moving across the top of the fridge. I try to grab it before it goes over the edge, but it slips out of reach, falling and hitting the floor with a sharp thud. The stool creaks loudly as I jump down, grab the pin, climb back up, shove it in the cabinet, and throw the door shut. I look over my shoulder, certain someone will be there, but the kitchen remains empty.

I hesitate at the end of the living room, remembering Dad's warning—*You have no business in here unless you're entertaining guests*—but the key to Mom's secretary is sticking out of the lock, urging me forward. I go directly to the cubby on the right. But when I open the envelope, there's nothing but stamps inside, the prime minister's black-and-white face staring back at me, taunting me.

"Darn it," I say out loud.

I pull everything out of the cubbies: envelopes, note cards, more stamps. Everything but cash. I start on the drawers next. There are notebooks, pens, pencils, rubber bands, paper clips, binder clips, old letters, and printer paper. *Dozens* of letters. They all have the initials R.S. in the upper left-hand corner. Who is R.S.?

I open one and read the first line.

Dear Mary Beth,

I was just thinking about that class we had with Professor Wilhoit...

They're from one of Mom's college friends. I put the letters back in the drawer.

I take in a deep breath. What will I do if I can't find enough money?

I have to take everything in the flour sifter. Mom is too smart not to notice half is gone. Why not take it all?

I'm on the step stool reaching for the Ziploc bag of cash when I hear it.

The sound of creaking stairs.

Someone is coming down the stairwell. I contemplate my surroundings, but there's nowhere to hide. When I was little, I hid in the bottom of the pantry all the time, but I'm too big for that now. There's not enough time to run to the annex either.

I'm going to get caught.

I put the money in the front of my pajama pants. I have nowhere else to hide it. Dad flips on the overhead lights at the exact same moment I shove the flour sifter back in the cabinet.

"Stella? What are you doing?"

A lumpy plastic bag is all I can find. I turn around with it still in my hands.

"Is that chocolate?"

I examine the bag. Semisweet chocolate chips. "I had a craving."

His head tilts.

"I'm feeling kind of…you know…emotional."

"Is everything okay?"

I close my eyes and let out a dramatic sigh. "It's, you know, my period."

"Oh." Dad leans back on his heels. Even though they teach boys how to talk about menstruation at school now, older men like Dad never learned those kinds of things. Mentioning my period is the easiest way to throw men his age off guard. "I understand." He turns halfway around before pausing. "But don't overdo it, Stella. You've got Visitation with Joseph Clarke this weekend."

I want to scream but swallow my anger. "Of course, Dad."

He turns back around. "Speaking of Joseph, I want you to consider making a commitment of some kind."

"A commitment?"

"Yes, a commitment to a future with him. It would be wonderful if you could be engaged by Freedom Day." *Freedom Day?* Freedom Day is just over a month away. Only two days before I'm supposed to leave. Is he out of his mind? "That's when I'd like to announce it. So don't go overboard."

"What?"

He points at the bag of chocolate chips still in my hand.

I want to throw the bag at his head so hard it leaves a dent. I'm still trying to work up the tremendous amount of courage it would take to do it when Dad walks away.

"Good night, Stella," he calls to me from the dining room.

I stand there processing what just happened. No way I'm getting engaged by Freedom Day, and no way I'm marrying Joseph Clarke. I put the chocolate chips back in the cabinet and return the step stool to the pantry. Before I flip the light off, I let my hand go to the giant wad of bills tucked inside the elastic of my pajama pants.

The cost of my freedom.

CHAPTER 61

S ister Laura will be the first person the authorities contact
once I'm gone. She needs an airtight alibi and can know
nothing of my escape. If she were involved, she'd be charged
with treason and sent to prison. Or worse.

I have to do this on my own. Meet with Angel. Review the
plan. Memorize each carefully laid out step. And then actually *do*
everything Angel planned.

We meet in the bathroom at State Street three times a week for
the next several weeks. I lock the plywood door as soon as I shut it
behind me. I don't ask Angel how she gets in, and she doesn't tell
me. There's a cracked window on the far side of the small space.
Could she be climbing through it? At her age?

Angel has maps and phone numbers and lists. She spreads
one of these on the bathroom counter every time I meet her. I
take it home and commit it to memory. Angel says it will happen
November 5th, two days after Freedom Day. I have just over four
weeks to get it all down. Just over a month to prepare. And then I'll
burn it. Every last shred of paper will go into the fireplace the night
before I leave.

238 of M HENDRIX

But I've always been good at studying. Each time she gives me a new document, I hide it inside *Lord of the Flies* because the boys in that book remind me of the Minutemen. In the library, I read the document over and over. When I get home, I recite it out loud until I've committed it to memory, whispering the words in a low voice so no one can hear. It takes all night, but I always get it done.

"It's hard to know what to talk about now," Sister Laura admits when we go hiking at Shanty Hollow a little more than two weeks later.

The lake looks incredibly inviting. I'm baking in the sun even though it's mid-October. If only we could take a quick swim.

Sister Laura goes on. "I don't want to put you in the position of having to lie."

I step carefully over the thick tree roots that line our path. "Good idea."

"We should talk about something unimportant, something that has nothing to do with what's really going on."

"Like what?"

"Mateo?"

My chest tightens. I've been trying not to think about him. "Who says he's not important?"

"Well. Not unimportant. But unrelated to...you know."

"Yes."

"I actually have news about him."

"You do?"

Sister Laura focuses on something in front of her with great concentration, as if glimpsing the future. "But you have to promise not to be angry."

"Why would I be angry?"

"Because I finally got what you wanted, and now you're leaving. I regret it took me so long."

"What do you think I want?"

She comes to a stop and studies the water in front of us. A blue heron lurks in the cove just beneath the trail. We see them every time we come here. Sister Laura turns toward me, her face squeezed into a frown. "Mateo. He's going to be one of your callers. The second Sunday in November."

I can't believe what she's telling me. "What?"

"It wasn't easy. Joseph Clarke has requested several weeks in a row. We'll schedule them an hour apart, so they don't cross paths. You were right. Mateo is a good match for you. He's a good student, comes from a good family. His father is a very successful neurologist." She lets out an angry laugh. "As if any of this should matter."

"A neurologist?"

"A neurologist is a doctor who treats people with diseases of the brain."

I turn back to the loon. "So what you're telling me is Mateo thinks he's going to call on me, but before that happens, he's going to believe"—I drop my voice to a whisper—"I've been kidnapped?"

Sister Laura flips her head toward me. "Stella!" Her voice is only loud enough to express disapproval. "I cannot know *anything* about what you're doing. Not even *when* it's happening." She looks over her shoulder. "The punishment for helping a girl escape is prison. Do you understand that?"

I'm horrified. I'm supposed to protect Sister Laura, and now I've put her at risk. So I do what I have to do.

I lie.

"You don't think I'd tell you the truth, do you?" I use the most casual voice I can muster. "I was just trying to throw you off."

Sister Laura lets out a breath of relief. "Thank goodness. You scared me."

Lying isn't hard at all. In fact, it's easy.

And I know I'll be doing a lot more of it soon.

CHAPTER 62

Not twenty-four hours later, I'm sitting across from Joseph Clarke for the fourth Sunday in a row.

Joseph rambles about the weather, but I'm not listening. Why doesn't he get I'm not into him? It's exactly like Bonita and Olu.

"This is actually my favorite time of year," he says. "The crisp air, the fall leaves—"

I cut him off. "I would hardly call it crisp." The temperature is still in the nineties even though it's mid-October.

He ignores me. It's something he does more and more. But I don't pay much attention to him either.

"We should do it soon—before it gets cold. I'm thinking Freedom Day. For the rest of our lives, we could share an anniversary with this great country."

It's the word *anniversary* that gets my attention. "What are you talking about?"

"I'm talking about the two of us starting our lives together, Stella."

"You mean, getting engaged?"

"No." When he leans across the coffee table, I instinctively lean back. "Get married, Stella. I don't want to wait. I want to be with you now."

A chalky substance pushes its way up my esophagus until it reaches the back of my tongue and coats the inside of my mouth. I'm going to throw up. I search for a glass of water, but the living room is like a museum. No drinks or food ever come in here unless Mom and Dad entertain.

"I hope that's what you want too, Stella."

Joseph stares at me, waiting. I don't remember what his last words were. I do know I have to tell him I have no intention of marrying him.

"Joseph—" I start, but he interrupts me.

"Stella, just let me get this out."

"Get what out?"

Before I know what's happening, Joseph is standing from his chair, moving around the coffee table, and dropping to one knee on the floor in front of me. The chalk lining the walls of my mouth gets thicker.

"Stella Graham." His voice betrays a ridiculous amount of sincerity. "I know we're just getting to know each other, but I'm sure you're the girl for me. I know it."

I wince when he says *girl*.

"You'll be the perfect wife, someone to stand by my side through everything yet to come."

I hold my hands up to him, willing him to stop. I need to stop him before he says it. I need him to *not* say it. "Joseph, I—"

It's Dad who interrupts me. "Oh, good! We're here just in time."

Mom is right behind him. Dad has an uncharacteristic smile

on his face, but Mom's lips are pressed together. She knows something's wrong. I'm trying to figure out how to prevent this from happening when Joseph clears his throat and again says my full name like he's taking attendance.

"Stella Graham." He's still kneeling in front of me. He reaches into his pocket and pulls out a small turquoise box, holding it out to me. "Will you marry me?"

If I open my mouth, I'll throw up all over the expensive rug he's kneeling on. I put my hand over my mouth and try to hold it in.

"Stella?" Joseph says.

I jump up from the sofa and rush out of the room. I'm running by the time I pass Mom and Dad, who gape at me like I have two heads. I make it to the powder room just in time, the vomit hitting the water so hard it splashes back into my face.

I puke for what feels like forever. Sister Laura holds my hair back just like girls do in old movies. This is how real friends act.

After I get cleaned up, Sister Laura pushes her glasses up her nose. "Stella, you have to go back out there."

Is she out of her mind?

"Go back and tell him you value his service. He's a constable. You can't let him know how much you dislike him."

Is this why Sister Laura is always so nice to the constables?

"Why is this happening? You said Mateo was approved for Visitation. How can Mateo call on me if Joseph just proposed?"

"No one told me anything, Stella. Maybe Joseph found out about Mateo. Maybe that's why he's rushing things."

I notice a spot of yellow vomit on her white caftan. Her *white* caftan. White, I've learned from Angel, is the color of the resistance. Does Sister Laura know that?

"It won't take long," Sister Laura says. "I promise."

"What won't take long?"

"Saying goodbye to Joseph."

Sister Laura escorts me back to the foyer where Mom and Dad stand awkwardly next to Joseph.

Dad's eyes light up. "There she is!" His enthusiasm is as nauseating as Joseph's proposal.

We stop next to Mom, who pats my arm like I'm a pet. "She's just nervous."

I study Mom's face for any hint of insincerity, but her beauty queen smile gives away nothing. Does she really think I'm nervous? Or does she know the idea of marrying someone like Joseph Clarke makes me physically ill?

"That's okay, Stella," Dad says. "We understand how exciting this is. For all of us really." He turns to Joseph. "Mary Beth and I are so pleased, constable."

Pleased? Pleased about what? I didn't agree to marry him. I didn't take the ring. I didn't even answer the question. Dad can't just *act* like I said yes.

"We'll start getting everything together. Freedom Day is coming up fast, but Mary Beth knows how to work miracles with this kind of thing. We'll make it happen."

It's clear to me now.

Yes, he can. He really can.

Give obedience.

CHAPTER 63

I tell Angel the next afternoon.

"We have to move things up."

"What?" She shakes her head. "That's impossible."

"We have to."

We're talking to each other's reflections in the bathroom mirror. That's how I notice the dark half-moons under my eyes. I barely slept last night.

I turn to face Angel. "Joseph proposed yesterday."

"Oh, no, Stella."

"Dad wants us married by Freedom Day. I can't marry him, Angel. I can't."

"You can still escape...even if you're married. We can have it annulled when you get there."

"But if I marry him two days before I leave, I'll still have to..."

Her eyes are wide with questions.

"Don't you understand? If I marry him before I leave, I'll still have to go through with...with the...the wedding night." I squeeze my eyes shut, willing those images away. I open them and beg her. "Please, Angel. I can't."

Angel sucks in a breath of air so long I worry she'll run out of oxygen. When she lets it go, she stretches the word *oh* into one long exhale. "Ooooooh."

"Exactly."

CHAPTER 64

Two weeks later I'm ready. I know it all backward and forward. This is our last meeting before I leave. "The only problem will be," Angel says, "if something goes sideways." She squints at me from behind her reading glasses. "Do you know what I mean?"

"You mean we have to stick to the plan."

"Right. And pray nothing unexpected happens."

I don't tell her I'm no longer sure I believe in prayer.

CHAPTER 65

I don't have any doubts until the morning of my escape. Can I really give up these eight people forever?

It starts on the run with Dad.

Angel warned me about not doing anything out of the ordinary today. *Don't draw any unnecessary attention to yourself. Don't throw up any red flags.* That means no talking in class, no fighting the Master, no time with Mateo, no being honest with Dad. All the things I've learned to love since Sister Laura came into my life.

Can I really leave it all behind?

It's true Dad doesn't respect women. But he loves me. It's the one thing I've always known. My parents will never stop loving me. Never.

I can't cry again. I can't let Dad see that. And I can't say anything either.

So I just keep running.

———

Tiffany puts a plate in front of me when we get back from the run. "Eat this, sweetie. You're gonna need it."

Does she know? Or is it just a coincidence?

Mom has made sweet potato pancakes with over-easy eggs, roasted tomatoes, sliced avocado, and the tiniest slivers of goat cheese. Who makes this kind of breakfast on a weekday? Angel told me to pack rations for my journey. Granola bars and apples and peanut butter. I'll be eating like an animal for three days. And I don't have any idea what it will be like when I get to Old America. Who will cook for me? Will I ever have another meal like the ones Mom makes? Angel hasn't told me much about my life there. My host family will teach me everything I need to know. But what if they serve things I don't like? More importantly, what if they don't like *me*? It's all so overwhelming I can't eat a single bite.

Mom looks up from the stove. "Is something wrong, Stella?"

I have no choice but to fake it.

"No, Mom." I lift the fork to my mouth. "I was just thinking about how this is my favorite breakfast."

"Is it? I had no idea."

"I really love it, Mom." I smile at her as warmly as I can. "Thank you."

We make eye contact, and she smiles back at me. We've connected for the first time in months. But, even if I stay, it won't last. Mom will erect a wall before I get home from school. And we'll go back to being people who live in the same house but are never on the same page

Even Sister Laura doesn't know today is the day.

I don't want to talk on our way to school. I'm afraid she'll know. But I can't say nothing either. Then she'll know for sure. We pass two constables who nod at Sister Laura. She offers them her usual cheery greeting: "Good morning, Constables."

Luckily they don't make eye contact with me. Sister Laura's head follows them as they strut away. "We shouldn't talk," she whispers once we're past them. "It's too dangerous."

Does she know?

I need to throw her off. We pass two giant oak trees. The edges of the leaves have finally started to turn orange and red.

"You're right. For the next few weeks, we won't be able to talk much."

"Stella!" She looks over her shoulder and lowers her voice. "How many times do I have to tell you? You're not supposed to say things like that." She nods toward the two constables who are at the end of the block by now. "What if they had heard you?"

"I'm sorry." I hope my words sound genuine. "I have to get better at lying."

Sister Laura quickens her pace. "Yes, you really do."

At lunch, I try to act normal. I need to fly under the radar, not blaze across it like a comet. I pick at my plain chicken breast and raw carrots without really eating. I make small talk with Bonita and Liv. I watch for Mateo on the boys' side of the cafeteria. Lately he gets a hall pass so he can stroll by during my lunch shift.

Bonita stabs the chicken breast with her fork. "I'm sick to death of hamster."

Liv winces. "How am I supposed to eat this now?"

I let out a small laugh before glancing across the cafeteria again.

"Stella," Bonita calls out. "You're going to give yourself whiplash."

"Leave her alone, B."

I sigh quickly. "She's right, Liv. It's just—"

"I get it," Bonita says. "You want to see him. You know I'm right there with you." Ever since homecoming, Bonita has spent less time with Mason and more with Olu. That's how she got him to drop the charges. Bonita grabs my hand across the table and squeezes it. I look at our interlaced fingers and am immediately overcome. The longing I feel for Mateo now is the way I'll feel about Bonita and Liv soon. How much I'll miss them is incomprehensible. What if no one in Old America gets me the way they do?

"What is it, Stella?" Liv asks abruptly.

I don't realize I'm gripping Bonita's hand so hard my knuckles have turned white.

"What do you mean?" I let go of Bonita's hand and pick up a carrot. A piece gets stuck in my throat, making me cough.

"You just seem… I don't know," Liv says. "Sad."

Hearing her say it out loud only makes it worse. It takes everything in me not to tell them. But I *can't* tell them. I have to protect them.

"There!" Bonita lifts her chin toward the boys' side of the cafeteria, and I follow her gaze. "There's your boy."

Mateo strolls through the cafeteria as slowly as he can, staring at me like I'm as bright as the stars in the country sky. Waiting to make eye contact. Because that's all we get. A look across a crowded cafeteria. A wave from fifty feet away. A smile as we pass each other in the hall.

It isn't enough.

Our eyes meet, and his smile drops. Does he know what I'm thinking? I hold my hand up to wave, but before he can respond, someone shouts, "Whore!" across the cafeteria.

Mateo's head flips from side to side, searching for the culprit.

But it doesn't matter who said it. All that matters is I can't live like this anymore.

I have to go.

Mateo tracks me the second I walk into Musical Expression. When I return his gaze, he tilts his head toward the back of the room.

I search my backpack for a pencil and head for the sharpener.

Mr. Jeffrey sits at his desk, lost in his smart screen.

A second later, Mateo is behind me.

He moves closer. "Stella." His voice is filled with so much long-ing it hurts. "I can't believe he said that…"

Does Mateo know about the rumors?

"It's fine," I whisper over my shoulder, my eyes on Mr. Jeffrey.

"It's not fine. It's idiotic."

I can't help but wonder if Mateo would feel the same way if he found out I let another boy, a boy I don't even know, put his hand up my skirt. "Honestly it's not the most important thing going on in my life."

"It's not?"

How am I supposed to *not* tell him? How am I supposed to let him show up for school tomorrow and find out I've gone missing? He'll think I've been kidnapped. Or worse. I have to give him some kind of clue.

I glance over my shoulder. "I need to tell you something."

He puts his hand gently on my hip. It's all I can do not to turn around and kiss him. "I have something to tell you too," he whispers. I feel his breath on my ear. "About Visitation. I was approved for next month."

He doesn't know about the engagement. Why would he? And I don't want that to be the last thing I say to him. "Sister Laura told me."

"I thought you'd be happy."

I turn so I can look directly in his eyes. "All I want is to spend time with you." Something passes between us. A wave of emotion surges through me. I check on Mr. Jeffrey. We don't have much time. "But you need to know something."

"What?" The concern in his voice breaks my heart.

"Did you hear about Willow Howard?"

"Of course." He nods. "It's terrifying. I don't know what I'd do if something like that happened to you." He grabs my hand and laces his fingers through mine.

Everything in me wants to kiss him. Could I kiss him if I stayed? Could I kiss him at Visitation? But someone is always lurking nearby, watching. Kissing Mateo is impossible. Sister Laura is right. I can't have what I want in New America.

"That's just it. She wasn't really kidnapped—"

"What in the *hell* do you two think you're doing?" Mr. Jeffrey's voice booms across the room, and Mateo immediately drops my hand. Mr. Jeffrey storms toward us like an ogre, his eyebrows arched in anger. Every person in the room turns to look at us. I realize too late I've done the one thing Angel warned me against. I've drawn attention to myself.

Mateo backs a foot away from me, his voice flipping from seductive to innocent. "Nothing, sir. Just sharpening our pencils."

Mr. Jeffrey lets out a maniacal laugh. "Nice try, de Velasco, but I saw you holding hands."

Mateo doesn't hesitate. "What are you implying, sir? That we're breaking the rules? Honestly I'm offended by that accusation, and my father would be too." He's so confident it's like he's practiced these lines. "As would Stella's father."

Mr. Jeffrey looks from Mateo to me and back at Mateo again, sizing us up. Mateo's point cannot be misunderstood. If Mr. Jeffrey documents us, Mateo will get our fathers involved. Two men who have far more power than a high school music teacher. It's the kind of comment only a boy could make. A boy who comes from money.

Mr. Jeffrey puts a hand on his face and shakes his head. I don't know if he's angry or resigned. He wipes his hand across his mouth before dropping it to his side. "Fine. I was wrong." It's obvious he doesn't mean it. "Get to your seats. Class is about to start."

Forty minutes later, the bell rings. I don't need to draw more attention to myself, so I move to the door without waiting for Mateo.

Before I leave, I look over my shoulder one last time.

His eyes are on me. I knew they would be.

I hold a single hand in the air, his signature wave. That's how it started that day in the library just two months ago.

Hello.

And now goodbye.

CHAPTER 66

It's not like in the movies.

I don't climb out the window or steal a car. I simply walk down the stairs and out the front door, leaving it open behind me. I want it to look like someone broke in. That way they won't blame Sister Laura.

It's well after eleven. Mom and Dad are in bed. Sister Laura at her meeting.

Outside the moon is hidden by clouds. Not enough light to see.

I'm through the gate before I have time to reconsider. But after I shut it, I look back and examine the house I've lived in all my life. Doubt surges through me. Will I ever come back? Will I ever see my family again?

The dog next door barks madly. Just like the night I lost my scarf. The constable fleeing out the gate. Could it have been Joseph? I don't have time for these questions. This is just the beginning of my journey. I have three long days ahead of me. I can't stop every time the past tries to slow me down.

I don't look back again.

It starts the same way it does every morning with Sister Laura: I walk from Gaslight to the high school. But tonight I keep walking—past the high school, past the library, past the square downtown, past State Street, past everything I've ever known.

I'm wearing what Angel described as gender-neutral clothes. A large blue Freedom Channel T-shirt, baggy jeans, and a white baseball cap over my new haircut. I chopped it off in the bathroom before I left, just like Angel instructed, flushing hair down the toilet a little bit at a time. Angel says they'll bring in a forensics team and find some of the stray hairs, but it will be too late. I'll have crossed by then. She says they'll enter my DNA into the system and, after that, be able to identify me with a simple blood test. But that's all part of the plan. I'll pass as a boy while I travel but give up my anonymity in the long run.

I walk not too fast. Not too slow. And like a boy. I review Angel's instructions in my head. *Keep your head down. Don't make eye contact. Don't swing your hips. Pretend you don't even have hips.* Still, anyone who gets close will have no doubt I'm a girl. That's the reason I'll travel only at night.

I'm out of Shake Rag in less than thirty minutes. The park is a mile ahead. I'm on the bridge over the river before I know it. The rapids rush below me like a hurricane, but the water will be calm just a quarter mile upriver.

At least that's what I hope.

Angel warned me about going near the park at night—it's too dangerous—so I stay in the middle of the parking lot. The evening is as quiet as one of those old zombie movies. I glance into the park a hundred feet to my right. Is anyone there? It's so dark I can't make out the trail that winds through the grass.

The boat ramp is straight ahead. I move toward it without hesitation.

The river seeps into my jeans like quicksand, even colder than I expected. Goose bumps spread over my arms. I force myself deeper, the water reaching my navel.

The Barren River is twice as wide as our courtyard and never deep, maxing out around twenty feet when there's been an unusual amount of rain. But it's been dry for months. It's no more than three feet deep tonight.

My wet jeans make it hard to move fast. Angel warned me, but I'm still surprised how much they slow me down. I check the waterproof smart watch she gave me. It's almost midnight. I have two hours to get to the takeout. If I'm late, I'll miss my ride. If that happens, the whole thing is off.

I can't be late. I just can't.

I don't see any sign of life on either shore. Even during the day, it's unusual for anyone to walk near the river. The hundred-foot cliffs sloping down to the water are all but impassable. It was rare for Sister Helen and me to see anyone when we kayaked here. I struggle out of my jeans, shoving them in my waterproof backpack. If someone sees me, I'll have bigger problems than the fact that I'm not wearing pants. I'll be arrested or sent home.

As soon as they're off, I move faster. A lot faster.

If I can keep up this pace, if nothing slows me down, I'll make it. But then I see it.

A cottonmouth swimming right toward me.

Cottonmouths aren't an unusual sight in the Barren. Sister Helen and I saw them more than once. But that was from inside our kayaks. If they got too close, we'd push a wave at them, floating them away.

But I don't have the protection of a boat tonight.

I shove a wave in the direction of the snake. Then another. And another. I put my head in the water and start swimming for real.

I need to keep moving.

A little more than two hours later I get to the takeout.

I have exactly twenty-four minutes to make it to the rendez-vous spot. A shiver runs through me when I climb out of the water.

Nineteen minutes pass as I climb the steep, muddy cliff. It's hard work pulling myself up the incline. I'm not sure I'd make it if Sister Laura hadn't made me run with Dad every morning.

When I reach the top, I'm in the middle of a hayfield exactly like Angel described. I pull my wet jeans out of my backpack and yank them up my legs before taking off in a sprint. I have less than three minutes to get to the highway.

I double over when I reach the interstate, trying to catch my breath. I stay back from the pavement, hiding behind a cluster of trees.

I check my watch.

Two-thirty exactly.

I'm still doubled over when a white semi rolls to a stop in front of me. I step out of the trees and dash for the door.

I grab the handle and pull myself up the cab, hoping it's Angel I see next.

CHAPTER 67

She never takes her eyes off the side-view mirror. "Hurry."

It takes two tries to pull the heavy door shut.

Angel's finger is on her lips. "Shhh."

In the mirror, a set of headlights streak toward us like a double comet. In a few seconds, they'll reach us.

Five, four, three, two…

"It's okay." Angel finally turns to look at me. "We're okay, sweetie." She hooks her thumb toward the space behind her. "Now just climb back there."

I step between the two front seats and spin around just as Angel slides a wall in front of me like the pocket doors in Dad's office.

"Have to cut the interior lights, sweetie. It'll look funny if we're barreling down the highway with the cab light on."

When the lights go out, I flinch. It's darker than I expected. So dark I can barely make out my hand when I hold it up to my face.

"All right back there?"

Angel doesn't wait for my response, shifting into gear with a loud thump and pulling away from the side of the road.

"I promise, Stella. This will all be worth it."

The next thing I know Angel is knocking on the wall, waking me. I've fallen asleep slumped against the back corner of the cab. A sharp pain shoots up my neck.

"Stella?"

The truck is slowing. Have we really been on the road two and a half hours? Did I sleep that long?

"Are we there?" I ask through the wall.

"Not yet, Stella."

The possibilities run through my head. The constables have found us. The police are pulling us over. The truck is breaking down.

"Nothing to worry about, Stella. Just the police."

At least it's not the constables.

"Don't make a sound, and we'll be fine. I'm sure of it."

CHAPTER 68

The truck rolls to a stop. "Not a peep, Stella."

We sit in silence so long I wonder if Angel is still there. I turn my wrist, lighting up my watch. Almost four in the morning. The sun will rise in just over three hours. Angel's window whirs down.

She speaks in what sounds like her most respectful voice. "Yes, officer?"

I can't hear him well but make out the words *routine* and *missing*.

Did someone else go missing?

Angel gasps. "That's terrible, Officer. What did you say her name was?"

His response is as clear as if he's right next to me. "Stella Graham—"

They already know about me. I haven't been gone five hours, and they know. How did they find out so quickly? Someone must have woken up, seen the front door. Was it Mom? Dad?

I hear the truck door open, and it's all I can do not to whimper.

"Can you give me a hand, Officer? These old bones don't like steps, but I need to stretch my legs. Would you like a cookie? Made some snickerdoodles for my granddaughter."

Why is Angel getting out of the cab?

The two of them continue talking, but I can't make out what they're saying. I put my ear against the wall and wait for something to happen.

When I hear the sound of creaking metal, I know someone is climbing into the cab.

"I'll be sure to keep an eye out, Officer." It's Angel. "I just hate it when this kind of thing happens."

I barely catch the officer thanking Angel before I hear her window whir back up.

Is he letting her go?

Angel puts the truck in gear. "We're okay, Stella. We're just fine."

CHAPTER 69

'm too anxious to fall asleep again. I stay alert, listening for trouble. But the only sound is the low rumble of the engine. I can't even hear other cars pass.

When Angel knocks again, my body fills with the exhilarating sensation of relief.

"We made it, Stella. We're in Shiloh."

The truck slows to a stop, the gears clunking down. I wait for Angel to slide the wall away.

Before she can do that, I hear her say the words, "Oh, no," out loud.

"What is it?"

"Try not to worry, Stella, but a red SUV just pulled up behind us."

A red SUV. A constable.

"What do we do?"

"I'll handle it. You stay quiet."

A minute later, the window goes down again. *It's going to be okay. Just like last time.*

Angel is her chipper best. "Good morning, Constable."

"Angel Hightower?" This time I can hear clearly. He's that loud. "Of Bull Run?"

"Not me. Name's Janie Archer."

"We know who you are, Miss Hightower. I need you to step out of the truck."

"But what did I do?"

"Now." The constable's voice is insistent.

"Just need to find—" Angel shuffles something in the front of the cab. It sounds like she's moving things around.

Just do what he says, Angel.

"It's on the floor here somewhere." She's looking for something.

"Ma'am!" the constable yells, his voice even louder. "Keep your hands where I can see them!"

Just do it, Angel. Just do what he says.

"Can you feel it, sweetie?" That's when I get it. She's not talking to the constable. She's talking to me. "On the floor?"

I reach down and run my hand over the sticky floor. My hands find the metal bar at the same time I hear it.

Pop pop.

One after another. Like firecrackers.

Angel lets out a long, weary groan. I know without seeing. She's been shot.

Everything in me wants to knock down the wall and help her. But if I do, we'll both be caught. Angel told me exactly what to do in this situation. *If something happens to one of your drivers, Stella, don't try to help. Just get out of there as fast as you can. Fight your way out if you have to.* I grip the metal bar and wait for the constable to find me.

CHAPTER 70

When I hear glass breaking, I put my hand over my mouth to stop from screaming.

The door squeaks open on the other side of the cab. The passenger side. He's gone around, so he doesn't have to deal with Angel.

He's going to find me.

"Stella?" His voice booms through the cab. "Where are you?"

A part of me wants to give myself up. He shot Angel. Will he do the same to me?

"Stella, I know you're in here. Just come out. I promise I won't hurt you."

I close my eyes and force myself to breathe. *Quiet your mind. Focus.*

He knocks on the wall in front of me like it's a front door. "Stella?" It's only a matter of seconds before he finds me. But I'm ready.

His palms slap against the wall as he works it open. And when it slides away, I come face-to-face with him. His eyes flip from searching to satisfaction just as I pull back and swing the bar toward the side of his face. I hit him square in the temple. Like it has a bullseye on it.

He falls back against the dashboard. The thud is so loud my hands go to my ears. I hesitate, making sure he isn't moving before turning to Angel.

"Angel!" I shake her arm, but she doesn't respond. "Angel, are you okay?"

I climb into the front of the cab and face her. That's when I see it. The bullet hole on the far side of her neck. Blood bubbles out of the wound. I put my hands on either side of her face. "Angel! Wake up!"

I hear her voice in my head again.

Stella, don't try to help. Just get out of there as fast as you can.

The constable moans. I need to go.

I check the highway, looking up and down the pavement, before I jump. There's no one else around. Just the one SUV behind the semi, its red lights flashing in the still-dark night. I put one foot on the first step and launch myself to the ground.

I have to hurry.

I don't have much time.

CHAPTER 71

I t looks exactly the way Angel described. A patch of grass slopes to a wire fence. I rush down the small hill and search for the white bandana. *It will be attached to a piece of fencing you can pull away. Remember to take the bandana with you.* I do exactly as Angel instructed, shoving the bandana into the pocket of my jeans before I pull the wire grid back, squeezing under it as quickly as I can. It snaps back and hits my arm. I yelp out loud and glance up at the cab. Even from here, I can see the constable lifting a hand to his head. I dart across the backyard on the other side of the fence and come to a residential street lined with tract houses as small as apartments. There are literally thousands of them. Maybe more. It's a maze of vinyl and cement. I've heard about these neighborhoods. This is where people like Mason live. People who work in factories. People who send their daughters to govie.

I look both ways, searching for the T intersection. Ransom Trace and Warren Pass. It's just one house down. I sprint forward and turn left, running up the road as fast as I can. I'm moving so fast I almost miss it. 102 Warren Pass.

The first shelter.

The front door opens even before I get to it.

Inside, a tall man in tortoiseshell glasses closes the door behind me. I stare at the small silver pistol in his hand.

"This?" He holds the gun up. "Don't worry. It's not for you." He peeks through the blinds. "It's for them."

The woman standing next to him in matching glasses turns from him to me. "Are you okay, Stella?" My name sounds strange in her unfamiliar voice. "We heard the shots."

"You did?"

"Yes, and we can't be the only ones."

The man scoffs, pointing out the subdivision is a massive labyrinth. Ten thousand homes on twenty acres. It would take days to search them all. He insists half of their neighbors would shoot anyone who stepped on their property. "No offense, but you're probably not worth the effort."

The woman shakes her head at him. "Paul, please."

Their names come back to me. *Paul and Ana.* "You're the Cristos?"

"Technically it's Cristobal, but no one can remember that, much less spell it."

Ana turns back to me. "You must be hungry. How about cereal? Do you like granola?"

"I'll eat anything."

~~~~~

After breakfast, they show me where I'll hide. A secret room behind a fake bookshelf in their bedroom. An air mattress sits on the floor next to a camping lantern, a stack of books, and a paper bag overflowing with chips and pretzels, food I'm never allowed to eat.

"We'll be home early," Paul says as Ana puts on a jean jacket that makes her look much younger. "But it'd look suspicious if we didn't go to work."

I didn't realize this was part of the plan. I knew I had to wait out daylight here, but I had no idea I'd do it alone. A whole day alone in a place I don't know. It's better than Angel's cab but not much.

CHAPTER 72

jolt awake to the sound of a door closing.

I'm sitting on an air mattress. There's an empty bag of potato chips and a beat-up copy of *Their Eyes Were Watching God* next to me.

This is not my room.

"Stella?" a man's voice calls out.

Heavy shoes clap against stairs.

"Stella?"

Is he going to find me?

"Stella, it's Paul and Ana. We're home."

Paul and Ana. The first shelter.

I exhale the balloon of fear in my mouth.

It's okay. I'm okay.

For now.

⌇

When Paul says he'll start dinner, I almost ask why. My dad has never heated a can of soup, much less made an entire meal. Paul seems proud of his skills, detailing how long it's taken to perfect his pork loin. While he cooks, Ana asks questions about my life in Bull Run. It's unnerving to tell her about a world I'm leaving behind.

Paul reviews the plans while we eat. I know them by heart, but I can tell it makes him less anxious.

I help Ana with the dishes while Paul takes a nap. Two hours later, he finds us downstairs. "It's time." He pushes the small pistol into the back of his pants.

Paul pops the trunk of a brand-new Corvette Roanoke sedan in the garage. White, of course. It's the kind of car a wealthy person would drive. The kind of car my dad drives. Not what I'd expect from a vigilante in a small house.

Ana and Paul are what Dad calls car rich.

"Nice car."

"Thanks. Just got it."

Ana jumps in. "We decided to splurge."

"You ready?" Paul stands in front of the open trunk.

"You want me to ride in there? Are you kidding?"

"I don't kid." He lets out a quick sigh. "You know they're already looking for you, right? Your picture is all over the Freedom Channel. They put out a Red Alert."

"They still think I'm missing?"

"They always will, Stella. People believe what they're told."

I look to Ana as if she can help me.

She frowns, tilting her head to the side. "It'll be fine, Stella." She steps closer and pulls me into a hug even though she doesn't really know me. "I promise."

Paul holds out a flashlight.

I look into his face, hoping he'll change his mind, but he just nods at the trunk. "You know as well as I do we have to stay on schedule."

I glance at Ana, hoping there's another way.

"Promise me you'll both stay safe." She touches a finger to her eye. This is hard for them too.

I take off my backpack and hand it to Paul before climbing into the trunk. I can almost straighten my legs. He hands me the bag and puts his hands on either side of the trunk. "It won't be too long." He pushes the lid down. When it clicks shut, I gasp out loud.

I can't see *anything*.

CHAPTER 73

I try to stay awake, but it's useless. The car vibrates beneath me, rocking me to sleep. I don't open my eyes until Paul pops the trunk again, bright streetlights hitting my pupils so hard I squint like a vampire.

"What's going on?"

"We're here." He pulls a pack of cigarettes from his shirt pocket. Did he have cigarettes at their house? "Leeville Rest Stop."

"Already?"

"Yup. We crossed what used to be the state line an hour ago. Now you've just got to cross one more state and the river. Then you'll be home free."

"State?"

"Well, it used to be a state." He holds his empty hand out to me. "Come on, get out of there."

I lift one leg out of the trunk at a time. Every inch of my body is stiff. My legs throb, my hips ache, my shoulders are tight. "Everything hurts."

Paul lights his cigarette. "I can imagine."

"I can't believe we've already made it this far."

He takes a drag on his cigarette. "Already? We've been on the road three goddamn hours."

I wince, and Paul says, "Sorry, I forgot."

"Forgot what?"

"That you people don't curse."

"You people?"

Paul gives me an exasperated look. "These questions will go on all night if we let them, Stella."

I crane my neck around the parking lot. "Are we safe?"

"Not a soul here. Used to be rest stops were manned around the clock, but now...the Minutemen are too cheap for that."

He checks his smart watch. "It's three o'clock. Where the hell is she?"

I must wince again because he says, "Sorry" in a voice that implies he only says it out of obligation.

"I have to go to the bathroom."

He simultaneously shakes his head and blows out smoke. "No time."

"I didn't know you smoked."

"I don't know what you're talking about, young lady." He takes another drag. "I don't smoke."

I let out a small laugh, but that only makes me have to go more. "I really have to go."

"Goddamn it." Before I can wince, he adds, "You might as well accept that I'm going to curse. A lot. Especially when I'm stressed."

"I'll try not to be a baby about it."

"Glad to hear it." He lifts the cigarette to his mouth again as he scans the parking lot. "Damn it, where is she?"

I follow his gaze but see nothing.

"Fine, let's go." He moves toward the small building. "But make it fast."

The driver still hasn't arrived when we walk out. Paul checks his watch just as a set of headlights swing into the entrance.

"Finally. Can you believe this shit? It's seven minutes after three."

But the headlights are high, like an SUV.

"Shit!" Paul flicks his cigarette to the grass. "That is *not* our guy."

CHAPTER 74

A red SUV screeches to a stop in front of us, and I turn to Paul, terrified. What are we going to do now?

Both doors fly open at the same time, two constables spilling out. One is tall and scrawny, the other shorter than I am.

"Good evening, Constables ." Paul uses a voice I've not yet heard from him. A TV announcer voice. He's straightened up too. Gone is the guy who sneaks cigarettes and curses every time he speaks. This is the guy who drives a brand-new Roanoke.

Paul is a chameleon.

"What the hell are you doing out here?" the short constable asks.

"Would you be so kind as to watch your language, constable? There's a young lady present."

"What?" The constable studies me, and his face reddens. "I didn't realize. But you still haven't answered the question."

"We're driving home from Sewanee. My daughter's first college visit. Got a late start."

"You two?" the gangly one says.

"That's correct, sir." Paul doesn't sound like he respects them. More like *they* need to respect him.

"You want me to believe *you* are *her* dad?"

Paul considers me. Apprehension appears in his eyes for the first time. He doesn't look old enough to be my father. He's barely thirty-five. And he's a giant. At least six foot four with deep brown hair and sepia-colored eyes. I'm short. Only five foot four with honey-colored hair and gray-blue eyes. We look nothing alike.

Paul is quick on his feet. "She's adopted."

"My ass, she's adopted."

"Gentleman, I don't want to have to ask you again not to speak that way in front of my daughter."

He speaks with such confidence I wonder if this is how it always works. Paul pretending to be the father of a girl on the run.

"I know who you are." The short constable points at me, and fear squeezes my chest. "You're that girl they're looking for. Stella something."

I don't respond, too afraid of giving myself away.

"That's right, isn't it?" He steps onto the sidewalk, moving closer to us. "Come on, Harlan. There's a reward for this one."

The tall, skinny one—Harlan—doesn't move, and Paul puts his hands out in front of him. "Gentlemen, please."

The short constable hesitates, and for a split second no one moves. Then Paul rushes forward, knocking him to the ground like a stuffed animal. They wrestle while Harlan looks me up and down.

The short one shouts, "Get her, Harlan!"

This time, Harlan listens, lunging toward me. As soon as he's close enough, I throw a jab straight into his nose. He puts a hand to his face, and I launch a side kick to his gut. He stumbles back two steps, and then I hear it.

A shot.

A loud pop just like the ones I heard twenty-four hours before.

Paul holds his silver pistol in the air. The short guy is clutching his leg and screaming like a sick infant. Paul points the pistol over my head. "Don't even think about it, asshole."

I spin around just in time to see Harlan's nightstick in the air above me.

Paul shakes the gun at him. "Drop it."

Harlan obliges.

Paul pivots his eyes toward me while keeping the gun trained on Harlan. "Stella, catch." He tosses me his keys with his empty hand. "Get the handcuffs out of the trunk."

The short constable stops screaming. "I knew it! You're her."

"Shut up, dumbass," Paul says.

"You'll never get away with this."

"We just did."

CHAPTER 75

We lock them in the janitor's closet, handcuffed together, with the keys we found on a cleaning cart.

Outside, another set of headlights appears. They're lower to the ground. A small white hatchback flies up to the curb in front of us. I can barely hear the engine idling.

"It's so quiet," I say to Paul.

"It's a hybrid. Gas and electric. They don't make them here anymore. This is one of the last models. A vintage 2023 Prius."

Our guy, as Paul called her, turns out to be a woman with short spiky hair and tinted glasses. Her window is rolled down. "You two okay?"

"We had an issue." Paul nods at the red SUV, its doors still hanging open. "But we handled it."

"That's a relief."

"More importantly." Paul makes a show of looking at his watch. "It's 3:30. Where the hell have you been?"

"I'm so damn sorry. There were constables all over the on-ramp. It's like they knew I was coming. I had to take a different route."

"Shit." Paul looks over the roof of the hybrid as if he can see their red SUVs in the distance. "That's not good."

"Don't I know it."

"They're everywhere tonight."

"Yup."

Paul shakes his head. "We have to create a diversion."

Paul shoves paper towels into the gas tank of the Roanoke while simultaneously shouting instructions at us.

"Dr. B, alert backup." It takes me a minute to realize he's talking to the woman in the hybrid. "Tell them to meet me at the next exit."

"On it," Dr. B says from the driver's seat while Paul lights a cigarette.

I turn to her. "You're a doctor?"

She looks me in the eye for the first time. "Kind of. I'm a professor. I mean, I used to be. Before."

Before. Everything was different before.

Paul keeps talking while he trails the paper towels out of the tank of the Roanoke like a tail. "Stella?" He nods toward the hybrid when I look at him. "Open the back door."

I do what he says.

"Now get in and lie down. There's a blanket. Put it on top of you."

Paul lights the tail of the paper towels and shoves the cigarette into the tank of the Roanoke. Smoke curls away from the SUV while Paul rushes to the passenger door of the hybrid. The paper ignites just as he jumps in. I throw the blanket on top of me.

"Let's get out of here." Paul's voice is almost as calm as if he were asking someone to pass the salt.

Dr. B peels out, swerving onto the highway. That's when I hear it. The Roanoke exploding behind us like a volcano. I throw off the blanket and jump to my knees, peering out the back window. We've left the rest area, but it's still visible, the night sky lighting up in a giant tower of orange flame.

"Stella!" Paul yells over his shoulder. "Get down!"

CHAPTER 76

I can't see them from under the blanket, but I hear them.

The sirens.

There must be dozens of them. Dad could always tell the sirens apart, but I never learned to distinguish them. All I know for sure is there are way too many of them. Are they looking for us? Are they headed to the fire?

I raise my voice so he can hear me from under the blanket. "I'm sorry, Paul."

He doesn't respond at first but eventually says, "It's not your fault." His voice is subdued, resigned. "And this will make it harder for them to find us. Give Ana and me some time to get away."

Get away? Will they really have to leave? And then I remember Angel. Of course, they will.

"I'm so sorry."

"It's fine." He lets out a bitter laugh. "That's what I get for spending that kind of cash on a car. That and not leaving sooner. We've been wanting to get out. This is just the kick in the ass we need to do it."

Dr. B jumps in. "It's hard to leave." I hear the longing in her voice. "It's hard to walk away from everything you've ever known."

It never occurred to me that people their age would be unhappy here. It's challenging for everyone. Neither of them says a word after that, their silence filling the air with regret.

Ten minutes later, the car veers off to the right. We must be at the exit.

We haven't even come to a complete stop when I hear the passenger door fly open.

Before it closes, Paul's voice reaches me in the backseat. "Good luck, Stella." I peek out from under the blanket, so I can see his face one last time. "Ana and I are pulling for you." He looks at the driver's seat. "Dr. B too. We're all pulling for you."

I'm too moved to speak. Who are these people? Helping someone they don't even know. Blowing up their cars. Risking their lives. Why would they do this?

Back on the highway, we pass more sirens. The hybrid speeds up.

I lift the blanket again.

"Hold on, Stella," Dr. B says over her shoulder. "We gotta haul ass."

CHAPTER 77

Less than thirty minutes pass before the hybrid slows again.

I hear barking. Loud barking.

"You can come out," Dr. B says over her shoulder.

I throw the blanket off. A sunrise the same orange as the flames engulfing Paul's car is peeking over the horizon. There's just enough light to make out the beat-up trailer in front of us. A German shepherd barks madly, pulling against a fat chain tied to the stairs.

"Where are we?"

"Appomattox, a place formerly known as Charleston."

Appomattox. The Ward Hallow train yard. Shelter number two.

"My hometown," Dr. B says. "Also home to some of the most evil men in the world."

Before I can ask if she's talking about the Appomattox Six, the door of the trailer flies open. A uniformed security guard steps out. I gasp without thinking.

The man touches his head with one finger.

"It's okay, Stella," Dr. B says. "He's one of us."

The security guard struts over to Dr. B's door. She rolls down the window.

"Hey, Sam." There's real affection in her voice. "May I present our latest renegade?" She hooks her thumb over the seat at me. "This is Stella."

Sam leads us to a grid of abandoned train cars, the German shepherd straining at the leash five feet ahead of him. We walk down one row and turn right and then left and then right again. Like we're climbing flat stairs. Pretty soon I'm all turned around, my sneakers covered with dust. I'd never find my way out alone.

Sam stops next to an old white train car with the letters *CSX* painted in red in the upper left-hand corner. I'm studying the peeling paint when Sam says, "This is it, Stella. Home sweet home. At least for the next sixteen or so hours." He throws open the car door. "I got a cooler in here with rations. Some books and a monster flashlight. Heard you like yoga, so I got you one of those rubber mat things. Give you a chance to work those muscles." He nods at a sleeping bag in the back corner. "Something to sleep on too." A thin blanket and pillow are folded perfectly on top.

"Where do I—"

"Other end." He points to a cardboard box in the opposite side of the car. "Like a litter box."

"A what?"

"A litter box. That's where a cat—" He starts to explain, but I interrupt him.

"I know." I look from Sam to Dr. B. "I just…"

Dr. B offers me a shrug from behind her dark glasses.

Sam scratches his forehead. "Did you feel safe at home, Stella?"

The truth is, I should have felt safe, but I never did. "Is it safe here?"

"I'll be watching the gate all day, and Killer here—" Sam nods at the German shepherd.

"Killer?"

"She'll have the run of the place. No one's gettin' past her. Not alive anyway."

My eyes roll over the grid of train cars, the dusty rows, the piles of trash. I really don't want to get inside.

Dr. B senses my reluctance. "I know it's frightening, Stella. But isn't this what you wanted?"

Is it? Is it what I wanted?

"It's just one day."

Sam interjects. "Half a day."

Dr. B agrees. "The fact is your life up until now has been incredibly privileged."

Sam dips his head. "The question is, do you trust us?"

I consider the two of them. They both have thick dark hair and matching violet-blue eyes. They must be related. Brother and sister or something like that.

I do trust them. And even if I didn't, what choice do I have?

CHAPTER 78

I lock the door from inside like Sam showed me. Only a thin line of sunlight seeps into the train car. I find myself longing for Paul and Ana's clean space and carpeted floor, things I took for granted until today.

I devour the food Sam left in the cooler—a bologna and cheese sandwich, potato chips, a massive chocolate bar, two cans of soda. More food I'm not supposed to eat. I relish every bite. It tastes better than Mom's New America Strip steak.

After that, I'm not sure what to do. I start one of the books Sam left me. *Bless Me, Ultima*. I get through fifty pages without even realizing it.

When I get sleepy, I do sun salutations. Sam is right. I need to stay at my best. Sister Laura was training me for this, and I didn't even realize it. I have to keep up what she started.

After a half hour of yoga, I drop to the sleeping bag and try to read again.

I fall asleep without finishing the page.

I wake to the sound of barking in the distance.

Where am I?

I can't see anything except a thin line of yellow light. The barking is getting closer. That's when I remember.

Killer. Sam. The train yard.

Someone shouts over the barking. "We need to get the fuck out of here!" The voice is not far from my car.

I tiptoe to the crack in the door. Two men in gray pants and shirts sprint right for me.

Constables.

I back away, praying they didn't see me.

Praise God for protecting women from harm.

Please please please, God.

Please protect me from harm.

Each time their feet hit the dirt, it sounds like Shea clapping with her mittens on. They're close. Too close.

The clapping is replaced by a long sweeping sound. I peek out. One of them has slid to a stop right outside my car. He's gasping for air and soaked with sweat, his face almost the same pink as his lips. I step back without letting out a single breath.

He yells at the other constable. "Hurry the fuck up, would you?"

Does he notice the car I'm in is white? Does he know that means something?

The other constable's feet sound more like brushes than claps. He's sprinting. A few seconds later, the barking is so loud I can't hear either of them. Killer is right outside my car. I step up to the crack. The constables are gone. Killer turns her face toward me. Protecting me like Sam said she would. She lets out a single bark and takes off after the constables.

My heart is beating harder than it ever has before. I stumble to the sleeping bag and put my palm to my chest, willing it to slow to normal. But it's no use.

Nothing will ever be normal again.

CHAPTER 79

My eyes open, but I can't see anything.

The crack of sunlight is gone. Did I really sleep that long? I turn my wrist, lighting up my watch. 8:14 p.m. Thursday. Two days since I left.

If I were home, I'd be in my room reading, maybe talking to Sister Laura. By now the dinner dishes have been cleared. Mom is putting Shea to sleep. Dad is in his office. Or the garage.

Then again, maybe none of this is happening. Maybe nothing is the same. Maybe they're out looking for me right now. The thought of Mom and Dad walking the streets with flashlights, calling my name overwhelms me with guilt. Is this what I've done to them? Made them the parents of a missing person?

Of course, this is what I've done.

It never occurred to me how they would be affected. I only thought about how it would affect *me*. How much I needed to get out.

I pray out loud this time. "Please, God, please help them move on. Please help them let me go. I *want* them to let me go."

Three hours later the air inside the train car smells like a portable toilet. I'm sitting in the corner with my knees pulled up to my chest, worrying about what comes next, when Sam knocks on the door. The sound bounces off the walls like I'm inside a giant metal lunchbox.

"It's me, Stella."

"How do I know it's you?"

"You're wearing blue jeans and a Freedom Channel shirt so big it looks like you could fit a whole 'nother person in there."

I undo the lock, and Sam slides the door open. When I jump down to the dirt, Killer licks my shoes.

A beat-up white delivery truck sits outside the front gate. Shelter number three.

A haggard-looking man and woman stand in front of it. The man is chewing tobacco, and the woman stares at me like I've got a sign on my nose. When she catches Sam's eye, she touches her forehead with a shaky finger.

Sam walks to the back of their truck and throws the doors open with both hands. A bright yellow blanket sits on top of a dirty mattress.

I look at Sam. "Is there a flashlight?"

"Well—"

I put my hands on my face in a futile attempt to stop tears that are bound to come.

"Stella." Sam rests his hand on my back the same way Dad did when Sister Helen died. "You're going to be okay."

I drop my hands and stare into his eyes. But what I see there isn't empathy. It's admiration.

"You don't know that."

"No, but I believe." He hands me a threadbare handkerchief. "In six hours, this whole thing will be over. You'll be on the other side."

I contemplate the dark, empty truck. "I'm not getting in there."

"We got to give her something." The woman digs an orange bottle of pills out of her purse and hands them to Sam.

Sam holds out a small peach-colored pill, and the woman passes me her water bottle. Sister Laura told me to never take something if I don't know what it is.

"It's just a Xanax," the woman says. "It'll help you sleep. You need the rest for what comes next."

The last leg of my trip. I'll have to run through the woods and swim across the river.

"I don't know if I can do it."

Sam rubs my back. "You've trained for this, Stella. You're just shook up. And dog tired. It's all right. Lots of girls get cold feet at this point."

"They do?"

All three of them nod though the woman looks more impatient than understanding. Sam still holds out the pill. I grab it and gulp it down.

"Not too much." The woman reaches for her bottle. "We won't be able to stop."

Sam offers me a hand. I take it and climb into the back of the truck.

"Stella." He grabs my ankle before I flop down on the mattress. "Don't forget." When I look at him, he says, "I believe in you."

As soon as he closes the door and locks me inside, I'm surrounded by darkness.

The tears start for real now.

CHAPTER 80

I cry so hard I choke on my own sobs. When I can finally breathe again, I'm too tired to cry anymore. My throat is dry and raw.

I need water.

The back of the truck is completely devoid of light. For the second time since I left, I can't see *anything*. I remember my smart watch, flipping my wrist until light washes over my face. Ten after one in the morning. Just over three hours to go. I run my hand over the mattress to see if they've left me any supplies, but there's nothing except the small backpack I've been carrying since I left home.

Four hours without water. I gather as much spit in my mouth as I can and swallow. It doesn't really help.

I dump everything inside the backpack on the mattress in front of me. There's a tube of Chapstick, some tissues, a couple leftover granola bars, a handful of panty liners, an emergency pad, and a small bottle of hand sanitizer. *Is that it?* I twist my wrist, illuminating the space just long enough to make out the white baseball hat and a small wrapped box. When I pick up the box, the paper is coarse under my fingers. Newspaper.

Sister Laura put it in my hand more than a week ago, closing my fingers around the box. "Take this with you when you go, Stella. But don't open it until you're ready to give up, until you have nothing left."

I wanted to open it at Paul and Ana's. Then in the train yard. But I told myself to wait. I told myself I'd need it more later. I was right. Right now I need whatever Sister Laura has given me.

The newspaper rips right off. Underneath is a delicate wood box with a white stone top. I pull as hard as I can, but the lid won't budge. I flip it over and try to knock it loose with the heel of my hand. Nothing works. I turn it over and over in the dark, running my index finger along every side until, finally, something gives, the top sliding away from the bottom.

Inside is a piece of yellowed paper.

The flyer from the church office.

There are words typed on the front, but they're cut off by a tear on the right side of the paper.

STOP THE MINUTE

Stop the Minute? On the back of the flyer is a handwritten note. I use the light from my watch to read a few lines at a time.

Dear Stella,

If you don't recognize this, it's the piece of paper I showed you the night I told you what happened to my sister. I'm giving it to you now because you're finally ready to know what the flyer said.

Those men who attacked my sister that

day in the church office? They were Minutemen,
Stella. We were trying to fight them. But
we lost.

I flip the flyer over.

STOP THE MINUTE

The Minutemen. STOP THE MINUTEMEN. That's what it said
before it was ripped out of her hand. I turn it over and keep reading.

They got what they wanted. They destroyed us.
They formed their own country. And they took
our freedom. But the fight isn't over yet,
Stella. We're still fighting. We never stopped.
And we won't give up until we win. But we
need people like you on our side. We need YOU.
*   If you're reading this, you probably feel*
like you can't go any further. Like you have
no fight left in you. But you're stronger than
you know. You have more fight than anyone
I've ever met. I know you can do this. I know
you can be the person you so desperately
want to be.
*   I believe in you, Stella.*

She didn't sign her name. She couldn't risk it. But I still hear
her voice in my head. *I believe in you, Stella.*

I press the flyer against my chest, lie back on the mattress, and
close my eyes.

I need to rest if I'm going to be ready.

CHAPTER 81

The doors of the truck open. How long have I been out? The last thing I remember is reading the note from Sister Laura.

Someone shines a flashlight in my face. It's so bright I have to cover my eyes.

"Stella?" It's the old woman. I can't remember her name. Did I ever know it? Did I memorize it before I left?

"Where are we?"

"Green Spring. A town so small they didn't bother to stick it with a new name."

Green Spring. The place where I'm supposed to cross.

"Put this on." She holds out a pile of clothes. A super tight jog bra, a white T-shirt that say MOUNTAINEERS in green letters, and a pair of running shorts. All of it smells like fabric softener. "Now be quick about it." She closes one door of the truck for me to change behind.

The shorts are shorter than any I've ever worn. I might as well be naked. But I want out of the truck so badly I don't care. I move to the back and jump to the ground.

She points her water bottle at me. "You ready?"

"I guess."

"I only got one piece of advice. Whatever you do, don't hesitate. You can't afford doubt."

I want to tell her I've hesitated the whole way. I'm hesitating now. "Okay."

"And Godspeed to ya."

Godspeed. This is her way of saying she cares. Of course, she does. Why else would she risk her life to help me?

"Thanks," I say too casually, quickly adding. "I mean it. Really. Thanks for all of your help. Both of you." I nod toward the front of the truck.

"Can't let the bastards win, can we?"

A twentysomething man with black hair cropped close to his head and wire glasses walks up.

"Good to see you, Vicki Lee." He puts a finger to his forehead, and she does the same.

Vicki Lee. That's her name. And the guy driving is her husband, Vince.

The man is wearing the same shorts and white shirt with green letters that I am.

"I'm Max, Stella." He must see me staring at his shirt because he points to it. "Our cover. The local university. You ready?"

Whatever you do, don't hesitate. "Ready."

Max waves over a group of men wearing the same basic outfit the two of us are wearing. One of them looks only a few years older than I am. The other two appear to be at least seventy. "I'll let the guys introduce themselves."

"I'm Irving," one of the older men says, "and this is my brother Simon. We're from New Jersey." They could be twins: both thin and tall with gray curly hair.

"And I'm Michael," the young guy says. "From Oregon."

"You're not all from here?"

"We come from all over the United States. To run with girls like you," Max says. "I'm from North Carolina."

"You mean Old America?"

Max lets out a little laugh. "That's not what it's really called, Stella. It's still the good ole U S of A. They only call it 'Old America' here. But you'll learn all that soon enough."

I'm confused but have a more important question. "Why do you do it?"

"You haven't heard about us?" Max asks.

"No." I'm shocked by how much I still have to learn. "Angel only told me what I needed to know."

"They call us Night Lights." He gestures toward Vicki Lee and the others. "All of us. We're the people who get girls out at night."

A surge of emotion moves through me as I think of all the people who've gotten me to this point. Angel. Paul and Ana. Dr. B. Sam. Vicki Lee and Vince. And now this group of men. Max. Irving. Simon. Michael. I had no idea so many people cared about girls like me.

"Shall we?" Max asks.

I nod in response, and before I know what's happening, we're going.

We're running.

CHAPTER 82

We run a mile right down the side of the road, the almost-full moon lighting our way. Just as Angel predicted. When we get to a white No Parking sign, we veer off the roadway. It looks like dark brush, but pretty quickly a path comes into view.

We run in silence another few minutes until Max speaks. "We all think you're very brave, Stella." The others murmur their agreement. "Coming all this way by yourself."

I'm caught off guard but manage a weak "thanks."

"You must have been trained well."

"I was."

It's true. Sister Laura pushed me. Fighting at State Street. Sitting alone in the library. Running with Dad. My chest tightens when I think of Dad. This will be the third morning I'm not there when he and Mom wake. They've slept three nights without me. They must be beside themselves with worry.

"Will my parents find out what really happened?"

Max smiles, but I see the heartbreak in his eyes. "That would be too dangerous." Max pauses when we come to a clearing, holding us back with one arm while taking a pair of binoculars from his belt. He examines one side of the open field and slowly rotates 180 degrees, taking in the entire area. He touches his forehead. "All clear."

We run along the perimeter. We were protected by trees before, but now we're exposed on one side. No one says a word, and I tell myself they know what they're doing. They've done this more than once. But before we reach the other side, we hear it. Only a whisper at first.

Rustling leaves and snapping twigs.

Max stops and holds a hand out while pointing to the ground with the other. "Drop, Stella."

CHAPTER 83

Max motions for Irving and Simon to drop with me and touches Michael's arm, pointing to the woods on the other side of the clearing while pulling a pistol out of his belt. "Let's go."

The two of them dart straight across the clearing. Seconds later, they disappear into the tree line. My instinct is to follow, but one of the brothers says, "Stay down."

Before I can respond, shots ring across the clearing in rapid succession.

One.

Two.

Three.

Four.

The air goes quiet for a drawn-out moment.

And then one more shot splits the darkness.

CHAPTER 84

The three of us look at each other with the same questions in our eyes. *Who was shooting? Who got shot?* Irving turns from Simon to me. "Wait here, Stella."

Vicki Lee's words play in my head. *Don't hesitate.* "No."

He gives me a resigned look. "Fine."

The three of us jog back around the perimeter, taking cover behind a giant osage when we get to the spot where Max and Michael went in the woods. The area in front of us seems darker than when we were running through the trees just a few minutes ago. My eyes have already adjusted to the moonlight.

Irving's mouth flattens into a line of determination. He counts down on his fingers—*three, two, one*—and at the exact same moment, we step from behind the tree and run into the woods.

We find them less than a thousand feet inside the brush. Michael on the ground, clutching his shoulder like it might fall off if he doesn't hold it there. Max on his knees, unrolling a bandage.

Simon studies something in the distance. "You got him."

You got him? I follow Simon's gaze. Not far in front of us, a guy in a camouflage jumpsuit lies flat on his back, blood leaking all over his stomach. His eyes are open, but nobody's there.

"You *killed* him?"

Max lifts Michael's arm to slide the bandage under it. "I had no choice. He wouldn't stop shooting."

I don't argue, suddenly more horrified by Michael's shoulder, which is entirely red now. Like he's wearing a cape of blood.

"You need to keep moving," Max says to Irving. "Our cover's blown. There might be more of them. I'll text backup to meet us at the road."

Irving points out the obvious. "That's over a mile away."

"I'll get him there." He sounds certain.

Michael's eyes start to close.

Max puts his hands on either side of his face. "Stay with me." Michael's eyes flash open, and Max turns back to us. "Go now. Before it's too late."

CHAPTER 85

The three of us move away from Max and Michael with hesitation, but then we commit, taking off in a sprint. Simon and I follow Irving. We run through the trees at an angle, cutting the corner to the other side of the clearing.

"This way." Irving leads us down another path.

We run faster than before, making up for lost time. I'm out of breath in a few minutes.

"Slow your breathing, Stella," Irving says. "Count it out. One, two. One, two."

I do as he instructs, timing my breaths with the heartbeats in my throat.

A minute later we come around a large maple and nearly run into a deer stand. We all stop without speaking.

Simon moves around the stand. "No one's here."

I'm not as confident, inspecting as we pass. It isn't a minute later when we hear a branch breaking somewhere ahead of us.

We freeze.

And then we hear it again.

Irving opens his mouth to speak, but Simon shushes him.

We hear more twigs snapping. *This is it. This is when it all goes wrong.*

Another stick snaps right before the culprit steps right in front of us. A deer big enough to feed my whole block.

Simon drops his head. "It's just a doe."

She looks right into my eyes, staring deeply.

Does she know I'm running?

Does she know they're hunting me?

Her eyes grow bigger. And then, before I can take it all in, she leaps away, effortlessly clearing the growth to our left. I let out the breath I've been holding as she scampers away. I'm still watching her when another deer flies across the path in front of us. I cover my mouth to stop from yelling.

When the second one is out of sight, I start to move forward, but Irving holds me back.

Another deer leaps in front of us. And then another. And another. We watch without moving as a half dozen more of them leap past us.

Simon gasps. "My God."

The way he says *God* is not in vain. It's gratitude. An acknowledgment. There are things greater than us in the world.

"We're lucky." Irving glances over his shoulder. "This is a good sign."

And then we're running.

I'm not counting my breaths anymore. I'm gasping for air. I come to an abrupt stop.

"We're almost there, Stella. Just to that curve." Irving points to a turn a ways ahead of us. "And then it's all downhill."

We start running again. When the path curves right, Irving pauses, pulling back a tangle of tall plants in front of us. "This way." He walks into them. Simon and I follow. The brush is too thick for running. Tree limbs and offshoots slap our faces. We tolerate it until the area clears, the ground sloping down to a wide river.

"Is that—" I ask.

"Yes." Irving smiles. "That's it."

CHAPTER 86

Simon's next words come out in a whisper. "We made it."

The two of them pull pistols from their belts, glancing up and down the shoreline like they're fleeing the scene of a crime.

Irving doesn't look at me when he speaks again. "You have to hurry. There could be more of them."

"More deer?"

"No."

I know what he means. More of the man who shot Michael.

Irving speaks in a hushed voice. "The current's not bad, but still swifter than I'd like. You'll have to move fast. Or you'll get dragged downstream."

"Where do I go on the other side?"

Simon points across the river. "They're waiting for you."

At first, I see nothing, but then a light flashes. Then two more. Their faces come into focus above the lights. Like they've been switched on too. Three faces with three sets of wide eyes. Waiting.

Irving looks both ways up and down the bank of the river. "Go now. It's clear."

"Thank you so much."

They tap their heads at the same time.

I tap mine in response and turn back to the water, thinking again of Vicki Lee's words. *Don't hesitate.* This all started in the water, and now it will end the same way. One way or the other. I look right, left, right like I'm crossing the street. Light filters through the trees. The sun is starting to rise.

It's clear. There's no reason to wait.

I run down the slope and dive in.

CHAPTER 87

The water here is even chillier than the Barren.

The cold hurts my head, and dizziness quickly overcomes me. I force myself to keep going. *I'm so close.* The current is stronger too. A lot stronger. I have no sense of how far I have to go. It feels much farther than it looked from the shoreline.

I tire quickly and pause to look for the faces on the other side. When I see their eyes on me, it gives me the will to keep going.

But the next time I look, I can't find them.

Where are they?

I see something moving in my periphery. One of them up shore, signaling me. I've drifted farther than I realized. I force myself to swim harder. I'm almost there.

But I'm swallowing too much water. I pause to catch my breath one more time. I've come too far to give up now. I will myself forward, lifting my heavy arms. And then I see it in front of me. The shore. It's so close I could throw a rock at it. I push myself harder, swinging my arms over my head like a windmill.

I'm five strokes away.

I'm going to make it.

I throw another arm forward, but as soon as I do, my knee slams against something under the water. A sharp pain shoots up my leg.

I pull my knee to my chest, trying to make it stop. But, when I do, I drift farther downstream. If I hold on until the pain is gone, who knows how far off course I'll be?

I have to keep going. I have to try.

I let go of my knee, the pain rushing back, and do the only thing I can. I finish those last few feet with just my arms, paddling my way to shore like a kid learning to swim.

I drag myself out of the river and check my knee. Blood streams down my leg. I glance up and down the shore, trying to get my bearings straight.

I'm not safe yet. I could still be shot.

I hear people racing through the trees, thrashing through foliage to get to me. I can't run—my knee is killing me—but I hobble as fast as I can for cover, propelling myself forward like a wounded animal. When I'm absolutely certain I'm safe, I fall to the ground, exhausted and out of breath.

When I look back, I can't see the river anymore. I can't see Irving or Simon either. But I know they're watching me. I know they witnessed what I did. And then it hits me.

I did it.

I escaped.

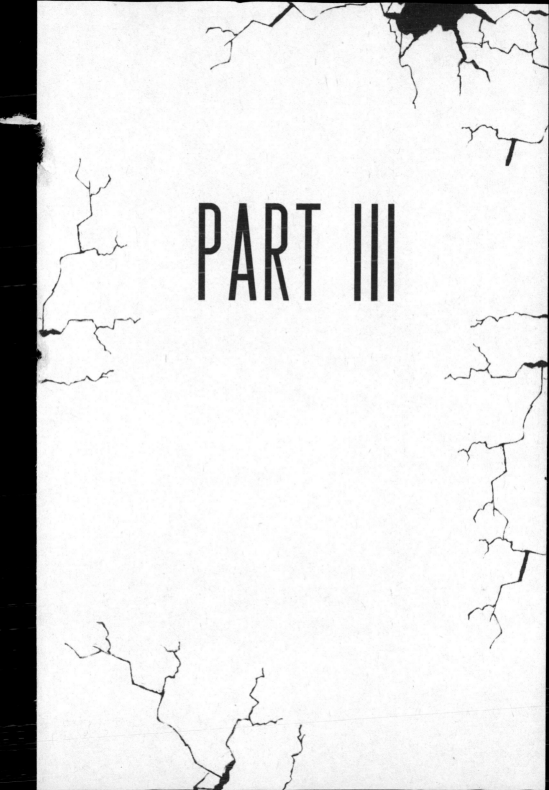

PART III

CHAPTER 88

The Jacobs Center smells like paint.

They're making improvements. A new wing will be finished by spring.

The resistance movement is growing quickly.

A week ago I didn't know there was a movement. I've learned so much in the past nine days I haven't had time to process it. And that's only what I've gleaned from my host family and the few higher-ups who've stopped by to check on me. This is my first official day at the Jacobs Center, the day I start my deprogramming.

I still have a lot to learn. In just over a week, it's become obvious how much they don't teach girls in New America. Just because we're born with another X chromosome. The two teenage girls in my host family—Zoey and Alex—know things about the world I can't even imagine. Like what photosynthesis is or why climate change means everyone here has solar panels. Or even what a chromosome is. I was horrified to learn extreme temperatures are not natural like they teach us in New America, but something much more harmful.

I didn't know any of this before I got here.

Nor do I know how to speak another language—Zoey speaks

Spanish, Alex Chinese. I don't have the slightest comprehension of advanced math either. Zoey showed me her calculus homework one night, and it looked like hieroglyphics, another word I didn't know until a few days ago. Thanks to Sister Helen and Sister Laura, I know a lot about books, but almost nothing about art and music since Mr. Jeffrey never told us what all those songs were really about, just providing the barest details. What's even worse is how little they taught us about history. Even though I read Anne Frank's diary, I'd never heard the word *Holocaust* before I got here. We were all watching the news one night, and I had to ask Ms. Ervick, Zoey and Alex's mother, what they were talking about when someone said the situation in New America was becoming more and more like the Holocaust.

Once she explained it to me, the newscaster's comment seemed ridiculous. New America isn't *that* bad.

The truth is, I'm learning my perception has been shaped by everything they taught us. It's hard to unlearn all those lessons, and sometimes I get overwhelmed. It's like I was living a fake life before, and I'm living a real life now. The only problem is my old fake life felt real and my new real life feels fake. Or maybe not fake. Just completely incomprehensible. Not to mention bigger than I ever imagined possible.

At home, I only interacted with my family and my classmates. And after grade school, I *barely* interacted with the boys at school. But now, in the real United States of America, I can interact with literally anyone I want. I can go to the mall with Alex and Zoey and talk to girls, boys, men, women. There are people here who don't define themselves that way too. And people who were told they're girls but feel like boys. And vice versa. The whole idea of gender is different. It's not the most important thing about you. It doesn't define you. Nor does it determine how you look. Zoey's hair is asymmetrical—long on one side and shaved on the other, showing off a small butterfly tattoo below her ear, while Alex's hair stops at her ears and is dyed green at the ends. If it weren't for their matching hazel eyes, I couldn't even tell they're sisters.

It's the same with dating. I can go out with anyone I want— boys, girls, anyone. And if I choose, I can have sex. I can get free birth control. There are even places where girls can get something called an abortion if they get pregnant. I'm pretty sure that's what they call infanticide in New America, but I'll admit I'm kind of confused by that. Zoey says only a woman can decide what happens to her body, and when I asked her about the baby, she said it's not a baby, which I'm not sure I understand, and that just makes me feel stupid. Or ignorant, as Dad said.

I'm desperate to leave my ignorance behind, but it's a slow process.

The thing is none of this was possible before. No one even talked about it. I'm so glad we can talk about *everything* here. But sometimes, the avalanche of possibility scares me. How am I supposed to figure out what I want?

All of this is going through my head as Ms. Ervick walks me through the halls of the Jacobs Center. I have an appointment at nine with Dr. Fineberg. She's the psychologist who will oversee my transition. Even though I met Dr. B during my escape, I was still shocked when I learned women could be doctors here. Ms. Ervick and the girls were equally shocked by my response. "Don't you think women should be allowed to be doctors?" Alex asked me.

"I don't know."

"You don't *know*?" She didn't bother to hide the skepticism in her voice.

"I guess I never thought about it." I pull on my bottom lip without thinking but force myself to let go when I realize I'm doing it. "It's not that I don't think they should be doctors. It's that it doesn't seem real. It just happens on TV."

That's the only thing I'm even remotely knowledgeable about besides books—TV shows and movies. If it weren't for those things, I'd be even more ignorant than I already am.

"This is it." Ms. Ervick pushes open a glass door with the word DEPROGRAMMING etched across it.

While she holds the door for me, I notice again how she dresses. She's wearing a tight skirt that stops an inch above her knees with high-heeled boots. Women in New America aren't allowed to wear skirts or dresses that short. And even if they were, I doubt anyone would. But Ms. Ervick, who's in her forties, wears clothes every day that would get you arrested where I come from. I've never known a woman who kept her maiden name either. She's Ms. Ervick, and her husband is Mr. Koffi. Each of the girls has one of their parents' last names: Zoey Ervick and Alex Koffi. I've also never known a woman who has a job like Ms. Ervick's—a career, not just a job. She's a biologist and not only went to college but also graduate school. Then there's her confidence. Ms. Ervick is the single most confident woman I've ever met. That might be why she doesn't seem to notice me examining her as she tilts her head in the direction of the waiting room.

I could use some of Ms. Ervick's confidence right now. I'm about to start my new life, and it feels like the first day of kindergarten all over again. What if I can't do it? What if I'm not smart enough?

What if I liked my life better before?

CHAPTER 89

t turns out Dr. Fineberg is easy to talk to. It's almost easier to talk to her than Zoey and Alex, who sometimes laugh at me when I admit what I don't know. Dr. Fineberg never laughs. She tells me she understands. It's her favorite thing to say.

On my second day, Dr. Fineberg jumps right in, not even bothering with the small talk we made the day before. "Stella, we need to talk about Sister Helen."

"What about her?"

"About what happened to her."

A shiver goes up my spine. *About what happened to her?* Now I know for sure. Sister Helen was murdered. Why else would Dr. Fineberg say it like that?

"Do you know what happened, Stella?"

"I don't *know*, but—"

"You suspect?"

I nod before glancing out the window. Dr. Fineberg's office has a view of the bay, and I could stare out the window the entire time. It makes me think of Mateo in Musical Expression, gazing out the window with longing. "So who did it?" I ask without looking at her.

"We don't know yet, but the autopsy did show she was poisoned—"

"Poisoned?" That's what those police officers, Poole and Alvarez, thought too. "Was it my mother?"

Dr. Fineberg takes in a quick breath, but when I flip my attention in her direction, she recovers quickly, hiding her surprise. "Your mother? Why would you think that, Stella?"

"She always hated Sister Helen." For the first time, I realize how true it is. Mom couldn't stand Sister Helen. "From the moment Sister Helen arrived, Mom hated her, but she couldn't do anything about it. So she gave up on me."

Dr. Fineberg leans back and writes something in her file. "That doesn't mean she killed her, Stella."

"No, it doesn't." I glance out the window again. Small waves crest into foamy white caps. If this is how beautiful the bay looks, I can't even imagine what the ocean will be like. "But I found something."

"What kind of something?"

"Well, it wasn't really a *thing*. It was a message."

"Yes?" Dr. Fineberg asks.

I'm supposed to go on. But going on means telling on my own mother. What if Dr. Fineberg alerts the authorities? What if it goes in her file? If Mom wants to come to real America someday, am I ruining her chances?

"If you're not ready, Stella, you don't have to tell me. Wait until it feels right. But don't forget—whatever you say to me will stay between us."

I gaze out the window again. "Someone sent her a message." I turn back to her. "One of her friends. Right after Sister Helen died."

Dr. Fineberg doesn't respond. She's strong enough to wait forever if she has to.

"The message said, *I guess this means there's one less chaperone in the world.*"

Dr. Fineberg offers me a frown. "That must have really hurt you, Stella. I know how close you were to Sister Helen."

I don't answer. I don't have to. She knows she's right.

"But, in reality, we don't really know what that message meant. It could've meant something different than you thought. It could have been about your mother's perception of the chaperone system as a whole, not *your* chaperone."

"My mother loved the chaperone program. It gave her an excuse to ignore me."

I want Dr. Fineberg to respond to my harsh words, but her face remains impossible to read.

"I understand it may have seemed that way, Stella." I must not look convinced because she adds, "It's always possible your mother was involved with what happened to Sister Helen, but it's unlikely too."

"Why?"

"Whoever did this was a Minuteman. They're the ones we're fighting. Not people like your mother."

"But why would they kill Sister Helen?"

"Oh." Dr. Fineberg puts a finger on her chin. "I thought you knew."

"Knew what?"

She hesitates, but now I'm the one who waits her out.

"Sister Helen was one of us, Stella. She was part of the resistance. A sleeper chaperone. And we have reason to believe she'd been found out. The only thing we don't know yet is if the powers-that-be sanctioned her killing. Sometimes individuals in the party act on their own. They have the authority to do so if the situation warrants itself. That's another reason we're glad you got out. Once the Minutemen learned about Sister Helen, we worried they'd started watching you more closely too."

"A sleeper chaperone?"

"That's what we call chaperones who work to change things from the inside."

"How?"

"Well, it's different for each of them. Some of them are sending us information. Others are teaching their charges to think for themselves. Maybe even resist."

I touch the pendant at the base of my neck. The *white* pendant. The color of resistance. All of the books Sister Helen and Sister Laura gave me. We spent *hours* talking about the women in those books. How strong they were. How heroic. Sister Helen was the first person who gave me a book written by a woman. Harper Lee. I'll never forget it. And Sister Laura is the one who taught me to embrace change. "That's what Sister Helen was doing?"

"That was some of it, yes."

I sense Dr. Fineberg is hiding something, but the set of her jaw tells me I'm not going to get it out of her. Not yet.

"And Sister Laura? I know Sister Helen chose her for me."

"She's a sleeper too."

"Wow, I guess I got lucky twice."

Dr. Fineberg clears her throat. "It wasn't luck, Stella."

What is she talking about?

"We look for certain kinds of people. We've recruited a number of chaperones to the resistance. More and more all the time." Sister Laura said the same thing. *There are more of us every day.* "And young women too. You were chosen, Stella."

I feel my mouth drop open. "Me? But why?"

"You tested very well as a child. Your IQ is higher than most, but not too high, which is often a disadvantage."

I've never heard anything about this. *Never.* "You're kidding, right? I would know about something like that, wouldn't I?"

"I'm not kidding at all. They didn't tell you because they don't want girls who are smart to know it. You're good with people too. You can read situations, think on your feet." Dr. Fineberg taps her pen against her pad of paper. "There's something else. Do you remember when you refused to continue with ballet? In kindergarten?"

"I hated those classes. They kept telling us to swirl around and pretend we were leaves. It was like they thought we were stupid."

"We look for that kind of behavior too. We flag girls like that."

"You picked me because I refused to go to ballet?"

"Refusing to do something everyone else is doing is a sign of being able to think for yourself, Stella. Don't underestimate what you did. In your own way, you were resisting. That's one of the reasons Sister Helen was assigned to you. And Sister Laura too. And that's why it was important to keep her in the dark about your escape. If they found out, who knows what would happen?"

"They'd kill her too."

It's like the story about the cave. They kill anyone who talks about life on the outside.

"Maybe," Dr. Fineberg says, "but there's no question for me anymore. I know it's true.

If they find out about Sister Laura, they'll kill her too.

CHAPTER 90

After I meet with Dr. Fineberg each morning, I attend training with the other escapees. There are nine of us right now, and more are on the way. Apparently hundreds of girls have already been through this.

The girls they told us were missing? They weren't missing. They escaped. The Minutemen just wanted us to believe they were kidnapped to scare us, to keep us in line. That's what they teach us at the Jacobs Center. The truth about New America.

I walk into the training room the next morning, wondering what new secrets they'll tell us. Then I see her.

Willow Howard.

I was right. She wasn't kidnapped. She escaped.

She's wearing tight jeans, black boots, and a T-shirt that falls off her bare shoulder. There's no sign of a bra. The only noticeable difference about the way I dress is Sister Helen's white pendant. I wear it every day now that I'm allowed to wear what I want. Willow appears to be adapting better to her new surroundings. I'm still studying her from the door when Willow's eyes land on me.

"Sequins?" she yells across the room.

I am instantly overcome, fighting tears I never expected. Willow is the first person I've seen who I know from New America, and hearing her call out to me like that—even a nickname I can't stand—takes me back to all I've left behind.

Willow jumps up from her desk and runs across the room. When she reaches me, I immediately notice how good she smells—like someone who just stepped out of the shower, a sharp contrast to the musty scent of her clothes back home.

"Is it really you?"

"It's really me."

"I never thought you—" She holds her hands up in front of her. "Wait, when did you get here?"

"Last week. Yesterday was my first day."

"I had to get my physical yesterday."

"How was that?" My physical is scheduled for a month from now, and I'm terrified.

"It was like being probed on an alien spaceship."

I let out a little laugh.

"It was not fun. Let me tell you."

For the first time, I get that Willow is funny. I couldn't see her clearly when we were in a world that didn't make sense to either of us.

"But I don't understand," she says. "Why are you here? I thought you liked being the queen of Bull Run Prep."

"I was hardly the queen."

"You were one of them, Sequins. Wait…is this because…is it because Russell wouldn't let you talk in class?"

"I mean, that's part of it. But there's so much more."

"You just seemed so…I don't know…into it. You really acted the part."

"I was trying to make the best of it. I thought if I played along, it wouldn't bother me as much."

"Wow." Willow's eyes grow big. "I guess that proves you can never really tell about a person."

"No, you really can't."

The last time I saw Willow she was walking out the door of the HH party with a wad of cash in her pocket. A wad of *my* cash. The money could not have been better spent.

"I can't believe it's really you. I can't believe you're here." Willow lets out a tiny sniffle and wipes her eyes. "It's just such a relief to see someone I know."

All of a sudden, I'm sniffing too. But instead of feeling sad, it seems like a win.

CHAPTER 91

Winning isn't hard in real America. It happens every day. After I finish at the Jacobs Center, Zoey talks me into going to the mall with her, and she drives us there.

By herself.

In her own car.

She doesn't even make a big deal about it. This is *normal* for her. I don't know *any* girls who drive, but teenage girls in real America do it all the time.

Zoey's engine turns on as we walk up. The doors unlock. I've never seen an electric car before. Zoey asks what kind of cars we have in New America.

"Just regular cars. You know, with gas."

"You mean, like the kind old people drive?"

I don't admit that everyone drives them no matter how old they are.

At the mall, we stroll through store after store, holding earrings up to our faces and trying on T-shirts over our clothes. I've never been shopping without my mother or a chaperone. Zoey has no

clue what a big deal this is for me. We're about to get on the esca-
lator when two twentysomething guys stop right in front of us,
blocking our way. The one with long hair stands closer to us while
his friend hangs back.

"You girls looking to party?"

"We're *only* seventeen." There's so much indignation in Zoey's
voice only a person in the parking lot couldn't hear it.

"We can help you out with that. Buy you some beer. Hook you
up." The long-haired guy elbows his friend and smiles. "I mean, for
a price, of course." He winks at Zoey.

"That's disgusting." Her sour expression sends the same message.

"It doesn't have to be."

"Why are you even talking to us? You're, like, fifty years old."

My mouth drops at Zoey's audacity, but she's just getting
started.

"What happened? Did you strike out with all the senior ladies?"

A funny look appears on his face. An I-didn't-see-that-coming
look. His friend drops his head with a shake, embarrassed.

Zoey doesn't wait for a response. She turns to me, says, "Let's
get out of here," and walks right past the guys as they watch us go.

I'm completely astonished by her behavior, but I don't dare tell
her. Instead I follow her and wonder how long it will be until any
of this makes sense.

CHAPTER 92

During lunch the next day, Willow drags me to a table at the edge of the cafeteria.

"So what happened, Sequins?" she asks. "How did you get out?"

I look over my shoulder before I answer, a habit I can't seem to break. "I asked my chaperone—"

"Wait." Willow drops her fork. "You asked *your chaperone* for help? Like you could trust her? Are you kidding me?"

"No, I'm not kidding."

"How is that even possible?"

I search the room again.

"What is it? Tell me." She sounds insistent, but I don't want to betray Sister Laura.

"I guess it doesn't matter what I say. No one is listening, right?"

Willow shakes her head. "I seriously doubt it."

"Dr. Fineberg told me Sister Laura...well, she's..."

"Out with it, Sequins."

"I guess she's a sleeper chaperone."

Willow leans back in her chair. Admiration oozes out of her. "Oh, that is so badass."

I work hard not to flinch. "You know about sleeper chaperones?"

"Sure, everyone here does. They're *amazing*. There's not much braver than going undercover with all those creepy Minutemen, is there?"

"Probably not."

Willow lifts her chin to the ceiling. "Jesus." This time I do flinch, but at least she doesn't notice. "I would never even *consider* doing that myself."

"Me neither."

"So what did she say when you asked?"

"She couldn't help me herself. It's too dangerous. She introduced me to someone who could. A woman named Angel."

"Angel? That's who got me out too!"

"I think she did it for a lot of girls."

"I'm sure."

"So I wonder who's helping them now."

"What? Why would you say that?"

I try to swallow the food in my mouth, but a piece of meat gets stuck in my throat. I choke the words out. "You don't know?"

"Know what?"

I can't say it. I can't say out loud that Angel is dead because of me.

Willow puts both hands on the table and leans forward. "Tell me, Stella."

It's the first time she's ever called me Stella.

How can I tell her the truth? She'll hate me.

"Are you crying?" Willow offers me her crumpled napkin, studying me while I dab my eyes. Then she puts it together. "Oh my God." She looks away, her gaze roaming frantically across the cafeteria. She's clearly trying to hold it together, but when she looks back to me, her eyes brim with tears. "She's dead, isn't she? Angel's dead."

I nod the tiniest bit.

"You were there?"

I nod again, too horrified to speak.

The two of us sit there. Not talking. Not eating. Just crying and remembering the brave woman who saved us.

CHAPTER 93

A t the mall that weekend, Zoey leads me to the food court, where she says a bunch of her friends are *dying* to meet me. Is this what it's like to be free? You decide you want to go somewhere or do something, and then you just do it. You don't have to ask permission, you don't have to drag your chaperone along, you don't have to plan weeks in advance.

You just do it.

Five tables in the food court are pushed together. I expect to meet a couple of girls. Maybe three or four. But there are *dozens* of people. Girls *and* boys and people I can tell are what Zoey and Alex call nonbinary. I've never had a friend who isn't a girl in my entire life, much less someone who isn't defined by gender.

The chairs are askew. Two boys sit cross-legged on top of a table gazing into each other's eyes. One girl has her feet propped up. Another girl sits in someone's lap. Zoey introduces them all to me. Her best friend, Sara Ann, says, "You are *so* amazing, Stella. I want to hug you. Can I hug you?"

"I guess." I shrug because how can you say no to a hug?

Sara Ann's hug leads to more. Soon everyone is hugging me.

I haven't touched this many people in years. Since kindergarten when you couldn't go a day without another kid running up and embracing you for no reason.

The result is electric.

Their acceptance ricochets through my body like lightning. Is this connection? Is this what other people experience their whole lives?

Is this what they've stolen from us?

We see an R-rated movie about a gorgeous female superhero who makes really sarcastic comments while saving the world. She reminds me of Zoey. There's a ton of sex and violence, and I can't believe we're all sitting in the theater watching this together, laughing and screaming the whole time. Like it's perfectly acceptable behavior.

Zoey orders extra-large popcorn and slushies for both of us on her phone, and it sends her a message when they're ready. I've never seen anyone pay with a phone before. Mom always used cash, which Zoey calls "super old school." I don't tell her sometimes Mom ran out of money and had the bill sent home to Dad. Or that I wasn't allowed to buy *anything at all* until I turned eighteen. She already thinks I'm the weirdest person she's ever met. Though she also says she likes that about me.

"Let's go now," Zoey whispers in the dark. "This fight scene is going to last *forever.*"

Even though I don't see a single person working in the lobby, our food waits for us. Where did it come from? Who put it there? Zoey takes a bite of popcorn, so I do the same. It doesn't taste like any popcorn I've ever had before. It's warm and thick with butter. At home, popcorn tastes like salted cardboard.

"Why is this so good?"

"I got it with real butter." Zoey winks at me.

I shake my head in awe. Popcorn with real butter?

Back in the theater, several of Zoey's friends have their arms wrapped around each other and not just boy-girl couples. Some are boy-boy and girl-girl. One couple kisses every time there's a slow scene. Even a few rows away, I can hear them slobbering all over each other. No one else seems to notice. They all act like this is acceptable behavior. Like it's *normal*.

Maybe Sister Laura was right.

This is all perfectly normal.

Maybe this is how normal teenagers act.

CHAPTER 94

We get back to Zoey's house around eight. An unfamiliar vehicle is parked in the driveway.

Inside we find Zoey's parents sitting with a woman who looks the same age they are.

"Stella!" The woman jumps up, crosses the room, and pulls me into her arms. "Oh my God, Stella, I am *so* happy to see you."

I try not to cringe. When she lets go of me, I say, "Do I know you?"

"You have no idea who I am, do you?"

I shake my head.

"I figured you would've seen my picture."

"Your picture?"

"From college. Your mother and I were roommates. At Baylor."

I know Mom went to Baylor University, but she never said anything about a roommate, never mentioned college at all. She and Dad graduated before New America was founded, and they never talked about life before then.

"She didn't tell you about me?"

I don't know what to say. How do I tell this woman Mom never uttered a single word about her?

She nods. "I guess it makes sense. It's not like your mom could tell you about our days living in a coed dorm and getting drunk at frat parties every weekend."

My mouth drops, but the woman doesn't seem to notice.

"The truth is, she probably can't talk about me at all. But I did want to meet you, Stella." She holds her hand out to shake. "My name is Rose. Rose Stallard."

I ignore her hand. "I'm sorry I've never heard of anyone named Rose."

"Your mom and I message each other all the time. I'm so sad she never told you."

"You message each other? You mean, on the internet?"

"Yes, almost every day."

"Wait…are you…are you RoseinReality?"

Rose smiles at the same time that my jaw clenches. "So your mom *did* mention me?"

"No, she didn't." Everyone is staring, waiting for me to explain. "But I saw what you said about Sister Helen."

Rose's hand drops back to her side. "What are you talking about?"

"The message you sent Mom." Rose's face doesn't convey recognition, so I go on. "After Sister Helen died, you said you were glad there was one less chaperone in the world."

Rose shakes her head. "I didn't say that."

"Yes, you did. I saw it."

Rose puts her hand on her head for a second like she has a headache. "Oh, no, Stella, you completely misunderstood. I didn't say I was *glad*. I merely pointed out there was one *less* chaperone."

"Exactly."

"Meaning one less person indoctrinating young women into a life of subservience."

Zoey and her parents look from Rose to me, waiting for my response. But Rose's words don't make any sense. Why would my mother care about that? She's one of the most subservient people I know.

"What?"

"Stella?" Rose steps closer to me and grabs my arm. "Your mother is very worried about you. She messaged me as soon as you went missing. I posted about you right away, but it took me weeks to find you." Rose smiles at Ms. Ervick and Mr. Koffi. They smile back, but I can tell they're nervous. "Still, I promise I won't tell her anything without your permission. I wouldn't do that. It's up to you."

"Is she going to make me go back if you do?"

"Of course not, Stella." Rose finally lets go of me. "Why would she do that?"

"Because escaping is against the law. I'm sure she's furious."

"Your mother is *not* angry, Stella." Rose's hand goes to her mouth. "Your mother *wanted* you to get out."

"What are you talking about?"

"She always dreamed you'd escape."

"She did?"

"Of course. She doesn't want her daughters growing up in that...that..." Rose's words come out like spit. "That place. With those...those fascists."

The equilibrium drops out of me.

Mom didn't want me to stay in New America?

"I know a big part of her wanted to leave too."

Mom wanted me to leave? I put my hand on the back of the leather chair in front of me.

Zoey turns to me. "Are you okay, Stella?"

"I'm okay." I look directly in Rose's eyes. "When did she say she wanted to leave?"

"Back when New America started. When women were leaving in droves. But she was in love with your father. I'll admit he's quite a force. And honestly he worships her. She was always so beautiful. He put her on a pedestal, which is not always the best foundation for a healthy relationship. So she stayed. And then it was too late for her to get out. But she would've done anything she could to help you, Stella. She told me about the money—"

"What money?"

"Didn't you find the money? Isn't that how you got out? She said she left money for you to find."

I flash back to the first time I saw Mom putting a roll of money in the flour sifter. And the time I saw her carelessly drop the stamps, one-hundred-dollar bills falling to the floor like leaves. I caught her doing things like that all the time. Had I really caught her? Or did she *want* me to see it? "She did?"

"Of course, Stella. It's sad that's all she felt like she could do for you. She certainly couldn't talk to you about leaving. Not with your father around."

"What do you mean?"

"I mean, your dad, Stella…" Rose looks away from me for the first time since I walked into the room. Her gaze moves from Ms. Ervick to Mr. Koffi to Zoey and then back to me. "You do know about him, don't you?"

"No." I look at Zoey and her parents to see if they know what she's talking about. But all three of them have blank looks on their faces. "I don't."

Rose takes a deep breath and wraps her arms around her torso. She looks out the window, as if someone might be out there listening. "He's one of them, Stella. He's a Minuteman."

CHAPTER 95

I can't fall asleep.

It's a problem I've had every night I've been here. Except for the first night when I fell into bed like a zombie and slept for sixteen hours straight. My room at the Ervick-Koffis' is nice enough even though it's less than half the size of my room at home. I have a comfortable bed with a soft mattress and organic bedding, a beautiful antique desk, and my own smart screen with access to the internet whenever I want it.

But I'm still not comfortable here.

I feel like an imposter. Or maybe it's more accurate to say I feel like a visitor. A visitor to another planet. An alien among kind strangers.

Tomorrow is my eighteenth birthday. No one here knows that. I'm not sure how to bring it up. I'm not even sure I want to. What would happen if I did? Zoey and Alex would plan a party of some kind. Ms. Ervick would bake a cake. Actually she wouldn't bake it. She'd buy it. Ms. Ervick doesn't cook at all. Most nights dinner is delivered to the front door. And if she knew about my birthday, she'd order an expensive cake from a bakery online, and, like everything else I eat now, it would be the most delicious thing I've ever tasted in my life because it would be made with real ingredients. Real sugar. Real butter. Real calories. And then they'd all get together and sing "Happy Birthday" to me, which would just make me want to cry.

How can I be so happy and so sad at the same time?

I stare at the ceiling and listen to the noise machine. Ms. Ervick bought it for me when I mentioned I was having trouble sleeping. Everyone here has them. Its constant hum reminds me of the humidifier Mom used to put in my room whenever I got sick.

Every night I lie in bed and wonder what's going on at home. Is anyone worried about me? Are Bonita and Liv freaking out? Did Mateo figure out what I was trying to tell him? Do any of them know I escaped? Or do they all believe I've been kidnapped? Have I become a cautionary tale? Are the Minutemen using me to scare girls into submission?

But every time I long for home, I remind myself how much more I know now.

Dad is one of them.

A Minuteman.

Like Joseph. Like the men who raped Sister Laura's sister. Like whoever killed Sister Helen. Does he know what they're capable of?

That's why the constables were always coming to see him. That's why it seemed like *he* was the one giving *them* orders. That's why he wanted me to marry Joseph. Why he didn't like Sister Laura standing up to him. And if he's one of them, he has power. They *all* have power. Even the constables. And Dad is no constable. He's head of one of the biggest companies in New America. He probably gives them money. He's probably one of the biggest donors in the country. That's why Mom said we'd never be shunned. She knows. Of course she does.

Dr. Fineberg said teaching me to think for myself had been *one* of Sister Helen's roles with the resistance. Was the other spying on Dad? Is that why she was killed?

And if he really is one of them, does he know I wasn't kidnapped? Does he know I escaped? I always knew Dad would be angry when he got up in the morning and found me gone, but if he's really a member of the Minuteman Party, I can't imagine how enraged he must be. Or how hard that must be for Mom. I'm sure he's taking it out on her.

Mom.

I can't get over what Rose told me about her. Is that why Mom never said anything? Is that why she kept her mouth shut when Dad went on his rants about Old America? Was she afraid of him? As Rose hugged me goodbye, she said she couldn't wait to tell Mom I was okay.

Mom always kept Shea close. She was always holding Shea's hand or patting her back. As if they were attached. Mom was like that when I was little too. But she erected a wall between us once Sister Helen arrived. She was never cruel, but she kept her distance. When I picture the two of us, I always imagine space between us. As if touching each other would be painful. Was it painful for Mom to be near me? Or was she pushing me away for a reason?

Was she pushing me away so I would leave?

CHAPTER 96

When I return to the Jacobs Center Monday morning, I come face-to-face with Sister Helen.

Or a photo of her anyway.

Someone must have hung it over the weekend. There are hundreds of photos on this wall. Everyone who's died fighting the Minutemen. Only it doesn't say *Sister Helen* under her photo. It says, HELEN SIMPSON, SLEEPER CHAPERONE.

I put my finger on the pendant at the base of my neck.

She died exactly three months ago today. How long will it be until they hang Angel's picture?

Next to Helen—it's hard not to think of her as *Sister* Helen—is a photo of a girl who looks to be my age. There aren't many pictures of teenage girls on this wall. Under the photo, it reads GINGER REEVE. We learned about her yesterday. She tried to escape but got caught in a current and drowned. I could've ended up like Ginger.

At least she'll be remembered.

At least no one will forget she tried to get out.

Our team leader, Ms. Norrod, tells us about the chaperone program. How it came to be, how it works, what they don't want us to know about it. It's weird how much I love training here. Every day brings a new revelation. I can't wait to get here each morning.

"It's not as hard as you might think to flip chaperones and recruit them to our side."

I'm surprised to hear Ms. Norrod say this, but the indifferent looks on the other girls' faces tell me nothing would surprise them.

"In fact, that's our goal. To turn the chaperone program into a wing of the resistance."

Like Dr. Fineberg, Ms. Norrod has an eerie sense of calm about her. Nothing seems to rattle her.

"Many of the women who become chaperones hate New America and all it stands for."

"Then why become chaperones?" Willow asks without raising her hand.

This is something we do here. Jump in without raising our hands or asking Ms. Norrod's permission. It's not unusual for the nine of us to devolve into an intense debate. After what happened in Russell's class, it's one of my favorite things about my new life. The freedom to speak.

"They don't have much in the way of choices, Willow. Women in New America can get married and have kids, they can work as a servant of some kind, or they can become a chaperone."

"What about college?" I ask.

A couple of girls in the back laugh. Willow shoots them a dirty look before turning to me. "College is just for show, Stella."

"For show?"

Ms. Norrod jumps in. "It's not that simple, Willow." She turns to me. "Since they don't let women hold professional jobs, Stella, there isn't any real reason for women to go to college. Of course, they can go for the sole purpose of becoming more educated, but even then—"

"It's a joke," one of the girls in the back says. "Trust me, I tried it."

I turn and look at her. Her name is Tracy. She's wearing a strapless white jumpsuit. I can't imagine her in New America.

Ms. Norrod holds a hand up in disagreement. "I wouldn't say it's a joke."

"You wouldn't?" Tracy asks.

Ms. Norrod lets out a quick sigh. "Okay, you're right. It's a joke. Just like high school, all they teach you is to behave."

Is it true? Is college just as worthless as high school?

"Then why even let girls go?" I ask.

Ms. Norrod turns back to me. "I'm not sure, Stella. Maybe they think it will distract them. Maybe they think girls who go to college will feel better about their lives. Did you plan to go?"

"Yes, of course."

"They push smart girls like you toward college to keep you happy. If you're focused on studying, applying to college, graduating, they figure you won't think about the fact that you'll never have a real career."

"It's a pacifier," Tracy says.

"Pretty much," Ms. Norrod admits. "That's why they teach you gossip is a sin. So you won't talk to each other or compare notes. Like you're doing now. It's another way to control you." Ms. Norrod shakes her head. "Of course, some girls figure this out. I'm sure you all did. Isn't that why you're here? You realized something was wrong."

"Thank God," Willow says under her breath.

"And that's why some women who hate the system still choose to become chaperones. They don't see any point in going to college. They don't want to get married and have babies."

"Is that why so many chaperones are gay?" A girl named Rafaela asks. She's the one who got here the same day I did.

I turn to Willow. *Are they?*

Willow shrugs. It might be the first time she's admitted to not knowing something.

"Well, I wouldn't say 'so many,' but yes, some women who are gay choose to become chaperones," Ms. Norrod admits. "If you were a gay woman, would you want to get married to a man and have his babies?"

Everyone laughs. I immediately think of Liv on homecoming night.

I can't do it. I just can't.

"That's why it's not terribly difficult to recruit chaperones to our side. Yes, chaperones have more freedom than other women in New America, but they're still not free. They still can't do things women can do here. No matter who you are, being a woman is dangerous in New America."

"What do you mean?" a girl named Jamaine says from the front of the room.

Ms. Norrod lets out a slow breath before she continues. "I know you're all well aware of the things women aren't allowed to do, but what you may not realize is how the Minutemen enforce those rules."

I flash back to all the red SUVS racing around town.

Ms. Norrod looks each of us in the eye, making sure she has our attention. "What you may not know is they've killed women who dared to resist."

No one says a word. I peek at Willow. Her eyes are as wide as mine. She shrugs at me for only the second time in her life.

"What I'm trying to tell you," Ms. Norrod explains, "is that every woman in New America is in danger of being murdered. Men there can legally kill a woman they believe has broken the rules of their society. They don't even have to prove it. They can merely say they felt it to be true."

The room is so quiet I hear the second hand of the clock whirring around its face.

Ms. Norrod continues.

"The worst example of this happened when you were still girls. In a town now called Appomattox."

Appomattox?

"Six men in that town decided they were going to put women in their place. They went from house to house searching for women they could arrest. Or worse. They were vigilantes, plain and simple. They were out for blood and wouldn't be stopped. They wanted to find women they could kill. They called themselves the Appomattox Six."

CHAPTER 97

W hat did you just say?" Every head swivels in my direction. "Did you say the Appomattox Six?"

"Yes, I did, Stella. Do you know about them?"

I don't answer, searching the others' faces to see if anyone else has heard of them. But no one shows any sign of recognition. Instead they all stare like my face has turned blue.

"I've heard of them, but I don't know what they did."

"As I said, they went out looking for women who were not going along. In under a month, they killed two different women." *Killed? Did she say killed?* "But that was just the beginning. Before they were caught, they killed eleven more women."

Several girls in the room gasp, but I can't even move.

They killed eleven more women?

"These women were holding secret meetings. Trying to get a movement started to fight the Minutemen."

"Good for them," Willow says, pulling my attention from Ms. Norrod for a split second.

"Yes, I agree, Willow, but unfortunately, they didn't succeed. These men learned of their plans and went after them."

Are these the men Sister Laura and Dr. B were talking about?

"They gathered in an abandoned Episcopal church. No one knows exactly what happened that night. What we do know is these men went to the church with the intent of putting an end to their meetings. And that's exactly what they did. They stormed the church, launching a Molotov cocktail into the nave."

"A what cocktail?" Rafaela asks.

"A Molotov cocktail. A homemade bomb you make with just a bottle, a gas-soaked rag, and a match."

Jamaine lets out a soft whimper. "Oh, no." She's the sweetest in our group but also the most prone to tears.

"Precisely. The church was under construction. The bomb hit some scaffolding inside the front door, knocking a can of paint thinner to the ground. The lumber on the floor immediately caught on fire. According to testimony, the front entrance of the church was engulfed in seconds. The men who were responsible claimed they figured the women would flee out the back. But what they didn't know—or *said* they didn't know—was that the rear doors had been removed and plywood had been nailed over the opening. That was their story anyway."

Someone in the back lets out a noise that sounds like a cross between a growl and a cry.

"The women were trapped inside. The front entrance was blazing, and the rear was blocked. They couldn't get out."

"What about the windows?" Tracy asks.

"They were very high. Over ten feet off the ground. Impossible to reach."

"So what happened to the women inside?" Jamaine asks.

Doesn't she know? Doesn't she get it?

"I'm sorry to have to tell you this, Jamaine, but those women...
they were burned alive."

I can't sleep that night.

Every time I close my eyes, I picture those eleven women.

Frantic. Trapped. Terrified. Their knuckles raw from banging
furiously against the back wall. Screaming to be let out.

What kind of person would help those men?

What kind of person would come to their defense?

What kind of person is my father?

CHAPTER 98

The next day I tell Dr. Fineberg everything.

Everything.

Rose. Dad. Sister Laura's sister. When I get to the part about the A6, Dr. Fineberg reaches out and puts her hand on my knee.

"Stella, look at me."

I lift my eyes.

"Stella, you need to slow down. Just breathe, okay?"

Her words trigger an inhale. I count to ten, hold my breath, and then count backward as I exhale.

"Feel better?" I nod, and she leans back. "I'm not sure what to say, Stella."

"Aren't you shocked?"

Dr. Fineberg's eyes narrow. Either side of her mouth pulls up, but she's not smiling. She's thinking. "I understand, Stella, why it might surprise you to learn this about your father, but the truth is, we've known he was a Minuteman for some time."

So it's true. Dad really is one of them.

"You knew?"

"To be honest, Stella, that's another reason why you were chosen. So we could get closer to him. We target households like yours."

"Why didn't you tell me?"

"You weren't ready."

It's the same thing Sister Laura said when I asked her about the A6. *You're not ready... Knowing what happened would only hurt you.*

"I was working up to it," Dr. Fineberg explains. "And this"— she gestures toward me—"is why. It's formidable. You're processing a lot of information. On the one hand, you feel relieved to share all of it. On the other, you feel overwhelmed by how big it is. And how awful."

"It *is* awful. Completely awful." I'm talking too fast again. My voice is getting louder. I take in another slow breath and look out the window. The water in the bay is violent today, the waves rolling on top of each other. Like it says in that song Mateo gave me, *a boat could go lost.*

"He helped those men. He helped them get off. Murderers. What kind of person would do that?"

"I want you to know, Stella, that even though he was clearly in the wrong, I believe your father thought he was doing the right thing."

"But how?"

"You told me he claimed he was trying to solve a problem. I think he was referring to what was happening in New America at that time. The A6 tore that brand-new country apart. Even skeptical people were willing to go along with things they didn't think were right, but not that. Not burning people alive. Not killing those women. For a while, it seemed like the country might descend into chaos and maybe even civil war. Honestly, I wish the resistance had been up and running back then because that's when New America was at its most vulnerable. We could've easily taken them down."

"I wish you had."

"Me too." Dr. Fineberg lifts her pen to her mouth but doesn't bite it. "But we can't go back and play the What If? game. What we can do is work through your feelings about your father. He knew how vulnerable the country was. He was worried it would fall apart. So he helped those men by paying for their defense. I don't know everything about the case, but I do know they initially weren't going to plead guilty. And when they did, people felt vindicated. I'd like to think your dad played a role in that."

"He was still wrong."

"Perhaps, but another part of becoming an adult is realizing that even people who do bad things sometimes have good intentions. And that's true of those in the Minutemen Party too."

"I hate them."

"I understand, Stella."

"How can I just sit here and do nothing?"

"You're not doing nothing, Stella. You're training to be part of the resistance."

"But how much can I really do on the outside?"

"More than you realize."

"It's not enough," I insist, and suddenly I realize how right I am.

If I stay here—in real America—my life will be easy. No, I won't ever see my family or friends again, but I'll be free. Free to go to college. Free to get a job. To drive. To have my own bank account. To have sex. Free to speak whenever I want. And even though some part of me will always be back in Bull Run, I'll still be able to make my own choices.

But if I go back, I can try to change things. I can be a spy. A sleeper chaperone. Like Sister Helen. Like Sister Laura. I can help people. I can teach girls to think for themselves, show them the truth about New America. Maybe even help them escape. I can recruit people to our cause. Bonita. Liv. Maybe there'd be so many of us they'd have no choice but to change things.

But can I do it? Am I brave enough to risk my life? I might end up shunned or in prison. Or worse. I might end up like Sister Helen.

The truth hits me like a jab to the throat. *How can I not do it?*

"What are you saying, Stella?"

I focus on Dr. Fineberg. I'd almost forgotten she was there. I look her in the eye.

"I'm saying I have to go back. I have to go back and fight."

CHAPTER 99

I t happens five months later.

That's how long it takes to finish my training at the Jacobs Center.

This time I cross at Harpers Ferry. When we get to the water's edge, our caravan leaves the roadway for the gravel towpath. Our SUV moves slowly over the bumps and grooves. A hawk swoops over the steel-colored water.

There are about fifteen of us. Zoey and Alex and their parents are allowed to come with me, but it's not safe for Willow. The rest of our group is FBI. They've helped with my training too. Today there are ten agents, the first people I've seen in real America with guns. They don't look *that* different from constables. They wear suits and carry automatic rifles. They even drive SUVs with tinted windows, but theirs are black, not red.

We park under the bridge that connects real America to New America. The FBI agent in charge is a woman. "Are you ready, Stella?" Her voice is even.

"I am." I've been training for months, but the lining of my stomach still feels like it's been scraped with a razor blade.

"And you know what to do if there's a problem? An emergency?"

"I memorized the protocol."

She raises her eyebrows. "Impressive."

"I had to memorize everything last time too."

"I should have guessed. You really are quite gifted, Stella. I hope we have the opportunity to work together again."

I smile. It's the first time I've felt a sense of calm all morning.

"I hope so too."

She nods at me before abruptly turning around. "Okay, people, let's do this."

A giant spiral staircase takes us from the towpath to the bridge. I watch the earth move away through the open grates as we get higher.

The view is stunning with gray-blue water on all sides. A chain of tiny islands sits just beside the bridge. But I can't enjoy the scenery. I have to focus on what's ahead.

We stand at the end of the bridge. A narrow walkway for pedestrians sits next to two rail tracks. I can't see across to the other side.

Before I start the long walk, I turn back and take one last glimpse of freedom. I want to remember all of this when I'm back in Bull Run—not allowed to go anywhere alone, not allowed to drive, barely even allowed to speak, much less go to college or have a career.

"At least I know it's a cave," I say out loud because, for at least a few more minutes, I'm still allowed to say what I want.

I take the first step forward. The agents step with me like our movements are synchronized. We walk slowly.

With purpose.

I face forward but catch flashes of the two rivers crashing into each other like warriors. If the water where I crossed had been this rough, I wouldn't have made it. I would have drowned. Or maybe I wouldn't have even tried.

About halfway across the bridge we see them. The group on the other side marching toward us like they're going into battle. There are at least a dozen constables and two men not in uniform. Even though the temperature is still hovering around freezing, they're not wearing coats. The sight of their gray uniforms causes my throat to tighten. Am I really going back to this?

As we get closer, I start to make out their faces. That's when I see Joseph Clarke.

The man I was supposed to marry.

My throat constricts even more.

Not Joseph. Not him.

I force myself to calm. I am *not* marrying him. There are some things I won't do. I already have my out. I'm not going to get married at all. I'm going to the conservatory. Mom and Dad won't like it, but they won't be able to stop me either. Doing so would mean admitting the chaperone program is not a public good.

I keep my eyes on Joseph until we're close enough that he can see me watching him. When his gaze catches mine, I shift my attention away from him. I will not give him the satisfaction of looking into my eyes. I have at least that much choice. Even in their world.

My gaze lands on the person in the middle. A thin middle-aged man in a green-and white T-shirt with the word MOUNTAINEERS across the front.

A Night Light.

This is who they're trading me for. He's been in prison for months.

This is another way we've tricked them. By making them believe they have to trade someone. The truth is, I'm allowed to leave real America whenever I want. No one's blocking my escape. I could walk over this bridge any day of the week, and no one would blink, much less stop me.

But why do that when we can save someone's life?

I cannot appear sympathetic to the Night Light. I don't want to give them reason to doubt where my loyalties are. So I keep my face flat and focus on the man next to him. He's wearing a dark gray business suit and a striped tie. Dad's uniform. Clearly he's in charge.

The suit stops walking, holding his left palm up like he's halting traffic. "Stop! Stop!" We obey his instructions. He lifts a megaphone to his mouth.

"The trade is off."

One of the FBI agents puts his hands around his mouth since he doesn't have a real megaphone. "Why?" he yells down the bridge.

The suit holds up the megaphone again. "The girl is a spy."

It feels like the bridge drops out beneath me. An FBI agent grabs my arm to steady me. In his clear eyes, I see for the first time how young he is. He can't be ten years older than I am.

"I'm okay," I tell him, and he lets go of my arm.

"We need to get her out of here," the agent in charge says. "This situation is no longer secure."

"No, wait—" I try to say, but they close in, forming a human shield around me.

"We have to move fast," she says.

"No," I say, "I'm *not* leaving." But no one listens.

"Now!" the agent in charge yells. "Go!"

I can't leave. If I do, the Night Light will be sent back to prison. Or worse. They'll kill him. They've killed others. What incentive do they have to keep him alive?

I have to go back. I have to try.

I break free. It's not hard. No one has their hands on me.

As soon as I've left the pack, my jog turns into a sprint. There's less than a hundred feet between me and the Minutemen. The suit drops the megaphone and stands there gawking at me. A few of the constables reach for their pistols. I slow to a stop.

I'm not stupid. I don't want to get shot.

I'm close enough now that they can hear me. I hold my hands up in the air like I'm under arrest. "I don't want to hurt anyone. I *just* want to go home."

The suit lifts his megaphone before thinking better of it, passing it to a constable behind him.

He starts walking toward me, and when he's twenty feet away, he shouts at me. "We know you're a spy!"

"I'm not!" My voice is so pleading I almost believe my lie. "I swear I'm not."

He's only ten feet away now. "You have no way to prove it."

"I can." I say this though I have no idea how. "I swear."

The suit snaps his fingers at one of the constables, signaling him. The constable approaches the prisoner from behind, pushing him forward until he's standing right in front of me. The suit pulls a pistol off his belt and puts it above the Night Light's ear.

"No!" I yell. "Please!"

I hear the FBI agents behind me drawing their guns. In response, the constables pull theirs out. Is this where it all goes wrong?

The suit levels his gaze at me. "Admit you're a spy."

"But I'm not a spy. I'm not!"

"You have three seconds to admit you're a spy, or I'm going to shoot this man. Three…"

"No, please!"

"Two."

"No!"

"One."

"I'm not a spy! You have to believe me. I'm not!"

The suit drops the pistol. The Night Light bends at the waist as if he's going to throw up.

The constable kicks the Night Light in the leg. "Go."

The Night Light straightens and glares at the constable. The only sound is the furious hiss of the water beneath us.

The suit breaks the silence, waving at the Night Light. "Go on. Go!"

The Night Light takes a cautious step, his eyes on the suit the whole time. When no one stops him, he takes a second tentative step. And then another. And another. It feels like the whole thing could fall apart at any moment. Someone will stop him. Someone will shoot.

But none of these things happen. And seconds later the Night Light passes me on the bridge.

I watch him go by. Fear colors his face as clearly as paint. He's the reason I have to go. If I don't, he'll be sent back.

So I do what I have to do.

I turn back around and take a step forward.

CHAPTER 100

My statement is going to be broadcast live on the Freedom Channel tonight. Everyone in New America will be watching. Everyone in real America too. They'll all know what happened to me.

Or what we want them to think happened.

At first they didn't want it to be public. The Minutemen.

But after I told them my story, they wanted everyone to hear it. They're using me to help their cause.

I never would've thought I'd be good at acting, but apparently I'm a natural.

I stare right into the camera and tell them exactly what the real Americans told me to say.

"Hello." I clear my throat. I want to reach for the glass of water they put in front of me, but instead I keep going. "My name is Stella Graham, and I'm here because I was brainwashed by my chaperone."

I pause, letting my words sink in for an audience I cannot see nor hear.

It's strange to sit here in this tiny room and speak to a camera, knowing my words are being broadcast all over the world. They expect an audience of twenty million. Maybe more. But none of it seems real.

I don't make eye contact with the men who are filming, keeping my gaze trained on the camera lens, as if I can see the faces on the other side. "Sister Helen was assigned to me when I became a woman. Right before my twelfth birthday. For six long years, she taught me to hate New America and everything it stood for."

It isn't easy to say these things about Sister Helen. I'm only able to do it because I know this is what she'd want me to do.

Fight.

Resist.

"I hated our country so much that when Sister Helen died and my new chaperone, Sister Laura, replaced her, I hated her too. I even told my friends how much I hated her. I was so brainwashed I eventually decided I couldn't live without Sister Helen and had to escape to Old America, which is what she'd been pushing me to do for years. I was too afraid to do it before she died. I didn't want to leave her. But once she was gone, I felt so alone it was almost like I had no choice. Sister Helen had turned me against my mother and father and told me she was the only person I could trust. She isolated me so completely I felt like there was no reason to stay. But when I got to Old America—"

I have to concentrate at this part. I've been saying "America" for months, and even when I know I'm playing a part, calling it "Old America" feels wrong.

"When I got to Old America, it was all so different. Women wore revealing clothes. People cursed and smoked. I hated it. And I missed everyone so much. My family, my friends. I love them all so much. Even Sister Laura, who I'd grown closer to than I realized." This part is to make Sister Laura look innocent. "I just wanted to go home. And I wanted everyone in New America to know what happened to me. So it wouldn't happen to them. No, I wasn't kidnapped, but in some ways what happened to me was much, much worse. I became a different person. I became someone I was ashamed of being."

My words bounce off the walls of the room and back into my face. This is the hardest part. Yes, it was hard to lie about Sister Helen, but lying about myself? About how I feel? It's like a blasphemy on my soul.

I've hesitated too long. The Minuteman behind the camera is flipping his hand in circles. *Wrap it up.* Everyone watching must be wondering what's wrong. Why did I stop? I have to finish, but I can't remember what's supposed to come next.

I look into the camera one last time. "I just want to go home."

For some reason I can't fathom, my words are followed by a long sniff, and then, without even realizing it's happening, I start to cry.

CHAPTER 101

The broadcast is a success.

Reporters on the Freedom Channel praise my courage. The prime minister calls me a hero. They all buy it. Everyone in New America buys it. And they love me. *The girl who just wants to go home.* That's what they're calling me. It's such a lie I don't even know who I am anymore.

When it's finally over, I find myself back at home.

In my bedroom.

Alone.

It's like a dream. My bed, my things, my books. Is this really my life again? I shiver even though there's a small fire going in the fireplace. A fire I know was made by Tiffany. None of this would happen in real America. There'd be no fireplace in my bedroom. No Tiffany. But there'd be a car outside I could get into and drive away now that I know how to do that.

I need to practice for tomorrow—my first day back at school—but all I want to do is lie on the bed and contemplate the enormity of what I've done.

I run my fingers along the shelf, thinking about all the secrets hidden there. *In the Time of the Butterflies* disguised by *Love in the Time of Cholera*. *Incidents in the Life of a Slave Girl* hiding behind *Uncle Tom's Cabin*. "Omelas" lurking inside *The Collected Poems of Langston Hughes*. *Fahrenheit 451* buried between the pages of *Dante's Inferno*.

I was getting ready.

I'm running my finger over *The Scarlet Letter*, camouflage for "The Lottery," when someone knocks on the door.

"Come in," I say from across the room, turning to see if it's Sister Laura. She moved back in this morning. What I said on TV worked. Everyone in New America wants to see us reunited.

But it's not her at the door. It's Dad.

He hasn't been in my room in years. Not since Sister Helen moved in. At least not that I can remember.

He enters the room with caution, as if it's booby-trapped. Does he sense I know the truth about him? He gets to the fireplace and picks up the Russian nesting dolls on the mantel. I flinch. The song lyrics Mateo gave me are hidden inside.

"I remember these." Dad says, examining the dolls. "I got them for your fifth birthday." He sounds like he's visiting a person he hasn't seen in years.

"Mm hmmm." I don't trust myself to say more. It's one thing to put on an act with the constables. It's another thing to do it with my own father.

He sets the dolls back on the mantel, and I let out the breath I've been holding.

Dad turns to face me. "I need to tell you how proud I am of you, Stella. How proud we both are. Your mother and me."

Rose's words appear in my head.

Your mother wanted you to get out, Stella.

He's lying. Has he always lied? Can I ever trust anything he says again? I'm not sure, but I know how I'm supposed to respond. "Thanks, Dad."

"It took real bravery on your part." He tilts his head to the side. "To be honest, the whole thing must have required an unimaginable amount of fortitude. Making the plans to escape, following through with them, living in Old America, and then being strong enough to see it wasn't for you."

He's right. The whole thing took everything I had. Everything and more.

"I'm also so pleased to know you've finally embraced everything we've worked for here in this, our brilliant new country."

Everything we *have worked for here.*

We.

He's admitting he's one of them.

"I know you've struggled with what's expected of you in the past, Stella." Dad holds his hands out to me, as if asking for peace. "The Visitations. The rules. Even the idea of marrying Constable Clarke, which I'm willing to let go. For the time being anyway. But now we know why." I must have a question on my face because he adds, "Sister Helen," like she's the entire reason I escaped. I'm relieved. I *want* him to think that. "And all the lies she told you. All the harm she did. I bear some of the responsibility for that."

"You do?" I shouldn't have said that. He's caught me off guard.

"I wish I'd seen it. I wish I'd sensed she was not a believer. I blame myself." He shakes his head and looks to the windows at the far end of my room. Fat snow flurries fall from the sky outside. It's been like this ever since I got back even though it's almost the end of April.

I can't help myself. I feel for him. He shouldn't blame himself. It was my decision. "It's not your fault, Dad."

He turns back to me and smiles. "No, I should've known. I regret very much that I didn't."

I don't know what to say. Any words I utter might give me away.

"But that's all behind us now. You're home. And the truth is, you're stronger than ever, Stella. I can see that."

"Thanks, Dad." I say this even though I'm certain there's something else. Something he isn't saying. There's a half smile on his face, but his warmth isn't genuine. When he smiles for real, his eyes soften so much the skin around them crinkles. When he's pretending, they go flat. And right now his eyes are completely dead. Ever since I've become someone who puts on a show, it's a lot easier to recognize when someone else does it.

"And now that I know how strong you are, Stella, I promise—" His eyes lock on mine. His scrutiny is so intense I want to look away but don't. I hold his gaze and let him finish. "I promise I won't underestimate you. Not ever again."

He knows.

He knows everything.

He turns away and walks toward the windows, leaning forward when he gets to them as if trying to get a better look at the snow.

I take solace in the fact that he still doesn't know what kind of books are lining the shelves on either side of him.

"I'm going to be more involved with picking your new chaperone. I'm not going to let the constables choose on their own. I don't want anything left to chance. I can't have you led astray a third time."

"What do you mean a *third* time?"

He glances at me before slowly making his way back across the room, talking the whole way. "I need to be vigilant about making sure we find the right person to replace Sister Laura."

"What do you mean? Why is she being replaced? She just got back."

He swivels in my direction before he gets to the door. "She can't very well be your chaperone if she's in prison, can she?"

"What?" I take a step toward him. "What are you talking about? Sister Laura had nothing to do with my escape. It was all Sister Helen. I swear."

"You don't think we're stupid, do you, Stella?" He slants his head at me. "We know she was involved. She had to be."

His stare is so fierce it's painful.

"You can't send her to prison, Dad. You just can't."

"Oh, it's not me, Stella." He shakes his head and lets his eyes rove over the room as if he just walked in. "It's the Minutemen."

CHAPTER 102

s soon as he's gone, I hear them. The sirens.

I run to the window, praying it's not true, praying I'm hearing things, but they're already screeching into the driveway. Three red SUVs. Just like when Sister Helen died. Are they going to kill Sister Laura too? Are they going to kill me when they find out why I came back?

I sprint to the hallway and see Sister Laura's door standing wide open. Her door is *never* open. I move closer. She's sitting in the center of the bed. A small suitcase rests at her feet, her hands folded in her lap like a child.

She looks different than I remember.

Younger. Smaller. More vulnerable.

When I peer into her face, she moves her head from side to side the tiniest bit. She's warning me. *Don't.* Don't what? I'm about to ask when her eyes flip to the left. That's when I see him. Dad. He's hiding behind her open door.

He doesn't move his gaze from Sister Laura, doesn't even glance at me, but he must hear me because he says, "Go back to your room, Stella."

"But—"

"Now!" Dad's voice is so loud I'm sure Tiffany hears it downstairs.

Sister Laura puts an index finger to her forehead.

Think, Stella. Think.

What does she want me to think? What does she want me to do?

I have to calm down, think about why I'm here. I'm here to fight. To spy. If I act too upset or try too hard to stop him, it will seem like I'm on her side. I can't do anything that might be read as disgruntled or disrespectful. I can't let them know the truth about me.

But why would Dad let her come back if he was just planning to have her taken away? Why would he do that to me? It's almost like…

Like he's doing it on purpose. To hurt me. He wants to break me. But I won't let him.

I do what I have to do.

I wipe the fear from my face and go back to my room.

I have no choice.

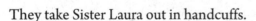

They take Sister Laura out in handcuffs.

I expect Mom to walk up behind me and tell me to back away from the window or Dad to look up from the driveway in anger. But I'm left to do as I please. I don't realize I'm crying until Sister Laura glances up and frowns at me before they put her in an SUV.

I take in a breath and try to keep my emotions under control, but it's useless. Pretty soon I'm sobbing, wiping my eyes with the sleeves of my sweater. That's when I see him.

Joseph Clarke.

Our eyes meet, and he actually has the nerve to smile.

I spin away from the window, not wanting to give him the satisfaction of seeing me cry.

I don't know if I've ever hated anyone more.

CHAPTER 103

The next morning I wake before everyone else. Now that I have a purpose, I have no desire to sleep. I know what I came back here to do. I want to avenge Sister Helen. I want to help Sister Laura. I want to stop the Minutemen.

I'm more focused than ever.

Mom knocks on my door at the time Sister Laura normally would. Sister Laura always had to wait for me to finish getting dressed. But now I'm the one waiting.

Now I'm ready.

Mom's eyes meet mine. This is the first time we've been alone since my return. She doesn't say anything, but now that I know she's on my side, everything has changed. I'm not sure I can completely trust her, but I do believe she wants what's best for me.

"You ready?" She doesn't add the words, *for school*. I can see in her eyes her question is bigger.

I don't hesitate. "Yes, I am."

~~~~

The sight of Bonita and Liv causes a wave of regret to pass through me. I didn't realize how much I missed them. Bonita's face relaxes into a subtle smile, and Liv's eyes alight with joy. But I cannot go back to who I was before. The girl who just went along with what was expected. I have to lead now. Without letting them know I'm doing it.

Like Sister Laura.

Like Sister Helen.

Liv dashes across the courtyard, and everyone turns to watch, their mouths dropping open when they see me.

I'm famous now. Or maybe *infamous* is a better word.

Liv pulls me close, her cheek warm against mine. Bonita wraps her arms around both of us, squeezing so tight Liv lets out a little yelp. This is my real welcome home. But I don't give in to the moment as much as I'd like. I hold part of me back, unwilling to let my emotions take over.

When I pull away, Bonita looks over my shoulder. "Is that your *mother?*"

I squint at Mom, still standing at the gate. "Yes." I don't say more. Anyone could be listening.

"So...Sister Laura?"

I only nod in response.

Liv wipes a tear away. "We were so worried about you, Stella."

"I know. I'm sorry." I lower my voice. "We can talk about it later."

"Yes, we can. You have a lot to tell us." Bonita says this even though she knows as well as I do I'm not allowed to reveal what real America was like. I'm supposed to stick to the talking points. *It was strange. I didn't like it. I missed everyone. I just wanted to come home.*

I won't lie to Bonita and Liv, but I won't tell them the whole truth either. I'll tell them only what I must for them to see things for what they really are. After that, it will be up to them to decide if they want to stay or get out.

Or become someone like me.

"I guess I can't put this off any longer," I say, lifting my eyes to the school.

The brick building looks exactly the same and totally different. Grand on the outside. But small compared to what I've seen.

I'm no longer the ignorant girl Dad accused me of being.

I know he's behind me even before I turn around.

I feel him. A force I can't ignore. I rotate slowly, drawing out the anticipation. When our eyes meet, it happens exactly the same way it did all those months ago. The air between us electrifies. I'm a far cry from the person I was the last time he made me blush, but some things are still the same. My body flushes with longing. I want nothing more than to touch him.

Mateo offers me the sweetest smile in the world. "You're back."

"I am."

For a moment we stand there, staring at each other across the hallway. Any minute a teacher will show up, but for now, we're connected.

"I'm sorry if I worried you."

"I wasn't worried."

"You weren't?"

"No." He squints at me. "I heard what you said. Before you left." The story about Willow. He understood.

"Mr. de Velasco!" a voice calls to us over the other students. I know it's Mr. Washington without even looking.

Mateo backs away slowly, his eyes never leaving me. "I'm not giving up on you."

This is going to be the hard part.

CHAPTER 104

The last few weeks of senior year go by in a blur.

I go to school every morning, yoga and the library every afternoon. A week after I return, I'm even allowed to spend the night with Bonita and Liv. I share what I can, giving them books to read and telling them how the Minutemen use fear to keep us in line. But I'm never fully there. I'm in my head, somewhere else. Back in real America. Training at the Jacobs Center. At homecoming with Mateo.

I do this most often during Visitation.

This is the third Sunday in a row Joseph has been here even though I've told him explicitly how I feel. Or rather how I don't feel. I'm not in love with him. And I never will be. I've spared him the list of feelings I do have for him—fury, contempt, disgust, anger, pity—because I know Dad's always hovering nearby. Listening.

The other boys have finally stopped trying to arrange a visit. My new chaperone, Sister Meredith, got dozens of requests the first week I was back. Every one of them except Mateo was approved. Dad insists I have to pick someone, but the constables have not allowed the one person who might sway me inside the house. I'm sure Joseph is behind it. He knows somehow. Of course, I'd choose Mateo over him. I'd choose any of them over Joseph Clarke if I were interested in marriage. But I'm not.

Once the others figured out I wasn't going to tell them anything about Old America they couldn't hear on the news, the requests for Visitation slowed. But they didn't disappear completely until word got out that Joseph was granted a visit indefinitely. Dad's doing, I'm sure. A way to pressure me into commitment.

I'm not getting married, but I haven't told Dad that yet. The time isn't right.

In the meantime, I've been filling out my application for the conservatory and continuing the training I started at the Jacobs Center, watching for clues from Dad and the rest of the Minutemen, reading the banned books someone forgot to remove from the library—or maybe some rogue librarian put back.

Of course, I have to be careful. If they find out, they might kill Sister Laura. She's in prison now, but women go missing in prison all the time. They might kill me too. So I never breathe a word about it to anyone. I just keep watching. And reading. It's frustrating. There's so little I can do while I'm still in high school. But in a few weeks, my whole life will change.

Again.

***

"Joseph is your *only* caller today, Stella." Dad lectures me as he crosses the foyer to the front door. "Be a good sport. If you don't have callers, it will look like there's something wrong with you." He wants everyone to think I'm normal. Doesn't he know no one in New America thinks I'm normal anymore? It takes all I have not to throw a cross-hook at his face. But I remember the Master's words. *Don't pick a fight you can't win.*

"Besides you owe me. That dress probably cost me a small fortune."

I look down at my dress and suddenly hate it. If I could rip it off and stand here naked, I would. I can't believe what he's saying. I can't believe this stupid dress came with strings attached. Has it always been this way? Was I too ignorant to notice?

"This is an important time, Stella. For you. And"—he turns to Mom and uncharacteristically puts his arm around her, squeezing her like she's a stuffed toy—"for all of us."

Mom echoes his words. "It really is, Stella." Her voice sounds totally artificial. It's like he pushed a talk button on her back. I used to think she *tried* to sound fake because she wanted to come off as haughty, but now I know she's just faking it. I see the resentment in her eyes. She doesn't like the rules any more than I do.

Dad ceremoniously throws opens the two front doors and holds his hand out to Joseph. The two of them shake for what seems longer than necessary. Joseph looks down at their clasped hands, and I follow his gaze. That's when I see it. Dad's index finger tapping the place where Joseph's palm meets his wrist. It's some kind of signal. That's why the Minutemen always shake hands so long. They're communicating.

"I thought Stella and I might sit out back today," Joseph says with all the subtlety of a bull in heat. "If that's okay with you, sir."

"Yes, yes, of course."

"Alone?" I ask.

Dad shrugs. "Why not? You two have spent enough time in

this stuffy house with all of us looming over you. You're almost finished with high school. It's time."

I glance at Joseph, trying to conjure a way out of this, but he speaks before I can.

"I brought this so you wouldn't get cold."

He lifts his hand and holds out a white scarf to me. I look at it for a long moment. That's when it hits me. The scarf he's holding is my white scarf.

I pull back from his outstretched hand, horrified. It *was* him in the courtyard that night.

All three of them watch me, waiting for me to accept his offer. Before I can respond, Dad takes the scarf from Joseph and drapes it over my shoulders. He leans toward me as if he's going to give me an illegal peck on the cheek but instead whispers in my ear. "Do this now, Stella, or suffer the consequences later. It's up to you."

"Fine."

I glare at Joseph with contempt. "Let's go."

Joseph holds out his arm to me. I have no choice but to take it. But putting my hand on his arm makes my skin crawl. Am I giving in too much? Is he getting the wrong idea?

In the courtyard, violet lilies stand at attention around the stone fountain. If I were with anyone but Joseph, it would be incredibly romantic. I keep moving, so he can't get too close.

"I just want you to know, Stella." He catches my eye against my will. "You're the prettiest girl I've ever seen."

A shiver runs down the length of my back. I don't even bother to hide it.

"I'd like to ask you something, Stella."

He's right behind me. I peer over my shoulder and search his hands for any sign of a ring, but they're empty.

"Do you know someone named Mateo de Velasco? He's in your grade at school."

So Joseph does know about Mateo. Does he also know how I feel about him? I glance at Joseph, not sure what to say. Should I tell him the truth? Would that make things even worse?

"He's requested a visit with you every week. I don't know why he would keep doing that. Unless you're encouraging him somehow. Unless you two are breaking the rules."

I stop moving and turn to face him. *Is he threatening me?*

"Of course not, Joseph. I would never—"

Joseph's head shakes so hard it seems broken. His gaze roves over the courtyard, glaring at nothing, like the strange person he is. I know what he's thinking. *I could have him arrested. I could end this right now.*

I need to appease him. "Joseph," I say, regaining his attention. When he squints at me, I lean toward him the tiniest bit. "You don't have to worry about Mateo. He hasn't even been to Visitation once. And I spend time with you every week."

Joseph grabs my wrist, cuffing it the same way Dad did when we were running last fall. His grip doesn't cut off my circulation, but it still hurts. "You'll have to do more than that."

My gaze meets his involuntarily, and I can see in his dead eyes that he's as serious as he's ever been. When I don't answer, his grip tightens.

I drop my eyes to his hand.

His attention follows mine, and he reluctantly lets go. "Stella," he whispers with so much longing it sucks the oxygen out of my lungs. He takes up all the air, leaving none for me.

I make the mistake of glancing at him, and he reaches for my face. I pull back, but not fast enough. His hand grazes my cheek. I flinch at his touch, and he narrows his eyes at me. He's angry again. I never knew he had such a temper.

"I know you saw me that day." His voice is filled with more hate than I expect. "Outside your window. The day Sister Helen died. The day she was murdered…"

Heat takes over my body. Everything in me wants to hit him, I call on my training and count down from ten to calm myself.

I turn away from him, take a step toward the house.

"Where do you think you're going?" Joseph yells after me. His tone sounds like he really believes he's my father.

"Where do you think?" I say over my shoulder, not bothering to hide my frustration.

"But—"

I pause and glance back at him. "But what, Joseph?"

"I just got here."

"And now it's time for you to leave."

I start walking again, and Sister Meredith opens the door for me. Was she watching us?

"Stella." Joseph starts after me. "Wait. I want to—"

I spin back toward him. "Don't, Joseph. Just don't."

"But—"

"There's nothing you can say."

I must get through to him because he doesn't try to argue. He just stands there, frowning. If he weren't so creepy, I might feel sorry for him.

Out the corner of my eye, I see Sister Meredith's mouth drop open. She's never heard anyone talk to a constable this way before.

A few months ago, I hadn't either. I would have never imagined I'd be brave enough to do it myself. But after everything I've been through, Joseph Clarke seems as threatening as a fly.

"Is everything okay, Stella?" she asks.

Joseph answers for me—"She's fine"—as if I can't speak for myself. "I shouldn't have said that." I look at him and wonder if he finally gets that I have a voice, opinions.

But then he says, "You're a lot better than fine, Stella. You're exquisite." Disgust rises in my throat. To Joseph, I'm nothing more than something to possess. A piece of art. A trophy.

I turn away from him and climb the brick steps into the house. Inside, Mom and Dad wait in the living room, Dad in a club chair with a drink in his hand, Mom at her secretary.

I lead Joseph to the door, and Dad jumps up to say goodbye.

After he closes the front door, Sister Meredith whispers in my ear. "Are you okay, Stella?"

"It's fine. He's harmless. Just a pest."

The truth is, I'm no longer sure.

CHAPTER 105

I t seems like graduation will never come, like the days I have left in school will last forever. But then, all of a sudden, it's the week of graduation and everything that goes with it. The cap-and-gown fitting, the senior luncheon, the baccalaureate, commencement.

At first I'm not interested in any of it. It's Bonita who changes my mind. We're in the cafeteria, eating Tofurky, overcooked lima beans, and a pear. Everything tastes like cardboard now that I've had real food.

"Do you realize this is the last time we get to be kids?" she says with wide eyes.

I put my pear down. "What do you mean?"

"We're graduating. After that, we'll be adults."

"Finally." Liv has been counting down the days more than any of us.

Bonita goes on. "I know we've been looking forward to growing up for a long time, but—"

Liv interrupts. "I *cannot* wait to get rid of Sister Sophie."

"But that also means responsibility." Bonita mashes her lima beans into mush on her tray. "Right now we don't have to worry

about planning a wedding or making babies or anything like that."
She doesn't mention college. I've told them the truth about that.

Liv puts her fork down. "Don't ruin my appetite."

I turn to Bonita. "And? What's your point, B?"

"My point is this is the last time in our lives no one is expecting
us to act like grown-ups. We need to enjoy it. You already missed
prom, Stella. That was a big deal."

"Was that right before I came back?"

Bonita nods, her face blank.

"How was it?"

Bonita blinks at me and turns to Liv with a look I've never seen
on her before. Is it disbelief?

Liv reaches across the table and puts her hand on my arm.
"Bonita was crowned prom queen, Stella. Didn't you know?"

"Prom queen?" I look at Bonita and see only disappointment
on her face. "That's amazing, B." I grab her hand and squeeze it.
"I'm so happy for you."

A trace of joy appears in Bonita's eyes.

"How did I not know?"

Bonita shrugs. "You've kind of been in your own head a lot. I
mean, ever since you came back."

"Yeah, I know. I'm sorry."

"You don't have to apologize, Stella. I get it." She squeezes my
hand back. "You missed *a lot* while you were gone. There were
more than a dozen promposals too."

"Oh, God. It's getting worse."

"Stella!" Liv squeals at the same time Bonita looks past me to
the constables stationed at the doors.

"Sorry, I forgot."

"You know we love you, Stella." Bonita's voice is pleading. "But you can't say that word. I know high school's almost over, but you still have to be careful. This isn't Old America."

I cringe when she says, *Old America*. I haven't told them what it's really called. Not yet.

"That doesn't mean you can't enjoy it, Stella." She lets go of my hand and sits back, a look of total seriousness on her face. "This is our last chance to be young."

She has a point.

If there's anything I want to do before graduation, I have to do it now.

CHAPTER 106

I wait for him outside Musical Expression.

When he sees me from down the hall, he quickens his pace, striding toward me like a missile. My face gets warmer with every step he takes.

When he stops in front of me, I tilt my head in the opposite direction.

He mouths the word, "What?"

I whisper back one word at a time. "Follow. Me." I tilt my head again just as two Climbers come strolling around the corner. Their eyes land on me like I'm more prey than person. I look away, but sense them taking in Mateo standing right in front of me. They know something is going on.

I turn sharply away from all three of them, walking briskly down the hall. When I get to the girl's multipurpose room, I pause at the last door, looking over my shoulder, before I push it open. Even this far down the hall, I can see Mateo lingering in front of Mr. Jeffrey's classroom, watching me.

Inside, I'm all alone at the end of bleachers that rise twenty feet in front of me. I tiptoe toward the gym. Girls stream into the middle of the floor from the locker room in the opposite corner, waiting for Gynecological Fitness to start. They're too busy talking to notice me. I move back until I'm out of sight, making sure no one sees me. I duck under the bleachers and wait. I have no idea if he'll show.

But I had to try.

Class starts, and Mateo still isn't here. Mr. Tidmore gives the girls the same instructions he gave my class last period: *Drop to the floor and start stretching.*

The door across from the bleachers opens slowly, Mateo's eyes peering through the crack.

He made it.

I put a finger to my mouth and wave him forward as I step backward under the bleachers. He follows me, the two of us disappearing into the shadows like explorers crossing into another dimension.

The bright gym lights bleed between the wood slats overhead, painting the dark space with narrow stripes.

I stop when I reach the middle of the bleachers, but Mateo doesn't pause until he's so close to me we'd be touching if he got any closer. We're only six inches apart. I could put my finger on his lips. I *want* to put my fingers on his lips.

He leans down and whispers in my ear. "I can't believe you." He shakes his head the tiniest bit. "I can't believe we're really here. *Alone.*"

Our eyes meet. "We only have two days until graduation," I whisper back. "I don't know when I'll see you after that."

His mouth drops into a frown. "No, Stella." His voice is filled with desperation. "Don't say that."

I've already told him my plans. He knows where I'm going. And I don't want to talk about the future right now. I want to make the most of what little time we have left.

I raise my right hand and gently put it in the center of his chest. "Shhh," I say, lifting my face to his again. I feel his heart thumping under his shirt. Have I ever felt the beat of another person's heart?

"Is this for real?" I say out loud.

"Oh, it's real."

We're alone.

Really alone.

But we don't have long.

Mateo puts both hands on my hips and pulls me to him in one slow, careful motion. He smells like a cross between clean laundry and fresh-cut cedar. We're touching from our knees to our shoulders. Heat floods my body. I move closer, letting myself feel every part of him. The last time we were this close was homecoming. Six full months ago. And we weren't alone. We were in the middle of a packed dance floor with chaperones in every corner.

This is different.

This is so much more.

He leans toward me again. His mouth brushes my ear, and a wave of euphoria passes through me. "You're the bravest person I know, Stella Graham."

As he pulls back to look into my eyes, his stubble brushes my cheek, scratching and thrilling me at the same time.

My eyes meet his, and we lock on each other. I can feel his

body responding at the same time as mine. His muscles tense, his grip tightens.

We lean closer.

And closer.

So close I can't see him anymore.

I feel the warmth of his skin radiating against mine. I turn my face to his, and he turns his to mine.

We move closer...closer...until finally...his lips touch mine.

Finally.

We don't stay long.

It's too risky.

After a few minutes, his mouth pulls away from mine. Losing contact is physically painful. My body aches to touch him again.

"We need to go," he whispers, his mouth so close I feel his breath on my face. "Before they come looking for us."

I nod even though there's nothing I want less.

He looks over his shoulder before letting his gaze fall back on me. When our eyes meet, my whole body floods with emotion. I've never felt anything like this before. He picks up my hand and kisses it without taking his eyes off me. I'm dizzy with joy.

"I'll never forget this, Stella. Never."

I wish more than anything we could stay in this moment forever, that we could forget everything and just be together.

But this is not the path I've chosen.

This is not why I came back. No matter how tempting it sounds right now. It's like that song he gave me. *When a woman learns to walk / she's not dependent anymore.*

He kisses my hand one more time and then abruptly drops it, turning away from me, away from us. I watch him slowly make his way out from under the bleachers.

It's over so fast it's almost like he was never here.

CHAPTER 107

On Sunday, the doorbell rings while everyone else is still at church. I've gotten permission to stay home and practice wearing the new heels Mom gave me for graduation.

Mom told me to expect flowers, but when I open the front door, it's not a delivery person I see, but Joseph Clarke standing on our front step with a dozen red roses cradled in his arms like a baby. *Why is he here?*

I don't hide the skepticism in my voice. "What are you doing here, Joseph?"

"I wanted to surprise you."

He's a terrible liar. He wouldn't be here without Dad's permission. The two of them must have planned this.

"You shouldn't be here, Joseph. It's against the rules."

"Not after tomorrow." Technically he's right. Tomorrow, I graduate from high school, and everything changes. Sister Meredith moves out. I'll be allowed in public without a chaperone. Though it's still highly unusual for an unmarried woman to be alone with a man. Nor is it safe.

"We shouldn't be alone."

"Isn't your guardian here?"

I look over my shoulder in the direction of the annex. I *think* Sister Meredith is in her room. But that's at the other end of the house. Upstairs. *Didn't she hear the doorbell ring?* "I guess."

"So we're not breaking any rules, are we?"

He knows this isn't true. He knows we're not supposed to be alone together. We shouldn't even be talking.

"And your father gave me his blessing."

What is he talking about? His blessing for what? My eyes go to Joseph's hand, praying he's not holding the turquoise ring box, but there's nothing there besides his chubby fingers. "His blessing?"

"To be here with you. Alone. He said we're practically engaged anyway."

It hasn't been cold since the week I returned, but a shiver travels down my back.

He puts the roses on the pedestal table in the foyer and looks right into my eyes, a violation of its own. "And don't forget what you promised me."

I know immediately what he means. The last time he was at Visitation. When he said, I'd have to do more than spend time with him.

I have to distract him from what he really wants. "Do you want to come in?"

He nods rather than answer with words, more Neanderthal than human.

I'd hoped Sister Meredith would've shown up by now, but the foyer is dead quiet, the living room furniture empty, the dining chairs pushed under the table. It's as if the entire floor has been evacuated. Normally Joseph and I sit in the living room, but it's possible Joseph will sit next to me there. The dining room is safer.

"Would you like some tea?" I ask over my shoulder as I move in that direction.

I'm not even out of the foyer when he grabs my arm, yanking me back to him like a yo-yo. Before I know what's happening, he's pulled my body to his, clutching me so tight I can't breathe.

"I don't want any goddamned tea," he hisses down at me.

I'm too stunned to react.

I stare into his tiny eyes. All I see there is violence.

"You're hurting me, Joseph."

"I don't give a rat's ass."

This means all the rules—all the things they teach us—are just for show. When he's alone, he'll do whatever he wants. Curse. Grope me. Hurt me. I see how wrong I was to assume he was harmless.

Where is Sister Meredith?

Of course, when I really *do* need a chaperone, no one is around. The truth is, they don't want to protect me from someone like Joseph. A constable. A Minuteman. They only want to protect me from myself.

Joseph hisses again. "You promised me something, and you're going to give it to me."

I pretend I don't notice the vitriol in his voice, that I'm still in control, even though my heart is pounding so hard I'm sure he can feel it through our clothes. "I said we could spend time together. You know that anything else—even what you're doing right now—is against the rules."

"Like you care about the rules. You're the one who left."

My heart pounds even harder. I didn't know Joseph felt this way. I didn't know he didn't believe my story that it was Sister Helen who led me astray. I tell myself to go back to my training. "I was tricked, Joseph. That's not what I wanted."

"You're full of shit." He squeezes me harder. "I want what you gave him."

"What are you talking about?"

"I know what you did. I know you went under the bleachers together."

The bleachers. Did someone see us? Another constable? One of the Climbers?

My only option is to lie. "I don't know what you think you saw, Joseph, but nothing happened."

"Bullshit." He squeezes me even harder. That's when I feel his erection pushing against my thigh.

I twist from side to side. "Let me go."

His grip is too tight. I can't get away. I wriggle my hands free and push against his chest as hard as I can, but he doesn't move an inch. I have to do something. I have to stop him. I can't beat him physically, so I have to outsmart him. And I need to do it in a way no one can question.

Abstain from sin.

I give up fighting and look into his face. "If you don't let me go, I'll scream."

"You wouldn't dare."

Whatever you do, don't hesitate.

I stare into his eyes and scream at the top of my lungs. He tries to put his hand over my mouth, but I squirm out of his grasp.

"Stop it!" Now he's yelling too.

But I don't care. I want to be heard. I want Sister Meredith to come running. She must have heard us by now. I scream as loudly as I can one more time, and then I stop.

I don't try to get away. I just listen. And, finally, I hear it. The sound of a door flying open.

That's when I play my part: "I renounce you, Joseph. I renounce sin in all its forms."

"What's going on?" a voice calls from the back door. But it's not Sister Meredith. It's Dad. They're home from church early.

Joseph shakes his head at me in disgust. "You fucking bitch." He shoves me away, sending me crashing to the floor.

Dad steps into the dining room. Did he see what happened?

"What's going on here?" His eyes land on Joseph before moving to me. "Stella!" He lunges across the room. "Stella, are you okay?"

"She tripped, sir." The vitriol has been erased from Joseph's voice. He's a better actor than I gave him credit for. "She was going to get us some tea, and she tripped."

Dad drops to the ground next to me. It's like Sister Helen's death all over again. Dad kneeling beside me. That was the last time he tried to reach out to me. The last time he showed me physical affection.

Joseph's voice cuts through the air. "Don't touch her, sir. Don't give into temptation."

He's only a few inches away, but Dad stops himself, shifting his attention to Joseph.

"It's against the rules, sir. I'd have to arrest you."

Mom appears behind him. "Mitchell?"

Dad turns to her.

"Mitchell, let me do it."

Mom rushes across the room and falls to her knees on my other side. She pulls me into her arms. I can't remember the last time she held me. Dad watches us for a long moment before getting to his feet and stepping in Joseph's direction, making up the distance between them in no time. Is he angry or relieved?

Joseph throws the DANGER method back in my face. "It's those high-heeled shoes she's wearing, sir. They're totally inappropriate."

"Why didn't you help her?"

"You know I can't do that, sir." Joseph steals a look at me. "I would never lay a hand on Stella." The tiniest spark appears in his eyes. This is funny to him. It's all a big joke. He'll do what he wants in private and play his part when other people are around. But he doesn't believe any of it. I could call him on it. I could tell Dad what really happened, but what good would it do? Women are never believed. A man's word is always taken over that of a woman. I say nothing and wait to see if Dad will ask more questions. Joseph goes on. "Unless we were married, of course."

"Of course." Dad puts a hand across his mouth.

Does he really believe what Joseph is saying?

Finally Dad turns back to me. "Is that what happened, Stella?"

I probe Joseph's eyes. There's nothing but fury there. If he wanted, he could have me arrested for dressing provocatively. He could have my name smeared even more. Or he could make things difficult for Mateo. For any of us.

I have to let it go.

"Yes, Dad, that's exactly what happened."

CHAPTER 108

Our house is aflutter on graduation morning. There are cleaning people and caterers and florists. Mom wants everything to be perfect. Vases full of gasp-worthy tulips rest on every surface while giant trays of imported lobster and shrimp, expensive cheeses and meats, and disgusting foie gras are lined up on the dining room table. It's all for me, but I feel removed from it, as if this celebration is happening for someone else. I told Mom I didn't want a party, but when she insisted, I let it go. It's the least I can do for her since there will be no wedding.

I've chosen a white silk dress that doesn't have a single sequin on it, hoping Willow would be impressed. There's a slit up the front and a scoop in back. I'm no longer interested in subtlety.

Sister Meredith is packing her things in the annex. Dad moved Shea back to her room after Sister Laura was arrested. Once I'm dressed, I go to the annex to say goodbye. Sister Meredith has only been here a few weeks. I barely know her. I'm standing in the door a full minute before she sees me. She's not as observant as she should be. When she finally notices me, she frowns.

"What's wrong?" I ask her.

"You look so grown up."

"I *am* grown up."

"I know." She nods as she places another folded caftan into her suitcase. "Sometimes you seem years older than your age." She smiles at me. "No surprise after all you've been through."

"You've been through a lot too. The conservatory, the work. It can't be easy."

Sister Meredith picks up a ceramic mug from the dresser, the one she's carried with her from room to room ever since she moved in. Her security blanket. "You're very sweet, Stella. Your parents did a good job with you."

I want to say it was Sister Helen who did a good job. And Sister Laura. But from the minute I met Sister Meredith, I wasn't sure I couldn't trust her. She's more shadow than confidante.

"A chaperone can teach you lots of things, Stella," Sister Meredith adds as if she can read my mind. "But your parents get the credit for teaching you how to love. I know your mom is especially good at that."

For the first time since I got back, regret swells inside me. It's not just Sister Meredith who's leaving. I'm leaving too. I'll move into the conservatory in less than a week. In some ways it was easier when I escaped because, back then, I had no idea how Mom really felt. But now that I know she never wanted this kind of life for me, I can see she's always looked out for me. Even when I thought she was just going along with Dad, she was protecting me.

I wipe away the tears forming in my eyes as Sister Meredith says, "Your mother will never forgive you if you ruin your makeup, Stella."

"Do you think I care?"

"No, but she does. And it's nice for a daughter to do things for her mother sometimes. Especially when she's about to lose you again."

CHAPTER 109

The auditorium is sweltering.

Beads of sweat appear on my forehead before I get to my seat. The boys are spread out in front, the girls packed in back. We sit so close our arms touch. When we process to the front, I wave at Mom, who's sitting in the front row of the balcony next to Dad like they're royalty. In Bull Run, they are. By the time it's my turn to walk across the stage, there's sweat under my arms, across my chest, between my legs. All this for a ritual that's nothing more than performance. A diploma that might as well be meaningless.

After the ceremony, so many guests and servants crowd our house I have to turn sideways to make my way into the kitchen. This, even though my real friends weren't invited. Dad insists they're a bad influence. Mom gives orders in the kitchen. She's dared to wear her racy Manolo Blahniks. Maybe her vintage wardrobe is a nod to the past, a silent rebellion. She certainly doesn't look like other mothers.

I try to get by without detection, but she catches me staring. Her mom radar is on.

"Stella, what are you doing in here?" She walks around the

island until she's in front of me, putting her hands on her hips. "You need to talk to the guests. You're the one they're here to see." She doesn't literally push me out of the kitchen, but she might as well.

Back in the dining room, someone touches my arm. One of my many relatives, Aunt Rachel, has a crease in her forehead so deep it looks like it's been there since she was born.

"Stella, dear, I can't believe how grown up you are. Let me get a look at you." She grabs my hands and holds them out at my side like I'm a doll. "You are such a beautiful girl. And what a figure." She spins me around ballerina-style. "What I wouldn't give for that little behind."

A few of the people standing nearby laugh, and one man I don't know raises his eyebrows. Zoey's rebuke of the older guys in the mall pops into my head. The thought of Zoey helps me focus, reminding me there's a world outside this buttoned-up formality and outrageous decadence. A world I'd almost forgotten. I need to remember that world. I need to remember why I've chosen to be here. To play my part.

"That's sweet of you to say, Aunt Rach, but you've got a lovely behind yourself." I tilt my head and peek at her butt, which, in truth, is perfectly shaped.

She contorts her neck as if she can see her own backside. I take the opportunity to pull out of her grasp, nearly running right into Douglas Jones, a cousin of Dad's who works with him at Corvette.

"Hello there, young lady. Or should I say congratulations?"

"Thank you." The words are barely out of my mouth when his wife spins around and clutches his arm.

"Oh, Stella. It's just you."

Who else she was expecting to find at my graduation party?

Mr. Jones ignores his wife. "Well, young lady. What are your plans? Heading off to college in the fall?"

"No, sir."

The corners of Mrs. Jones's mouth drop. "Oh, that's a shame." I wonder if she knows how rare it is for girls here to go to college. Bonita and Liv still haven't heard about their applications, but Mateo found out he got in everywhere he applied back in April. I still don't know one single girl in New America who's gone to college.

"Did your daughter go?"

"Unfortunately, no." Mrs. Jones takes a quick sip of her champagne. "She got married."

Mr. Jones furrows his brow at his wife before turning back to me. "Planning a wedding then? Your father claims you have a suitor who's been coming here for months."

From his point of view, those are my two choices: go to college or get married. It's time to start telling people the truth. "No, sir, I'm not getting married."

"He didn't propose?"

He assumes if I'm not getting married, it means no one proposed. He can't even *imagine* I would turn down a proposal. I relish the idea of telling him the truth. "Oh, he told me he wanted to marry me." I pause when the confused looks appear on their faces. "More than once."

"He did?" Mrs. Jones's surprise cannot be missed.

"Yes, he did." They both stare, waiting for an explanation. "But I'm not interested in marriage."

"You're not?" Mr. Jones gapes at me like I'm covered in ants. The irritation in his voice tells me I've gone too far. Douglas Jones is almost as powerful as Dad, and I don't need to push his buttons. I say what I have to say. What they told me to say. "If I marry, sir, I'd only be able to have so many children, but if I become a chaperone, I can help dozens of girls start down the path to motherhood. I feel like that's the best way for me to help make New America stronger." Now that I've said it out loud, I'll have to tell Mom and Dad too.

Mr. Jones holds my eye. Can he see through me? I brace myself for an interrogation that never comes.

"I see." He breaks away from me to look at his wife, whose mouth is twisted in disapproval. He shakes his head at her just once, making her scowl disappear, before turning back to me. "A noble choice, Stella. And not one many girls of your, well, of your upbringing would choose. I have to say I admire you."

"Thank you, Mr. Jones. I genuinely appreciate it."

It's not a lie.

I do appreciate how easily I've fooled him.

A half hour later I'm done.

Just done.

I've had enough. Enough small talk. Enough answering questions about my future. Enough of being sized up. I sneak up the stairs without Mom noticing. I almost have the door of my room shut when I hear her. "Stella Ann Graham, you still have guests. Get back downstairs." I open the door and come face-to-face with my mother's pout. "Please."

Give obedience.

I decide my best bet is to keep moving. I float from one group to another, picking up salmon bites and cheese puffs as I go. It works. I move from the living room through the dining room and to the kitchen without getting cornered again. Eventually I make my way outside where more guests await. The fountain is gurgling, and tiny string lights crisscross the courtyard.

Even I have to admit it's stunning.

If only I cared. If only I didn't want to be anywhere else. If only I had a place to hide.

That's when I see my out.

The garage.

CHAPTER 110

Dad is the one who usually hides in the garage. Strange since he's never been one of those fix-it kind of dads. Still, he spends most weekends and some evenings here. It's where he was when Sister Helen died.

Three cars sit in front of Dad's workshop: a navy Corvette Roanoke, a black Corvette Wilderness SUV, and Dad's prized possession: a 1963 red Corvette Stingray convertible. The kind of car spies drive in the movies.

Even though in real life, they drive beat-up old Mercedes.

It's a rare occasion when Dad takes the Stingray out for a spin. Almost no one in New America drives a flashy car. Dad keeps his hidden away, only taking it out early in the morning or late at night.

I stroll over to the Stingray and run my hand over the rough texture of the canvas cover. What it's like to sit behind the wheel? I can't wait to drive again at the conservatory. In real America, I fell in love with acceleration, the feeling I could escape simply by pushing my foot to the floor. I've only seen Mom drive once. The time she picked up Dad after he had too much to drink at the Corvette track.

I long to get behind the wheel, feel the leather against my back. It's my graduation party after all. I want something more memorable than the birdcage full of checks waiting for me inside.

I pull on the cover, but it doesn't fly away like I imagined. I have to yank on each corner to get it off. The red paint is so bright it hurts my eyes. Once the car is free, I relax into the driver's seat like I belong there. Dad would kill me, but he's too distracted by all the bigwigs in our living room to care. I lift my hand to the ignition and let out a little yelp of surprise when I feel the keys hanging there.

If my life were a movie, I'd turn the key, back out of the garage, and drive into the sunset. But this isn't a movie. And I'm not going anywhere. Not yet anyway.

I pull the keys out of the ignition and examine them. Could I get them copied? There are three different keys on the keychain. Two of them—an oval one and a rectangular one—have the letters "GM" embossed on their silver surface, but the gold key doesn't say anything. It's not a house key. It's smaller. Probably for a lock, not a door.

That's when I lift my face and notice what's right in front of me. Dad's shop.

My gaze moves along the wall until I get to the padlock that's been hanging on the door in the corner as long as I've been alive.

I look at the small gold key in my hand.

It's the key to Dad's shop.

CHAPTER 111

'm inside before I know what I'm doing, gently pushing the door behind me as if someone might hear. *Why am I in here? What do I think I'm going to find?* The truth is, I know exactly why I'm here. They trained me to do this. To investigate. To look for things. To find out everything I can about Dad.

Never in my life have I been inside Dad's shop. He doesn't ever leave it unlocked, nor does he invite us in. It's his private space. Even more private than his office.

It isn't what I expect. There are no tools. No beer fridge.

There's a narrow Formica table sitting against the outside wall with bottles and jars along the back of it. A small wood desk sits at the far end of the space, but it holds only papers and a massive smart screen. Nothing that could be used to build things or do repairs.

I go right to the desk and start flipping through the papers. I pause when I see the word *resistance*.

Dad knows about the resistance? The Minutemen know about us?

I keep flipping, but there's too much to read in just a few minutes. Soon someone will come looking for me. I have to get back to the party. I can investigate more another time. Now that I know where he hides the key.

I glance at the smart screen. What would Dad's password be? It won't be as easy to guess as Mom's. I'll have to try to figure out before I come back. Why is this happening now? Only a week before I move out?

I'll be home on weekends. There will be time.

I move away from the smart screen. That's when I see them. The glass jars sitting along the back of the table. I hadn't processed how out of place they are. They look like they belong inside a medicine cabinet with cotton balls or Q-tips in them. I pick one up and inspect it. It has white coffee filters inside.

Coffee filters?

Why would Dad have coffee filters in the garage?

I reach for another jar. This one has a clear liquid inside with a powerful smell. Some kind of rubbing alcohol. The kind they use in doctor's offices and hospitals. The next has a tiny bit of white powder on the bottom. Like confectioner's sugar but with no scent.

Should I taste it?

I need to get back before people notice I'm gone.

My eyes move down the row of jars and stop at the last one. It looks like there are brown bugs in it. I move to the end of the table. When I lift the jar to my face, I can't see them clearly through the glass. I unscrew the lid and peer inside. They're not bugs.

They're beans.

Brown and gray beans.

Have you ever seen any funny-looking beans around the house? Maybe in the kitchen. Maybe somewhere you wouldn't expect. Castor beans. They're brown and gray.

My entire body goes cold. It's like I've been dipped in a bath-tub full of ice. I see it all over again.

Sister Helen on the floor.

Clutching her throat.

Taking her last breath.

A shiver goes through me that shakes my entire body.

I gaze into the jar again. Are they really the same kind of beans…?

But that would mean… But how could…?

Unless…

Unless it was him…

Unless it was Dad who…

Unless he was the one who killed Sister Helen.

I try to screw the lid back on, but my hands shake too much.

That's when I hear the door to the garage creak open. Is it Dad? What will he do if he finds me?

I try to close the lid again, but the beans cascade out of the jar, clattering to the table like firecrackers.

"Hello?" a muffled voice calls from the other side of the wall.

I look around the small space, searching for an escape, but there's no way out and nowhere to hide. Another creak and then the door clicks shut. After that it's dead quiet. I stand frozen in place and wait.

Just when I think the person might have left, I hear a squeak. And then another. Someone is walking across the garage. It's not Dad. He doesn't wear shoes that squeak. Dad wears shoes that tap-tap-tap on the floor.

I inch to the door of the workshop, barely cracking it open. My eyes roam over the space. No one is here. I start to push the door all the way open when a person steps in front of it, his back to the door. I put my hand over my mouth to keep from screaming.

He's so close I can make out the individual white-blond hairs on the back of his head.

Joseph.

I hold my breath, but he doesn't seem to be listening as much as looking. His face swivels. He moves forward, tilting his head in between the cars as he slowly travels the length of the garage. At the Stingray, he studies the cover on the ground, rests his hand on the hood of the car, as if checking for a heartbeat.

Then, without warning, he spins around, dropping his hand to the gun at this hip. I pull back from the door, praying he doesn't see me.

Please please please don't let him see me.

"Who's there?" His voice echoes through the quiet. "Stella? Is that you?"

My instinct is to pull the door shut and lock it—there's a latch on the inside—but I can't risk it. The blood rushing through my ears is so loud I'm not sure I'll hear his footsteps if he moves again.

What is he doing?

I hear another squeak. And then another. He's coming toward me.

The squeaking stops on the other side of the door. He's right in front of me. He's going to open the door. He's going to find me.

"Stella," he says through the door. "I want to apologize—"

He stops midsentence.

"Mr. Graham? Is that you? I'm sorry, sir. I thought you were Stella."

I don't say anything, and he continues.

"I'll get out of your way, sir."

His shoes squeak again, this time moving away from me. The door creaks open. Another creak and then the door clicks shut.

He's gone.

I'm safe.

I look over my shoulder. Beans lay scattered across the table and the floor.

Until Dad finds out who I really am.

CHAPTER 112

When I step back inside the house, Dad is at my side.

Does he know what I found?

"Stella," he hisses in my ear. "We've been looking everywhere for you. Where have you been?"

My eyes land on Joseph. He's staring at me from across the dining table. *Did Joseph tell him someone was in the garage?*

Dad goes on. "We need to do the toast, Stella. People are starting to leave."

He doesn't know.

"The toast? What toast?"

"To your engagement, of course."

My engagement? What is he talking about? "But—"

He leans closer, cutting me off before I can finish. "Don't start, Stella." The smell of hospital crossed with aftershave hits me as he talks. Now I know where it comes from. The rubbing alcohol.

An artificial smile covers his face, but his head shakes the tiniest bit. He isn't budging. He's making me do this.

Waiters offer trays of champagne to the guests. A glass is put in my hand.

Mom walks up and passes Dad a flute of champagne. "We're ready, Mitchell." Dad leans down and whispers something in Mom's ears that makes her blush. She turns to look at him, and their eyes connect for the briefest second. I flash back to Rose's words. *He worships her.*

Dad breaks away from Mom and picks up a spoon from the table, clinking it against his flute. He doesn't say anything to quiet them. He doesn't have to. His mere presence commands obedience. Dad always gets what he wants.

But I can't let that happen this time.

Dad clears his throat. "I want to thank you all for joining us on such a special day."

Joseph offers me a satisfied smile and moves around the table until he's standing next to Mom. That's when I see the small turquoise box in his right hand. The ring box. The same one he had when he first tried to propose.

I have to do something. I have to stop this.

"It's been a long time since she first started kindergarten, but the day has finally come when our eldest daughter has finished her education."

Finished her education. He sounds so certain. So smug.

One person starts to clap, and the entire room breaks into applause. The two men standing on either side of Dad give him long handshakes. Are they Minutemen too? Are they *all* Minutemen? When the noise dies down, Dad turns to me with a smile.

"Stella Ann, I am so very proud of you." My mother is standing by his side, but he doesn't mention her, as if her role in my upbringing isn't worth a side note. "I also have some news to share."

If I don't stop him now, it will be too late.

"It's actually wonderful news." Dad turns to Mom, doing the bare minimum to acknowledge her presence. "Mary Beth and I want to announce that Stella is going to—"

I jump in before he finishes. "There's nothing to announce, Dad."

Dad cuts me a look that says he could kill me. I shouldn't be speaking at all. *Don't speak unless spoken to.* Especially when he's got the floor. I ignore his glower and continue before he stops me.

"What I mean is there's no need for a big announcement. Enrolling in the chaperone conservatory is an honor, not an accomplishment." Several people gasp out loud. Joseph tries to step forward, but Mom puts her arm across him like a child, holding him back. I keep going. "Besides you already congratulated me—"

I turn so I'm looking directly at Dad. But he's studying the guests, evaluating their responses. I wait until he turns back to me.

When his eyes finally meet mine, I go on. "In the garage."

The tiniest bit of concern flickers across his eyes.

"When we were in your workshop."

His mouth closes, his smile creasing into a straight line.

"Remember?" He doesn't say anything—he's actually speechless—so I ask again. "You do remember, don't you, Dad?"

His eyes never leave mine, but the joy that was there a few minutes ago has vanished. His pupils are completely flat. I've crossed a line I've never crossed before. This will change things between us. I can never undo it. It's not the way I want things to go, but I have no choice. I came back to be a chaperone, and that's what I'm going to do.

No matter the cost.

He holds my gaze another second before turning away from

me and back to his audience. "That's true, Stella." An artificial grin returns to his face. "I did congratulate you already." He closes his mouth and pauses an index finger over his lips. "And you know what?"

I have no idea what he's going to say.

"You are absolutely right. It *is* an honor to attend the conservatory. Not because of anything *you* have accomplished but because of the accomplishments of the men who built our great society."

My whole body relaxes. If this is how he'll get back at me, so be it. As long as I don't have to marry Joseph, who is now glaring at me so hard I can't imagine people don't notice.

"It's an honor *bestowed* upon you. We shouldn't toast you. We should toast *them*." He lifts his glass in the air, and everyone in the room, except Joseph, mirrors his movements. "Here's to the Minutemen, and the formidable nation they've created. The greatest America ever. *New* America."

Several men yell, "Hear! Hear!" across the room, and Dad throws his entire glass of champagne back in one swallow. When he drops it to his side, he steals a look at me. I lift my glass to him in salute and do the same, slugging the champagne back as if it's water.

I hope he wonders how I learned to do it.

CHAPTER 113

M om hires movers to take my things to the conservatory, and Dad comes home early from work. We haven't been in the same room since graduation.

But he has to drive me to the conservatory. That's something Mom is not supposed to do.

I'm sitting in Sister Helen's chair by the window, trying to imagine what it will be like to leave home a second time. Will it be different now that I'm only moving across town?

Dad's Roanoke pulls up. When he steps out, I'm amazed by how normal he looks. How could someone who looks so normal be capable of murder?

I've run through every possible scenario in my head, but no matter how much I try to avoid it, I keep coming up with the same answer. It had to be Dad. The beans were right there.

In his shop.

With his things.

Behind a door to which only he has the key.

I'm not going to let him get away with it either. He has to pay for what he's done. I'll make sure of it.

He must feel me staring because he glances up, spotting me in the window. Our eyes meet, but I don't wave or smile. I'll put on a show when I go downstairs, but I'm not ready to do that yet.

I'm not ready to pretend.

I walk right up to him and play my part.

"Thanks for doing this, Dad." I say this even though we both know he has little choice.

He considers me, a question in his eyes. Is he wondering how much I know? But a second later his face shifts from distrust to warmth. He's either playing his part or falling for mine. "Of course, Stella. I wouldn't miss your last day at home."

"I'll be back every weekend. Until I'm confirmed anyway."

It's Mom who answers. "It won't be the same."

Shea is right behind Mom, but she's not smiling. Is Shea glad I'm leaving? Now she'll really have Mom all to herself. At least until her chaperone arrives. But that's still a few years away.

"Well, we should go." Dad says *we* even though Mom and Shea are not going with us. There's no reason for them to do so.

Mom pulls me into an embrace. She's been more affectionate since my return. She squeezes me tighter, and emotion wells up inside me. It *is* harder this time. Now that I know so much. I was desperate and angry before. Now I'm just sad.

Mom pulls back and turns to Shea. "Say goodbye to your sister."

I hold my arms out to her. Shea's hug is quick, obligatory. She's not going to miss me. I regret we've never been close.

"See you this weekend," I say to all of them when I pull back.

Mom's face brightens. "I'll make New America Strip."

"You don't have to."

"But I want to." This is all Mom thinks she can do for me. Make my favorite dinner. How awful.

I want her to go with me. I want her to become a chaperone, join the resistance. But it will never happen. Maybe knowing she wants me to fight is enough.

Dad and I move toward the front door. I turn around to take one last look at the magnificent house where I've lived all but a few months of my life. This will never be my home again.

My home will be an idea, not a place.

The idea of resistance.

CHAPTER 114

The conservatory could not be more different than our house. It's cold, sparse, utilitarian. Cement blocks line the walls. The floors are linoleum. It's almost prisonlike. Have I made a mistake?

The receptionist working registration is friendly when I get to the front of the line, but she seems baffled by Dad's presence at my side. "May I help you?" she asks him after highlighting my name on her list.

"I'm her father."

She stares at him, still confused, and he adds, "I'm helping her move in."

He says this even though two young men stand behind us holding my things. They are the only men in sight besides Dad. Every other girl is holding her own suitcase. I noticed some of them saying their goodbyes in the parking lot. Everyone else arrived alone. How could I know I was supposed to do this on my own? I've never been allowed to do anything on my own.

"Oh, I see," the receptionist says. "I just have to make sure that's okay." She picks up the handset of an old-fashioned phone and hits some numbers.

It's strange for Dad to be questioned. Normally he's the one in charge. The receptionist is young, only a few years older than I am, but she has the power to turn him away. He must not know what to make of a place overrun with women deciding what he can do.

A minute later, she hangs up the phone. "Okay, Stella." She talks to me, not him. "It's fine if your dad goes with you today. But just today. Orientation starts at two o'clock. He'll need to be gone by then."

I look to Dad for approval since that's what I've always done.

He nods at me, and I smile back at the receptionist.

She squints her eyes and hands me a folder. "Here's your welcome packet and your key. Peggy will show you to your room." She nods toward a woman wearing overalls with a pink T-shirt.

"Thank you."

The receptionist leans to one side and peers at the two men holding my suitcases and boxes. "Are they with you too?"

I'm so embarrassed. Why did I come here with an entire entourage of men? Why couldn't I carry my own things? I'd take the boxes myself, but I couldn't possibly hold them all. "They'll leave as soon as they drop everything off. I'm so sorry. I didn't know."

The receptionist's eyes open wider. "It's okay, Stella. You're new. And there's no wrong way to start here."

I thank her again.

In my room, we find three beds, three desks, three dressers. They are set up in groups. Each bed sits between a desk and dresser, an exclamation point between two periods. My roommates haven't arrived yet.

"Put her things near the desk by the window," Dad says to the two young men after he shuts the door.

I swivel toward him. "I don't want to take the best one."

"Why not? You're the first one here, aren't you?"

It's a waste of time to argue. He'll never let it go. I take the bed by the window. I can always switch after he's gone.

The men Mom hired stack my boxes in front of the dresser and put my suitcase on top of the desk. The space still looks uninviting. *Can I really do this?* I glance at Dad for support, forgetting what I know about him and just thinking of him as my father.

He must read the doubt on my face. "You don't have to do this, Stella. You could still apply to college. It's only May. Or you can get married. I'll find someone else—"

I interrupt him. "That's not it, Dad." I want to tell him college will be as useless to me as high school. I want to tell him I long to learn about the world, not be protected from it. But it would give me away. So I say what they trained me to say. "I don't want to go to college, Dad. I can't help people there. If I become a chaperone, I can help so many girls become women. That's the best way I can do my part for New America."

There is real pain on his face. He takes a deep sigh and lets his eyes close. Is he sad I'm leaving? Or does he think I'm foolish? Does he know chaperones are just another way to keep women in their place? He opens his eyes and turns to the young men waiting for him in the doorway. "We should go."

I hesitate because, even though I'm horrified by what he's done, there's a part of me that doesn't want him to leave. There's a part of me that still wants my dad. "I guess so."

He lifts his hand in line with my shoulder but pulls back, offering a kind of half wave. He was going to put his hand on my shoulder. But then he remembered. That's not allowed. And we're not alone.

"Well, call if you need anything. You have my number, right?"

"I do." I've had his number memorized since I could read, but I've never once dialed it. If I need something, I call Mom.

"And I'll pick you up Friday. On my way home from work."

"Okay, Dad."

He surveys the room as if he's forgetting something. As if there's something else for him to say or do. "This is just so different." His eyes drift over the space I'll be living in for the next year. "It's so different than when my parents took me to college."

"A lot of things are different now."

He jerks his head back to me. I've said too much. I'm not supposed to know how much it's all changed. But I've seen how things used to be, how they *can* be. And I'll never forget.

"That's right." His eyes narrow at me. "You know about the world now, don't you? I keep forgetting. But don't worry, Stella. I won't forget again."

CHAPTER 115

O rientation is in the big hall.

I go with my roommates, the two women I'll be living with the next year. I've never shared a room with anyone in my life, and now I'm sharing it with two strangers, one of whom already accused me of taking the best bed.

She did follow her accusation with a grin. "I don't blame you or anything. You got here first."

Other than that, they both seem nice and relatively normal though I'm shocked by how comfortable they appear in our new room, flopping down on their beds like they really are home. I remind myself they moved straight from govie. Sharing a nondescript room in a government building is nothing new to them.

We go to orientation together. As if we're already friends. I like knowing I have people going through this with me. Maybe that will make it easier to recruit them to our side. We step out of the stairwell on the first floor, and I see her. Sister Meredith. She's here waiting for her new assignment. Sister Laura should be here too, but she's still in prison. Not for long though. The resistance is already planning how to get her out.

"Good afternoon, Stella." Sister Meredith sounds like she's greeting a stranger, but her smile is wide and warm. "Welcome to the conservatory. It's a pleasure to have you here."

My roommates turn to me after she's gone. "Who was that?"

I don't think to lie. "My last chaperone."

"Oh, you're one of *them*." She says *them* like it's a dirty word.

There's no denying it, so I don't even try.

"Is it true your *dad* was here?"

I put my hand on my forehead. "Yes, okay, I admit it."

"Might be the first time a man has ever stepped foot inside this place. Did all the estrogen freak him out or what?"

I let out an involuntary laugh. "He didn't seem comfortable, that's for sure. Too many of us, I guess."

There are a lot of us. There must be one hundred girls in the big hall. At least as many girls as in my graduating class at the high school. I'm surprised it's this many. The sad truth is I have no idea how many girls my age went to govie. I only know boys vastly outnumber girls at Bull Run Prep. And I've heard govie girls try very hard to get one of those boys to propose before they finish high school, so they can get married and avoid work altogether. But who knows if that's true? That might be something else they tell us to keep us from trusting each other.

Still, I can't forget most of them are here for different reasons than I am. Most of them are here because they have fewer choices. They aren't getting married, so they have to work. Being a chaperone is one of the only decent jobs a woman can get in New America. No one wants to be a laborer, cleaning houses or working in a factory for hours on end. It's the kind of thing people say wears a woman out before she's forty.

Some of the girls sitting near me already look worn out, and almost every one of them looks resentful. What have they been through? Will I be able to convince any of them to join me? The idea that I might fail is terrifying.

I'm surrounded by women my own age, but I still feel like I'm in this alone.

Each trainee is assigned to a smaller group called a community. Our communities will be our home away from home. Mine meets in a small field behind the dorm. We sit in a circle right on the grass. I can't remember the last time I sat on the ground outside without a blanket or anything to protect my clothes. Probably back in grade school. The grass tickles my ankles, and the scent of honeysuckle hangs in the air. I'm wearing a new blue sundress Mom bought specifically for today, but almost all the other girls are in jeans and T-shirts. I make a mental note to take home my dressier clothes this weekend.

Our community leader introduces herself as Sister Lacretia but insists we call her Cre. She passes out plain gray notebooks and pencils, asking us to write something about why we're here. I open my notebook and stare at the blank page.

Am I supposed to tell the truth?

Sister Cre explains. "What you write in your journal is just for your own eyes, sisters, but I do want you to share *something* about yourself. Even if it's just a small detail. Your favorite food or hobby. Whatever."

I glance around the circle and see the other girls scribbling. What if I have nothing to write? But then things start pouring out of me. How my mother is an amazing cook. How I had no idea she didn't want me to stay in New America. Even why I want to be a chaperone. Once I start writing, I can't stop, and when Sister Cre tells us to wrap it up, I'm disappointed. I could do this all day.

We put down our pencils, and Sister Cre goes first. While she's talking, I notice her clothes. Black jeans and a black zip-up sweatshirt with white stripes down the arms. She's casual and stylish at the same time. Besides Sister Laura, I've never seen a chaperone in anything besides a caftan. I'm studying Sister Cre's black boots when she says, "I have to tell y'all that I'm a diehard yogi." Her eyes light up. "I seriously can't get enough of it."

A girl wearing a T-shirt with a rainbow prism and the words PINK FLOYD across the chest nods her approval. "Namaste, Sister Cre."

Sister Cre bows to the girl, and I start to bow back. Maybe I'll have more in common with the others than I realize.

"But I guess the more important thing," Sister Cre says, "is why I'm here. I'm here because when I was young, I felt very alone. I had no one to talk to or guide me. I had no one to help me become the woman I wanted to be."

It's not lost on me that she says the woman *she* wanted to be rather than the woman she was expected to be.

There are more of us every day.

"So when I finished at govie, I wanted to be that person for other girls. I wanted to be a chaperone."

I can already tell Sister Cre is someone I'm going to like.

She turns to the girl next to her and asks her to share something.

The girl's face turns red. She tugs at the grass while talking but manages to get out that her favorite food is a glazed donut.

"It doesn't seem like you'll get any argument about that one." Sister Cre is right. If Dad were here, he'd give me a disapproving frown, but every single person in this circle nods her approval. "Thank you for sharing, Sister Julie."

The girl sitting directly across from me squeals, lifting her hand to her mouth. Everyone turns in her direction. "I just…it's just…it sounds so strange. To hear you call her that."

"But that's why you're here, isn't it?" Sister Cre says. "To become one of us? To become a sister?"

A breeze passes over me, goose bumps popping up on both arms. She's right.

The next girl rotates her head around the circle like she's sizing us up. "Hey, y'all. My name's Leann. Listen, I'm not going to lie. My reasons for being here are not necessarily good. Not necessarily bad either." She picks up her gray notebook and shakes it at us. "I wrote it all down, but the thing is, I just don't know what else to do. I'm not getting married. *No way* I'm getting married."

Right away I get it. Leann is like Liv. Gay. Or maybe trans or nonbinary. I learned all about that during my training. They told me to look out for people like Leann and Liv, to help them stay safe or even escape. I don't blame Leann for coming to the conservatory. That's what I'd do too.

"So what choice do I have? I mean, I dig everything Sister Cre is saying, but I just want to be honest, you know?"

Everyone nods, and Sister Cre thanks her. "That was very brave, Sister Leann. I so admire your honesty."

Leann *is* brave. I've never been anywhere in New America where a girl could admit out loud she didn't want to get married. Liv shared that secret with Bonita and me, but she never told anyone else. She never once uttered those words at school. She never told it to strangers. And that's when it hits me.

Something is different about this place.

I look up, and everyone is staring at me.

It's my turn.

A breeze blows across the field. Individual blades of grass ripple in the wind. I have to decide right now whether I'm going to open up to them about why I'm really here.

"My name is Stella Graham."

For a second, I regret saying my full name. If they didn't already know who I am, they do now. The girl who escaped. *The girl who just wants to go home.*

But I'm certain now. I want to be honest. I want to be me.

"I know some of you might be wondering why I'm here. Why would someone who can go to college attend conservatory? Well, as strange as it sounds, I didn't really learn anything in high school."

Some of their eyes grow bigger, but I keep going.

"I mean, I learned how they want us to act, but I didn't learn anything about the world. And I know college won't be any different."

Leann nods every other second. Like she hears a drumbeat in her head. I take this as a sign I should keep going.

"I want to help girls the way my chaperones helped me." I lift a finger to my pendant. "I want to help girls learn to be themselves. Not who the Minutemen think they should be." I hesitate and consider their faces.

Everyone is staring with wide eyes now.

"And I want to do that even if it comes at a cost. Even if I lose my life the way my first chaperone did."

No one says a word. My eyes drift around the circle, hoping

for at least one smile, but no one returns my gaze. Not even Leann. They're all studying the ground, unwilling to meet my eye. When I finally land on Sister Cre, her eyes are closed, her hands in the prayer position at her chin.

Have I given too much away?

Sister Cre's eyes flash open.

This is it. This is the moment when I'm found out.

Sister Cre tilts her head and utters a single word—"Wow"— before dropping her head into her hands. When she lifts her head again, she looks directly at me. "Sister Stella." She shakes her head.

Am I supposed to respond?

"That was *truly* beautiful." She switches from shaking to nodding her head. "I believe you put into words what many of us are thinking. Am I right, sisters?"

Several girls look up and nod.

"Thank you so much for your honesty."

I let out a long breath, and everyone in the circle does the same, lifting their eyes from the earth and returning my gaze. Some of them even smile at me.

As their approval washes over me, relief floods my body. I finally understand what's different about this place.

There are no men here.

It's just us.

There's no one watching. No one telling us what to do. No one telling us what we do wrong. We can be ourselves here. *We* are different here. *Everything* is different.

My eyes sweep over the other girls in the circle, and my body fills with warmth.

I'm not alone anymore. I'm part of something bigger now.
I'm one of them.
I'm a chaperone.

STELLA'S LIBRARY

"The Allegory of the Cave" by Plato

Bird by Angela Johnson

Bless Me, Ultima by Rudolfo Anaya

I Capture the Castle by Dodie Smith

The Collected Poems of Langston Hughes by Langston Hughes

The Complete Poems by Emily Dickinson

The Color Purple by Alice Walker

Darius the Great Is Not Okay by Adib Khorram

Deenie by Judy Blume

The Diary of a Young Girl by Anne Frank

Fahrenheit 451 by Ray Bradbury

The House on Mango Street by Sandra Cisneros

Incidents in the Life of a Slave Girl by Harriet Jacobs

Inferno by Dante Alighieri

In the Time of the Butterflies by Julia Alvarez

Jane Eyre by Charlotte Brontë

Little Women by Louisa May Alcott

Lord of the Flies by William Golding

Love in the Time of Cholera by Gabriel García Márquez

"The Lottery" by Shirley Jackson

Of Mice and Men by John Steinbeck

"The Ones Who Walk away from Omelas" by Ursula Le Guin

The Outsiders by S. E. Hinton

Pride and Prejudice by Jane Austen

A Room of One's Own by Virginia Woolf

A Room with a View by E. M. Forster

The Scarlet Letter by Nathaniel Hawthorne

Their Eyes Were Watching God by Zora Neale Hurston

To Kill a Mockingbird by Harper Lee

Uncle Tom's Cabin by Harriet Beecher Stowe

A Wrinkle in Time by Madeline L'Engle

ACKNOWLEDGMENTS

The race is not always to the swift but to those who keep on running.

My father had a poster with these words on it that hung in our home when I was growing up, and it's this belief that has kept me writing for twenty-eight years. I'm incredibly sad my dad will never see this book in print, but so glad he was sitting next to me when I found out it would be published. He was not only a wonderful father, but also a tireless cheerleader. I miss him dearly. My mother is an equally supportive cheerleader, giving away copies of my books to anyone who will have them. She holds me to high standards and simultaneously tells everyone how much I exceed them. I cannot possibly put into words how invaluable it has been to have these two people in my corner since the day they adopted me.

I am equally grateful to my exceptional agent, John Cusick, for not only believing in me and this story, but also for making it even better than it was when he first saw it. Your patience, persistence, and warmth are deeply appreciated, John.

Thanks as well to my incredibly insightful editor, Annie Berger, who saw Stella's potential before anyone else and pushed me to make her story the best it could be. And she did all that while having and raising a baby. Thanks, too, to editor Wendy McClure for stepping in to help us hone the manuscript while Annie was away. How many writers are lucky enough to have two excellent editors?

A big thanks to everyone at Sourcebooks, especially Aimee Alker, Cristina Arreola, Rebecca Atkinson, Susan Barnett, Laura Boren, Gabriell Calabrese, Cana Clark, Liz Dresner, Emily Engwall, Ashlyn Keil, Chelsey Moler Ford, Keri Haddrill, Kelsey Kulp, Caitlin Lawler, Karen Masnica, Madison Nankervis, Valerie Pierce, and Molly Waxman as well as Dominique Raccah for creating such an amazing publishing house. I feel like I won the lottery the day Annie offered me the chance to work with this outstanding team.

I'm indebted to everyone in the kid lit community for welcoming me into their world and teaching me how to write a book like this one, especially Hope Bissell, Sharon Cameron, Denise Deegan, Caroline Dubois, Susan Eaddy, Meg Griswold, Rita Lorraine Hubbard, Rachel Kenyon, Alisha Klapheke, Rae Ann Parker, Shauna Reynolds, Erica Rodgers, Kris Sexton, Corabel Shofner, Diane Telgen, Kim Teter, Kristin O'Donnell Tubb, Mary Uhles, Ismée Williams, and Jessica Young. An extra big shout-out to Debbie Dadey who invited me to her cabin for a writing retreat where I outlined every chapter of this book.

Thanks, too, to Laney Becker, Beth Browne, Roy Burkhead, Danielle Chiotti, Scott Douglass, Alyssa Jennette, Julie Kingsley, Jen Klonsky, Bess McAllister, Danielle Perez, Craig Renfroe, Jessica Sinsheimer, and David Hale Smith as well as all of the librarians and booksellers who have supported me over the years.

I feel incredibly fortunate to have so many additional friends and writers to thank for their support. Thanks to Kelcey Ervick for being on this journey with me every step of the way, to Tracy

Williams for having my back ever since that day at the Fun Center, to Cyndi Crocker for being my eyes and seeing things I don't see, to Ben Crocker for keeping everyone grounded, to Michelle Losekamp for helping me construct my sets, to Craig Losekamp for his expertise in all things medical, to Tomitha Blair for holding us all together, to Bonita and Ryan Dearbone for making something beautiful with me, to Jeff and Cristy Weems for giving me a place to crash, to Kara Thurmond for being my sounding board, to Linda King for playing the believing game, to James Weems for making me look good, to Ginger Cleary for letting me finish my stories, to Joey Coe and Mount Saint Elias for creating music that makes me want to be a better writer, to Katie Brandt for being by my side for forty-nine years, and to Skylar Baker Jordan for helping me take my writing to the next level. Thanks also to Sara Ann Alexander, Shelly Arndell, Al Bardi, Kristin Czarnecki, Peggy Davis, Susann Davis, Pam Eisert, Julie Ellis, Laura Beth Fox-Ezell, Sherry Hamby, Rachel Hardwick, Meredith Love, Sandy McAllister, Alex Montenegro, Katie Pickens, Barry Pruitt, and Sara Volpi Woods, all of whom helped get this manuscript across the finish line. And a big thanks to my Gen Z consultants: Melanie and Emma Brandt, Jennifer King, Sophia Koppensteiner, Samantha McAllister, and Madeline Williams. Finally thank you to the Parran/Parenti family for welcoming me with open arms.

I can never thank David Bell enough, but I will try: thank you for working tirelessly all these years, thus making it possible for me to write and take care of my dad when he was sick. Thank you, too, for all you did for him and continue to do for my mom and me. I'm well aware this book would not exist without you giving and sacrificing so much for all of us. I will never forget it.

AUTHOR BIO

Photo credit James Weems

M Hendrix is the author of two previous books. She lives in Bowling Green, Kentucky, with her husband, novelist David Bell. *The Chaperone* is her first novel. Learn more at mhendrixwrites .com.

FIREreads

#getbooklit

Your hub for the hottest young adult books!

Visit us online and sign up for our
newsletter at FIREreads.com

 @sourcebooksfire

 sourcebooksfire

 firereads.tumblr.com